"I really loved the entire overall plot, the characterization as a whole, and the gory, action-packed scenes. This is a good, solid zombie book and I highly recommend it."

—Rhiannon Frater,
author of *First Days: As the World Dies*

"A raging tale of zombie carnage with characters who's story lines work on a much deeper level. Check it out!"

—Eric S. Brown, author of *Season of Rot*

"Mr. Long is defiantly a writer to watch and *Among the Living* is definitely a zombie novel to check out."

—HorrorNews.net

"Well told story and finely drawn characters battling the swiftly mutating risen dead for survival."

—Stephen North, author of *Dead Tide*

"The book is excellent ... If you are a fan of zombies or just of apocalyptic fiction in general, this is definitely one to pick up."

—Patrick D'Orazio, author of *Comes the Dark*

Sean,
Seattle and
lattes and
zombies ...OH my!

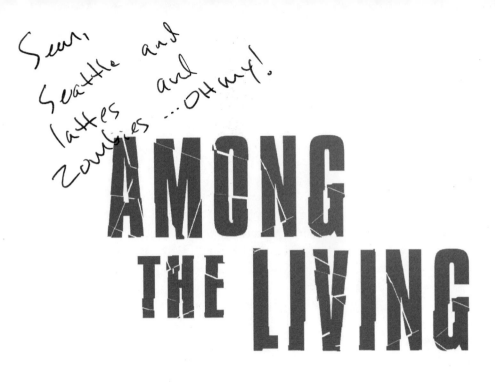

AMONG THE LIVING

TIMOTHY W. LONG

Permuted Press
The formula has been changed...
Shifted... Altered... Twisted.
www.permutedpress.com

= crypticon 2012 =

For Kayoko

A PERMUTED PRESS book
published by arrangement with the author
ISBN-13: 9781618680068
ISBN-10: 1618680064

Among the Living copyright © 2009, 2011
by Timothy W. Long.
All Rights Reserved.
Cover art by Zach McCain.

PRELUDE

Lost, and for a time so is he. Breath rasps in and out as her lungs begin to fail.

Cold, and so is she. Her hand is ice, a rigid claw that grips with the force of a newborn. Skin translucent, wisps of gray hair that struggle to rise as he strokes her arm. Bone thin, old, past her prime and yet barely in her fifth decade.

Hours spent by her side, and for it her eyes opened but once. She stared past him at the ceiling as if it held less recrimination than his gaze. Milky and gone to smoke, at least the one on the left, while the other is clear and the bluest blue he has ever seen. They pulled him in from the first, dug into his soul and now, twenty-two years later, it continues to haunt.

The syringe is cool as he rolls it across the tabletop. He picks it up again to feel the weight of the world. Clear and languid, the liquid rests, unassuming.

If it does what he asks, what he hopes, it will be her savior and perhaps his.

The brush of alcohol, but she doesn't stir. Then a stab and the deed is done. Just a waiting game now, and for all the long months he has been away, he will not leave her side until it works—or kills her.

It may be some time before the tumor shrinks. That thing that looks like a balloon in her head. It grows daily as if pumped full of air; the pressure must be immense.

The virus is 'programmed' to seek out the tumor and enter it. There it will begin eating the thing with a vengeance, his vengeance. Minutes are all it needs to start working, maybe days until she is coherent.

She sighs and her head stirs. He leans over and presses his lips to dry skin next to her pale mouth. Then she is silent once again, and he waits.

The light from the window paints landscapes across the blankets. Mountains made of knees, hips for land fall, waist a pool of lake water. Later, night slips in and the painting is reversed.

She stirs again, and one eye drifts open. It is clear for the first time in as long as he can remember. The other is still milky and may never recover from the damage.

"Herb ..." Just a whisper, and he has to lean close.

"Ruth?"

"Herb, I feel strange ... like my blood is on fire."

"Try to relax, my love. Everything will be back to normal soon. Very soon now."

"It's not okay; it hurts. My head feels like it's going to explode. "

"I did it, Ruth. All those years of research and I have the cure. Finally. I gave you a shot that is killing the tumor."

"I don't think so, Herb, I don't think so." Her eye moves back and forth as if trapped. Her head shakes, and her body shifts under the blanket. The dead eye turns and looks past him at a spot on the wall.

Blood pours into the other one, beneath the surface of the cornea. Within seconds, it is crimson. One side of her face slopes down as if it is about to slide off her head. Oh God, a stroke! He grabs his bag from the floor and paws through it as she starts to shake. She thrashes on the bed, foam bubbling from her mouth.

He flips the bag over her body and continues to look through it as he holds her down. He is sure he has Coumadin, but Aspirin will do as well, just in case, oh God—just in case. She writhes, and he feels her heart beating through her chest. It rumbles, pounds and then, to his horror, slows down and shudders to a halt.

"Ruth, my God. RUTH!"

"Herb," she sighs then sits up in bed and sinks her teeth into his exposed neck. He screams, but not for long.

Dead, and so is he.

PART ONE
DAY 0

MIKE

The day starts with a blast of rain that matched my dark mood, a teasing precursor to what will, much to my surprise, be one of the best days of my life. Bus so full I'm left standing in the aisle for the twenty-minute ride to Seattle. A portly man who reeks of mothballs bouncing against me with every bump and turn. He carries an old-style briefcase that keeps bashing into my knee. I want to slap the top of his shiny bald head and tell him to pay attention to his stuff, but he has a pair of white ear buds pushed so deeply into his ears that they look like wires running into his head. I keep imagining they are electrodes and I hold the controls so I can zap him every time he touches me.

There is a woman standing behind me who looks pissed because none of the men offered her a seat. Probably because she is wearing a skirt that barely reaches mid-thigh, and they want to stare at her legs. Hell, pissed or not, I wish I could stare at them too. Beats looking at a shiny head.

Headphones cup my ears, but the morning show guys are just a droning buzz of background noise. I don't know what they're saying, because other things weigh heavy on my mind. It is the third of July, and it is the third anniversary of my son's death.

The day before Independence Day. We used to spend it shopping at the reservations for fireworks. I would come home with a box of them to Rita's disapproving eye. But she would relent later, after a few drinks; then we would sit outside and fight the bugs while we launched rockets into the sky.

I was haunted from the moment I opened my eyes to the second I stepped into the shower. Every movement thereafter was mechanical. I went at the morning like an automaton, convinced that if I just got some momentum going, the rest of the day would fall into place.

A trip to Starbucks saw me staring slack-jawed at the barista when she asked for my order. I knew she was talking, but I had somehow zoned out. I snapped back to attention and babbled that I wanted a latte, tall. Not my favorite drink, but it was the first thing that popped into my mind.

I waited in line behind other customers and remembered a time when Andy had been with me, mouth armed with a big grin for a cup of hot chocolate. He wanted extra whipped cream, which made me stop and think of what Rita would say; only she wasn't there, so she never had to know.

He got his cup from the smiling woman and blushed at her "You going to work with Dad today?" then sipped at the pile of cream puffed on top. He got some on his nose, which elicited another 'ah' from the girl. It was a greeting card moment, the kind of thing you see on TV and brush off as too melodramatic. Only it wasn't; he was my son and he was beautiful.

We did spend the day together. I gave him a tour of the office and the press where we printed the tiny Seattle Metro Weekly newspaper. It wasn't running at full tilt, it was just spitting out some of the middle sections like entertainment and want ads. He marveled at the machine, at how fast it worked, moving paper, pressing and folding. It was a good day. He kept me entertained when I broke away from writing, and I kept him busy with our laptop when I was working on something.

The name is Mike Pierce, by the way. I used to be a reporter for one of the Seattle bigs, but downsizing led to layoffs a year ago. I don't blame the paper for the run of bad luck. I understand. I'm the first one to log into the PC in the morning so I don't have to read a real paper.

The Metro Weekly has been good to me. I maintain a small section that focuses on some of the weirder lifestyles around Seattle. I meet interesting people like restaurant owners who put dollops of maple syrup in their martinis, and professional dominatrices who run things we aren't supposed to call brothels. I was assured over and over and OVER that no payment for sexual services was ever rendered. Instead, I was told to think of it as a massage. Right. A massage where a guy gets the shit beat out of him.

After zoning out at Starbucks, stumbling on the bus and then jumping off at the wrong stop, I had a half-mile walk ahead of me. At least Mr. Mothball left the bus three stops ago.

The sun is making an appearance, and the mugginess of July is just starting to settle over the city. The smell is pure Seattle. A breeze wafts off the waterfront, carrying with it the scent of seawater mixed with an undercurrent of piss and old booze from alleys along Second Avenue.

The traffic moves right along, barely stopping at red lights before zipping up and down side streets. I approach Bell, a cross street I can take down to the waterfront. I'm still in a daze, thinking of the past, walking an all-too-familiar route on autopilot when a series of honks interrupts my reverie. I turn, expecting to see someone driving too slowly or asleep at a green light. Thanks to the countless coffee stands in the city, people tend to be highly caffeinated and a bit on edge.

But they are making a fuss at a homeless man who is fighting with a guy dressed in a suit. The two are locked in combat, arms reaching for each other's throats. They move around in a circle, neither giving ground, like they are performing a waltz. A red stain soils one side of the well-dressed man's suit jacket, and he is grunting as if in pain. I turn to help out, then wonder what I can do. A car stops, and a pair of younger men gets out.

Not my problem, I decide, and walk the rest of the way to work.

* * *

I step into the office a few minutes late. Jim is always cool about it. In fact he never mentions my hours. He is the sort who expects stuff to get done; if it takes longer to do it, then you burn the midnight oil. The office is darker than usual, but a steady stream of daylight pours from multiple windows. It is a green day for us, and the lights will be off until the sun goes down.

Erin has her long legs up on her desk, skirt riding dangerously high. What is it with the skirts today? She also has on what she calls 'smart-girl' glasses, which have a catlike frame and look like they came straight out of the sixties. Locks of her dark hair have fallen across half her face; a folder lies open on her lap. She is the closest thing I have to a best friend. It doesn't hurt that she is very attractive.

"'Sup, Chuck." Her favorite greeting. She looks up, and I get a quick smile.

"Another day."

"Have you seen this? Some guy down by Fort Lewis said he saw a guy die from a virus. Said they got it while taking care of that big gas leak up on Queen Anne. He claims the guy lay dead for more than five minutes before rolling to his feet and attacking another soldier."

"What? Like those horror movies?"

"Right? Only those movies are bullshit. You can't come back from the dead. Unless you're Jesus, I guess."

I'm trying to wrap my head around this. Ask anyone I know and they will say that, despite reporting the weird, I am the biggest skeptic they know.

"Do we know anyone there, any contacts?" Then again, what would we do … look into it and write a feature that wouldn't even hit the stands until next week? By then people would have forgotten about it.

"Jim doesn't want us to get involved; it's too far outside of Seattle."

"Good. I got enough stuff to keep up on without a trip to Tacoma."

I plant myself at my Dell and fire up the old rig. I've had the same machine for a while, and it was a hand-me-down when I started. It works well enough as a web surfer and word processor, so I choose not to complain.

My desk is covered in crap. I have printouts from web searches I did months ago. About twice a year, I like to gather the stuff up, flip through it, remember I didn't mean to save ninety percent of it and then toss it all in the recycle dumpster.

My desk is opposite Erin's, so she is always at my back. The cubicle walls are low and don't provide much privacy. She and I have been confidants for a year. Her face is hidden behind a newspaper, so I take the opportunity to study the line of her lean legs. They are an olive tan that seems to be the same color all year. She has some Italian in her, but you wouldn't know it from her last name, Stafford. God I need to get laid. Since Rita left, I haven't had the best luck with women, not that I would try anything with Erin. She isn't really my type. She has her shit together.

"I'll let you get away with it this time." She smiles, paper in her lap once again. I wonder how long I have been staring.

"Uh, sorry. Just wondering if they go all the way up," then I choke on the stupid shit that just came out of my mouth.

She laughs and spins around to stare at her computer screen. Jim wanders over with a fresh cup of coffee under his nose. He milks that thing all day. Drinks it by the gallon. I wonder if he ever sleeps.

"Pierce, what's new?" Jim's a good guy. Older than I am, wears flannel shirts like it's still the nineties. He has a massive gray beard that hangs a good six inches from his chin. His large frame lends him the air of a fishing boat captain. He isn't really overweight; he's just a big guy.

"Not much. I just walked in the door and the beast is starting up. I'm finishing up the story on the seven most intimidating dives in

Seattle. Are we looking into the gas leak at all?" I'm wondering because we are close to the bottom of the neighborhood. It's blocked off right now with police vehicles, barricades and tons of yellow tape. There are more police arriving every hour; I even saw a military truck trundle past us last night.

"Like we could get you up there." He sighs. "The local media is having a field day with that one. They're crawling all over the place like ants at a picnic. Not that they are being provided with all that much info."

"Well I'm ready if you need me to go by; maybe I could get some statements from some of the folks who are displaced. Let them have a voice since the cops have been the spokesmen for the whole mess."

"Let me think about it. Anything else?"

"He was checking out my legs; I think I need to talk to HR," Erin says while staring at me with a frown, but one I know is all sarcasm. Like I said, we have been confidants for a while.

"Then you'll probably have to file a complaint against half the guys here. The way you wear those skirts, it's a wonder we don't have more people walking into stuff and filing workers comp claims," Jim says.

Erin jumps to her feet and wraps an arm around Jim's shoulder.

"Did you just pay me a fucking compliment, boss?"

"As long as HR isn't involved, I guess I did." The smile turns into a frown when he realizes what they look like standing together.

"Someone's in a good mood. You must have scored last night."

Jim puts on a crooked grin and actually blushes under all that beard. It turns his cheeks ruby red, and for a moment he looks like a serial killer version of Santa Claus.

"You two think you can get some work done today?" He untangles himself from Erin's arm and goes back to his office. I focus on my computer screen. I need to get that damn story done.

My cell phone buzzes in my pocket. I dig it out and check the display. It's Rita, but I'm not in the mood to speak to my ex-wife just yet. Not this early on the anniversary of Andy's death. I send her to voicemail.

The morning passes quickly as I wrap up the piece. I had to visit a dozen or so bars while doing my 'research,' which meant I spent a week going home on the bus half drunk. I add some humor and point out which of the places bothers having anything close to mid-shelf, let alone top-shelf liquor. I can't get my mind off the problems on Queen Anne. A gas leak sounds dangerous, and the media has had a good bit of coverage on it, but the facts are scarce. They are saying a lot about the dangers and why they evacuated, but they aren't providing any facts.

The phone rings. Rita again. I'd put her call out of my mind and didn't bother to check my voicemail. I stare at the blinking screen as it reaches the fourth ring. If I wait one more, I won't have to talk to her at all. I won't have to deal with the pain and the drunken babbling.

I want to feel sorry for her. After all, we were together for almost nine years. A couple can go through a lot in that span, but the last two broke me. I tried and tried to reconcile our feelings, to make her see that Andy's death was not her fault even though, in the back of my mind, I curse her sometimes for letting him wander away in the parking lot. I would never say that to her face, and even if I did, I doubt she would see past the bottle of vodka to the depths of my soul, which I used to bare on a consistent basis.

She wasn't always like that; there was darkness at times but never as bad as it is these days.

"Hi, Rita," I answer after popping the phone open.

"Hi, Mike. Are you going to stop by this Sunday?"

"I'll try." I doubt she'll remember the invitation.

"I thought I saw Andy at the store the other day. He was all smiles. Then I realized it was a kid that just looked like him. You should have seen his smiling face; it was just like the old days." Her words are heavy and slurred. They drip with sadness. They tug at my heart and make me wish I had the right words for once in my life, the words to make her see how much I care, but my cynicism would only temper them—make them cold and harsh. So I resort to reason.

"Is that so? Rita, how much have you had to drink today?"

"Not much; it's still early." Then she sobs into the receiver. "It's just hard to wake up sometimes, and even when I am awake, I feel like I'm still asleep. Why did it happen? Why did I take my eyes off him? I should have had him at my side every second. Oh God, why couldn't I have been a better mom?" She trails off in misery.

I know it is hard to read these words and not feel pity, but the truth is she has much worse days. Days when the guilt and dread weigh her down like an anchor. I've seen it and I've fled from it. I've spent entire nights at her side, seen her take enough uppers to make an elephant smile. I've seen her study a gun, and I don't remember which was colder, the barrel or the look in her eyes.

"Rita, do you need me to come over?"

"I'm okay. I have to go." And just like that, she hangs up.

LESTER

"Oh my God, what is she wearing? It's like a cross between a robe and a big ol' cow."

"Don't know, babe. She looks like a sleepwalker to me."

Angela lies sprawled between two chairs with her legs poking out of a summer dress so she can soak up the afternoon sun. She studies the shambling figure through reflective sunglasses. A floppy pink hat shades the rest of her perky face even though the line of sunlight cuts her torso neatly in half.

The street has been quiet for a couple of hours. Neighbors used to poke their faces out of similar houses along Cole Avenue. They used to walk by with heads held high, aloof, as if oblivious to the fact that they had renters such as Lester and Angela near their precious property value.

Then those fuckers in trucks showed up, drove around yelling through bullhorns about a gas leak, get out, go somewhere else, get a couple days' clothes, the Red Cross are standing by, so are hotels—bring your credit card. Screw that was Lester's opinion. There was no way he was leaving his rented house, his supply of weed and alcohol.

A quick call to his attorney informed him that they couldn't make him leave. They can't make you, and don't you let them fucking try it! He could picture Jerry in his office, walking around with that headset plastered to his ear while he screamed about Lester's rights. He gets worked up because he is a good lawyer, also because he does coke, which he buys from Lester by the truckfull.

So they stayed inside while the guys passed by in their trucks with their green clothes that provided about as much camouflage as if they were dressed in bright red with 'Eat At Joe's' balloons over their heads.

Some of the people who looked like sleepwalkers had been rounded up. That's when Les knew something was not right in Dodge. Not fucking right at all. Other men came. These were suited up in puffy white outfits, sealed up like they expected a chemical attack at any moment. They patrolled the streets after the soldiers and rounded up a couple of the people who were acting strange. Les had just hit his bong for the second time when one of the walkers attacked a guy in a space suit. He was crazy, like a rabid dog, thrashing and trying to bite the guy. A soldier jumped out of a truck and shocked the guy with a Taser. He hit the ground like a brick, then flopped around like a fish out of water.

But he was back on his feet in half a dozen heartbeats. Lester started giggling at the guys in white—the guys in green for that matter.

Then they brought out the electric guns. Poor bastard. That laid him out for the count. They wrapped him in some kind of plastic that covered him from chest to toe. Then they put something that looked like a hockey mask on the guy like he was Hannibal Lecter himself.

"There are guys who would pay big money to be tied up like that," Les chuckled.

"That's sick, Les." Angela frowned.

Lester and Angela were lying upstairs, peering through slits in the blinds. This let them watch the action without being seen, or so he hoped. They lay side by side, and she kicked her legs up and down like a hyper kid who'd gotten into the chocolate chip cookies. She was also smiling from the weed, a big dopey grin that must reflect the one on his face. Not even the horror outside could crack their glossy stoned smiles.

The house was locked up tight as a drum. When the soldiers came to pound on the door, he and Angela stayed silent except for the sound of the bong gurgling. They fought down giggles as they played grab ass on the guest bed. The invaders yelled and banged on the back door next, but they didn't break it down.

A shot rang out crisp and loud, shattering the already fucked-up morning with its retort. This would pretty much set the pace for the next two days of Lester's life.

He slid closer to the window. Did they just shoot someone? And, sure enough, there was a man down in the street bleeding from a shot to the chest. Then the poor injured bastard struggled to his feet, and one of the soldiers shot him in the head. Just stepped up with his M-16 and put a bullet in the guy's brainpan like he was going for a walk in the park. Blood and gore exploded outward, splattering the street. The noise was gruesome, like a bowl of spaghetti dropped on the floor, and was somehow louder than the actual gunshot. Suddenly the pot was no barrier to shock.

"... the fuck?" he muttered. He stared as the men moved on, but they left the guy in the street. That was yesterday. No one had returned to claim the body.

Now a couple of the walkers have come to make a social call.

Lester raises the rifle to his shoulder and looks into the scope. The figure leaps into view, red from scalp to sternum with a red stain down her robe. She is not a small girl; her neck seems to merge from her chin into a steady flow of skin that marks the beginning of her chest. The white robe is covered in cow spots and blood. Lester can't help but think of a slaughterhouse.

"This ain't a damn gas leak. They're hiding something from us. All those soldiers here yesterday, driving up and down the road in their Humvees." He lowers the gun and looks at Angela. "It's bullshit. They're covering up whatever made these people sick." He says people because a few of them have wandered past the house. Some walking, some shambling, and some loping like dogs.

"Deader is missing an ear and part of her left arm," he says in a cold voice. They'd escaped to the shade outside after sitting in the stifling house all morning, but Angela moved her chairs closer to the edge of the porch to tan her legs.

Lester is in a shitty mood. After the power went out in the middle of the night, he started sweating from the humidity and had a hard time going back to sleep. Finally he split an Ambien in half and washed it down with some lukewarm water. He would have taken a full one, but he didn't want to be a zombie in the morning. So he woke up to sheets drenched in sweat, body awash in its own perspiration.

Then he tried to make coffee with hot water from the tap, but it tasted like shit. He ran it until it was steaming, too. He even let the grounds sit in the water for a few minutes and then strained the mess through a coffee filter. It tasted like some weak-ass tea. He contemplated boiling water in the fireplace, but that would just heat the house and add to the misery. He dug out an old bottle of caffeine pills instead, and chugged a couple.

"Deader?" Angela asks.

"Heard one of the soldier dudes call them that yesterday when they were in the yard looking around my house. I should sue the bastards for trespassing."

"They were trying to help, Les. They were trying to evacuate everyone, including us."

"It's bullshit, babe. Do you smell a gas leak? I sure as hell don't. Someone fucked up, and now these people are sick. We saw them execute one like he was a criminal. Do you really want those guys 'escorting' us off Queen Anne?" In his contempt, he practically snarls his words.

"I don't know, Les. I'm scared is all."

"Don't be, babe. We got food, we got booze, we got weed and we got fucking guns … and the guys with guns always win."

He watches her as she sighs and looks toward the end of the street that curves down the hill. The hill that leads downtown, the hill lined with trees and cars, other houses and the only exit out of the cul-de-sac.

"Do you think we can go to town tomorrow? I really need some new polish. I hate this shade, I just hate it," she points at her feet while wiggling her toes.

"We're going to need food soon enough, but I don't think that's such a good idea yet, babe. I'd rather those soldiers not see us."

She sighs heavily and looks toward the end of the road again. "If they see us now, they might kick us out."

"They can't! Jerry said they can't make us leave, they can just advise us that there is an emergency."

"Don't we have, like, a radio or something?"

"Got rid of it when we got the satellite." He stands up for a stretch.

"When this is all over, we should get a radio that runs on batteries or something. You know, for emergencies."

"What the fuck is this? If it ain't an emergency, I don't know what is."

"I know, but we are safe, I mean it doesn't feel like a real emergency. Hey, maybe we could get one of those windup radios; they charge when you crank them."

"Good call, babe. It'll be the first thing I buy when we get to a store. Meanwhile, I have something you can crank on." He reaches down and shifts his junk in his shorts.

"So," she lets the syllable hang in the air as if considering it. "Are you saying that if I crank your cock, news will come out of you? Where will it come out of exactly?" She shoots him a full pearly white grin.

Lester takes his seat and reaches into the cooler. The ice melted off yesterday, but the water in it is still reasonably cold. He extracts a beer, a microbrew with a red label. They are running out of the cheap stuff, but he has been saving this one.

"It's not even noon. Isn't it too early to start?" Angela whines.

Bubbles hit the back of his throat, rough and bitter. After the first swallow, the rest goes down clean, so he drains a quarter of the beer and lets out a long belch.

"Hand me a Diet Pepsi."

"Won't taste good warm," he says.

He pushes cans and bottles around until he locates one on the bottom. He pulls it out and pops the tab in one smooth motion before handing it to her. She smiles over the top and takes a few swallows, then belches with the back of her hand over her mouth.

"'Scuse me."

Lester reaches over and pats her bare knee. He lets his hand linger, sliding up her smooth leg.

"Oh look, here comes another one!" She jumps up excitedly like a little girl at an ice cream parlor. Lester glances to the side and watches the cloth fall down her legs, covering her tanned skin.

A figure comes around the corner and stumbles over a body. It's another girl, but this time dressed in a business suit with a button-down shirt. She wouldn't attract attention if it weren't for the blood staining the white and black clothing. She seems to be missing part of her forehead, and she is limping.

"Oh my God, is that Marlene?"

"Marlene with the big fake boobs?"

"Is that how you remember our friends, by the size of their tits?"

"In her case, it's the only thing she has going for her. She is kind of a bitch. At least to me."

"I think she is into women … well, sometimes. She usually has a guy with her, though."

"She's into women? Fuck, that's hot."

"Sicko."

"What's sick about it? Have you ever been with a woman?"

Angela puts her hands on her hips and swivels to meet his eye. He can't tell if she is mad at the question. The shade of her hat droops over her eyes so they look half lidded.

"No, and I don't want to."

They are quiet for a moment, and then she says, "Why, do you want to see me with a woman?"

"Of course I do, but only if she isn't a deader." Lester laughs aloud, sits back in his chair and clutches his stomach.

"Men. Jesus," she sighs and then turns her attention back to the new deader. "I think it is Marlene. Hey Marlene!" Angela yells.

The woman continues to stagger toward the fence. She stumbles over the body of the dog they had to shoot yesterday because it was chewing on the ankle of the guy left to rot. It was worrying at the flesh like a bone left in its kennel. Big sucker too. Rottweiler, or so Lester thinks.

Marlene recovers and does her mindless waltz toward their house. Moo cow girl turns to look at her but continues stumbling around in a full circle until she is staring at Angela again.

Lester raises the rifle and studies the other girl's chest.

"Yeah, that's her."

"Oh my God. Oh my God. Poor Marlene. Remember when we had that picnic last summer with her and that guy, what was his name?"

"I called him assclown, but I think his name was Chuck. All he did was talk about his stupid Mustang, like I can't afford one of the new ones. Is she still with him?"

"Babe, she isn't with anyone. She isn't even with herself right now. Oh my God! Poor Marlene."

"Should I take her out?"

"No! She used to be our friend."

Your friend, maybe.

Their friend—make that Angela's friend—reaches the fence but keeps trying to walk forward like a retarded kid. The chain link fence forces her to stop, but she swings her arms in their direction as if trying to reach the twenty or so feet. She bares her mouth in a horrid visage of broken teeth, tongue held on by a hunk of muscle, and a splatter of dried blood on her lips and chin. Her shirt hangs open, but not enough for Lester to get a glimpse of those big boobs. Not that he wants to; her skin is the same putrid gray shade as her swollen tongue.

A bag dangles from one shoulder as if she were on the way to the store.

"Is that her Coach purse?" Angela moves down the stairs.

"What?"

"That purse, it was her pride and joy. She told me once it cost a grand."

"You're fucking kidding me. For a bag?"

"Get it for me, babe," she pleads, studying him up and down, her eyes promising him great things if he does. Great things that happen in bed.

Another figure marches the drunken waltz around the entrance to the cul-de-sac, this one a large black guy wearing only a pair of pants. With each step, he leaves a bloody footprint. He pauses midstride, takes in the scene and approaches Marlene.

"Hurry, get it for me!" She turns and leans over so he has a flawless view down the front of her dress. She isn't wearing a bra, and he marvels at the sight even though he has seen her large breasts countless times. There is something about a peek, that taste of voyeurism of which he never tires.

"Okay, but you need to cover me."

"What do I do?" She does a little dance in place, clutching her hands together in front of her stomach like a child getting an allowance.

"Take the pistol and follow behind and to my side. If she gets too grabby, I want you to shoot her."

He has his guns laid out on a little table with bullets and cleaning gear. He just went over the 9mm, figuring he may need to use it in the near future. He got the thing in a deal when one of his regulars didn't have the scratch to pay for some coke.

Angela picks up the pistol and studies it for a moment.

"Where's the safety thingy?"

He takes it from her hand and slips the magazine free, then peers at it. It's packed with copper heads. He slams it back home and jerks the barrel back so there is one in the chamber. Trigger cocked, he slides the safety off and hands it back to Angela.

"Careful, that thing is ready to fire. All you have to do is aim and pull the trigger. Make sure you have a clear line of sight; don't shoot me in the back."

"Okay." She raises the pistol in both hands and sights along the barrel, one eye squinted, head cocked to the side, looking sexy as hell as far as Lester is concerned.

"After this, we should go inside. I want to show you my other pistol."

"Get me that bag and I'll do anything you want, babe." She grins.

Lester steps off the porch and into the muggy July sun. Even Seattle has brutally hot days when it decides not to rain. This is one of them, and he is not looking forward to this evening, when the sun will heat the house to a hundred degrees. With no power, there is no need to haul the air conditioning units upstairs like he has been promising to do for the past week.

Angela steps behind him and to the left, gun raised and pointed at her friend.

"Sorry, Marlene," she whispers.

Lester steps up to the fence and bats Marlene's hand aside. He grabs at the purse, but she flails her arms around, trying to get a grip on him. Her mouth opens and closes mechanically, chewing on the chunk of tongue that hangs loose. He tries not to look at the bloody gums, the broken teeth, but her terrible breath draws his eyes. It smells like rotten meat. Garbage left in the sun too long. Death.

He turns his head to the side, trying to avoid her breath, then he smacks her grasping claw away and grabs at the purse again. There is a little blood on the shoulder strap, but the rest seems to have avoided being splattered. He tugs the strap down her arm, but her other hand comes around and nearly cracks him across the face.

"Fuck, Marlene, just gimme the goddamn thing. You don't need it anymore." He slaps her hand as he gets ahold of the strap again. He yanks back and then falls down as she leans forward to take a bite out of his cheek. She snaps forward quicker than he thought possible, nearly gets a taste too.

Lester's teeth click together painfully as he lands, but he has the leather Coach purse his girlfriend wants. The other deader has approached the fence, but only one arm seems to work. He collides with Marlene, and the two stagger. He groans loudly, eyes fixed on Lester. Marlene stumbles into the large woman in the moo cow robe, and they both go down in a heap.

Then Marlene is back on her feet and reaching over the fence for him. Lester scoots back on his butt, hands doing a crab walk as he tries to scurry away. The big guy is leaning over the fence when Lester gets a look at the guy's eyes. They are rimmed with gray, filled with blood. It's like something out of a horror movie.

"If you shoot him, I don't think it will improve his looks," he calls to Angela. "Fucker's got the worst case of red eye I ever saw."

The shirtless man sets his gaze on Angela and starts grunting while pushing against the fence like he is humping it. Lester is disturbed. The guy has a medium build but is completely bald. The way the guy is going at the fence reminds him of a child molester or something.

"I think he likes you, babe." Lester frowns as he comes to his feet. He carefully extracts the pistol from her hand and points it at the ground.

Angela studies the man, then steps closer. Lester grabs at her arm, but she slides away with a little shooing motion.

"I just want to get a closer look. I won't let him touch me."

"Just be careful."

She ignores him and approaches the fence but keeps a cautious foot or two from the man's grasping hands. Marlene joins the guy at the fence, and they wave their arms like a pair of drunks reaching for last call at a bar.

"Hey Marlene, you in there?" his girlfriend asks.

The deader shuffles back and forth, putting more pressure on the fence. The black guy reaches forward so far that he has to raise one leg to make the stretch. It comes up and close to the top of the fence. Then it makes the connection between the tiny barriers holding him back from the couple, and he practically staggers over the chain link.

"Get back, Angela, I'm gonna take him out!"

Angela stares at Marlene for another second as if transfixed by her eyes. She stares and stares and doesn't see the other deader fall forward, hand outstretched toward her. He lands face first but not before grabbing the top of her dress and ripping it down her chest. Angela takes a hasty step back and covers her now-bare breasts as if there were any need to be modest in front of the mindless things.

Lester doesn't really care for a peek now; all he can think about is the fact that one almost got his girl! He pulls her back roughly and then shoots the guy a few times. The deader thumps and bashes into the ground as the bullets strike. Puffs of blood rise from his back, neck, and head as they punch through his body. Then, with a groan, the guy goes still.

"Son of a bitch!" Lester howls. "Don't you get it? You stay on that side of the fence and you get to live." Fucker fell in his yard. How many more will figure that out?

KATE

Fever dreams rip dread horror through her skull.

She bolts upright to light shining through the curtains over the bedroom window. Home after a long night, home and safe in bed in her tiny studio. Time to get up and make breakfast. Some frozen waffles would be good with blueberry syrup pooling around the edges. Maybe some bacon in the microwave. Did she buy bacon last week? She must have, because she can smell it. She must have left it out when she got up earlier. Then the dream pops into her mind, and she shudders. Why now, why can't she just sleep in peace?

He had been there, the old man, crazier than ever. He had been tearing into her flesh with a belt this time. She tried to hide her face behind her forearms, but the leather struck everywhere. Blows fell over the rest of her naked body, and she screamed in agony until she was hoarse. Almost as bad as the beating was the smell of whiskey as he leaned over to scream profanities at her. He called her things she didn't understand, a word she had heard referred to as the C word. Bitch, over and over, always bitch and she didn't even know what it meant. She was eleven years old, and she wanted to die. She wanted to find a real father who treated her like a father should. She was too young to fight back, so she just curled up and hoped it would end soon.

Fucking pathetic!

That was the 'her' of fifteen years ago, the 'her' who gave in to the old alcoholic. He had been insane when he drank, which was most of the time. If it was noon and he hadn't tipped the bottle into a glass yet, it was going to be a good day. Then he would stare at the marks on her arms and legs and look away as if shamed, but it didn't stop him from doing it again.

Every once in a while, he was her best friend. He would take her to the drug store and let her buy anything she wanted from the toy rack, cheap little things in crinkling plastic containers that she would open in the car as he beamed at her. He would do this to make up for the bad times. But nothing made up for them. He could have bought her a pony and it wouldn't put a dent in his quota. Truth was she hated the toys, hated how cheap they were, but didn't want to risk angering him even if he was sober.

She takes a deep breath as she lies half off the bed, feet on the floor, upper body resting while she shifts her head to the side and studies the man's thigh drenched in crimson. With a gasp, she is on her feet and away from the blood. The room was familiar when she opened her eyes, but that was owed to her view of nothing but white ceiling.

It was the smell that should have given it away, should have clued her in to the fact that she was not in her usual reality.

Last night, she had been the other, and it had been wonderful.

The imagined smell of bacon is the body. Blood is congealed all over the bed, on the man, on the headboard, on the wall. She glances down at her naked body and sees drops there as well. In her hair, she is sure of it, and she is also sure that it is completely fucked up to pass out on a bed with a butchered man.

He is bound to the bed by his wrists, which are pressed tightly together and wrapped in white nylon rope. She picked the stuff because she knew from experience that it would chafe. After he had his fun, was beside himself with need, only then had he consented to having his hands tied so she could straddle his chest and take his enraged cock in her mouth—or so she had promised. She promised him she wanted to tease him, draw out his pleasure, all the while her striped back and ass presented to his hungry eyes.

They always complied. They always gave in. Tying his legs together had been a different matter. Lucky for her, he was in terrible shape and didn't have the energy to put up much of a struggle. Not with her fondling his cock and whispering words of devotion to his livid eyes.

Even though he made her call him master, had taken a belt to her, then a flogger while she straddled a straight-back chair so that her ass hung off the end, even as the pain started, built, overwhelmed her then turned to pure undeniable bliss, even then she had still been the other. The cold, calculating bitch who would have the ultimate climax.

He started on her thighs, whipping them red while she bent over, belt lashing across them over and over until she cried out for—more. Then the chair and the flogger, on her back, across her ass cheeks as they hung over the edge of the seat. Delicious agony that was nothing like the beatings of old. She was a masochist in the truest sense of the word. She found great pleasure in pain, in submitting to the men she would later truss up like pigs.

"Was it good for you?" she asks the corpse. She studies the bloody wounds and remembers each one like a snapshot in an old photo album. The first cut had been on his leg, the next on his chest. Not deep, just enough to bleed. The next had been on his neck, each side but not close to his carotid artery. His eyes had nearly burst from their sockets when she started slicing.

The blade was razor sharp, honed by her hand the night before. She sat on her couch and ran it over a stone until it was sharp enough to lift the downy hair of her forearms. Then she ran it over the stone again.

Like a medical student learning on a cadaver, she had punctured his body at various points, but none that would cause him to die. In his thighs, calves, feet, arms, and hands. She avoided his chest for now, because she wanted him to bleed. She had straddled his chest as she said she would, and lined his eyes with black lipstick so he looked like a raccoon.

Those eyes had pleaded, no longer looking on her body with lust, his cock flaccid like an old sausage. She turned to play with it, fondle it, tease it, but she couldn't get him up, not anymore. When he failed to get excited, she put the cold knife under it, which stopped his struggling. He moaned, begging her to stop.

"If you can get it up, I will let you go." She smiled as she applied his blood to her cheeks. She rubbed it around in a circle like the world's reddest blush.

He strained, tried to beg for her to let him go, begged with his eyes, which were filled with tears.

She would have none of that. In fact, she was just getting warmed up.

"You don't want me anymore, baby? You don't want me to beg for more pain?" she asked as she drew around her little nipples with the lipstick. And of course the pig didn't answer her; he couldn't with a washcloth stuffed in his mouth then taped up with silver duct tape. She drew a tongue where his lips were, wagging to the side with drool marks. He watched her with giant eyes shifting back and forth in silent reproach, begging her to let him go.

"Bet you would promise me the world right now. Bet you would promise me money, maybe a car, anything just so I would let you go. But I'm not going to. I'm going to kill you tonight, Fred or whatever your loser name was." She smiled.

"Did you enjoy beating me, you bastard? Did you enjoy using your belt on me? Fucking asshole. I bet you thought I liked it, that I came for you." He shook his head, eyes as big as saucers.

"I saw the mark on your finger where the wedding ring should be. Does Mrs. Asshole know you answer ads on Craigslist? That you like to meet girls and hurt them? Maybe I should have taken pictures to share with her."

She ran the knife over his chest, and it was razor sharp still, judging by the way it lifted the hair right off his sweaty skin. Puffs of the stuff, gray and wiry made tiny mounds. She blew on them and then cut a letter into his flesh, a big A.

He thrashed as she dug in, his eyes squinting in pain. He screamed against the cloth, but it sounded mute, so she cut a second outline around the letter. She moved the blade around the triangle in the A, then slid it under the skin. She slipped a finger against the broad part of the upper layer, and then she tore it off.

She spent the next five minutes finishing her artwork, making the letter more or less square. Blood welled around the angry wound, skin puckered like a pair of lips.

"Wakey wakey, time to meet a painful end." She grinned and cut his penis off. As the blood poured out, she opened his nut sac and removed both of his balls. The knife cut them cleanly, quickly, so she could show him her handiwork before he bled out. She slapped him, hard, because he might have passed out.

His eyes popped open, and he bellowed against the gag.

She placed his member on his chest inside the A and put his still-warm balls over his eyes. She held his head tightly so he couldn't shake them loose. Blood and body fluid leaked into his eyes, and he went crazy, but it didn't last for long as the bed soaked up his life fluid.

She moved the severed penis aside and listened to his chest as his heartbeat staggered to a slow crawl and then stopped. She retreated from his body as he died, just before he let go of his control.

A sickening sound as his bowels released, leaving a river of shit around his legs. The smell of blood and crap made her want to puke, but she stood over him and maintained control.

She took the gag out and put his severed dick in his mouth, then his balls back in his eye sockets, which were wide open and locked in pain.

She made it to the bathroom, calmly lifted the lid, leaned over and tugged her black hair back behind her neck just before a furious stream of vomit erupted from her mouth. She gagged around the burning fluid, then vomited again. The shakes set in, so she sat on the edge of the tub and waited for them to pass.

* * *

Showered, she cranks up the heat in the little room so she can move around naked. She takes the bag out of the closet and lays out her tools. She sorts his clothes and folds them neatly. She checks his wallet, which informs her that his name is Walter Smith and not Master M as he so blithely told her before he flogged the shit out of her.

She folds her clothes carefully and placed them in a plastic bag, then she combs the room, picking up anything that looks out of the ordinary. She puts the flogger in a separate bag, and the belt joins it. Her lipstick goes into the same bag, then she takes the binding off his wrists and ankles. She bought the rope at Home Depot and uses several sizes so that none is from the same manufacturer as any other. Let the CSI guys figure that one out.

She extracts the small vacuum and plugs in the AC adapter. Transferring the tiny device from outlet to outlet as she runs out of slack on the short cord, she cleans every inch of the tiny room, the chair, the bed, the couch. She slips to the ground and runs the cleaner under the furnishings.

She packs everything away and then pours a bottle of hydrogen peroxide over his entire body to confuse the scene. She does something different every time because she knows from reading books about serial killers that the way they get caught is by using the same MO, or modus operandi. She takes a lint-free polishing cloth and goes over the entire room with it. Then she does it again.

She showers one more time in scalding hot water and then dries off with the already wet towel, which she folds and puts in the bag. She dresses in a pair of gray slacks that burn as they slide over her thighs and ass. Then she slips on a pair of dark red pumps. A bra cups her tender breasts, covering the welts that still stand out from the night before. A blue silk blouse whispers over her bruised back. She buttons it up demurely and then goes into the bathroom to put on a blond wig. She applies a tint of pink lipstick to her full lips and studies her face in the mirror. Pretty, not beautiful, maybe a bit too long in the chin. Eyes ever so slightly upswept, possibly from an Asian relative a few generations ago. Brown eyes shine without the thick layer of eyeliner she wore when she came in. The half dozen clip-on earrings she wore last night are gone, and it looks odd to leave that side of her head bare.

Who are you? she asks silently. The one you couldn't be all those years ago, she answers just as silently.

MIKE

"Jim needs to see you," Erin says before I have a chance to sit down. She studies me for a moment but doesn't say a word. I suppose she is waiting for me to offer up a hint about my conversation with Rita. She has always been a good listener in the past, offering advice on my ex-wife and my feelings for her. But today I'm not in a sharing mood. I feel stifled, depressed, like I need to be two people at once, and I don't have the energy for it. I think about how many times I have been the sounding board for Rita, how many times I have listened to her rant and rave in the middle of the night while offering nothing but lame sounds like 'oh' and 'I'm sorry.' The truth is I'm not sorry, not anymore.

Erin's eyes meet mine again, and I feel it, like an electric current passes through me. I feel like I should do something, say something, but I end it with a lame "Cool, thanks." And walk away.

Jim's little slice of heaven is the epitome of an editor's office. Stacks of old papers skulk in every corner. Piles of printouts obscure the surface of his desk. He has layouts plastered to the walls, hiding the handful of journalist awards on his 'me wall.' An old ceiling fan hangs over the desk like a decrepit set of arms complete with dust and detritus trailing from the blades. I'm sure it hasn't been turned on in years; in fact, if it came on, we might have to evacuate the office to avoid a massive allergy attack.

Jim perches on a four-legged wicker stool, leaning over so his forearms rest on his desk. He is peering at an old computer monitor that is as big as a tube television. It's bulky and supported on a small stack of telephone books. His room smells of old paper and smoke. When he isn't in the office, he puts away at least a pack a day.

"I've been thinking about this gas leak. I called 911 and acted like I lived up on the hill, asked them when I could go home. She put me on hold for a minute, and then some guy comes on the line, smooth as butter. He assures me the neighborhood is still too dangerous, that the leak could explode with little provocation. He is calm, and when I try to ask questions, he just deflects them and talks about my safety, concern for my well-being. And the whole time, you know what I'm thinking?" He takes a breath and keeps going before I can get a word in. "I'm thinking that these chuckleheads need to spend a little more time being straight with us and a little less time making up a bunch of bullshit, 'cause we both know there is no way a gas leak caused them to evacuate an entire neighborhood for two days. No way."

"Want me to go up there?" I'm thinking about how ridiculous I will look when I flash my press pass for the tiny newspaper I work for. Wonder how hard they will laugh when I bust out some hard-hitting questions like 'What are you covering up?'

"Nah, just call around, hit up some friends. Don't you have a buddy who used to be a cop?"

"He's still a cop. Works for Bellevue, so he probably won't know anything."

"I bet you can find out stuff. You're good at that; hit up Google and see what kind of crazy rumors you can turn up."

"You're the chief, err, chief."

* * *

I'm back at my desk when my cell rings again. It's Rita, but I ignore it and go back to scouring the web. Sure I can call on friends and old associates to see if I can get a lead, but Jim is right: nowadays all the action is on Google.

The only problem is that reports are weird. A man claims he was chased into his house near Queary Park by a guy with red eyes and gray skin. He said he looked like a corpse and smelled worse. I discount it immediately; the neighborhood borders Fremont, and I know how those guys like to party. In fact, every year there is a naked parade through town that makes the conservatives nuts.

I back my browser up a couple of pages so I can read that message board again. It's devoted to sushi shops in Seattle, but the guy seems like a regular poster. The only problem is that I can't find it now. Their message board must have gone down. I go to offline mode and grab the story out of my browser's cache. Once it is on the screen, I hit print and grab the warm copy off my little desktop inkjet printer.

"What is this?" Erin asks when I show her the copy.

"Can you check that link? I'm having trouble finding it again."

"What do you mean?"

"I mean it won't come up. I did variations of the same search with no luck. I grabbed the old link from my history, but it gave me a 404 error." 404 is the universal 'screw you' that web pages display when they don't exist anymore.

She spins around and stabs at her keyboard with lacquered nails that clatter across the keys like plastic dominoes falling on a card table.

"Rita keeps calling me," I say quietly. I don't even know why I utter the words. Erin pauses but doesn't turn around.

"How is she?"

"The usual. Delusional, drunk, probably on enough pills to choke a horse."

"Mike, you need to leave her alone. You divorced her years ago, but you pander to her needs every day, and you hate yourself for it. Don't you want a normal life?" Same old conversation, same old Erin, and sadly … same old me.

She isn't the only one. I have heard it a hundred times from a hundred different people. Even the big guy on TV who dispenses advice would say the same, and still I know I can't leave Rita alone. She needs me. She needed me then, before Andy, and she needs me now more than ever.

Erin turns around and hands me the paper. "Nothing, dead link." Her eyes study mine, and suddenly I feel shy under her gaze. We have been co-workers for a year, and I won't say that I haven't had feelings for her. But she is smart, beautiful, and young, too young to get mixed up with me.

I take the paper from her, and our hands brush each other. Her fingers are soft and warm as they trail across the back of mine, sending a shiver up my spine.

"Thanks for checking."

She doesn't say a word. She just stares at me, and I can feel the pity radiating from her like a furnace.

"No problem." Again I feel like something passed between us, as if I missed an important moment. I know I should ask her what's on her mind, but I don't have the guts, not today.

There is a picture on my desk of me, Rita, and a very young, very toothless Andy. He was at that age where he seemed to be missing teeth like lost toys. He was smiling, a big cheesy grin that surely came from my side of the family. Rita was radiant in a white dress, shoulder straps hanging over her pale but shapely frame. I'm behind them, arms draped around both. This picture is from a trip to Florida to see the big mouse. It was one of the best weeks of my life. I miss them, both of them, and I don't know how to get over them.

I throw myself back at the computer and widen my search to blogs. That's when I hit the jackpot.

A guy who calls himself SilverSurfer57 writes:

It's a cover-up, folks; I can confirm this for at least as long as this blog stays active. I'm guessing that the guys in suits have some sort of program scouring the web for certain words, so I'm going to keep this as generic as I can.

There is some crazy shit going down in my neighborhood, which is in the Emerald City. This neighborhood is not for kings, and it was the other sister. Okay, enough hints?

It's a pretty clever reference to Queen Anne.

I have been holed up in my basement (hold the laughter, assholes) for a day and a night. I locked the doors but cops and soldiers have been by several time. They walked all over my property and smashed my wife's flowers. Bastards. I don't know what they are looking for but I did see them rounding up some sick looking people.

I don't know what the sick guys have but it's bad enough so that now they have the CDC fuckers in town and they are dressed in white suits that zip all the way up to their masks. I think you know what I am talking about here, folks. Who didn't see that Dustin Hoffman flick Outbreak? So what is it exactly? I'm guessing it's bird based, are you catching my drift here, folks? Get it, drift?

"Fuck me!" I exclaim as I collapse back into my chair. It rolls back a foot and comes to a stop.

"Smooth talker," Erin calls over her shoulder.

I turn and look at her; she has her back to me, so I whisper.

"Erin, can you help me with something?"

She rolls back and gives me a serious stare. "Yes, Agent Pierce?"

I roll my eyes. Our heads are close together, but our backs are still to each other. I can smell her scent again, clean, fresh, like she just showered. I have never known her to wear a hint of perfume, for which my allergies are eternally grateful.

"If the bird flu hit the U.S., what do you think the government would do?"

She spins around and stares at me. "I hope you aren't suggesting ..."

"I don't know what I'm suggesting. I hope I don't."

"Well, I think they would go on TV and have the Centers for Disease Control make some statements about safety, what to avoid, what to do, word on vaccines—I think they have some sort of vaccine for that stuff now, don't they?"

"But what if they don't and it hit a certain community hard, so hard that they had to lock it down, make up some bullshit story about a gas leak. Are you with me here?" My eyebrows are arched, and I think my voice may have a hint of hysteria to it, because her eyes have gone wide, but I can't read her look. It may just be pity since she knows what today is to me.

"Mike, you can't be serious."

"I don't know. I was just reading a blog; this guy is hiding out in Queen Anne and writing about people in white suits collecting sick people. The big CDC suits that cover them from head to toe with gas masks, the works."

"A blog? Oh Jesus, Mike, I thought you were onto something there."

"What about the site that worked a few minutes ago but now is down? Isn't that weird?"

"Right. Websites never go down."

I sit back, turn around to face the computer and look at the blog again, then I burst out laughing. She is right. What am I getting so worked up about? I'm not some ace reporter in a book who discovers something the rest of the American public has missed. It's absurd, but I know what it stems from. I don't want to think about today's date.

I look over my shoulder at Erin, and she is smiling at me with her arms crossed.

"You're right, it's silly. I'm just a little … off today."

"Off your rocker, maybe."

"Would you have me any other way?"

"I would take you that way … any way for that matter," and then she winks, which makes me blush until I turn around and try to concentrate on work.

I wish I were a drinking man so I could have a liquid lunch.

* * *

Noon rolls around. I have poked and prodded the web, contacted friends, and finally called my buddy who is a cop. Dale sounded distracted; he has been on the force in Bellevue for a couple of years. When I asked him about the excitement in Seattle, he blew it off, claiming it was way out of his area. I asked him if he'd heard any rumors, and he replied with a curt "no" and said he had to go because he was on duty. We have chatted while he was on duty before, but he sounded harried today. Maybe he was about to pull someone over.

I head out to a local deli to grab a bite to eat. The wind whips my shirt around my back as I step out of the small office space on Denny Avenue. It is colder than usual, and I'm betting rain. It's a pretty safe gamble in Seattle. Some kids light off fireworks, and I jump at the sound of firecrackers in an alley. It sounded like gunfire for a moment, and all the paranoia of the morning has set me on edge. Last night was bad enough, and it is still a day before the fourth. Kids were blowing stuff up for hours as I tossed and turned and finally fell asleep around 1:00 a.m.

I usually go out to lunch with Bob in advertising, but today he brought something to eat. I didn't bother with Jim, because he was busy screaming into the phone at a vendor that screwed up an order of paper. Erin broke out a huge salad before I could ask her if she wanted to grab a bite to eat.

So I venture out alone and walk the warm three blocks to the deli. Lou isn't behind the counter, but his wife is. She is a tall Korean woman who smiles all the time and is in the habit of experimenting with new meals to unleash on her regulars. She once made a batch of coleslaw with kimchi in it, only she didn't tell me about the hot stuff. I thought I was going to have a heart attack right in the tiny store. She laughed so hard that my tears of pain turned into tears of laughter for her.

I order a turkey, bacon, avocado sandwich and wait with a couple of other guys. We all stand around trying to look interested in the candy bars and bags of chips so we don't have to look at or talk to each other. I wander over to the news rack and scour the front page for any weird stories, but it is the usual bad news about the economy. I must be a sight, a newsman reading a rival newspaper. Except that they aren't even a rival. They could swallow our little rag with barely a burp of indigestion.

I move to the window while the woman works on three orders as fast as she can. She tends to be a perfectionist, which is fine with me. All I have to go back to is a stuffy room with buzzing computers.

A couple wanders past the deli hand in hand, but they don't look very happy. The man keeps glancing behind him as if being followed. I move to the corner and try to peer around it, but I don't see anything except cars rushing by. Then the couple is past the window. I watch them and it dawns on me, the weird feeling I have had all day. It's like a sense of dread hangs over the city, like it is waiting for something to happen.

I hope it's just my nerves.

LESTER

The smell of gunpowder hangs in the air and then is whisked away by a breeze. Marlene stares on. Lester raises the gun and pulls the trigger again like another bullet will make a difference after the three that are already in the deader's neck and face. There is no boom, and he remembers that he is dry. Angela grabs his arm and pulls him back. She shivers and makes an attempt to cover herself with the ripped fabric of her dress. She pulls him back to the porch, where they collapse into their respective seats. Lester sighs, and then the shakes start for real.

"Oh shit." His voice is harsh from yelling at the corpse. "That was sick."

"God, he just came right over the fence. Do you think he's dead?"

"Oh yeah, he's dead all right. I just put a shitload of lead into his body."

Angela sobs once, stares down at her torn dress, at her breasts, which she covers with one arm. She lifts her other hand to tug at the fabric, then drops it and breaks out in tears.

"Ah come on, babe. Let's get you some new clothes, then we'll smoke a bowl and things will be different."

"What about the deaders? If we go inside, we won't know if they get into the yard or not."

"The only reason he made it over the fence is because he saw us. If we go inside, they won't have any reason to get in."

"Oh."

She follows him into the small house, which is stifling. She stares out the window, her torn dress clutched in one hand. She smells faintly of sweat and whatever cream she puts on her soft skin. He moves behind her and runs his hands along her arms.

"She's leaving," she mumbles.

"Marlene?"

"No, my gay sister Frieda. Of course Marlene. She watched the house for a minute, and then she just walked off like she had a hot date."

"Maybe she's meeting another deader for drinks." Lester tries to find humor in his own joke.

She watches the window for another moment, curtain pulled to the right, but gives up on this fairly quickly and plops down on the couch. Angela opens the new purse after wiping at the bloodstains with a tissue for a few seconds. She pulls out Marlene's wallet and flips through the contents. Checking out her friend's ID, she clucks at the picture.

"That lying bitch. I knew she was older than 28."

She yanks out credit cards and tosses them in a heap. There is some money, but it barely looks like enough to get a few drinks at Starbucks. She also has a small packet of blue pills.

"Oh fucking score, babe, got some free X."

"Great," Lester says while staring at the top of Angela's torn dress where her breast is barely covered.

She takes out lipstick and removes the cover, rolling the color up. "Hmm, streetwalker red, my favorite." The lipstick joins the other treasures on the table. She pulls out a box of condoms and shows them to Les with her eyebrows raised.

"I knew she was fucking around on Chuck."

"How do you know that? Maybe they're for him."

"Because he had a vasectomy," she states.

"Poor bastard."

"Chuck or her lover?"

"Um, both?" he turns the smile into a question, his head cocked to the side.

"Hah."

She pulls out an iPhone and holds it up. She unlocks it and looks through Marlene's contacts.

"Shit, no signal."

"They cut everything somehow. We're completely isolated."

"Babe," Angela pleads. "We need to get out of here."

"Tomorrow, babe, promise."

He heads upstairs to the bedroom with Angela in tow. He studies what is left of their clean clothes. He had planned to wash today, but with no power, that plan fell apart just like pretty much everything else. He may be a drug dealer, but he hates dirty clothes. He stares down at his own shorts, which he has worn for several days, and grimaces. If the power doesn't come back soon, he plans to fill the tub with water

33

and wash their clothes by hand and then hang them up in the house like they are trailer trash.

Angela drops her new purse on the dresser, then shrugs out of the tatters of her dress and stands gloriously naked in the center of the room. Lester's eyes are hungry as they rove over her body from calves to round hips, over her full breasts with pencil eraser nipples to her pert face with its sprinkle of freckles. Though she likes to bleach her hair blond, it is a shade of light brown that shows at her roots. She doesn't have to worry about the rug matching the curtains, because she is smooth as a baby down there. Hardwood floors all the way, baby.

Lester slips behind her and runs his hands up her stomach to cup one high breast. The bubble of her implant is detectable, but he ignores it and rubs her nipple between thumb and forefinger until it grows hard as a little pebble.

She sucks in a breath and leans back into him, her hand going down to cup his balls in his shorts. If he weren't hard as a rock already, that would have done the trick. He loves seeing her naked. He has pictures on the computer, posed, candid, some taken in secret. When she runs off to her part-time job, he likes to go through them while waxing poetic with his cock.

"Oh wait." She giggles and dives across the bed. Their pipe is on the nightstand on her side of the bed. She picks it up and loads a fresh green bud from a baggie. Lester wriggle out of his shorts and climbs onto the bed as she lights up. He straddles her legs so he can caress her ass with both hands. He wants to dive between her legs, but he will be patient, wait until they are both good and high.

She coughs out a stream of smoke and hands the pipe up. He takes a deep hit and then passes it back while his other hand moves across her lower back, ass, and the top of her thighs. She parts her legs just enough for him to slip his hand through so he can finger her.

She takes another hit and holds it as long as she can before exhaling the smoke in a long, lazy stream. She sighs as he plays with her sex.

"Go down on me!" she begs, and Lester thinks that is a pretty fucking good idea, so he slides off her and hits the pipe one more time. She rolls over and parts her long legs. His eyelids grow heavy as the pot kicks in. His heart beats faster, but that may be because he is about to get laid. His ears ring, and sounds warble in and out of his brain.

He sighs and sinks his head between her thighs and smells HER over the burning smell of pot on his breath. She giggles as his goatee rubs against her thighs, then her hands are in his hair and she is pulling his face down to grind into her.

*   *   *

"I love fucking when we're high." Angela stares at the ceiling. She cups his now-flaccid cock, stroking it gently while she waits for it to wake up again. She feels content and warm all over. Her sex is still throbbing, wanting him to sink into her again. She has always had this need for more and better sex, and Lester fills it pretty well. Other lovers have tried, and failed. Of course none of them had access to the drugs that Lester does.

She grabs a bottle of fruit-flavored rum from the side of the bed and takes a swig. The liquor burns its way down her throat in a line of fire that erupts in her belly. She grimaces but swallows another shot of the coconut-flavored fire.

"Goddamn, that is good." She exhales. She hands the bottle to Lester and waits for the booze to mix with the weed. It feels like the room is pulsing around her, and she has the sudden urge to crank up some music and dance naked for him.

She struggles to her feet and stands over his waist, legs parted so he can gaze up at her. The lack of electricity casts the room in midday shadows from the wide slats in the blinds. The window above their bed is wide open, but she doesn't care if one of their pervy neighbors wants to watch. Not that she has seen anyone else today except the deaders, and they don't really count. Some people walked by the other day, cautiously creeping by the house as if escaping from jail or something. Bags and boxes in hand like a bunch of refugees.

Soldiers stood on either side as they left the cul-de-sac. The same soldiers who pounded on the doors earlier in the day, then walked around the house like they owned the place. She had to hold on to Lester, because he was pissed and he had that big machine gun in hand, and she knew nothing ever went down like it did in the movies. If he tried to kick them off the lawn, she was pretty sure things would have gone downhill fast.

Putting the nasty thought out of her mind, she starts humming a song out loud, puts her hands above her head, and sways back and forth. The room spins, but she moves with it as if she were a dancer in front of a crowd.

She can see them in her mind: a big Las Vegas show where everyone's eyes are on her body. The women stare, jealous; men watch in lust. She waves her hands at them and then steps over Lester so her legs are spread over his face.

He smiles and claps his hands in appreciation, takes a pull on the rum bottle and hands it to her.

"Like what you see, baby?" she teases.

"Look down."

She does and is pleased to see he is hard again. She settles down slowly on his lap. Then she rides him for the audience. She drinks from the bottle and lets some dribble between her lips to splash down her chest. He struggles upright and laps at her breasts, trying to clean them of the alcohol.

Her moans grow louder. "That's it, right there, do it! Fuck me!"

He thrusts up into her, hard, and she rides him, hips flexing back and forth. Much sooner than she wants, he unleashes a stream inside her with a long and loud moan. But that's okay. She knows where the Viagra is, and within a half hour, he'll be ready to go again.

She collapses against his chest and bites at his neck. She wants to stay in the bedroom for the rest of the day, smoke, drink and fuck. The world is going to shit, so it seems like a great way to give it the middle finger.

KATE

She walks to the elevator with a cool, confident step. High heels click clack as she strides with purpose across the lobby. She ignores the sign advertising continental breakfast in front of the elevator door, steers around the tiny restaurant tables with their assortment of muffins, breads, carafes and bowls of sugar and creamer laid out in perfect symmetry. It strikes her that an employee must have good discipline to line up little packets so perfectly. It smells good, like a combination fresh bakery and coffee shop.

She drops her bag on the floor and extends the sliding handle with a click. Then she tilts the combination overnight bag and laptop case back on its wheels and pulls it behind her. There are only a few people in the lobby, and the men turn to check out the chick in heels. What would they think if they knew her 'other side'?

It's not a classy hotel by any stretch of the imagination, nor is it a complete dump. It rides that area between the two in which she prefers to do her work. For one thing, it is big enough that the worker from the night before won't be on duty the next morning, but not so big that they have a security camera on every corner. In fact, a day of scoping out places revealed that this particular hotel only has security cameras on every other floor, thanks to construction.

She entered this hotel once as a businesswoman in town for a night.

The second time she came in was on the arm of large man who was sweating profusely. No surprise in the muggy July heat. His hand shook, just a minor tremble as he scribbled on the room information form. He slid a credit card across to a smiling attendant who had clearly seen it all. Then the two were off, and the desk worker couldn't help but follow the girl as she strutted across the floor in a tiny plaid shirt, torn-fishnet-clad legs on display.

She had checked in with the same attendant a few hours ago, but dressed in professional clothing with a pair of sunglasses to hide her eyes. She had an old plane ticket hanging out of her wallet so the guy could see it, just a little something to complete the illusion. She had worn a different pantsuit, a brown number with a plaid jacket. The expensive license Kate Osborne handed over proclaimed her Leslie Miller, the result of a forged birth certificate that cost her a quarter year's pay.

No one who saw the two women enter would ever guess that they are one and the same. She checks out with a disinterested look on her face and clicks out the door after shooting the attendant, whose nametag identifies him as Steve Bolling, a quick smile meant to dismiss, to say, "I'm far too busy to engage with you. I have other things to attend to."

The glass door slides shut behind her with a whisper, and she is on the street. The same dark sunglasses complete her disguise as she steps onto the sidewalk.

She glances around and wonders what is out of place. There is something in the air, as if the city just took a breath and forgot to exhale. People pass her, but they don't make eye contact. A young couple holds hands, but instead of looking carefree, they are in an awful hurry to get somewhere. The young man glances around but doesn't see Kate. He passes behind her, and the two turn right at the next corner.

Her eyes light on a man across the street. He hovers in an alley, staring at a wall, then staggers toward a green dumpster and walks straight into it. He backs away, then leans forward and bashes his head against it several times.

"Whoa, whoa, buddy, you all right?" A black guy with short dreads glances over at the lost soul. He turns into the alley and approaches the man. Kate continues to watch, half interested, as she flags down a taxi.

Second Avenue has a hundred yellow and green cabs on it. She shoots her hand up as one passes, but another pulls up, and the driver hops out so fast the trailing end of his shirt nearly catches the corner of his car door.

He pops the trunk and drops her bag in quickly. She jumps in the back and says "Airport please," then commences to stare at an old Blackberry. She looks up at the two men still in the alley. The black guy leans forward so his hand can rest on the other man's shoulder. He has a concerned look etched on his face as he asks a question.

"What the fuck?" she gasps as the taxi pulls away. Did that confused-looking man just attack the black guy? For a split second, it appeared that he spun around and bit the guy's arm. Then the taxi speeds down the street as her eyes follow the action for as long as she can.

Must be imagining things, she assures herself. Nothing to see here, move along. Don't mind the biters. She stifles a giggle at her weird humor, then turns her attention to the dead Blackberry as if checking the stocks or maybe texting her significant other. This may be an unnecessary part of her disguise, but she follows it every second or third time she makes a kill. Anything to mix up the MO.

Traffic is light on I-5, which isn't unusual for this time of day. She stares out the window at the city of Seattle, its waterfront that teems with life as freighters arrive day and night. She has seen old black and white pictures of the city from decades ago when it was all wooden structures and people in funny hats. Now, high-rises cut into the landscape against a background of white-tipped mountains. On a clear day, you can see all the way across the Puget Sound from here. On a normal gray and rainy day, you can't see shit.

Still, she can't think of a better place to live, what with the cultural Mecca aspect, the intellectual side and the green Nazis that crowd the neighborhoods with recycling containers. Then there is the nightlife, which she mostly avoids. However, she likes to take in a loud concert from time to time, preferably at El Cid—the darkest metal haven in the city. Bands from all over come to play the place; the beer is cheap and cold, and the girls who work there are fucking hot.

Her thoughts drift until a line of green cuts across the road on the opposite side of the highway. Cruising along the right-hand lane is a steady stream of camouflaged vehicles. They stretch a mile into the distance and look very, well, shocking against the normally peaceful city.

"What the fuck?" she mutters for the second time in ten minutes.

The driver actually slows down as the green snake makes its way along the other side of the highway. He stares at it and then speeds up and is revving down the highway once again.

"Hey, I changed my mind. Can you take the next exit and drop me along Airport Way? I'll show you the spot."

"Fine," he says in slightly accented English and shoots her a dirty look. She can understand; it means he will need to return after a short fare with no one in the car. She'll just tip him well to make up for it.

★ ★ ★

After a long bus ride from the SoDo district back to Queen Anne, she walks into her apartment complex as herself. Long black hair dangles free, but she is still dressed in 'work clothes,' having changed her plans. Normally she goes to the airport and changes in a bathroom, dumps the luggage and catches a bus back in her normal clothes. Just like at the hotel, she is being ultra-paranoid, entering as one person, leaving as another.

The reason for the long, slow bus trip was the congestion caused by the Army trucks moving up and down the streets. She saw men getting out and standing at attention, other trucks stopping, taking up entire lanes while they waited for something. Was it a terrorist threat? Surely a little gas leak wouldn't necessitate this many troops on the streets.

She takes the stairs, since there is no telling how long the old elevator will take if it is on the top floor. Besides, it's only a few flights, and every little bit does her legs good. She thinks they're a bit chunky, not that the men she killed ever complained when she stood or knelt naked for them. They are thick, sure, but that came with her training.

She leaves the stairwell and makes her way to her apartment. Passes the place belonging to the widow Mildred Jones, who is much younger than her name lets on. Her husband had died in the late eighties while working on the docks. A large settlement meant she didn't have to work, so she stays cooped up. Contrary to every stereotype of a widowed woman with too many cats, she is actually fun to hang out with and always had a bag of weed on hand.

She slides her key into her apartment door, number 203, and it pops open. Bob Brason opens his door, and for a second she thinks of Rick Moranis in Ghostbusters, constantly waiting for Sigourney Weaver to come home so he can pop his head out and hit on her in his pathetic way. She tosses her bag into her apartment, quickly, hoping he doesn't comment on it. "Gee Kate, why the laptop bag? Been on a business trip? That's kinda weird. I mean, don't you work at a bookstore?" She wants to pound on the voice that mocks her, the voice in her head that sometimes says the damnedest things.

Unlike Moranis, Bob is actually a cool guy who has the worst job Kate has ever heard of. Even her mindless existence at the bookstore downtown is better than what he does, although he does get to work from home.

Bob is in a bathrobe, as usual, and he sports at least two days' worth of beard. He has his glasses on, and he must have been looking outside, because the transition lenses are dark. The thin wire frames disappear into the bushy growth of black hair that hangs down to obscure his ears and neck.

"Hey, kitty cat, you have a rough night?"

"Don't call me that."

"Sorry, kitty cat."

"Yeah and your mom says hi," she teases. Bob likes her, she knows this. Bob knows this. She likes Bob, but she doesn't ever let on. In fact, she has made it clear that she is into women, even though she just fantasizes about that aspect of her sexuality. She can't ever let on to Bob that she likes him; it would be far too dangerous for both of them. Sometimes she senses there is a mutual attraction, but she always puts him off by talking about some hot chick she is seeing.

"Harsh! Did she say what she wanted for Christmas? I want to get my shopping done early this year."

"A new dishwasher. She's tired of doing everything by hand."

"That used to be my job. So she wants a seventeen-year-old kid who talks back a lot, got it."

Kate smiles and then giggles at the joke.

"You in the hallway in your bathrobe for any other reason than to see my pretty face?" she inquires. "Don't you have some pervs to call?"

Bob is a collection agent for a company that sells live porn feeds on the Internet. When the customers don't pay up or their credit cards end up getting declined after they have rung up a large bill, they send Bob in. His favorite collection method is to leave messages that can be overheard by their spouses. Sometimes Kate wishes she could see the faces of the women who hear: "Hello, Mrs. Smith, your husband owes the she-male fuck city club six hundred dollars in charges. Will that be direct withdrawal from your bank account?"

"Nah, I was staring out the little hole in the door when you came down the stairs. There is some weird stuff going on out there, and the news stations are being way too cool about it. They say the military is just doing practice drills, but did you see those assholes on every corner?"

"I know, right?" Kate exclaims.

"It's the gas leak, has to be. Half the damn city closed down, and they moved people out of the affected neighborhood. But why is everyone acting so weird? If it's just a gas leak, do we really need the fucking Army to get involved?"

"You are kidding, I hope." Kate sets her night bag down and leans against her door, kicks one leg back, foot arched against it so her knee sticks out. Bob leans against his doorframe and lowers his voice.

"Nope. But when you do searches, sometimes stuff disappears even as you look it up. I've been on the net for a long time, and I've never seen anything like it. Even cached pages are all fucked up. Like if I search for a page and it doesn't come up, Google usually has a stored version of it available. That isn't bringing stuff up anymore."

"Maybe Google is just having issues," she thinks out loud and wishes she still smoked so she could add a cig to this bullshit session. She really wants to go inside and go to bed, but Bob is one of her few friends, and she likes to listen to him. Sometimes he reminds her of what a college professor should be. Well, if a college professor collected for the porn industry.

"Maybe, and maybe the Army is just doing a practice drill that means they have to mobilize a few thousand troops and put them on the streets of Seattle. Come on, this is the most laid-back city in the world. You were on the street. Was that normal?"

That gives her pause as she thinks about the guys jumping out of truck beds, checking weapons, looking confused, waiting for orders. It didn't look normal at all. In fact, it looked downright screwed up.

"You go do some searches and then tell me what you think."

"I'm gonna get some rest first. I'm beat," she says, the irony of the statement not lost on her or the other. Kate spins around, knowing his eyes are on her legs but not caring. She glances over her shoulder and blows him a kiss.

"Who's the lucky girl?" he inquires as she opens the door.

"Just someone I met online. I don't think we're going to see each other again." Then she slips inside and closes the door. Home at last, and boy is she glad for the comfort. She can't help but feel dirty from the night before, dirty and used. Her back, thighs, and ass are a constant wave of pain as she moves. Pain that makes her focus her thoughts. Pain that makes her hot when she thinks of the night before, not the killing but the way the bastard made her sit in the chair and took the flogger to her with a passion. She wonders what it would be like to have Bob do the same to her and feels a warm rush between her legs.

Maybe she will go to bed and think about it a bit more while satisfying herself. Then she sees the image of the guy she butchered, and she is no longer horny. She just wants to curl up and die.

MIKE

"Turkey bacon avocado!" she calls out in accented English. She is the only one working at the deli, so it takes a couple extra minutes. It's quieter than usual; the other customers have long since departed. I go to pay and grab a bag of spicy chips on the way. When she zips my credit card, I notice that she looks haggard, keeps glancing at the clock, which hangs next to a full wall map of South Korea. There are pictures of military transports on the wall as well; the owner used to fly for the Air Force.

"Where's Lou?"

"He not feeling well." She clenches her face, which tells me he is probably sitting at home on the crapper. I feel sorry for him, but it's not like we are best friends. I only shoot the breeze with him while I wait for food.

The walk back is warmer. It seems like the sun is making a comeback over the morning clouds, so I take my time. There are others on the street, but I'm used to seeing more people. I walk toward Puget Sound. The mountains cut a beautiful sight against the backdrop of hazy sky. Boats flit here and there on the dark water, making bright white wakes. A ferry is powering toward the islands across the water.

When I get back to my desk, my cell buzzes again. Rita. I snap open the phone.

"You doing okay?"

"Yeah. There is so much yelling, though. There are police everywhere." I hear the clink of ice in a glass as she tosses something back.

"What's going on?"

"I don't know. There was fighting a few doors down, and then it stopped. I heard banging and lots of loud steps." She pauses to take a breath and then slurs into the phone, "Then all these cops were here with guns drawn. I think someone may be hurt or there was a fight."

The glass clinks again.

Rita lives in a small apartment on Capitol Hill. We used to have a house out in Auburn, but we ended up moving into different places during the divorce. After the settlement, I didn't have to worry about money to take care of Rita and the house, so in an unusual moment of clarity, I paid down our loan and refinanced the remainder at a honey of a rate. Now I have a mortgage that is less than most people's car payments, and she can afford a nice apartment near the city.

It's really pathetic that a woman who used to be an architect lives alone and is content to sit around her tiny apartment with her computer and a TV for company. Not to mention the ever-present plastic jug of vodka.

"Can you see anything?"

I hear her slide the curtains back. I can see the scene in my head, the circular parking lot full of cars. The road that leads out encompassed by trees. It may be an inexpensive place to live, but it is very well kept.

"There are some people moving around. I think the cops are trying to arrest someone. Um ..."

"What do you see?"

"He ... he's a big guy, and he's covered in blood."

This gives me pause. Should I leave work and rush over there? If I call a cab, it can probably get me there in fifteen or twenty minutes. The police probably have the situation in hand, and it will just depress me to see my ex-wife drunk in the middle of the day. I wonder if she would be seeing what she is describing without an alcohol-fueled sense of reality.

"He's, wait ... he's fighting. There are three cops trying to snap cuffs on him. He ... oh my God! He broke free and hit one of the officers. The guy fell down. I think he got hit hard. The other cops are trying to tackle him but ... oh what the ... the guy is biting one of them. Oh my God!"

"Rita, why don't you go sit down and see if there is anything on TV?" The words are stupid. I know she won't be able to look away. I wouldn't. Did she say biting?

"No. He is getting to his feet. The cops have their guns drawn. They're shouting. The other cop is lying on his back ... he's bleeding a lot. Okay, the first cop is trying to get to the biter."

There is a bang and then another; they resonate in the tiny speaker.

"Rita! Get down!" I yell into the phone, and for the first time I notice the entire office is staring at me. Erin's face is painted with concern, she half stands up, but I shoot her a small shake of my head, so she sits back down.

"It's okay. The guy is down, and the cops are taking care of the bleeding partner. More police are arriving and a couple of ambulances. It looks like they put a few bullets into the attacker ... wait, he's moving again."

"Where did they shoot him?"

"Chest, I think. He must be on something. He's on his feet and ... oh my God, he's attacking another cop. He's on top of him, biting him like the first one. The cop is trying to hit the guy but it ... Jesus, what is he on?"

"Rita, do you want me to come get you?" Her phone starts to fuzz and turn to static.

"I think it's okay now. The other cops are getting out of their cars, and they have more guns."

There is a series of loud pops that get lost in more static. I yank the phone off my ear like it is red hot and stare at the display. I have a row of full bars, so it isn't me. More bursts when I put the phone to my ear.

"Rita!"

"They got him, but I think they hit some of the other cops too. I need to rest now. Oh my God." Then the line dissolves into static and clicks off.

I redial a couple of times, but her phone just rings. I try her cell, but if I know her, the thing is dead and buried in the bottom of her purse. She never thinks to charge it, and just as I expect, my call goes straight to voicemail. I stare around dumbly for a few moments as I try to formulate a plan. If I leave now, I can be at her apartment in twenty minutes, thirty at the most, but what will I see? If there is a shooting, the road and apartment will be blocked for hours. Will I be able to get in?

I go back to my desk and look up the apartment building. I find it on the web and dial the office. After about half a dozen rings, the phone clicks over to voicemail, which informs me of the virtues of living at Casa De Monaco apartments. "Stupid goddamn name," I swear into the phone.

Erin is standing beside me. She rests a hand on my shoulder, and I look up at her.

"You okay?"

"Yeah. There's something going on at Rita's. She said the cops shot someone; he attacked and bit them."

"He bit them? Are you sure?"

"Yep."

"Druggie?"

"No idea."

"Are you going over there?" She leans against the desk with her arms crossed under her breasts. Her shirt is nothing fancy, yet it plunges ever so gently over her curves. For all its demure style, I struggle not to stare.

"I don't know. I mean I'm sure she'll be fine, but now I can't get through on the phones."

"Why don't we check Leonard's scanner, see what's going on?"

"You are brilliant," I say and stand up. She doesn't back away, and we are very close to each other. She is slightly shorter than I, but in heels she would look me in the eye—not that I'm a tall guy by any stretch. She is watching me, eyes fixed on mine, and I stare into those marvelous pools of brown for a few seconds. She doesn't speak, doesn't need to. Her eyes say it all; they look deep into mine and they smolder. For a stupid second, I see myself leaning over and kissing her, but the absurdity rocks me back. She can't be interested in an old guy like me; I'm used up and tired. She is young, beautiful; she probably has men knocking down her door.

The moment stretches. I don't know what to do, so I place a hand on her shoulder, something I wouldn't normally do, but I smile to say she is a good friend.

Then I turn and walk to Leonard's office. She follows me, shoes cracking across the floor. I sense that something has just passed between us, but I can't figure out what. Then it dawns on me. Pity. She feels sorry for me, and I fight not to turn around and tell her that I'm fine, but the words die on my lips even as they form. I don't have to explain myself to anyone.

Leonard keeps a somewhat tidy office. He mainly handles sports, but he also likes to run longer pieces on crimes that are overlooked by the main media feeds. They aren't hard to find. Mainstream news programs tend to focus on the sensational pieces, things that sell advertisements. He once wrote a three-part series about families that moved their loved ones into assisted living facilities and abandoned them while raiding their life savings. The piece garnered some national media attention, but 'Britney Spears' news quickly squashed it.

He's perched behind a giant monitor that looks more like a TV than a computer screen. He is the only one in the office who has one that large. As it turns out, he purchased it for himself. I asked him once why he went to such expense, and he rationalized it by saying he spent half of his day at the office, why shouldn't he be comfortable?

He is close to my age but is a barrel-chested outdoorsman with leathery skin from years in the sun. Premature age lines mar his face, making him look older than his forty-six years. They also give him a distinguished look.

"You got a minute?"

He stops banging on the keyboard with the first two fingers of both hands, and man does he pound on that thing. I have heard him typing from down the hall. He looks up from his display, eyes hazy behind glasses that are thick with a sheen of oil. Sometimes I want to take them off his face and subject them to a bath of Windex.

"Sure, what's up? Hey did you see the Mariners trade today? Man, we need another relief pitcher like we need a hole in the stadium's retractable roof."

"I thought they had that area shored up. What is management thinking?"

"Hell if I know. They don't pay me the big bucks to scour the west for new players."

"And it is a real shame; remember how well your fantasy football team did last year?" Which was miserable. He somehow ended up with three injured quarterbacks.

"Sure, dredge up my past and blare it in front of Erin."

"Hey, man, I don't know how the game works or how you can suck at it so bad." She grins, and Leonard can't help but grin with her. He is as big as a bear, but at heart he is more of a teddy bear, or so Erin has pointed out to me more than once.

"I was wondering if your scanner was working. There's some action up on Capitol Hill at my ex-wife's apartment. She sounds worried, but her phone cut out and I haven't been able to get through."

He stares at me for a long time, face an expressionless mask. Then he digs out the scanner from behind a stack of paper. He switches it on, and we are greeted with static.

"It's been like that since yesterday evening. At first the channels cut in and out, but then they all went dead. I think the police are using a different mode of communication for the time being."

"Why would they do that?" Erin beats me to the question.

"Million dollar question. I have been asking myself the very same, and I got nothing. All I hear are rumors, and even those are barely creditable. Just hints on the web if you know where to look. Videos on YouTube that get yanked as soon as they're posted."

I curse quietly. I didn't even think to check the video sites.

"I checked some blogs, but they're being obtuse, covering up words with other words like they're scared of being shut down," I think out loud.

"Wait a minute, what are you guys even talking about? You make it sound like there's some big conspiracy." Erin has a determined look on her face like she is pandering to us. I can't blame her; this is crazy talk.

"We already live in a world where people are used to ignoring stuff. Well, except for what the media tells them, and as a new paper, we know this better than most. 'Don't question, just live in fear.'" Leonard recites one of his favorite mantras. "Well, what if something bad is happening and it's being covered up?"

"Absurd!" Erin says loudly.

"There's something going on, I don't know what it is, but we have a responsibility to find out and report on it, and that is what I intend to do." And with that, Leonard turns his attention to his computer and starts typing again.

We leave his office and return to our desks. My mind keeps returning to what Leonard said. Erin also seems distracted. She keeps sighing and 'hmphing' every once in a while as she stares at her computer screen.

I still don't know what to do about Rita, so I sit down and try to focus on work.

INTERLUDE: SHYLAH RAE

Shylah Rae Parker stands in the sweltering heat of another humid day in Seattle and tries to be patient. Just as she approaches the street crossing, the light changes and she is forced to wait. Cars zip by on Westlake Avenue. She ignores the old ones and glances at the shiny ones. She has her shades slung low, purse held high and a look that grants nothing but disdain to those around her.

A couple stroll up alongside her. The man is dressed in some crap you might see at Walmart. She stares straight ahead, but she knows he is letting his eyes rove up and down her body, hoping his wife doesn't catch him in the act.

She doesn't have time for this! She needs to get in quick, pick up her dress at the new Cambria Boutique store and then get her butt home so she can go out tonight.

The dress is a slinky little thing with spaghetti straps and a bustline that plunges about three inches below the start of her cleavage. She also plans to stop at Victoria's Secret and pick up a new water bra. Sure, George says she doesn't need it, that she has the perfect-sized tits, but that's because he has to, especially if he wants to keep seeing them on a regular basis.

The light changes, and she steps into the road then has to jump back as a car belts past her, clearly running a red light. Asshole! She glares at the car, but the driver doesn't even look at her in the rearview mirror.

Then the way is clear, and she is safely within the cool vestibule of the mall. People stream past her on their way to the food court on the third floor, the game stores below, and of course the sinful chocolate heaven known as Godiva. Not that she will stop there today; her butt doesn't need any of that stuff. Again, not that George complains.

The smell from the food court one floor above is almost overwhelming. She has barely eaten today in preparation for going out tonight. A Power Bar for breakfast and a small salad for lunch. When they brought the salad, she almost started drooling at the sight of the bread they brought her friend Anne.

Anne had been married for a few years and ate whatever the hell she wanted to. Lucky bitch, but she would never be able to pull of the LBD Shylah is going out in tonight.

She takes the elevator to the second floor, hip popped out as it ascends. She avoids the glances of the men on the descending elevator on the other side, their eyes trying too hard not to stare at her cleavage. She puts on an air of diffidence, untouched by their stares. She loves the attention but won't recognize it.

At last she strolls into Cambria Boutique, and Helen is at her side in a flash.

"I know it came in this morning, give me just a moment." And she goes to a rack behind the counter. There are a few other items wrapped in fresh crisp plastic that crackle together as she checks tags. "Here it is," she pulls out the item and tugs the plastic up so Shylah Rae can get a look at it.

The dress is a wisp of nothing. Sheer silk, the black seems to reflect the light in the room and pull attention to it. Something about synthetic fibers wrapped around the silk. Some new process from Japan that will be all the rage in no time.

She touches the fabric, and it is as soft as she remembers, soft as a baby's rear end. George won't be able to take his eyes off the tiny thing that barely covers her ass. Her rear end that she has been perfecting for a month at the gym with squats and more squats, leg lifts and a personal trainer named Stephanie who might as well wear horns and parade around like the devil.

"It's beautiful," Shylah Rae exclaims, and Helen beams a smile at her that is all pearly white goodness and could stop traffic. She is taller than Shylah and older, probably well into her thirties, but she is also tall, statuesque and probably gets looked at by every geek who wanders by the store.

"Want to try it on?" Helen asks, but she doesn't have time. She has to stop for some undies and then get home, soak in a hot bath and get ready for the night. Her hair will take at least an hour.

"I'm good, thanks."

"Well you are all paid up, so enjoy your new dress. I bet your man won't let you out of the house wearing it, he'll be so jealous."

She smiles and nods, thinking that George is anything but the jealous type. He is sometimes so indifferent to her flirty manner with other men that it concerns her. What if he isn't serous about her? What if he is just in it for sex? Not that the sex is terrible.

He is very successful, vice president at a bank—even though he told her banks have more vice presidents than tellers. She knows he is joking about that, because he drives a nice car, a Lexus, and he always dresses in expensive clothes. In fact, he often looks like he just stepped out of a Hollister ad.

She clicks out of the store on her three-inch heels, skirt swaying over her hips. Her tanned legs look great against the maroon fabric, like she should be in a commercial.

Shylah Rae takes the elevator up one more level to stop at Victoria's Secret for some new goodies.

Her brand-new platinum Visa weighing heavily in her purse after an hour at the shop, she leaves with a handful of bags and crosses the street. Taking a right, she walks to the parking lot and her little convertible BMW. It's a deep blue and spotless in the fading daylight. It better be, for all the money she pays a detailer once a month at the Bear car wash.

A homeless man huddles near the pay machine, and she steers around him.

"Can you spare some change? Just a little?" He doesn't even bother to meet her eye. He probably has crabs and other diseases crawling all over his body. She pretends she doesn't hear him and walks out of her way to go around him. She skirts a silver Mercedes and then a Kia with a license plate that reads TOYBOYS.

A groan from the old man, and she turns to look at him. She doesn't want to, but he sounds like he is in pain.

He wears a faded Levi t-shirt and squats against a pole. One arm is wrapped around his knee, and he holds the other against his chest. He keeps looking down at something on his arm, but she can't make it out.

He is filthy, hair a frizz that goes in twenty-seven directions at once. A scraggly beard completes his look, and he even has dirt and smeared brown on his face that looks like dried Coke or something.

He shakes, and she feels bad for him. She works hard, sure, but her mother used to say it is good karma to share the wealth with those less fortunate from time to time. She hits the button on her key that triggers the car. Her hand slips under the trunk, and the lid pops up. She deposits her bags and then sets her purse inside. Leaning over, she takes out a few dollars and then slams the trunk.

A passerby averts his eyes as she turns, and she bets he was staring up her skirt as she leaned over. Well, let him look and let him imagine how soft her legs are. She holds the money out and walks toward the groaning man with her nose crinkled up as if she is about to root around in a trashcan.

The man doesn't move at all. His head has slumped to the side. Did he fall asleep like that? She will just drop the money in his lap and move on.

She struts across the parking lot and stands to one side.

"Here you go, mister. I hope you spend it on food and not booze," she says and then drops the money in his lap. Oh shit, was that a twenty? How could she be so stupid?

The dollar bills pile around his lap, and a woman walking by in a long sundress with a droopy yellow hat smiles at her in a clear attempt to acknowledge her generosity. Shylah Rae nods back, and when the woman turns, she reaches down with finger and thumb and grabs the twenty, then pulls it out as if extracting a receipt from the trash.

She lets out a little scream when the guy moves. Then she crinkles the twenty in her hand before he can see it and walks away. The man comes to his feet like a shot. She glances back at him and feels horror creep over her skin. His eyes are red, bloody, and the color around them has become a sickening gray as if devoid of any pigmentation.

He hauls himself toward her, and she notices he is bleeding from one hand where several fingers are missing. The sight of the bloody stumps is too much, and she cries out in dread.

On heels that are not designed for running, she attempts a little skitter step, but he is right there. She starts to scream when he lunges forward and wraps her in his arms.

"I gave you money, leave me alone!" she howls, but he sinks his teeth, his fucking nasty stinking teeth into her shoulder, and pain explodes in her head as she is borne to the ground. Her knees scrape against the hot black pavement. She manages to free one hand but not before a piece of broken glass rips it nearly to the bone. She hears a snap that concerns her, but her brain is still trying to come to grips with a man biting her.

The smell of him is like an alley filled with old piss and beer bottles. The overwhelming stench combined with the hot ground makes her want to gag. She swings her elbow back and manages to dislodge his teeth from her shoulder, and maybe it's not that bad. Then the pain arrives from that area, and she nearly passes out.

He digs in again, and this time there is a tearing sound as he pulls a chunk of flesh out. It is the same sickening sound as the time she cut up a whole chicken and had to pull the leg off the thigh meat.

Then the weight is gone as a man pulls the bum off her. Another man arrives, and they commence beating the crap out of the guy. The homeless man doesn't just resist; he goes crazy and swings his arms up to grip the first man in a bear hug, then his mouth snaps down to bite him as well.

Through tear-stained eyes, she watches him try to struggle free. Her other savior, a black guy with a shaved head, grabs the homeless man and tears him free. He grips him by the throat and thrusts him away with a loud "Back off!" but the guy only falls and then tries to stand again.

The first savior holds his own neck, and there is blood there, but it doesn't seem to matter to her as much anymore as she faints dead away. The last thought her living brain ever has is worry for the dress, which she forgot to hang up in the back of the car. Then darkness descends as a haze of red covers her sight.

LESTER

A crash outside makes Lester sit up in a panic and look around the dark room. He reaches for his gun, but it isn't there, and when his hand doesn't find the nightstand, he almost falls out of bed. Fell asleep facing the wrong way. How the hell did that happen? Then he looks over at Angela's naked form and remembers them fucking like it was going out of style.

The room is hot as hell, reeks of weed, booze, and sex. Lester grabs his arm and feels along it until he locates his watch. He brings it to his face and tries to focus on the digital readout, which if his gummed-up eyes aren't lying, says it is almost two in the afternoon. At least the day is passing quickly, getting closer to nighttime. That means it will cool off in a few hours. But they have been ignoring the deaders in the street, and Lester feels panic set in.

SHIT!

He slides along the length of the bed so his head is by his pillow. There are sheets everywhere, blankets on the floor; it looks like a tsunami hit. Then he swings his legs over the side, and now everything is where it should be. Shorts are next, then the shirt he has worn for two days. He sniffs it first, and it isn't too bad—a little sweat, a hint of gunpowder and a whole lot of Angela.

He grabs the handgun and a box of shells. Angela rolls over and tugs a sheet over her legs and ass. How can she be cold right now? It must be ninety goddamn degrees in here. He leans over and tries to kiss her but nearly falls over in the process. His hand shoots out to stop him from tumbling into her sleeping form, and he ends up mooching his lips into her shoulder. It's a wonder she doesn't wake up and slap the shit out of his half-drunk ass.

Where the hell is that rum?

He locates the bottle, the big half-gallon they have been working on for the last couple of days, but it only has an inch of liquid left. At least one of them thought to put the cap on and twist it tight. In this heat, it probably would have evaporated by now. Too bad there's no cold juice to mix it with, but the refrigerator is getting empty and is room temperature now. He takes a long pull and tries to ignore the burn. He holds his breath for a second until the urge to puke passes.

There is another loud sound from outside like someone banging into the fence. He grabs a box of shells from beside the bed and pops the magazine out of the pistol. He tries to focus on putting the bullets in the correct way. Unsteady fingers fumble with each one as he sets it in its little cradle, pushes down with a click and then loads the next.

Once the magazine is full, he slides it into the pistol with a snap and chambers a round. He fills his pocket with extra shells just in case he has to go to war. On his way out the door, he stops and looks at Angela. She is so out of it that a series of little snores matches a tremor before she turns over with a sigh and farts. That's my girl. He almost laughs out loud. He slips out the bedroom door, closing it quietly behind him with a click.

The hallway is empty and dark. The door to the guest room is closed because they had to dump the trash bags in there. No one picked up stuff this week, and he doesn't have a giant hole in the back yard in which to dump stuff. Still, he wants to crack the door and look in, make sure none of the things has somehow crawled upstairs and made a nest. Just paranoia talking, from the weed—no way one of those mindless things got inside. He creeps downstairs, head hung low, mind foggy, legs tingling, arms stiff, mouth feeling like a rat took a crap in it. Just another day in the life of Lester the drug dealer. Lester the druggie. At least he sticks to the mild stuff like weed and some occasional X. He refuses to mess with the really addictive stuff like meth and heroin. Leave that shit for the losers on the street.

The living room is dim from the drawn shades. This suits him fine, the darker the better. The blankets they sorted earlier are piled on one side of the couch. They pulled them out of closets in case they need them tonight, but the heat makes that unlikely. His mind fuzzy from the pot and booze, he brings the gun up, looking for anything or anyone out of the ordinary.

He wants to concentrate on the room, but the image of Angela dancing for him keeps intruding. Not to mention the image of Angela riding his hips and Angela pouring rum in his mouth while he rubbed her tits with his hands.

His mind turns to Marlene outside, wondering if she has wandered off yet. He thinks of the fantasy he had a few months ago where Angela was going down on Marlene, then he sees her empty face and shudders.

"Piss on that," he mumbles.

He walks to the front door and slides aside the curtains that are bound to bars on the top and bottom so that he has to push the middle together to see anything. Most of the old curtains came with the place when they rented it. He had to put in blinds in the bedroom the day after they moved in when he was woken at six in the morning by streaming bright sunshine. Besides, Angela refused to wear clothes in that room, and who was he to discourage such behavior?

The shrubs in front obscure most of the view, but he can see shapes out there. I guess Marlene didn't leave yet. He turns the knob and cracks the door. Stupid. In their haste to get to bed, they left it unlocked.

He slides it open a hair and peeks out. Then he slams it shut and yells "FUCK!"

There must be twenty of them out there, all milling around the fence. Has the whole world gone crazy?

Well, only one thing to do—he will have to go out there and get his AR-15. Ah, crap. That was another mistake, leaving his damn rifle outside. What if they were waiting outside the door? He would be well and truly fucked.

You were just well and truly fucked. He giggles and then smacks his own cheek to wake up. Concentrate!

His breath grows shallow as he prepares to open the door. He spins around, sensing movement behind him. But there is nothing there. The house is dark, and all his furniture and crap piled on the floor cast shadows that mess with his mind. The blankets on the couch, are they corpses? He imagines them moving, unfolding and creeping toward him with worms hanging out of their backs. Puckered red holes pulse as the creatures squirm into the shallow light.

His whole body shudders, and goose bumps break out across his arms and neck. Then a round of shivers hits, and he wants to sit down and rest. He shakes his head, trying to clear it of the pot and rum.

Then he takes a breath, cracks the front door and peers outside.

There is a clicking noise he can hear now that he is on the patio. In the front yard, his sprinkler stutters back and forth, spraying water all over the fence. Did the noise draw them? He hangs over the side of the fence and turns the knob until it shuts off. Now even the battery-powered automatic timer he put on the hose won't turn on.

The front yard is clear, but the deaders wander around like remote partners in a slow waltz. Some run into each other and push away.

Arms flop, some dangle, some drag legs, one woman's head hangs at an odd angle like her neck is broken.

He gets a chill watching them; they disgust him with their filthy bodies. He wishes he had a bomb so he could throw it at them and watch the parts fly. He does have one little surprise of the explosive variety, but he is saving that as a last resort.

Lester slips out the door and slides forward on silent feet. He isn't wearing shoes, and he imagines himself a ninja moving among the shadows like he is invisible to the deaders, like they can't even smell him.

He reaches for the low table, picks up the AR-15 by the barrel and brings it to his chest. He slips the Glock into the waistband of his pants so the cold metal is against his back. In the movies, they always look cool doing this. In reality, the heavy pistol tugs at his pants and is a cold, uncomfortable lump against his ass crack.

He turns the rifle over and clicks the magazine loose so he can check how many rounds he has. A box of ammo sits next to the chair, so he should be good. The magazine has a few rounds left, enough to get started.

But what if they surge over the fence like the black guy did earlier in the day? Thinking of this, his eyes are drawn to the corpse in the yard. He shudders and slides the magazine out again so he can reload it.

One by one, the deaders take notice of him and approach the fence. One leans forward as if he can reach the twenty or so feet to Lester's warm body.

"Stupid asshole," he mumbles as he pops the top of the ammo box open. He grabs a shell and loads it, then another.

Motion to his left scares the ever-living shit out of Les. A deader has fallen into the yard and decided to hang around the side of the house. Help, I'm dead and I can't get up!

When he sees the thing, a little scream bubbles past his lips like he is a six year old. It is in the direct light of the sun, and he has trouble making out its shape. He can't even tell if it is a man or a woman. Hell, it might not even be a deader at all. He has the magazine in hand, and he tries to ram it home, but it is upside down, and he can't seem to get it lined up with the hole. Come on, man, how many times did you play square peg, square hole when you were a kid? In frustration, he drops his thousand-plus-dollar rifle on the porch and whips the Glock around, which nearly tears his shorts off when the front sight catches on the waistband. His shorts leap sharply up against his balls, but he is too scared to recognize the pain that may race into his gut at any second.

His fingers shake around the safety. He has the handgun up and aimed before he can scream again.

"Who the fuck are you?" his voice rings scared, sounds hollow in his ears. "Hands up or I'm gonna bust one in your ass!" he yells.

The shape moans and slides forward, and as it comes out of the blinding light, he sees it's a two-hundred-twenty-five-pound kid with tattoos on both arms. Lank greasy brown hair hangs in front of his face, creating a curtain over a mouth that opens wide when he spots Lester.

He lowers the gun for a half-second.

"Ronnie?" Ronnie is a good kid. He helps out when he can. Sometimes he mules boxes of weed from the post office. Sometimes he buys from Lester, and sometimes he gets some for free.

This doesn't look like the Ronnie he knows. This one has a blood-red eye fixed on Lester, and the other is obscured by hair.

Lester steps back but raises the gun again. Ronnie moans and opens his mouth, coming toward him on feet that are suddenly much faster than remembers. The fat kid used to take a couple of tries to get off his couch. He would rock forward then back, and on the next heave he would come to his feet like a pumpkin dressed in black. Now he moves like someone is holding a blowtorch to his ass.

Lester takes a step toward the front door. He likes Ronnie and doesn't want to hurt him. But Ronnie isn't himself today; he's a deader. Lester trembles, scared, he hits something with the back of his leg and a bubble of horror brushes past his lips. He nearly falls, and in the process, the gun fires. He has his finger on the trigger, but he doesn't mean to shoot Ronnie.

The fat kid stumbles with a moan and falls backwards. There is no spray of blood out the back, and for a moment Les wonders why the hell not? There is always a satisfying spray of blood in the movies.

He steps off the patio and approaches Ronnie's body. It isn't moving, but he knows how this shit works. As soon as he gets close, Ronnie's arm is going to reach out and grab his ankle, sweep him off his feet and then it's goodnight sweet prince.

There is a little hole in the kid's chest, but his shirts obscure it. A ridiculous Hawaiian shirt hangs open over an old Morbid Angel t-shirt that would cover two Lesters. As sure as shit stinks, Ronnie's eyes open, and he sits up and reaches for Les's leg. Can I call 'em or what, folks? Lester's mind giggles wildly. Les likes his legs. He is attached to them, and when he thinks of losing one of them ... well, he sort of giggles again. He is still a little high, and the image of him hobbling around with a pirate's peg leg is pretty fucking funny.

Ronnie's eyes are bright red like he is more stoned than anyone has ever been in the history of the world. Like someone punctured his corneas and poured blood in them. He moans and tries to sit up, mouth opens wide, and the hiss of escaping air from his chest sounds like a balloon with a slow leak.

Lester has reached his quota for weird shit today, so he fires three times at his old buddy. Night, night, Ronnie boy, see you on the other side.

One punches into Ronnie's head just above the bridge of his nose. His head bounces back from the impact. One smashes into his cheek, and the other misses entirely, but they seem to do the trick, because Ronnie isn't moving anymore. Once again, Lester wants to know what happened to his satisfying spray of blood. There is blood all right, but it oozes out like congealed black grease.

Lester pops the magazine and checks it again. He tries to do the math in his head, but the numbers keep slipping away. Instead he grins as he reloads and grins as he considers how many of the filthy things in front of the house he is going to take out. Grins at the number of headshots he is going to pull off. Grins as he thinks of the pile of deaders that will soon litter the road in front of the house.

In fact, if he gets enough of them, maybe they will catch on and stay away. Sure they are dumb, but even a puppy learns not to piss in the house if you smack it with a newspaper enough times.

He fumbles the box open and jams shells into the automatic's magazine. The deaders stare at him, pushing against the fence. They shamble forward, some fighting to the front. His initial count of twenty may be high; it's more like ten or maybe a dozen. Where are those Army fuckers now? Sure could use a platoon of the guys in white to mop up this neighborhood, because it has gone to hell.

What if the rest of them figure out how to get in the yard? It's unlikely they will come through the back; that fence is over six feet high. Of course, if enough of them press against it, the thing will probably fall over. Maybe Ronnie was an exception. Maybe he remembered that they were friends and some part of his brain told him it was okay to pay a social call. That must be it. I bet the rest of them won't figure out how to get over. They are like children. Just look at those fucking brainless things.

He jams the full magazine into the rifle pretty sure there is one in the chamber. He raises it and watches the deaders as they push against the fence. His first target comes into view; it's a guy he thinks he has seen at the other end of the street from time to time. A man who always gives him a dirty look as he whips his expensive sports car around the corner and roars toward home. The neighbor must suspect Lester isn't exactly an outstanding member of the little community. Those judging eyes have caught his one too many times.

Now the asshole's eyes aren't so judgmental. They stare straight ahead, not even fixed on Lester. Here ya go, buddy, a nice 'fuck you' from your friendly neighborhood drug dealer. The gun's roar is a reassuring blast that resonates in his pot- and booze-addled hearing. The guy drops without a sound as the bullet takes him just below one eye. He falls without a twitch and is still. The others push over his body. A young girl in a bathing suit who is all of twelve if she is a day, with curly black hair and one lone flip flop, drops to her knees and starts to chew on Mr. Judgmental Eyes.

"... the fuck?" Les mutters out loud. He has seen it all today.

The smell of gunpowder is reassuring as it competes with the smell of death in his front yard. The sulfur smells like burned eggs. The oil that he uses on all the parts so the guns work as advertised. He loves to strip them when his friends are visiting. He shows them how the parts fit and how to load the magazines. It's something he is good at besides getting out a scale and measuring a gram or three of coke.

The door clicks open behind him. He spins around abruptly and scares a squeal out of Angela. She has donned a short robe that is barely closed in front.

"Hey, babe." He grins at her chest.

"Oh my God, what are you doing?"

"Goddamn Ronnie got in the yard, and I had to put him down. He was banging around, and I think it called a bunch of them over. Then I dropped one in front, sort of a warning to others passing by."

"Won't the soldiers see the bodies and wonder if someone is in the house?"

"Ah crap, I didn't think about that."

"Maybe you can drag him and the black dude's body to the back. I bet the things will wander off."

"I don't know, look at the little one." He points at the child, who is chewing on Mr. Judgmental Eyes's leg like she is a dog. There is blood all over her face as she tugs a tendon out of the hole she has created, sucking at the chunks of flesh that stick to it. Then she rips a fresh piece of leg off, which makes a tearing noise like ripping the sleeves off a t-shirt. Lester gets a chill.

"Let's go in, babe, this is too gross."

Angela follows him inside, and they wander to the couch in the living room. Light pokes in from the closed blinds, and the room is still dark and murky but bright enough for him to go over the machine gun and Glock for a good cleaning.

She runs back upstairs and then comes back with the bag of pot and their long glass pipe. She hasn't bothered to close her robe in the heat, and Lester wouldn't think of complaining.

"This cool?" she asks.

"Sure, but I'll skip it for now." He is still dizzy from earlier and wants to get his mind straight in case more of the things come into the yard.

He reloads the rifle as the smell of pot drifts near. He starts salivating and wants a hit.

"What do we have to eat?" she asks.

"Some canned stuff. A few protein bars."

"God, how can you eat those gross dry things?"

"Just do. If you eat a couple and we open some fruit, it will be like real food."

"Fruit is real food, babe." She smiles. "But I want a burger and fries or a steak. That would be so good, a fat juicy steak cooked on the grill."

"If we had steak, I would go out back and start the grill. Oh damn, we're out of gas."

"That sucks," she sighs and hits the pipe again. "Don't we have a generator we can use to power up the house?"

"Nope, but John next door does. Or he did."

"Is he around?"

"I don't think so. I bet they piled into their car early on and got the fuck out of town."

"Maybe you can go over there and see if the door is open, just borrow it. I'm sure he would understand, and if he gets mad, I can always flash him," she laughs then kicks her legs up on the coffee table.

"Naughty girl." He can't help but smile. John would probably have a fucking heart attack. "Hmmm, I don't even know how heavy the damn things are. I don't know if I can move it by myself."

"So you're thinking about it? I want to take a shower and dry my hair. I don't like the way it frizzes out when I use the towel."

Her speech is slurring and slowing down. Taking a shower sounds great, but the water is freezing. The hair dryer is probably out of the question. The power has flickered more than once when she fires up the big thing in the bathroom. He can't imagine a generator powerful enough to keep up with that beast. She is quiet for a minute. Then she hits the pipe and holds it in for a long time, so long that when she exhales, there is barely any smoke. Her lids grow closer together, and her eyes are once again bright red but not the same blood red the deaders have, thank God. He would hate to have to put down the stoners while taking out deaders. That would be really fucking bad for business.

"Maybe, like, I could help. I mean we can take turns with the gun, just go in from the side, open the door and slip over there when it's dark."

"Maybe." He wonders if he is really thinking about doing this. It's a pain not having electricity; they can't cook shit. He could always build a fire in the fireplace and heat cans of food, but the house is too hot for that.

Ah hell. You only live once.

"Okay, stop smoking that stuff, though. We'll go over when it's really dark and drag the damn thing back."

"Cool," she sighs and closes her eyes.

"Cool," he echoes, pretty sure he is getting a contact high. Oh what the hell, one more hit before nightfall sounds like heaven right about now.

KATE

Afternoon arrives with a blaze of sun that sucks the early morning clouds right off the cityscape. Kate's tiny air conditioning unit chugs away at full speed, barely keeping up with the humidity. It sits in a window, and its ass end hangs out over the back of the building. When she rented the place, it wasn't quite what she had in mind.

She wears a t-shirt and nothing else, because her skin is still sensitive, throbbing with a dull ache that leaves her strangely satisfied. And the rush she got when the pain started, there were times when she felt like she was about to orgasm because the agony was so sweet. She isn't angry with old Walter for doing this to her, how can she be? She had the ultimate revenge when she sliced his dick off just as pretty as you please.

She lies on the floor on her stomach like she is thirteen again, except she is sipping beer from a straw down the long neck of a Red Hook. She loves how fast the bubbles go to her head and how fast she gets a buzz. She has a movie channel on, and it's a romantic comedy, but she isn't really paying attention. Instead, she is thinking of Bob and her fantasy earlier. Good thing it is a fantasy. *I'd probably chop his cock off when he got done with me, and that would be a real shame for old Bobby-boy, because he's a nice guy.*

It's been three weeks since she last killed—well, before last night—and that was her fifth victim. He had also been the dullest. Very little chitchat, just Yes, sir. No, sir. Harder, sir. I can take it. He had a hard-on the entire time, and when she dared to look back at him, he was usually stroking himself through the thin fabric of his boxers. There was a point where he ordered her on her knees before him, told her to take his cock in his mouth and suck on it. *Suck it, bitch.* Why couldn't these guys get a little more creative when requesting a blowjob? Hell, her third victim had been almost romantic about the whole thing, and she had felt sorry for him at times. However, he was just a little piggy like the others, and they always went along with her plans when she begged off by asking them to punish her some more, aim for my inner thighs, please make me a good girl again. And the sadist in the bastards couldn't resist.

She can't believe she is covering her tracks so well. Some nights she lies awake waiting for the knock on the door that will bring the police or FBI. Will she go out in a blaze? Grab her two best friends and take a few of them with her before they gun her down?

The papers have made note of the murders, but no one has connected them in the media yet. Sometimes there is great detail and speculation, other times there is almost nothing, the barest mention of "a brutal slaying in a Seattle hotel room that left one man dead and the suspect at large." Hah, at large. If they ever get ahold of her tiny frame, they will never use the word 'large.'

She is certain the police have labeled it as the work of a serial killer, but they don't want to come out on the news and announce it that way. But one night the five o' clock news will lead off with "The police think they may have a serial killer on their hands." And she will have to make some decisions. Will she have to move? Lie low for a while and not kill for a few months, or maybe a year?

Until then, she will continue her double life. In fact, it may be time to start looking at Craigslist again. She has a program on her laptop that masks her IP address, and she also uses an anonymous site to mask where she comes from. Sure it's overkill, but at least she isn't sneaking out to libraries and writing furtive notes to her prospective victims while glancing over her shoulder the whole time.

She will start hunting again. Soon. She will take her time and get to know the guy, get some pictures of him. The guys who send her cock shots get shitcanned the fastest. She wants the normal men who have another side, just like her. She wants the men who are husbands but "just don't get what they need from their wives even though everything else in the marriage is perfect." It's such bullshit. If they have such perfect marriages, then why the fuck are they cruising Craig's trying to pick up her alter ego?

The movie is boring, so she gingerly sits in her computer chair and starts lurking on some of her favorite forums. She was more than a little disturbed to learn there were forums devoted to serial killers. Some require logins, so she made up an account on one of the free email sites and used that for their flimsy verification. Some are open, so she reads them and tries to understand the people who follow serial killers like they are rock stars.

Kate has no morals, no sense of right and wrong. When it comes to taking a life, she accepts that it has to be done and lets the other do the deed. But the people on these forums seem to revel in the suffering of the countless victims, and yet she is all too aware of the paradox that comes with reviling these people even as she acts out their fantasy world.

There is something about her wiring that let her do these things. Something messed up in all that ganglia upstairs. She wonders if it is just plain evil. No doubt a psychologist would have a field day with her, probing the relationship she had with her father. Wouldn't they be surprised to learn that little Kate, at the tender age of fifteen and fresh from a beating, waited until the old man was passed out drunk and then held a pillow over his head? He didn't even kick his legs or flop his hands; he just died, went quietly, much more gently than the asshole deserved.

The police called it an accident, and she went to live with an aunt she hadn't even been aware of. Susan had been a pain in the ass. Strict. Made her go to church, and she was never ever allowed to speak of the things her father did. She once tried to confide in Aunt Suzy, but the woman shut her down with a firm "Don't you ever speak ill of your father. He was a good man."

He was good at beating her to a pulp. She ran away at seventeen and hitchhiked from Warsaw, Idaho to the big city of Seattle over the course of a few days. Along the way, she met the drummer of a band from Yakima named Madface Monkies. He had a big Suburban, and the second night she hung out with him, the bastard tried to rape her. He held her down, and when she said she liked him, that she would give in if he would just give her room to get her pants off, she kneed him in the balls and then backed up to the end of the big car and kicked him in the head until he didn't move anymore. Then she took a gas can from the back of the vehicle and poured it all over the inside and the drummer. He begged until the flames took him. Then he screamed until they finished the job.

She sighs at the memory and stares at the screen for a few moments before coming out of her fog.

She changes gears and searches for information on the gas leak that is just a few blocks from her. She comes across a local forum, but they are just speculating about all the police and National Guards. There are a lot of angry people talking about their civil liberties being infringed upon. Some complain that the soldiers were cold toward them, wouldn't tell them what kind of a gas leak it was or how dangerous it was. They just blew them off as cool as you please with a

"We'll have more information available tomorrow." But it has been two tomorrows since.

A shot rings out on the street below, startling her out of her chair. It is loud and different than the fireworks she's been hearing all week. She nearly knocks over her beer but grabs the rim of the bottle at the last second, picks it up and goes to the window. The street is bare of people, and there are only a few cars passing by. She cracks the window, and instead of the controlled chaos she is used to hearing— people shouting, cars screeching, bottles clanking—she hears barely a peep. Another gunshot rings out, and she is so startled that she slams the window shut and takes a deep pull on her straw.

A banging on her door scares her so badly that her lips come off the straw mid-sip, and some of the beer dribbles onto her t-shirt.

"Fuck me." She stares down at the stain. "Who is it?" she calls out and wonders if she locked the door.

"Hey, kitty cat, just seeing if everything is cool," Bob calls, his voice muffled by the heavy door. She used to tell him that she hated it when he called her kitty cat, but the truth is she loves the nickname. It's just a good thing for him that he doesn't know about her real-life claws.

"I think it's unlocked," she calls out.

The door pops open, and Bob's straggly face pokes inside. He has a glass of wine in one hand but looks concerned. "You okay?" he asks, his eyes doing their best not to wander over the short t-shirt that barely covers her ass. She looks down at her state of dress and turns bright red. She hurries to her bedroom to find a robe or pants or something that covers her from head to toe. Bob comes in, quietly, and closes the door with a click.

"Oh my God, Kate, are you all right?" He is right behind her. His arm goes to her shoulder, and she spins around to knock it off, how dare he ... but when she turns, his eyes are indeed on her legs, but they look far from interested.

Oh fuck!

She whisks the robe off her bed and slides it over her shoulders, letting the pink cloth cover her just past her knees.

"Who did that to you?" His eyes wide open, downright fierce. He stands back as if afraid to touch her, as if she is the victim of an assault. She knows that he is trying to be considerate of her feelings, but he has no idea how deep her masochistic tendencies go. He can't understand what a release they are. She can make up some lame story about falling and put up with pity looks for the next month, or she can tell him the truth ... well, part of it at least.

"Um, Bob, I know we're neighbors and friends and shit, but you really don't know much about me."

"I know enough. Now who the hell hurt you?" he demands in that voice that sends a shiver down her spine. She wonders for the first time if she can screw him and not want to kill him. Then she wants to giggle at how fucking stupid that sounds.

"Wait, let me explain." She sits down on the edge of the bed and crosses her legs. The robe falls open so that her thighs are exposed, but she is going to come clean. She stares down at her pale, smooth skin and runs a hand over the welts that will become bruises.

"It's this thing, it's … it's consensual, okay?"

"What?"

"Don't be so fucking naive, Bob. I like it. I have a friend … she" and she almost slips and says 'he,' "ties me up and takes a belt to me. Then she uses a flogger."

At his confused look, she goes on. "It's like a whip, but it has a bunch of tails on it. It's like having your back scorched by a trail of fire ants over and over."

"Fuck, Kate, I don't know if I'm confused or turned on."

"Shut up!" She struggles not to smile.

"So the secret Kate lets one loose. What next, are you going to tell me you like to dress up in furry animal costumes and have sex?"

"Oh that is really funny, pal." She laughs out loud, and just like that, the tension is out of the room.

"Why do you like it?" he asks in a quiet voice as though he weren't sure he was going to ask the question at all.

"I don't know. I just do."

"Is it about sex?"

"You sure do have a lot of questions."

He steps close and studies one of the bruises; she follows his gaze because he has found a dandy. It is red and livid, raised up on her flesh, and it will be blue by tomorrow. She will wear pants for the rest of the week, but she feels liberated now that she has told Bob one of her secrets. She feels free, and she doesn't stop him when he moves toward her and drops into a crouch. He raises the wine glass and takes a sip while his eyes rove over her pale skin.

He leans over to look at one of the marks where it comes up her inner thigh. She feels suddenly bold and lifts her leg just a bit as if offering it to him. He runs one hand over a mark on her lower thigh, just above her knee. His hand is soft and warm, and she likes how it feels. She has a sudden desire to part her legs and pull him down between them.

"So it's not about sex? Did you go to Catholic school?" He is trying to be a smartass, but she appreciates the humor and gives it right back.

"No, but I have a Catholic school dress. Want to see it?"

He stands up so suddenly that she jerks back in surprise. She shakes her head as if shaking off a dream and stands up just as quickly. What the hell was she thinking?

"Whoa, I'm really sorry!" he backs up, hands out. Lucky it's him. She knows half a dozen ways to take one of his proffered hands and break the elbow like a twig.

"Oh, it's not that. I thought I heard something outside again," she says hastily to cover how nervous she feels. She is flushed, and she is sure her face is glowing red. What the fuck is she thinking? She can't have a man, not in a normal way; the other won't let her!

"I should go." He turns toward the door so fast that his wine splashes around and some dribbles onto the hardwood floor. "Ah, hell."

He heads for the kitchen and comes back with a paper towel. He is dabbing up the fluid when more shots ring out. They both turn toward the sound and in a flash are at the window. She cracks it again, and now screams can be heard out in the night. Another shot crackles across the road, but this one is deeper, louder, a fierce sound spoken with conviction.

"Shotgun, probably a twelve gauge," Bob mutters.

"What the hell is going on?"

"They keep saying it's a gas leak, but that is such bullshit. Something crazy is going on out there. Please tell me you're staying in tonight."

She is so touched by his concern that she wants to wrap her arms around him, but the urge dies when she thinks of the other.

"I'm staying put, mister. I don't have a rendezvous planned tonight."

There is less than a foot between them, and she can smell the wine on his breath. They stare at each other for a few seconds, and she has a crazy desire to lean in and kiss him. How would that beard feel against her face? Would he kiss her hard, press her lips back, or would he be gentle and take the time to nibble at her tongue?

She breaks the look first and stares outside. "Why don't you have a girlfriend, Bob?"

"I did, but we broke up six or seven months ago. It was a bad relationship, unhealthy. She wasn't ever happy, wanted to argue all the time. After a while, I didn't like her anymore, all I liked was the sex."

"Oh. So that part was good?"

"I'm a guy. Guys are like windup toys. You turn the key, and when they run out of energy, they are content to just sit around."

"So where is your key exactly?" She surprises herself by flirting with him and then wants to bite her tongue in half. Shut the fuck up, her own voice screams inside her head.

"You have to get more wine in me before I reveal any secrets."

A few more gunshots echo outside, but they seem to be farther away, Bob's face shifts to concern again.

"I can stay, or you can hang out at my place if you like," he offers, his voice full of innocence.

"Stay for a while," she says and slurps the rest of the beer with her straw.

"Okay, let me grab something real quick."

He leaves for a minute, and she slides her robe aside and studies the welts on her legs. She runs her finger over one that is turning blue. It will be a beauty in the morning. What are you? she asks herself again. What are you doing? she asks when the first question remains unanswered.

"Just having a little fun," she whispers after a long silence.

KEN AND ALICE

The splash of burgundy is shocking against the carpet, red on tan like a tie-dyed t-shirt gone wrong. You try to roll over, but the pain makes you pay for the effort. Your hand is pressed to your neck so that you can still feel spreading warmth against your palm. It flows in a pulsing rush, and if you had a throat, you would probably scream.

How long until you pass on? How long until the blood stops pumping through your heart? It's going to sputter to a halt soon. Sure you've had murmurs before, but this is going to be the granddaddy of them all, the last shuddering pulse of the most complicated muscle in your body running on E.

A spasm rips along one leg and then the other. It's like a jolt of electricity that leaves both appendages numb. You wish you could raise them a few inches. This would make a little more blood available to your brain, but you can barely move your head. In fact, if you could do that, you would take your eyes off the form that lies next to you. The vacant eyes gray-lined, bloodstained, one off-kilter as it tries to stare at the red hole just above his nose.

You only let him in because he was your son. You let him in because you couldn't believe he was one of them. The moment you opened the door, you knew it was a bad idea. It's one thing to see it on the news; it's another to see it in a loved one's eyes.

It wasn't even his hand knocking. He used his head to bang on the door. He came in with a mumble, then a clawing hand that tried to grab you. The gun was in the waist of your pants, but you didn't want to pull it, refused to believe what your eyes were showing you.

You batted his hand aside, but he came on, mouth a rictus of horror from which a blue tongue protruded. Breath fouler than a hunk of bacon left to rot or a port-a-potty forgotten in the sun. You couldn't help but wonder if the flesh hanging from broken front teeth was human, those strands that swayed with his shambling steps.

The gun came up in two hands, the way you've seen it a million times on TV. It was pointed at his head, but you couldn't finish God's work. You stepped back and felt the stairs against the back of your leg. You tried not to stumble, but the horror before you made your feet unsure. Your flesh was crawling, heart pounding in your ears. Great ragged breaths through open mouth made your head swim.

You backed up the stairs until you reached the top. Undaunted, your son followed, that arm stretched toward you. You misjudged the last step and came down hard on your backside. His hand reached for your ankle, and you scooted back; a little gasp of horror bubbled out. Then you had a good and proper scream when your back hit the wall.

You rolled to your feet; adrenaline amped you up faster than a double shot of espresso. You made it to the living room, but the next flight of stairs proved your undoing. You were sure he was right behind you, like you had sprouted a pair of eyes in the back of your head. But you fought the urge to look back until you hit the second little step, the short flight that separated the kitchen from the living room. Your head snapped around in desperation.

Your foot caught on the lip of the room, and you staggered to one knee. Not so young and spry anymore; that ship sailed at least a decade ago. Your hand went to the carpet, and you tried to propel yourself forward, but your feet tangled together and you went down hard. John, your pride and joy, the goofy-haired kid you used to take fishing, fell on top of you.

He moved fast, and when you went down, he fell on you like a pile of bricks. Both hands on his shoulders, you tried push him off. You turned your head to the side because that foul breath brought bile to the back of your throat. You choked it down, but then your eye caught his, all dried up like a prune. At least the other one must work, your mind tried to assure itself. Can't really hunt down old pop with no sight, now can ya, son?

Then the puke was there, burning hot. It spewed out of your mouth, and as you pulled back from his descending teeth, a splash of it went up your nose. It was the last insult as you tried not to vomit again while preventing your son from tearing into your neck. The plan didn't work out.

His head thrust in, and you beat at it but didn't have a chance. The pain and sickening tearing sound almost made you pass out. You tried to scream, but there was no vocal cord left.

Gun came up, last resort, didn't want to use it on your own son, but is he really the boy you raised to be a man? Nope, he's a mindless creature that is only interested in feeding on you. You swung the gun around, and wasn't it a shock that something went right, just one thing in the whole terrible minute that just passed? The gun struck him across the temple with all the force of a man at death's door. It connected with a crunch that sent the thing tumbling to your side.

There was a loud boom as you twisted the gun to your side and put one right between his eyes. Then a sickening splash as the bullet exited with most of your son's brains behind it. You didn't look, just rolled your head upright and stared at the ceiling while the blood poured out of your ruined neck.

What time will Alice be home? She can't find you both like this, can't see her son now twice dead and husband soon to be undead. You have to use the gun again, just put an end to it all by gently squeezing that trigger. She will be shocked, heartbroken, hurt and disgusted, but it beats the hell out of the alternative.

Your arm stiffens as your stomach turns to lead. It feels like you are being pulled feet first from a hot bath and straight into a pile of ice. The order goes out from your brain, but your arms are no longer working. You try to lift your hand, you lift with all your might, but the gun is suddenly as heavy as an anvil. Blood loss is killing you as your vitality pumps out of your body.

Your heart thumps like a bellows, feels like it's going to rip free. Then it stutters, beats once more, and goes silent. The world turns to ash before your eyes; a gray ring filters the light from the room. You guess it's your corneas dying. You try to breathe one last time, to taste clean air before the end arrives, but your chest is stuck in exhale and refuses to comply.

Your brain grows foggy; things blur. You feel your tongue dry up in your mouth and are reminded of the first sight of your son when you opened the door an eternity ago. Your brain's last thought arrives like a revelation.

Time to feed.

* * *

The car purrs down the residential network of interconnecting streets like a tamed motorcycle engine. Her view is crystal clear through the expansive front window. The compact is plush, with electronics doodads everywhere, and the new car smell still hangs around a year after purchase. She glances at the colorful GPS even though she has been on this little stretch a thousand times.

Alice can't wait to get home and watch last night's primetime offering while zipping through all the inane commercials. She hopes

Ken will work at the computer so she isn't interrupted. Ken means well, but his stupid jokes about her cop dramas have worn out her last TV nerve.

Her mind wanders over the plot lines from last week when a kid on a skateboard rockets across the street right in front of her. She slams on her brakes, which brings the silver car to a screeching halt. Boxes of food flop over in the back of the car. All that time carefully stacking them up, and now she will have to do it again. Dammit!

The kid keeps going, braided hair flopping in a long ponytail down the child's back. She swerves when she reaches the curve and does some trick where the skateboard pops off the ground, spins to the right and then races down the sidewalk. Her head whips back, and their eyes meet. Scared, wide-open, mouth an O of horror, probably aware now of just how close she came to plowing into the automobile. Damned kids. One of these days she is going to hit one.

Now all of her food will be out of order, all of the supplies she picked up after getting regular groceries for Ken. Her sudden anger is tempered at the thought of her new diet. She is even more excited about the counselor she met with today.

She had a fifteen-minute session to discuss her goals, all the while the lacquer-nailed, stick-thin woman driving home how important Alice is. How she deserves to look the way she wants. How her husband will see her in a new light. But more importantly, he will want to see her skinny body in a lacy film of lingerie. He won't be able to take his eyes off me. She smiles to herself, remembering fondly. Just like the first years of our marriage.

Susan understood her, understood her need to lose the baby fat she gained after little Anthony was born. Little Anthony who is now seventeen years old and thinks he knows everything. Her sweet boy who rarely comes home. Where did they go wrong? He had everything he asked for, every gadget he could imagine. A new iPod every year. The laptop that cost $2,000, the one that he had to have for classes even though all it is used for now is games. How could he be so standoffish? If she had acted like that when she was a kid, her father would have laid down the law.

Although her trip to the clinic had been fulfilling, Alice felt unfocused.

Then the counselor had become somewhat distracted. She kept glancing at a computer screen and fingering a cell phone. She snuck peeks out the front window as if she were expecting someone. In fact, the entire trip had felt off somehow. The grocery store was emptier than usual, and the other shoppers slipped from aisle to aisle like wraiths. The checkouts were nearly deserted, and Alice had to resort to a self check stand to pay for her groceries. This had taken a good fifteen minutes, but it beat waiting in line behind seven people.

Even the receptionist seemed on edge behind her desk and computer screen. She wore a shiny bright blue shirt that set off her ocean eyes, but Alice was distracted by the way her buttons were open nearly to her waist, displaying an obscene amount of her perfectly tanned globes. Who dresses like that at work? she wondered with a trace of jealousy.

The kid jumps on her board and is away. Alice speeds off and switches the radio on. She finds a talk show and listens to the chatter that more and more is centered on the mystery of the Queen Anne neighborhood. The gas leak and people getting sick, some being brought out in ambulances.

And it is so close to her house. She saw an Army truck trundle by a few hours ago and heard men shouting in the distance. She even had to cut around the hill to get across town, and it had added a good ten minutes to her drive.

Alice rounds the corner and pulls into her parking space. The house is set back with a long wooden fence in front that blocks the view from the road. It adds privacy and also allows friends and family members to park out front. Still the neighbors are far too close in this neighborhood, just like most houses in this part of Seattle, which borders Fremont.

Ken's gas-guzzler is in the driveway, parked too far to the left so that it takes up part of her spot. She frowns but pulls around and backs in slowly, her car dwarfed by the big Suburban. The back is open, so he is probably bringing in some wood for the new floor in the kitchen.

She's been ignoring the radio, but a distressed caller catches her attention. She lets the car idle for a moment and turns up the volume.

"My son had a cut, not too deep, or so I thought. When it wouldn't stop bleeding, my wife made me take him to the hospital, but when we got there we were turned away. They said a chemical spill inside forced them to close their doors but a nearby clinic might be able to get us in."

"Did they say what sort of chemicals?"

"Chemical, they only mentioned one. I tried to get some information out of the guy, but he just walked back inside. I thought I saw a soldier with a …"

She cuts the engine and wiggles out of the car. Just another wacko on the radio. They don't turn you away at the hospital, that's ridiculous. She slaps the little electronic key into her purse and strides around the car. Her hip bumps into the side as she rounds it. She grunts and rubs the spot. She won't miss the weight when it's gone, not one little bit.

She gathers the spilled food containers and hauls them to the front door. It's open, so she walks in, calling, "Ken, honey, can you help me bring in some bags?"

* * *

Cold.

Cold glass crunches in your joints. Slivers of the stuff slide through your blood vessels. Each time you try to move, it is pure agony. Your guts are clenched up like they are stuffed with a wad of towels, but they make hollow gurgling noises as if they have never been full. You feel a river of shit spreading down your leg, warm against your cold appendages.

Blood.

It is growing cool against your neck. You move your head just a bit, and more of the stuff leaks out. A squish as you raise your head, another as you it drop it in agony. Heavy weight drags at your hand. You raise an arm, and it thumps down as well.

Confusion.

A jumble of half-thoughts that seem to fade with each slow second. Memories of recent events, a boom, a hole in someone's head. Someone you knew, dead. The smell of the gunpowder burned your nose, bitter and hot, but that memory is snatched away even as it forms.

Silence.

There should be a thump in your chest, but it just isn't there. You can't even breathe; your lungs should rise and lower. How will you get oxygen to your brain? Panic grips you, but you can't move. A scream rips through your mouth, only no sound emerges, and you are aware at some level that you need air in your lungs to exhale past your vocal cords in order to form that particular sound. The sound of a dead man screaming. Nothing comes out, so you lie there with your mouth wide open.

The pain passes, and it leaves numbness behind. You can sense your arms and legs, your head still attached, but they feel like they are injected with Novocaine just like when you go to the dentist. Then the memory of drilling is gone, the smell of ground teeth evaporates, and you want to bite your tongue in half.

Every fiber of your being wants to clench up, curl into a ball and die. Then the memory of dying slaps your brain and—just like that—is snatched away as well. You wonder if you will be able to think once the gnawing in your gut is gone. It's like a hollow just opened up, as if you have never eaten in your life.

You manage to move, to shift one leg then the other. Your arms are next, then hands. How are they working with no blood in your veins? Doesn't matter. In fact, as soon as that question arrives, it too is lost.

Some level of brain activity acknowledges what is happening. The synapses are dying, and as they perish, you lose more and more of yourself. You pull yourself up, out of the pool of blood, away from the body beside you. He looks familiar, but in a moment, you don't even care who he is as the memory fades to nothingness.

You stagger to your feet and immediately fall down the tiny landing, one stair, then the other. Your arm at your side, hand pointed as you land on it. A crunch, but you can't feel pain, so maybe nothing is broken.

The hunger strikes again. Your stomach clenches tight; you need to eat. You stagger around in a half-circle and stare at the shape on the ground. You lean over and sort of fall back up the stairs, then an arm is in your mouth and you take a hearty chomp. Cold meat, cold flesh. It is in no way satisfying, but what choice do you have? The hunger is all you have.

Tearing at the meat, peeling sinew and muscle as you try to feed faster, but it is getting harder and harder to chew. Your bites slow down, and it turns into a slow-motion feeding as what few brain cells you have left cycle through the act of eating another human being.

If you could grin, you are pretty sure there would be a big one on your lips.

There is a sound down the hall. Your head comes up, and you hear a door slam. You drop the bloody arm and stand up.

∗ ∗ ∗

"I picked up everything on your list except tomatoes; the ones at the store were old and soft," Alice calls out as she pushes the door closed with her hip. She has a couple of bags of frozen meals but many more to bring in.

She pauses in the hallway as the smell hits her. Something familiar about it, something she has smelled before, like a fresh chunk of meat you just brought home from the meat market. Copper, like blood. But what in the world could Ken be preparing? It's still too early in the day to roast a pork shoulder on the grill; maybe he is planning to cook one in the slow cooker.

She stomps down the hall and kicks her shoes off at the entrance to the master bedroom. Then it's past Anthony's room, which has been vacant for a few weeks now. She has stopped staring at it as she passes, stopped looking at the formerly warm room gone cold and empty just like the ache in her heart. He was such a good boy, where did we go wrong?

More movement comes from the kitchen. It sounds like a stumble. There is a moan. Oh my God, must be Ken. Is he hurt? Visions of him lying on the ground, clutching his chest race through her head. She speeds down the hallway and comes around the corner only to be met with horror.

The blood starts on the stairs and traces a path into the living room. The carpet used to be tan—it needed constant cleaning—but now it is drenched in blood. There is a shape lying near the dinner table, but her mind is having trouble comprehending what she is seeing. And there is Ken, standing by the entryway, hand held out toward her like a declaration of need.

"Honey!" she shrieks and stumbles toward him. His side is covered in blood, and a great ragged tear breaks the line of his neck. She stops in shock and then stumbles back.

Ken turns toward her and extends one arm. The hand is hanging the wrong way like it is broken. He extends his other hand, and a half-moan escapes his lips. Then her eyes settle on his, and the horror peaks.

Those eyes hold no life; they are empty, with blood-filled irises. Something that looks like a piece of raw meat hangs from his mouth. His maw is surrounded by even more blood.

Alice steps toward her husband in shock and disbelief. She takes another step, and they are close enough to touch. She stares at him through tear-stained eyes that distort his image. A loud sob bursts past her lips.

"Wait, I'll get a towel for your cut, Ken," she says and turns away to grab one from the kitchen. There is one on the stove. She reaches for it in a mechanical way.

Ken lurches toward her and grabs at her hair as she turns. He misses and is propelled forward by his momentum; he looks for all the world like a large toddler just learning how to walk. She shies away from her husband of twenty years and then ducks down and around him.

"Ken, I don't understand. What's wrong?" The phone is in the living room; she just has to reach it. He turns slowly and reaches for her again but catches only the strap of her purse. He grabs it tightly and pulls it off her shoulder. She staggers up the stairs, steps in the massive pool of blood and then settles her eyes on the shape on the ground.

A scream rips past her lips, and she falls. Stumbles and goes down, hands slapping into blood-soaked carpet. She crawls away as fast as she can, her body doing a herky-jerky shake as revulsion sends vomit spewing out of her mouth. She staggers to her feet and flees into the living room.

She snatches at the phone and sits on the couch as if it is just another day. She stares at the keys, then glances up at the TV on the wall, the TV in front of which she had planned to park herself all afternoon.

She hits 'talk' and tries to dial 911. Her first attempt has her pushing 812. She clicks the talk button again and then carefully stabs the correct three keys. Ken has found that her purse doesn't contain anything he can eat, so he drops it in a heap. Bottles of pills, makeup, a compact cell phone, Tic Tacs, all scatter across the floor. A small bottle of perfume clatters along with the mess; the cap goes skittering across the floor and the smell of perfume fills the room.

As she puts the phone to her head, she glances at the body on the floor, the pile of matter next to it, and she thinks stupidly that Anthony has left a pile of play-dough on the ground and spilled ketchup on it. Damn kid, can't he clean up after himself?

Her hand goes to her mouth as a sob escapes, then the phone connects and an operator answers.

"911 emergency."

"Help, my husband … there is something wrong with him!" She stifles the urge to shriek and instead holds on to a high-pitched warble.

"Ma'am, please tell me what is going on."

"There's something wrong with him. I think his throat is hurt … he is covered in something. I think it's blood. It's like he's drunk, but he doesn't drink. Not anymore, he gave it up years ago!"

She shifts to the other side of the house as he makes it up the stairs and stumbles toward her with a shambling gait. The hand that is impossibly bent hangs at his side. The other is outstretched. He moans and smacks his blood-drenched lips.

"Ma'am, listen, you need to get away from him and get out of your house. I can't stay on the line … we aren't supposed to talk about them. Just get away. Lock him in a room, and someone will be there as soon as possible."

"Them? THEM? What are you talking about? You're 911, you have to help. Send the police, oh God, send the fire department, send anyone!"

"I can't send the police if there is just one! Just get out of the ..." Then another voice cuts her off in the background.

"I have to let you go now, ma'am. Just get out of the house or kill the thing if you have to. It's not your husband anymore. We ... we don't even know what they are."

Ken has made it across the room; empty eyes settle on her. She watches in utter horror as he comes closer and closer. She sits in place as if mesmerized, as if a hypnotist has popped into the room and put her under a spell. She wants to move, but her legs ignore her.

She stares at his lips and tries to figure out what is on them. Then it hits her: his bottom lip is hanging half torn off, and he is trying to suck it back into his mouth. She glances between this new horror and the body on the floor. The shredded arm, meat hanging in ragged chunks, and the pieces fall into place.

"To hell with this!" she yells and rockets to her feet. She gags again as she runs past Ken. He reaches out but only catches air, and she steers around him. A tiny gasp of sound like a sob breaks past her lips, adrenaline amps her body up and she is past him. She gags again as the smell hits her, copper, raw pork, old meat. She jumps over her son's bloody body and comes down hard. She slips and nearly pitches down the stairs.

She hits the landing to the kitchen and pounds over the contents of her purse. Her hand covers her mouth, but vomit spews out anyway. Then she is down the hall, in the bedroom and slamming the door closed behind her. Her fingers fumble on the lock. They twist at it, slip off and then, fighting the shakes, Alice finally gets the thing turned.

She drops to her knees and pounds at her legs. Then she takes a deep breath that burns as vomit is sucked down her throat. She breathes in as much air as her lungs can handle and then screams until her throat is raw.

MIKE

The afternoon rushes by as I type up my story on Seattle dives. This is why I love my job; I get to write in-depth articles that involve drinking large amounts of beer. My favorite dive had been a place called Jeans, which featured the worst selection of alcohol I have ever seen. They didn't have top-shelf booze, in fact they didn't even have medium-shelf. It was plastic jugs all the way, but they had a hell of a deal for cheap Budweiser on tap.

The phone rings, and it's Rita. She found her cell phone and is charging it. She is more coherent. Now she paints a pretty clear image of what is going on at her place.

"The police have cleared out of the parking lot. Several ambulances arrived and started packing people into them. Some had to be restrained, but the medics looked like they knew what they were doing, you know, very professional."

"How badly were they hurt?" I doubt she saw enough to make a judgment call; maybe I am just asking her questions to keep her on the phone.

"It was hard to tell. They didn't go easy; the attackers had to be hit with those electric guns a couple of times."

After my panic earlier, I'm reassured by her words. She then rants for a few minutes about how her neighbor Ted is constantly snooping around, asking her questions about her health, how she is enjoying the summer. She doesn't like it. I think Ted is a nice enough guy, and maybe he is genuinely interested in her. It is sad to see her unable to recognize the attention.

I hang up the phone and stare at it, dejected. She could do so much if she would just get out of her damn apartment—the dark hole with old furniture from our marriage squeezed into every room. Things she won't let go of, including most of Andy's possessions. At one time she worked on a children's book as the illustrator. Her background in architecture went a long way toward how the book came out. How she could draw! She would show her creations to Andy and judge a piece's worthiness by the expression on his face.

She is so lost. I need to talk her into going to a psychologist again. She went for a while and felt better; the Zoloft helped, but she quit after a few months and threw the bottles away. I purchased books for her on how to deal with loss, and at one point her depression peaked and she bought a gun. I thought about having her committed. I loved Rita once upon a time, and we had a good life together. Now we are two lost people doing the best we can to survive.

With a sigh, I push myself away from apathy and go fetch a cup of coffee from the kitchen.

The story is done, so I do a few searches for random attacks, which turn up some prank videos. Then I try random violence, rage. Then endless variations of the words. The closest I get to a hit is someone's cell phone footage of a man who appears to have a chest wound and still tries to stand up. The video is grainy, blurred and shaky. It is hard to tell if it is even real. I watch it several times before it suddenly disappears. Damn it! There is now a message that the video violates the terms of use agreement. There wasn't even a write-up explaining where the video was shot.

I am starting to think I am in on a big hoax when a link comes to my inbox from Leonard. I open it to find a site that stores large downloads for free, provided you sit through a timer and stare at their ads. I go back to a search window until my time comes and then download the fifty-megabyte file straight to my desktop. It is in a common video format, so I double click and wait for Media Player to load.

The video is grainy, taken from a distance, probably on a cell phone. The sound is tinny, but I hear the unmistakable screams of several people. Erin leans over my shoulder while I hunt for the volume control. No reason to bring the entire office over.

"What is it?" she asks. I can smell her hair where it hangs near my face. I glance at her profile. She has her glasses off, and she looks very young to me. I find myself intensely attracted to her for the hundredth time today.

"Oh, something Leonard sent over. No message, just the link."

The phone's view jumbles around for a bit then comes into surprising clarity. There are half a dozen people surrounding the body of a man lying on the ground. Most of them are dressed in shorts and t-shirts; one of the women had a bikini top on. From the amount of trees surrounding the area, I guess it is a park.

A voice shouts over and over, "I had to do it! I had to do it! You all saw him attack my girl!"

One side of the man's head is caved in. There is blood on his tropical shirt, great spots of it that turn the white fabric a shade of crimson, which is in sharp contrast to the yellow and green flowers. The man's eyes stare straight up as the camera swings close. They are an odd color—the lids gray-lined, the eyeballs dull and lifeless. As the camera focuses, I sit back in my chair. I hear Erin gasp, and she puts a hand on my shoulder.

The man's eyes are filling with blood as we watch. The whites are completely consumed in a matter of seconds. Then the man shrugs his shoulders, a shudder seems to ripple through his body, he coughs and then foam—white and blood-flecked—pours from his mouth. The camera jerks back as others scramble out of the way.

Another man steps close and looks at the camera and then back at the body, which is struggling to its feet. "No way! That guy was dead!"

The 'dead' man is on his feet in a flash, and I can't believe anyone can move that fast. He springs forward and clasps one of the women to him. She is dressed in a halter top, and he tears out a chunk of her shoulder near the strap. Silence for a half-second as if the parties involved can't believe what they are seeing. She screams and thrashes against him. Hands flail, finding his face and neck. This isn't real! The guy digs in like a dog tearing at a flesh-covered bone.

One of the men tries to pull the guy off, but he doesn't have a firm grip. His face is screwed up in dread, and it is obvious he is trying to avoid touching any blood. What the hell is wrong with that guy? Is he really worried about a little blood on his clothes while a woman is being killed? "Goddamn moron," I mutter, and Erin squeezes my shoulder.

Then a smaller man steps up to the plate and grabs the attacker by the shoulder and neck. He pulls back hard, but he hardly budges the man. Screams make the microphone crackle as the pressure pushes the tiny diaphragm past its limit.

The crazy spins around and backhands the woman's would-be savior hard enough to break bones. He seems unable to stay on his feet, let alone strike that hard. There is a gurgle as the thin guy falls, his jaw probably broken. Then it is chaos as the entire group attacks. Someone gets the bright idea to grab a piece of wood from the ground. He lifts the branch high and uses a big overhand blow in an attempt to dislodge the biter. He screams, and for a second I wonder who is more insane—the guy they thought was dead or the enraged man.

The attacker is down, and it's all jumbled camera angles as the participants jostle and run into each other. There are screams and then the camera turns to the woman who was attacked, and I can see that huge pieces of flesh are missing from her chest. Blood streams out of her wounds, and I want to yell at the screen that someone needs to stop the flow.

She kneels on the ground, hands pressed to the wound, then she falls over, and her body spasms a couple of times before going still. There are gasps and more than a few 'oh my Gods.' It is silent, and I wonder if they managed to stop the crazy guy. Then, to my horror, the woman opens her eyes, and they are just as blood-filled as the crazy man's had been. There are more screams, and the screen dissolves into a scattered bunch of pixels as the cameraman takes off running. Then the image snaps to a close, and the screen goes black.

Erin reaches over and hits replay. I'm too shocked to stop her, so I watch the video again. Because the quality is so low, I feel somehow detached from it, as if the video is from a movie trailer and the action is staged. I think of the bad movies I have seen where mindless creatures roam in search of brains, but what I have seen is nothing like that. She leans over me, hand still on my shoulder. Her breath on my neck makes the hair there stand up on end. The madness spreads, and goose bumps erupt all over my body. It's probably the video that freaks me out. I want to concentrate on the screen, on the horror I am witnessing, but all I can think about is Erin.

"Why don't they do anything?" she breathes against me again. I can feel her breast on my shoulder, and the sensation is insanely erotic. Erin keeps chipping away at my resolve. Does she mean to? She is smart and beautiful, fun to be around, and she can tell a dirty joke like a sailor. If she were mine, I would never let a bad thing happen to her.

I click off the video in frustration and wait for her to move back. After a second, she does and I stand up. She doesn't move away, and I'm forced to stand face to face with her. She doesn't say a word, just stares at me expectantly. I want to say something. In fact, as I study her face, I have an overriding desire to take her in my arms and crush her to my chest. I want to taste her lips. I want to smother them in mine. But I worry that others are looking, and I move around her with awkward steps.

"Why do you hide, Mike?"

"What do you mean?"

"You know."

"No I don't. I don't hide."

"The way you look at me sometimes … I wish you would say what you're thinking."

"I can't, I …" and I don't know what to say. Why is she doing this to me? Am I supposed to tell her how attracted I am? Tell her how broken I am inside? She can't understand, she can't know how deeply she affects me.

There it is: the gorilla in the room that is my hidden feelings. I wish I could just tell her, but the words don't come. "Let's talk after work," I manage and then walk away with my dignity somehow intact.

I can feel Erin's eyes boring into me as I try to keep my cool. She is tempting me at every turn; everything I do seems to draw her attention today. What if I am being a fool and she has feelings for me?

I'm still unnerved by what I saw on the web. That video was a nightmare. I mentally draw a map to the parks I know in Seattle, realizing that it could be one of dozens. I go to Jim's office to tell him what I just saw, but he isn't there. He must have gone home early. I have done enough research for the day and decide to call it quits as well.

I swing by Leonard's, and when I walk into his office, he looks up at me and nods his head. "Told ya so."

"Okay, that was some weird shit. Is it real?"

"Did it look real? 'Cause I don't know how you fake stuff like that unless you have a movie studio. Even then, it's unlikely anyone would go through that much trouble for a hoax."

I sigh. "Then you have a short memory, my man. Remember the Bigfoot guys a few months ago? Got a gorilla suit and then killed some small animals and put the guts in the freezer with the suit?"

"Yeah, I remember."

"How about the UFO video in Peru last year. That kid put it together on his home computer and had a million YouTube hits in a day. If you're asking if that video could be a fake, then I have to say yes."

"Okay, but you have to admit there is some craziness going on in the city right now. Like the big gas leak that no one is talking about. I find it a little hard to believe they don't have that thing under control yet, and I heard military trucks are moving into the city. Not a couple, either. A lot."

That gives me pause, but I'm not ready to concede the point just yet.

"You can say that crazy stuff is happening any day of the week. We have constant terrorist threats, pirates near Indonesia, swine flu, but you know what I think now, man? I think there is a big conspiracy to create a panic for no other reason than to ..." And I trail off because Leonard is no longer looking at me. His attention is pulled away from me and shifted past the office window to the street outside.

I turn, expecting to see a couple of college girls wandering by in shorts; few things distract him like girls in skimpy outfits. But all I see is a camouflaged truck passing by filled with men in Army garb. Then another truck rolls by followed by a Humvee. We both go out to the front door to look, and the trucks swing right as if they are heading for Denny Avenue.

"Told ya so." He grins. "You were saying ... something about a panic?"

"Well hell."

"Yep, my weird-shit-o-meter just hit pay dirt. I'm going home to watch the news." Leonard grins again.

* * *

I thought I was brushing her off when I said we should talk later, but Erin has other ideas. She starts closing up shop for the day as soon as I do. Computers off, papers straightened, bags packed. I keep looking over my shoulder as I get ready to leave, and she keeps smiling at me with that lovely grin she has that reaches her eyes and crinkles the edges.

"Ready?" she asks, and I nod. We leave together, and I feel like everyone's eyes are on us.

Cars tear up and down Denny like they are on fire. Everyone wants to beat that long light at the bottom of the hill. The sun is still up, and it is cooking the city to the mid-eighties. We stroll past a dog park, and when I look back at a German Shepherd lying on her back, I catch a glimpse of Myrtle Edwards park and think of the video we watched earlier. With a shudder, I turn my attention back to the road.

We walk past Bandits, a tiny place I have dropped into for a quick drink and some amazing queso on late nights. If her condo isn't much farther, we can walk to Fourth Avenue and find a restaurant. I think, Flying Fish is nearby and start to crave fish tacos.

I try some small talk as we stroll toward my bus stop, but she has different plans. "So Mike, why don't you swing by my condo with me. I'll change, and we can go grab a drink."

Unsure what to say, feeling like I have been called out, I nod and try not to look too much like a lost puppy dog following her. So much for escaping to my comfortable and nonexistent life. She has told me that she lives close to work and—truth be told—I would like to see her condo, see the other side of Erin, not her work-self. I suspect I get the real deal from her every day. She is very up front, and I have always appreciated that about her. I don't have to play games, and I normally know where I stand ... At least I did before I had the bright idea to ask her out tonight in my half-ass way. I haven't been out in a while, and maybe if I have a drink or three, I can explain to Erin why I shouldn't date. Maybe I can tell her that I find her attractive but can't risk getting involved while Rita is sick.

Another side of my mind, the side that has a little devil perched next to my noggin, asks why I can't see her. Is it my fault Rita can't cope with reality and turns to booze to make it through the day? To hell with it, I'm going to play it cool and see what happens. I feel sad for Rita, and I miss Andy terribly, but I have a responsibility to see myself sane.

"Did you see the trucks earlier?" I offer as small talk. She takes full strides up the hill, and I struggle not to show her how out of shape I am.

"Yep, National Guard," she says.

I look at her with raised eyebrows.

"Had a boyfriend who was in. I remember the uniform."

"I never pictured you as a gun-wielding leftist."

"Maybe I am. Maybe I have lots of secrets." Then her stride increases so that I have to shut up and pant to keep up. She takes her sunglasses out of her blue purse and puts them on. She wears a shade of lipstick I didn't notice earlier, dark red, almost burgundy, and with the sunglasses, she looks like a movie star.

Away from the madness of Denny Avenue, the streets are quiet this evening. We stroll past an espresso place that has closed up for the night. A few cars race along Second, and we wait at light after light as we walk across Broad Street. There is a Mexican restaurant I love just around the corner. I point it out, and she says she eats there all the time. Well, strike one.

She smiles as we walk on a now-flat surface, so I catch my breath and chat about nothing in particular. She offers jokes and sarcastic remarks in return, keeping me on my toes as usual. At last I realize that there is nothing going on here, we are just two work buddies on the way out for the evening. Just like a couple of guys, except for the fact that my 'buddy' has an amazing sense of humor, is sweet, thoughtful and has a knockout body.

We arrive at her door, and she slides some sort of keycard into a slot, then the door clicks and she pushes it open. The entryway is tiny, just a hallway with mail slots and elevators. She hits 'up,' and we wait.

"Nice building." My voice is inane in my head as if I were observing a cloud passing by. She nods and explains that this particular company has a waiting list for most of their complexes and especially this location, but she lucked out by knowing someone who was moving out.

"It is very close to work. I bet you get your beauty rest."

"Do I need it that much?" She smiles at me in that charming way she has, that disarming grin that makes me speechless.

"Er, tell me what to say and I'll say it." I chuckle.

"Hmm, then tell me I'm already beautiful." And once again we are on ground that is outside my comfort zone.

My mouth doesn't seem to understand this, and I look at her as the elevator door dings and say, "You are always beautiful."

What the hell did I just say?

The door starts to shut, but neither of us moves to stop it.

"Well thank you, Mike. That is the nicest thing you have ever said to me."

I break her gaze by hitting the button again, and I'm rewarded with the door opening right away. I reach out and hold the sides to keep it open, aware of how stupid it looks since we don't have anything with us that would take a while to load.

The elevator takes us to the sixth floor, and then we are at her door. I struggle with the need to say something, anything, but she just stares at me. Her eyebrows are arched up, and under her attention, words fail me.

Her condo is small, just a one-bedroom, but it is very tidy, and she has done things to make it seem larger. The entryway has a mirror on the wall just as you enter, and the walls are white. The floors are hardwood, but they give a little with each step, and I wonder if they are Pergo, the soft material that looks like wood but doesn't need to be finished or sanded. Rita always wanted that in the house, but we never seemed to have time for it.

"Welcome to mi casa. Make yourself at home." She motions to the living room, which can be crossed in about three steps. There is a tan leather couch with a Persian rug in front of it, and on this is a delicate glass table on wicker legs. She has a bowl of fruit that looks about as real as plastic can.

"I like your place. It must be easy to keep clean," I say and realize it may come out as a jab, as if I am making fun of it. But as usual, I think in literal terms, and the words are there before I realize it. I wish my place were this easy to take care of; instead I have a house for four with only one soul in it.

"It is, Mike. I have a maid come in once a week and go over the place with a dust mop, and then I do inspections with my white gloves."

"I see, and does your maid have an accent and wear a little skirt?"

"Yes, he does, but it costs extra."

Touché.

She heads for the kitchen and comes back with a cool bottle of wine and a microbrew, then stands in front of me with one hip cocked. "What's your poison, sailor?"

"Scotch, single malt and old, but I'll settle for some of the white."

"Excellent choice, sir. I will be right back."

She hums some song that tugs at my memory, but I can't place it. Glasses click on the counter, and then there is a pop as the cork comes free.

She returns after a minute with two glasses that are already showing condensate lines on the outside. The condo is hot, but not stifling. She deposits the wine in front of me and then opens the curtains to a long window that looks out over the city. I can see the skyscrapers from here. Colombia Tower and Westlake stretch into the heavens, and of course there is the gigantic Bank of America building with its sleek back windows.

"So where are you taking me tonight?"

"I don't know. What do you like?"

"Mike, how long have we worked together, and you don't even know what kind of food I like, hmm? We could go for some Mediterranean. I know a place in the city, and it's a bit of a walk. But I'm in the mood for something much more exotic." She pauses dramatically.

"If you say haggis, it's off."

"I didn't know you liked Scottish food." She laughs. "No, I want an oven-fired pizza, but we'll have to go downtown for that."

"That sounds amazing," I say then lean over and toast her with a tip of the glass against hers. The wine is cold but a bit sour for my taste; still I sip it and then have another, deeper pull.

"Now that you've had a few hours to think about the video we watched earlier, what do you think?" she inquires.

"I think someone has a crazy imagination. I think it's a hoax just like those UFO videos in Brazil or the guys who lit flares and attached them to big balloons in Texas. Just some kids having fun, that's all. The only thing that really concerns me is that my searches on the web today turned up some very odd and conflicting information."

"I found the same thing." She leans forward, and once again we are talking in tones that echo conspiracy even though we are alone in her condo. "Sites that disappear without warning, and every time I typed in 'deader,' I got some very bizarre information ... or misinformation. When you told me about the websites going AWOL this morning, I blew it off, but Leonard's pep talk got me thinking, and investigating. But I have to tell you something. I was too afraid to talk about all of this earlier."

"If you're about to tell me you were once a man, I may have trouble looking at you the same way."

"That's not it, silly. Besides, I would look ridiculous in a French maid outfit."

"I beg to differ."

She sips her wine again and then her natural smile returns but just a hint, almost a smirk that makes her lip curl up in one corner until a crinkle hits her eye. "Mike Pierce, are you flirting with me?"

I wish I could come out and say no, and in a way I feel shy and my mind flashes back to earlier today when I had the desire to kiss her in front of our desks. I wonder what would happen if I set my glass down and attempted to do that now.

"I was going to tell you that if the National Guard is rolling into town, we may have a very big problem on our hands, one we should look into tomorrow, and I mean look hard."

"On a Saturday?"

"Yep. Let's stroll into Queen Anne like we own the place."

I laugh at her, and she smiles back. Then I take a huge swallow of my wine and hope the stuff goes to my head quickly. We talk about the video a bit more, then about the nature of hoaxes and what it takes for someone to pull something like that off. We spend a good fifteen minutes planning how we will drive up and demand to be let in. As we chat, she jumps up and goes to the kitchen, returning with a plate of crackers and some cheese. I am hungry, and the food helps temper the wine somewhat.

We polish off half a bottle of the stuff, and it goes right to my head. I don't drink often, so I have a low tolerance for alcohol. She gets up after setting her empty glass down and leans over the table. Her shirt is open so that I can't help but get a glimpse down her shirt. I look up into her eyes, and she doesn't look perturbed.

"I'm a dirty girl, Mike," she says in a low, husky voice.

I just about choke on the last swallow of wine. Some of it threatens to rush back up my nose, but I manage to hold it down with a will.

"So," and she lets the word hang in the air. "I need to jump in the shower." She stands with a stretch and hits me with an innocent grin. "There's more wine, help yourself."

She heads down the hall, and the door closes with a click. A fan kicks in, and I am left to my own devices in Erin's condo. I sit for a minute with my eyes wide open, staring at the blank TV before I decide to try to put the image of her in the shower out of my mind. I switch on the TV and tune it to a local channel, but they are running national news, which looks a lot like yesterday's news. Maybe I am just getting cynical.

Shouldn't they be talking about the gas leak? There are potentially thousands of people displaced, and they seem to be ignoring it. If I ran a local station, I would have my reporters all over it day and night. That's the kind of thing that keeps people glued to the TV, real-life drama in your back yard, with commercial after commercial served a la carte.

I grab another glass of wine, just a half, and as I am pouring, my phone buzzes. I open it with a flip and see it is a message from Leonard. He has sent me a partial article from a website. It went to my Gmail account, so I am able to read it on my touch-screen phone.

The article is long, in depth and filled with medical jargon, but the gist of it is that researchers at Trigenics had been working on a virus that was able to enter a brain tumor and kill it. There was a rumor that one of the doctors grew impatient with the progress and decided to try it on his wife, who was dying of a nasty growth near her spinal cord. Surgery wasn't an option, and a gamma knife had only halted the growth for a few months.

As she lay dying, he injected the experimental drug numbered VSV N16J, a modified virus related to the vesicular stomatitis virus. The active virus was modified so that single-strand RNA was used rather than double-strand DNA.

The story gets vague after that. They were both brought to the hospital with wounds, but no one would say what kind of injuries. Then the story ends with no real explanation as to what happened to the woman. It isn't even a real news article. Leonard must have cut and pasted the thing from somewhere.

I read the tiny screen and half watch the news, which starts to creep me out a bit. They are going on about sports, orders at Boeing, the president's stimulus package, a gruesome murder in a downtown hotel. There is no mention of anything out of the ordinary. I try to play it off again; my mind is just being paranoid, and that is all. The attack at Rita's place was probably too small to show on the news; I'll check the paper tomorrow.

The shower stops, and there is quiet from the bathroom for a few minutes, then the door cracks open and I hear bare feet padding on the wood floor. I want to turn around and see what she is wearing. Is she in a towel? A little robe? Some hot lingerie she wears from the bathroom to the bedroom before getting dressed? I nearly chuckle at this last image. I stare daggers at the TV, fixating on the screen rather than turning my head around to watch her. Pure innocence—after all, we are just friends.

"I forgot my wine," she calls. "Would you pour me a half-glass, please?"

"Sure." And then she goes into her room.

I pour with a steady hand due to the courage I have sipped over the last thirty minutes. I take the glass down the hall and stand outside the door, just a foot away, unsure what to do. Should I just walk in and hand it to her? I am almost overwhelmed by the fresh scent of soap and shampoo, and she is very likely dressed in something decidedly unshirt- and unpant-like. "Um," I say after a few seconds, and isn't that a brilliant piece of dialog for the woman I have wanted from the moment I laid eyes on her.

"It's okay, you can come in."

She stands near the bed dressed in a towel that is tied in front over her breasts and comes just below her bottom. She is still wet, her olive skin silky tan under the gleam of water. Her hair pulled back from her face as if she only took time to run her hands through it.

"I'm conflicted, Mike." She walks to me and takes the glass. She sips it while staring into my eyes, and I want to turn away, to look at anything but that smoldering gaze. I can't; it's like she can see inside me to the broken parts and put them back in order. I want her, I want to plunge my hands into that hair and pull her to me.

"Oh?" I say instead, which is just about the stupidest thing I can think of.

"Yes. I want to take this towel off and then I want to take your clothes off, and I want to see where that leads. I have a feeling it won't lead very far, since the bed is right there. But I worry about our friendship as well, or should I say where I want it to go, because I have to tell you, Mike, I am just about done being your friend."

"You are?" Is that a hint of panic in my voice? It is. What is she talking about? I can't seem to decide if she is joking or not. I feel my face flush bright red, redder than the wine is making it. I have desired

Erin for a long time, and to think that she has feelings for me is overwhelming.

"Yes. I'm ready for what comes next between a man and a woman who are attracted to each other, and I know you are too. So tell me what to do, Mike. Do I get dressed and we go find some pizza, or do you take door number two, which is behind the towel?" And get your life back in order, my mind adds. What would that feel like?

There is a moment when I want to run screaming as if I were on fire. I want to flee back to my neat and orderly life where the only complication is whether or not my crazy ex-wife is going to call me in a drunken haze. I have my pets, a lazy cat and a noisy bird, and they don't get along so well, but the life works for me.

I am not sure if I'm ready for a complication like this.

My hand remains lamely at my side until she takes it in hers. She pulls it to her lips and kisses the palm. I feel a fire burn where her lips touch my skin. I feel my body ignite, and I want her. I want her like I have never wanted anyone in my life. Like a barrier shattering, I seem to come out of my fugue, come out of the fog that has clouded my mind. I see her before me; I see her with a clarity I have never experienced before.

Her face is smooth where I run my trembling hand over it, cheek warm and flushed from the shower. Her breath catches in her throat, and I run my hand around her ear and into her wet hair. Then her lips are on mine, and she is devouring me eagerly. I pull her to me and crush her in an embrace that has been a year in the making. I can almost feel her smile around the kiss, which goes on for so long I wonder if it is night already.

We fall onto the bed together, and somehow her towel is lost in the mix. Her body is wondrous, soft in all the right places. She smells like a dream, and I take my time getting to know every nook, every bump, and every cleft of her skin.

GRINDER

The bus was late getting to Seattle thanks to some clowns in military vehicles. They were rolling down I-5 like they owned the thing. The beat-up tour bus had to slow to a crawl and follow like they were in some kind of caravan. The driver, Marcos, tried to get around the convoy a few times, but he kept getting cock blocked.

The band started the day pissed, and it got worse by the hour. First the air conditioning cut out and sure, Seattle isn't the hottest town in the U.S., but when it is 85 degrees out and you've got no cool air, it feels like you are in a fucking oven.

They left Portland late, missed breakfast and had to eat some shit from McDonald's. Now Grinder has to lie in his rack while the crap food roils through his guts, giving him a nasty case of gas. Lucky for the other guys that they are asleep; they don't have to put up with his six-foot frame letting out noisy fart after fart. Shit smelled like rotten eggs left in the sun.

They had partied until 4:00 a.m., so they were all passed out, and as usual Eric was snoring like a lumberjack going at a fresh copse of trees. Grinder had the windows pulled all the way open so that when they were moving, the wind blew through his waist-length bleached white hair. He is perched up against the back of the metal rack with a wad of paper in his hand while he tries to come up with lyrics for the new album.

This will be the band's third disc in four years, and he is looking forward to getting back into the recording studio. They have found moderate success in the states, but more overseas. The European markets love their brand of death metal, while Americans tend to gravitate toward what he calls corporate-approved masturbametal. The shit they play on the rock channels between cuts of the classics like Led Zeppelin and AC/DC.

They are Corpse for a Day, and they write what they want when they want, and the record company allows it. Still, they like to point out in interviews and on stage that they do what the fuck they want. They actually get to do what the fuck they want as long as their music keeps selling. If sales go down the tube, they can say adios to their meal ticket, not that it is much money to begin with. Half the time, the guys don't even know if they will have enough to pay rent on apartments they never see.

Grinder wants to scare the shit out of people with the new album. He has an old book of demonology he picked up in Rotterdam. It has a faded leather-bound cover around yellowing pages. Most of the stuff inside is about as scary as a Harry Potter book. Allegedly, it was written a few hundred years ago but had none of the modern-day shock values. So he draws inspiration from the pictures, which are quite disturbing. Men being forced to serve demons who bear giant cocks. Boys kneeling in the dirt with their asses in the air while they call upon a God who isn't there and women bleeding from their cunts but begging for more. The entire book is ridiculous, but the fans love this stuff.

The first disc wasn't easy to sell, and they had been forced to cut back on some of the shock lyrics due to, as the exec called it, 'current climate.' Once they outsold half the artists at the tiny label, they released the second album the way they wanted to. It was shocking, bloody, and gory. The guys go by their stage names and sometimes cover themselves in pig's blood for the encore.

Grinder is happy with the band. The drummer has been a revolving door, but the current guy, Deathpounder, is a champ. Even though he played for a jazz band at one time, he took to the double bass drum like he was born in one. His real name is Wil Anders, but the rest of the band came up with his stage name. Wil just laughed and proudly sported it from day one. He is from fucking Minnesota, of all places, but his name sounds European in a Dethklok sort of way. Only he doesn't have a cool accent. It's still amusing to see the fans assume he is from Sweden or somewhere like that.

Technical, that's what the critics call their music, shocking and still technical with complex guitar riffs and math metal-inspired skins. However there is no pretense at playing anything that sounds vaguely political. There is no overarching theme dealing with issues in the world. They don't focus lyrics on clever innuendo, they don't sing about hot chicks or how cool drugs are. They stick to what they love, and that is horror.

Their first single, Corpse for a Day, based on the band name, dealt with a guy who died and woke up in his grave—only to suffocate. They got the audience into the chorus night after night. Grinder would reach down, hock up a ball of phlegm, leave it in the back of his throat and then bellow the words over and over like Cookie Monster from Hell:

CORPSE! FOR! A! FUCKING! DAY!

Sid helped write most of the first album. He plays bass, and his stage name is Xerdruss, a name he claims he stole from a demon. Grinder and Sid used to get along better. Lately Sid has been undermining the band, trying to get them to change their sound so they can sell more albums.

Grinder will have none of that. They started almost a decade ago with the idea of making their own music, and he'll be damned if they are going to change now. The band goes along with Grinder because he is the leader, the front man. He is responsible for getting up on stage and being the face of Corpse for a Day.

If they have an off night, he will rally the boys, whip the crowd into action. If things are really dull, he will dive right into the mosh pit and show the locals how to do that shit correctly. Nor is he shy. If the girls in the front are hot, he'll get them to flash some titties, which is about as cliché as it gets, but who is Grinder to argue with tradition? Rock and roll, man. Rock and fucking roll.

Sid is getting on his nerves; every night seems to end with a fight. There was a time when they would end each set, go backstage to hang out while a few fans came to worship them, call them musical geniuses. He and Sid would pass a bottle of tequila, maybe share a girlfriend of one of the fans. Have her on her knees servicing them while they drank and drank, until they were staggering around talking about how they were going to rule the metal world.

Now they are cold to each other with the exception of on stage, where they put their differences aside and play together like the old friends they should be.

The lead guitarist, Allen Wise, goes by the name Bloody Axe. He can wield an ax too—the six-string kind. He pumps out chunky riffs night after night, and in the studio, he always pulls out memorable leads and tight rhythm sections to match the macabre lyrics.

Eric is a rhythm guitarist who tours with them. He is very professional and can also serve as a guitar technician if the other isn't able to make a gig. In fact, he knows more about guitars than just about anyone Grinder has ever met.

He is older than the rest of the band, mid-thirties and a veteran of the metal scene for fifteen of those. He has played all over the world with bands bigger than life and little ones like Palforce, Enslaught Enslaught! and Diedrer & Blood. Grinder is always grateful to have him along, because when the shit hits the fan, he and Sid locked in an argument over some petty crap, Eric steps up as the adult of the band and offers a solution. Of course, he usually offers at the top of his lungs, which are considerably louder than either of theirs. He also knows when to shut the fuck up and let the band sort shit out themselves. If Sid ever leaves, he plans to ask Eric to join full time, and they will tour without a bass player if they have to.

Eric has the shortest hair of the band. It falls to his shoulders, and there are hints of gray, so they have him dye it before going on tour. He is craggy faced, like a younger version of Alice Cooper, but when he gets on stage, all that fades away and he bangs his head harder than anyone else in the band. He was reluctant to take a stage name like the others had, so they've taken to calling him Afterbirth, since he joined the band long after they formed.

Grinder coughs loudly a couple of time and even hits the metal wall of his bunk with his fist so the sound rattles around the bus. But Sid still snores like a chainsaw across the way. Grinder slips on his headphones and sets the iPod to shuffle. A Metallica song from the eighties comes on, and at once he loses himself in the old school.

* * *

The club is a dive with black walls and a pair of bars, one near the stage and one in the back of the club where they sell Pabst Blue Ribbon and watered-down Jack. Grinder tastes the latter and is not impressed.

The place is done up like a scene from Hell with devils on the walls in the bar and the main floor. Sid had looked at the sign hanging over the back of the space, which read 'Capacity 799,' and scoffed. The show is a sellout, though. They always sell out the little venues. Grinder doesn't get Sid's anger. They make enough money to get by; none of them has a family except Eric, but he has been on the road so long, he doesn't know any other life. They've come a long way in just a few short years; early on, they would have been lucky to open for a local band to eighty people in a tiny club.

There are rumors of playing some festivals in Europe next year, getting on stage in front of thousands of people … So what is his problem? It would be the perfect road to Sid's dream of commercial success. They could play their music on their terms and still blast through a set for a sea of fans.

They have three full-time roadies, and the guys are doing their best to move all the equipment inside as quickly as possible. The band is always involved as well, dragging in crates, amps, cords, bags of picks. But only Wil moves his own stuff. Always has. He is downright anal about who touches his gear, and that is fine with the rest of the guys. He sets up his own drums, tunes them and will only let a technician sit at his kit after the opening bands have played and they are getting ready to take the stage.

Sid drops one of his amps on the stage with a thump night next to one of Grinder's PA amps and sighs loudly.

"'Sup, dude?" Grinder asks. He likes to keep it cool before a show so they play together like the friends they should be.

"Same shit, brotha."

"I got us a bottle of Wild Turkey stashed away. The bar guy looked away at the wrong minute." He chuckles.

"Sweet. Well, I gotta get more shit unloaded." Then he walks away, and Grinder wonders how much longer before Sid leaves the band. Life on the road can be rough, but it's the ultimate rush when the night arrives and they are on stage for the fans. It's what they got into the business for. Sure the albums sell, mostly in digital format unless the rat thieving fucks steal their music. They make most of their money from playing gigs. Selling merchandise like thirty-dollar shirts they get for two bucks from Taiwan. Stickers, belt buckles, all that stuff adds up in their bank accounts.

There were a few endorsement deals, especially for Axe, who likes a certain guitar manufacturer. They worked out a special deal with him so he only plays theirs on stage, and he has photos in magazines and on the web with the same guitar. Grinder would love a deal like that; maybe one will turn up after the third disc comes out.

He walks back into the July sun, and sweat starts dripping down his forehead right away. His long blond hair is back in a full ponytail, but it's still hot as hell on his neck. He grabs some more crates and hauls them inside with the rest of the guys.

A green camouflaged truck putters along the road next to the tour bus, and Grinder stops to stare. The truck rounds the corner slowly, then is gone.

"The fuck is that all about?"

"I heard it was some drill," Phil the sound tech says. He's covered in sweat and generally looks like shit. Working in the sun, hauling equipment around with a pounding hangover is a bitch. "Some local said the city is filled with them. Army dudes on every corner, sounds like a song in the making, eh Grinder?"

Everyone calls him by his stage name, his alter ego. He refuses to answer to his real name, Duane Jones, or as he used to refer to it, the most boring name in the world. It all goes back to the lifestyle he fully embraces.

"What, the Russians about to invade?" Eric says as he walks by with a rack under each arm.

"Dude, the fucking Russians couldn't invade a village in Africa if they tried, that's some old eighties thinking. Like that movie where the kids hide in the mountains and kill the bad guys that try to take over America." Sid laughs.

"Red Dawn!"

"Yeah, that's the one. Hey, one of you guys try to find us a copy the next time you're at some shit hole video place. I want to watch it on the road."

Great, Grinder thinks, a shitty old movie played on the shitty nineteen-inch TV. Rock and roll, man. Rock and fucking roll.

LESTER

Lester is getting worried about his rifle ammo. He does have a shitload of rounds for the Glock, but they won't last forever if the things start coming over the fence.

Angela strolls down the stairs, tugging on a black shirt that looks like it is meant for an aerobics class. A pair of dark blue pants that come to her knees complete her ninja garb. Like the shirt, the pants are skintight, and Les stares at her ass when she goes into the kitchen. She has her hair in a big ponytail poking out the back of a dark ball cap, and it looks pretty fucking hot.

He joins her in the kitchen and runs the water into a glass. They don't have power, but at least that works. The water isn't exactly warm, but it is a far sight from being cold. He drinks it anyway, imagining that the glass is also filled with ice cubes.

"I'll go over first. If there is any trouble, I want you to shoot at anything that gets too close. I'll call out when I'm on my way back, so don't shoot me."

"Okay."

"You just stay on the side of the house and don't let them see you. Stay in the shadows. The moon is on the other side of the house for now, so you should be in the clear."

"Got it," she replies and raises the pistol in both hands like she is in a Charlie's Angels movie. "Are there many out there?"

"I can't tell. It's too goddamn dark. I can hear some shuffling around, but I think the couple of bodies out front taught them a lesson. And that lesson is: stay the fuck away from the dude with the machine gun." He suppresses a chuckle and moves to the side of the house. The window slides up silently, and he fiddles with the screen for a minute before it pops loose. He carefully pulls it inside and then pokes his head out.

The moon hangs low, a tiny sliver of white that does little to illuminate the ground. At least there aren't a bunch of clouds pouring rain on him tonight.

He hops onto the sill, spins around, slides his body over the edge and drops to the ground. He lands flat on his feet in a pile of dead leaves that crunch like a bag of potato chips. He doesn't move for a half-minute, just waits and listens, but it is quiet. Not even a cricket is chirping, which isn't that strange; they usually go quiet at the first hint of noise. But when is the last time he heard them?

When no deaders rise up from the ground and tear him to shreds, he moves the couple of feet to the fence, hand held out so he can stop when he touches it. The night is muggy. So muggy that he feels like he is in the bathroom after a shower. The smell is earthy with an undertone of dead leaves. Les isn't exactly the gardening type. They don't even own a lawn mower. Once the grass got too high, the summer rolled in and most of it dried up to a brown and yellow patchwork carpet.

Angela should already be moving to the back of the house. She will check the door and call out if she sees anything. He slides along the fence, picking up a couple of splinters in the process. There is a loud thump from the back, making him go still as his heart beats faster. Then Angela utters "shit," and he breathes a sigh of relief. Wonder what she ran into?

He grips the gun tighter, slides the chamber down and double checks that there is a round in the chamber. He can tell the gun is full by the weight in the palm of his hand.

He goes into commando mode, at least his version of it. Gun held high, he creeps along to the fence. The wood slats rise at least six feet into the air, and it will be a bitch to climb if he can't get the old wooden gate open. He can't remember ever using the door, so he prays it will work. Over here, it smells like fresh bark. It's an earthy scent from the stuff John had hauled in a week ago.

He locates the door and feels around until he finds the string hanging out of a hole. Lester takes hold and pulls. There is resistance from the other side, and nothing happens. He pushes on the door, gently, but it barely moves. There is a click of metal on metal that sounds as loud as two trashcans banging together to his hyped-up brain. He looks toward the front of the house, which is obscured by low shrubs. There is still movement there, but nothing he can make out with certainty.

He yanks the string harder, and there is a loud click from the other side. The door loosens, so he pulls it open. He can't help but wonder what they are going to do if they are still stuck here in a week. They have been content to sit around, smoke, drink and fuck. And while it is fun, Lester is concerned about the food supply. Maybe John has a pantry full of goodies and is willing to share. Maybe he left and it is up for grabs. Maybe the world has gone to shit and he will have to kill his neighbor.

He closes the door until the metal parts of the lock barely touch, but he doesn't let it lock just in case he needs to haul ass. John's yard is as hard to make out in the pale light as Lester's was. The difference is that John gives a shit about his yard. There are flowerbeds, large roses that rise along the wall. He pushes one aside gently, doing his best to avoid the thorns, but like the wood wall earlier, they bite into his skin.

He and the neighbor have been on speaking terms and outwardly friendly, but Lester knows the man doesn't trust him and in fact looks down on him. John is aware of people coming at all hours of the night, but he and his wife are older, kids gone, they probably don't have much of a life. They seem content to let the next-door drug dealer do his thing as long as it doesn't affect them. They probably have date night and screw once a month. If Les gets that old and boring, he hopes someone will put a fucking bullet in his skull.

He slides around the back of the house to the screen door. It is dark in the living room, and he can pick out indistinct shapes that are probably a chair and a couch. He tugs the sliding screen door aside and tries the door. Not surprising—it is locked. He doesn't want to go around to the front, he can't be sure the things aren't surrounding the place from all the rustling around on that side of the house.

He finds a side window and tries it. Thing doesn't budge. He moves to each of the remaining two windows and tries them. All are locked shut. He's going to have to break one.

He is nervous because, although he assumed that John and his wife left, he never saw them depart. The garage has been shut, and there is no way to see if the big SUV is in it. He goes back to the sliding glass door and tries to peer inside.

Nothing but shadows. He taps on the glass lightly with the butt of the gun and whispers as loud as he dares, "John?" His voice is loud in his head, and he hopes it doesn't carry to the front. He also hopes John isn't sitting in the living room with a gun aimed at the window so he can blow away any threats at his back door.

A cloud passes across the sky, obscuring the pale moon. This in turn casts the back of the house into complete darkness. He sighs and slides to the ground, sitting on the little concrete patio. He doesn't want to break a window; they may have to move here, and he wants the place intact.

He snaps his fingers when he thinks of an alarm company rep who showed them an inexpensive deterrent a few years ago. Lester had gone with the competition, since they offered a better in-home service, but he remembers the guy walking around, showing him where intruders could get in. The man stood by Lester's door and told him why the older houses needed some TLC.

He takes hold of the big door's handle and with a gentle motion, lifts straight up and then jiggles it a bit. The door slides up into the track at the top, and the latch slips off the hook. He slides it to the left and then lowers the door. It worked! Fucking sweet! Now Lester is a drug dealer and a thief who can be charged with breaking and entering. If his dad were still around, wouldn't he be proud?

He slips inside and stops until he can get used to the dark. The house has an odd smell, like potpourri with an undercurrent of rot, sort of like food left out too long.

He nearly stumbles over a low glass table on his third step. His shin cracks into the edge, and he mutters a half-dozen 'fucks' under his breath as the pain races up his leg. That's going to leave a lump.

I should have brought a flashlight, not that I have one. One thing Lester has learned from this is that he was unprepared for a power outage, and when things are back to normal, he is going to stock up on supplies. He is going to become a fucking survival nut with tons of food stores, and jugs of water to go with the bags of pot and boxes of bullets.

"John," he hisses. "It's Lester. Anyone home?" Then he says it louder.

He jumps. Was that a thump upstairs?

"John?" he calls again.

Nothing.

He moves around the living room, careful this time so his shins don't meet any more sharp edges. The kitchen is backed into a corner of the house. It is darker in here, but he feels along the edge of the counter until he finds drawers. He pulls them out one at a time, looking for a flashlight. He shifts utensils around in one drawer and then junk in another. There are shapes that may be cookie cutters in one and a drawer full of knives. He slides his hand out of this one very slowly.

He locates a box of candles in one drawer. They are the long, skinny ones that are used for dinner. They are better than nothing. He slips his lighter out and hisses the thing to life with a click. Then the candle is lit, and he can see around the little kitchen. He lights another candle and holds the two together to get a better view.

Well looky here, he smiles. There is an emergency light in the wall outlet, the kind that charges all the time while plugged in. He pops it loose and tests it. A bright light stabs out and brings the room to life.

Things are looking up!

There is another thump upstairs, louder this time. He doesn't want to go up there; he wants to find the generator and go. He blows out the candles and sets them on the counter. Then, thinking that it would be a shame to burn down his neighbor's house, he drops them in the sink and even runs water over the wicks.

He probes the house, wandering into an empty bathroom. Then into a family room complete with big screen TV and hundreds of DVDs. There is a leather couch and a lazy boy in the center of the room. He moves on to the entrance to the garage, presses his ear to the door and listens for a few seconds.

He grips the doorknob and turns it slowly. He cups the flashlight against his chest and peers into the darkness. His heart is beating faster again; it thumps against his chest and is so loud he bets Angela can hear it. What if John and his wife are deaders? What if they have the disease that is fucking up the other neighbors? What if they are in the garage, in the dark; will he be able to hold the light on them and the gun at the same time? Too many bad horror movie images dance through his head.

He takes a breath, slides the door open a fraction more and slips his head in. The smell hits him right away. It's a horrid odor that reminds him of something he can't put his finger on. God, he hopes there isn't a body rotting in here! There is no movement. He lets out a breath that is loud to his ears and then calls out again.

"John?"

Movement to the right, something fast that shoots up. He fumbles back, and the flashlight smacks into his face as the door slams shut. "Fuck!" he yells louder than he intended. What the hell was that thing?

Then he hears a faint purr and chuckles to himself. That would explain the smell all right—cat shit. He slides the door open, and a small feline rubs its way through the crack and noses at his feet suspiciously. He leans over and holds his hand near the cat so it can smell him, then he rubs its head. Damn thing has a purr like a small engine.

"I'll get you some food in a sec, cat," he tries to reassure the little feline. He runs his hand along its arching back. How long has the poor thing been shut up? Well if the cat was cool in the garage, there must not be an infected John in there, so he enters and checks to make sure the door isn't locked from the other side. He finds a shoe on the floor and uses it to prop the door open.

The garage is clean except for a cat box in one corner. There is sand splashed all around the plastic liner. The thing is indeed full of little lumps, but he'll be damned if he is going to clean it out.

The big SUV takes up most of the free space. There are sets of shelves against one wall, big metal ones that look as if they could support tons of stuff. He wanders around the space feeling very voyeuristic. Sure this is a matter of survival, but he is getting a perverse thrill out of looking through his neighbor's things. They never speak much, but they're on friendly enough terms. The wife is older but kind of a cougar. Tall, thin, tending to dress in business suits but likes to go around in shorts and low-cut shirts in the summer.

He spots a generator on a lower shelf among some camping gear. Bingo! It isn't quite what he had in mind, but at least it is portable. There are some extension cords near the thing as well as a propane stove and a folded-up tent. More poking around turns up a big plastic container of gas cylinders. He starts moving supplies to the hallway outside the garage.

Sadly, he doesn't come across any guns, but he still has half a house to search.

He moves the pile over to the sliding glass door and then raids their pantry for canned goods. They have some corned beef hash, lots of veggies and canned fruit. There are Vienna sausages and even a few tins of chili. He moves stuff around until he comes a box of plastic trash bags. He doubles one up and piles the food into it.

There are boxes of noodles as well, which he puts in another bag with some health shit they call cereal. Beggars can't be choosers, he reckons. Maybe some sugar will make it edible.

He slips out the back door and moves to the fence gate. He peeks around it and whispers loudly, "Angela."

There is movement, then a shape appears around the side of his house. Having her dress in black wasn't such a good idea, since he can barely see her. He raises the gun just in case, but she steps into the half-light and waves.

Lester moves some of the bags into his yard and goes back for more. He lugs the generator over and then the gas. When everything is close to the house, he waves at her one more time. A glance at the shambling figures near the front fence tells him that some are still milling around. For the thousandth time that day, he wishes they would fuck right the hell off his property.

He goes back to John's glass door, slides it open and jumps again as the cat flashes by with a hiss. Stupid cat!

He points the light into closets and cabinets one last time, but he finds only the same shit you would find in anyone else's closet. Sheets, blankets, towels, boxes of crap, tennis rackets, golf clubs. Hey deader, how about eighteen holes with your head as the golf ball? He moves to the stairwell and pokes the flashlight up. After six stairs, there is a landing and then a left turn to more steps.

He takes a deep breath and lets it out slowly through his mouth.

Probably nothing, the little thumps earlier, might be an open window or the cat, which seems intent on scaring him to death. He takes one step and then another. When he reaches the landing, he darts the light up into the pitch-black hallway. There is the overpowering stench of flowers or incense that makes him want to gag. It's like someone took a barrel of the stuff and dumped it in a pile, then left it to decay.

As his eyes crest the stairs, he is able to see that one door is open and two are shut.

"John?" he calls out.

The house remains silent.

He moves to the first closed door on his left and presses his ear to it. There is no movement, so he wanders past. The next door is open. He pokes the light in, but nothing leaps out. If something did, he would probably shit his pants. Lester can't remember ever being this scared in his life.

He has the gun ready, but his hand is shaking so that the flashlight next to it rattles against the barrel. He moves into the large bedroom. Dressers have drawers hanging out of them, and there's half-filled luggage on the unmade bed. He pokes around, but they only contain clothes in which he wouldn't be caught dead. John tends to wear tropical print shirts, khakis and the occasional shiny golf shirt. On his tall, gaunt frame, it works, but Lester would never be mistaken for a golfer, what with his scraggly black beard and hair that hangs past his ears.

He goes through drawers filled with women's undergarments, lingerie in neat piles, stockings and panties by the handful. Jesus Christ, she must have a discount card at Victoria's Secret or own stock in the company. He holds one bra up to the flashlight and looks at the tag— 34C? Not bad, Jan. He locates a drawer full of Kama Sutra oils, powders, edible things to rub on a lover's body. A pair of handcuffs, and vibrators of impressive girth. He starts to pick one up, then jerks his hand away, realizing he doesn't know whose ass it may have been up—although that might explain why John is so stiff. He locates a stash of porn, but it is old—on videotape. John's probably had the stuff for years. He might take some back if he had electricity. Or an ancient VCR, for that matter.

He wades through every drawer he can find, but he doesn't locate any guns or ammo. There is a closed door at one end of the room, and when he listens at it, there is no noise. He turns the knob with a shaking hand, and when it is open a foot, he steps back and raises the gun and light. He would like to stand to one side and sort of peek in, but the door isn't cooperating. It keeps swinging open on a creaking hinge. That is great in the movies, but not in real life. He has a sudden urge to rush downstairs and go through the garage again until he locates a can of WD-40. That's right, John, I came, I saw, and I oiled your fucking hinges.

The door continues to open, and he pokes the light in every exposed inch until he can see the back. There are more clothes hanging from every pole, boxes stuffed onto shelves. Shoes galore are stacked on a tall shelf—heels, pumps, sandals, and sneakers. He steps in, and his foot squishes in something on the floor. He shines the light down, and even with the deep blue carpet soaking up the light, he knows the unmistakable color of spilled blood.

Lester spins around quickly, gun eye level. His breath comes ragged and rapid. He shines the light all around the room, but nothing moves. Probably an accident and the neighbors went to the hospital when it first started. There is no one else in the house. No one in the house, no one in the fucking house! Please, let there be no one in the house, at least no one of the dead variety.

What about all the closed doors, old son? Still, gotta check them out.

Lester wants to hightail it back to the house. There is nothing else he needs here. He has food, the generator, and gas. Just go, bug out and call it a day. Angela is there, and she is far from scary. So is a huge bag of weed. They can hide in the bedroom and smoke until they both pass out. Is the house really worth investigating if it gives him a heart attack?

But he knows he has to check it out. He hasn't become a successful drug dealer by being fucking stupid. They may need to switch houses if the deaders get over the fence, and he would rather have a surprise now than when he is running scared with Angela behind him.

He finishes his tour of the room by poking around the large attached bathroom. There is a full shower with a sliding glass door and a deep soaking tub. Looks like heaven. He wishes he could bring Angela over here and soak with her. She can wash his back, and he can soap up her tits.

He walks back into the hallway and contemplates the other doors. They are all closed, but he is determined to search each and every room. One is set against the back of the hallway, probably a bathroom. He listens at the door but doesn't hear any noise.

He turns the knob and slides the door open on another set of squeaky hinges. No movement, so he pushes it open quickly, gun and light held high. Movement! Something billows, something black. It rustles loudly, and he nearly screams. He staggers back as visions of a deader wrapped in plastic invade his mind. The back of his neck goes ice prickly cold, and the rest of his body breaks out in goose pimples.

Just a shower curtain, stupid—pushing the door open made it fly up. He frowns and chuckles with nervous energy.

There is a room to his right, so he repeats the process. He listens for a minute, then pushes the door open and—ah hah—it is a door that doesn't squeak. Note to John, nice work with these hinges. Love, Lester.

He is greeted with a room full of torture devices; they sit in corners, arms poking up in the air. Christ, an exercise room. There is a ski machine, a weight bench and a treadmill. Fucking hell, who even has time for that shit? He pokes around but doesn't find anything useful. The small closet reveals nothing but free weights.

He backs out of the room and considers the remaining doors. He tries to remember where the thump came from when he was downstairs. Was it to the left or the right? Oh what the hell, he sighs and listens at the door next to the exercise room. He doesn't hear anything, so he pushes the door open.

Another bedroom, the bright light tells him. Bed, dresser, and pictures of kids everywhere. Must be one of their children's rooms. John told him once that his son and daughter were both in college. He steps into the room and into another splash of blood. What happened here?

A noise draws his attention to the door that must be a closet. A quiet moan. "Oh Jesus, oh Jesus," he repeats under his breath over and over like a mantra that will save him.

Then there is a scraping sound, and Lester wants to turn and run.

Can't, gotta make sure the house is clean, just in case. Must be a deader in there. I'll just open the door and shoot it in the fucking head. Damn thing can't even figure out how to get out, can't be much of a threat.

He steps to the door and sets his hand on the knob. He feels pressure low in his gut and is sure he will piss his pants, he is so scared.

"Oh Jesus, oh Jesus," he mutters as he turns the knob. "Fucker!" he yells as he jerks the door open.

Shape on the floor. Looks like a person. The flashlight shakes in his hand. He waves it back and forth as he tries to focus. Adrenaline has him so amped that he can barely keep it straight. Did it move? Did something brush his foot? It's on the ground. What the hell is it?!

He jumps back, and another scream rips past his lips. He shudders so hard that the shot strikes the back of the closet, not the thing on the floor.

In the tiny space, the gun is like a cannon. It blasts away his hearing, leaving a buzz that reminds him of being stoned. He lets out a shout of revulsion, but it rings hollow in his ears. He pulls in some shaky breaths. Draws them deep, and his teeth chatter. Is it suddenly cold in here?

The shape doesn't move. He shines the light into the cavernous closet. It's John! He can tell by his glasses, shiny shirt, and long body. Oh fuck, did I just kill him? Why didn't you say something, buddy? Oh fuck, why didn't you say something?

Then he draws one more deep breath, closes his eye for half a second to clear his mind. He can do it. He has seen a couple of dead guys today, so why is this different? He doesn't want to know anything else, he wants to run back to the house, to Angela and then hit the rum until he can't see straight.

Hand shaking so badly he can't control it, he shines the light down with a quick motion that brings John into view. John has his arm cocked at a weird angle under his body. Part of his skull is missing, and Les spots a pistol in his other hand, close to his head. John had the balls to kill himself?

Lester drags in one deep breath and then collapses to the floor. He draws his legs up and leans back against the opposite wall. He sighs his relief that he didn't kill his neighbor. But he also feels a feels a sense of loss for the man. Poor guy has been dead for how long? Maybe a day, the blood is dry, but he is definitely dead as a fucking doornail. He is also a link to Lester's world that is no longer there. He was a neighbor, sure, someone Les never really took the time to talk to, but he was a constant, and now that constant is dead.

Or so Lester believes ... until the arm twitches.

He jumps to his feet. Moves back so quickly that his legs wrap around each other and he falls down for the second time that day. He jitters the flashlight around the room in a rapid, shaky manner that makes the light dance. He leans forward. Breath comes in explosive gasps between his lips. The light focuses on the body.

The arm moves again, then a leg. Poor John has lost part of his head but is somehow functional. Lester points the gun at his head and puts a little bit of pressure on the trigger. Not enough to fire, not yet. John's head doesn't move, but his blood-red eyes lock on Lester's and it's all Les can do not to scream.

John's jaw works up and down as if chewing, and a little sound escapes his mouth, like air leaving a tire from a slow leak. Lester has never been so terrified in his life. He wants to jump out the fucking window and take his chances with the deaders that are at least on their feet.

He can't do it. He has killed a couple of these things, but he doesn't want to shoot John. He runs the light over the body. It moves back and forth, wiggling like a giant earthworm lying on the ground. There is blood everywhere, like he took handfuls of the stuff and splashed it all over the empty closet. There are also a bunch of potpourri petals piled on his body. So that's where the smell came from, something to hide the stench of death. Good thinking, Jan. He shuts the door and backs away.

Then he pauses and thinks about John lying up here unable to move. Maybe the self-inflicted gunshot wound cut off motor functions. Maybe they will find John like this in a few weeks, still struggling to move one arm.

AH FUCK, he wants to scream.

He puts his hand on the doorknob and shakes his head. He smiles a little smile at what he is about to do, at how fucking stupid it is. Then the smile drops, and he jerks the door open. He points the gun at John's face and fires three times. His head is driven into the carpet with each shot, a smacking sound to echo the shots. His hearing was bad before; now he will have ringing for days.

But John isn't moving anymore, and there is more brain matter all over the floor. There is a hole in John's forehead right between his eyes, and Lester feels proud for that one. Sorry, John! The second new hole is in his left cheek and the third along his jaw line. The bullet furrowed a line of black along the skin and then punched into his throat.

Les needs a drink, bad. No, he needs a fucking bottle and a few grams of weed to wash away this madness.

He abandons John's body without a prayer and tries to push the image out of his head. He doesn't bother with the gun in his neighbor's hand either. There is no way he is touching that thing. Not even if he had a bottle of Clorox and a chemical suit like the crazy guys were wearing on the street the other day.

He moves into the hallway and opens the door to the last room. It is another kid's room, and he is about to abandon his search when a shape stumbles into view.

The thing moves faster than seems possible. Arms out in claws that grasp for his face. A scream rips past his lips. A ragged little squeal that sounds like a six-year-old girl who just saw the boogeyman. He fires the gun in reflex. Doesn't have time to aim, just opens up. The blast once again tears at the remainder of his hearing, and muzzle flashes illuminate the shape attacking him like an old movie. Like camera flashes in a dark room.

He manages to lean out of the way so the thing's hands pass over his head. Then he falls back as the gun continues to leap in his hand, hammering the deader with round after round.

The gun jams on one shot. I'm screwed!

He kicks out, a lashing move that has little real force behind it but stops the deader in its tracks, makes it fall down. The entire incident has taken seconds, but he feels like he is a few years older.

He spins around to find the stair rail, but he is too close to the first step and stumbles, goes down on his knee. He reaches the wall but doesn't manage to find the railing and instead spills down the short flight of stairs.

Then the deader is there and filling the hallway with a horrid moaning sound that raises Lester's hair on end. God, seriously, get me out of this hellhole and I'll right my ways. I'll only sell drugs to adults. I'll stop watching porn! I'll tell Angela I love her. Just in case he is listening. He comes up on one foot, but his leg is bruised from the fall, so he staggers to the next set of stairs.

The shape doesn't wait; it dives after him. Fuck, how is it still moving with half a dozen bullets in it? He pulls the gun up, slides the chamber back and ejects the jammed shell. He flies down the stairs as the thing rushes behind him. Misjudging the last step, he comes down hard on the floor and staggers forward into the wall. The gun presses against his chest. Damn lucky it didn't fire when he slammed into it. That would make a brilliant end to the day, shot by his own gun.

Out, he needs to get the fuck out! The deader stumbles down the last stair as well and slams into the wall where Les just stood. He slides away, raises the gun and fires blindly, backing up as he tries to find his target. One shot goes wide. In the dark, he is having trouble finding the thing's head so he can put a bullet through it. He readjusts his aim and fires three more quick rounds before the gun strikes empty.

Jesus fucking wept!

Hands grab his shirt, and a mouth is suddenly near. A gaping maw that reeks like old meat or garbage left to rot. He punches quickly, hand a blur as adrenaline drives his blows. He strikes a small shape, catching the thing a good glancing blow. He shoves forward into its chest, his hand sinking into a pair of hard, unyielding breasts. From the thing's height, he knows that this is John's wife. His mind gets a flash of her face just a few weeks ago—reasonably attractive; he wouldn't mind having a go at her.

She isn't so good looking now, and all he wants to do is take an ax to her head.

He kicks out again. Solid impact this time, but low on the body. The shape falls away and thumps into the floor. Yeah, yeah, you want some of me? He lashes out his foot again but only finds air.

Lester moves toward the door, but a hand hooks around his shoulder, and he stumbles into the family room. He drops the flashlight at some point, so he is fighting in a dark room that is barely lit by the tiny blur of moonlight.

His hand quests along the wall and comes across a metal DVD rack. He lifts the thing and finds that it is pretty heavy. She flies at him with hands hooked into claws. Was her name Jan? Jane? Maybe it was Jane.

"Jane, back the fuck off!" He means to use a big, deep voice, but it comes out shallow, hollow, a rasp that wouldn't scare a puppy. Then when she staggers toward him, he swings the rack across his body as hard as he can.

It mashes into the deader and sends DVDs flying in every direction. The thing howls and falls. He steps close and swings the rack overhead with real force this time, once, twice, a third time. The last manages to break the flimsy thing in his hand, so he is left holding two pieces of metal. He swings them against the shape over and over again until he feels nothing but pulped meat under the blows.

He stabs down, but the metal bars lack sharp ends, and they slide along the body. He stomps down where he thinks the head is, and indeed it feels like he strikes something round but hard that almost makes him fall, as though he'd stepped on a bowling ball. He stomps down again and again until breath whistles out of his mouth like a train struggling to get up a long hill.

"Die!" he yells and then wants to giggle at how stupid that sounds, telling a dead thing to die. Should be more careful with your insults, old boy, he thinks and then breaks into a fit of laughter.

He sits down and leans forward, hands on knees as he tries to catch his breath. Then he laughs until the smile is gone from his face, and he screams until his voice is hoarse.

Jan—or Jane—doesn't twitch, and it serves her fucking right. Bitch.

ALICE AND KEN

You make a grab for the warm body, but your limbs don't work like they used to. In fact, they barely respond at all. But none of that matters now; all you care about is the scent of real flesh. The hunger slammed into you the moment you saw her come into the room, an all-consuming ache that radiated from the center of your body and then out to all four appendages. Meat! Fresh meat!

The dead stuff you were chewing on feels like ashes on your mouth. You let the meat fall out and slide down your chin until it hits the ground in a bloody mess.

But she is fast, that one, several attempts to grab it result in you only grabbing air. You come after her on unsure feet. They stumble beneath your every step.

You shamble past the body on the floor and then carefully navigate the two large steps into the smaller room. Your eyes linger on the dead boy as you step past, but he no longer holds any appeal to you. All you can think of is the fresh meat down the hall.

You reach the door and push at it with your upper body. Then some part of you, some muscle memory grasps at the little metal knob on the barricade and makes a twisting motion, but the required coordination eludes you. Pressing against it has no result, nor does backing up and walking into it.

You try again, backing up until the wall is at your back and then moving forward. Smack, your head follows your body as it slaps against the wood. Then you pause and wonder what you are doing. Why did you need to get into this room in the first place?

"Ken, no, leave me alone!" a voice shrieks.

Meat!

You pound at the door, twisting your shoulder as quickly as you can to slam into the obstacle over and over. Then you smack your head into the wood a few times, but it won't budge.

Sobs again, but this only renews your lust. So you twist and thrash, and a hollow moan spills past your lips as the hunger drives another spike into your gut.

* * *

She sits on the edge of the bed and weeps. The last few minutes have been a living nightmare, her son on the ground, dead from all appearances. Ken insane and covered in blood.

How can a gas leak cause him to act so crazy? She should have listened to the news, paid attention to what they were saying last night, but she was too busy. Besides, she hates watching the evening body count, the bad news and celebrity gossip, so she avoids it and watches the shopping network or, better yet, a cop drama from her DVR.

She can't stay, and she can't venture into the hallway because Ken is insane, so she decides to leave, to crawl out the window and head for a hotel. She grabs a pair of comfortable sneakers and slips them on, then she jumps on the bed and slides the window back. She tugs at the screen and figures out how to slide it to the left in order to force it to release. It snaps loose, and she is able to pop it out. The thin frame clatters to the ground outside.

She tries to crawl over the frame when there is a much louder bang on the door. She tries to scurry up and onto the windowsill, but she can't seem to maneuver her body through. Another loud bang makes her do a little jump that takes her to the opening. She wiggles and squirms until she can get her body out through the frame. Then she struggles to sit up so she can swing her legs over. A last bang sends the door crashing open.

* * *

You step back and walk into the door. Nothing happens, so you get a better start and smash into it. The door holds. Both hands come up in frustration, and you smash them against the door as hard as you can. The hand that is twisted the wrong way flops back from the impact, but the door seems to move a little bit more. You back up and barrel into it, and the tiny lock gives way. The door falls open with you behind it. You fall to the ground but look up to see your meal escaping. As quick as your limbs can manage, you are on your feet and crawling on the bed.

The thing is rotating one leg out the window, but the other is hanging there, beckoning, a morsel that may stop the gnawing hunger that is eating at you. Another spike drives itself into your stomach, and you nearly double over from the pain.

Pain, that is something new. Before, it was a hollow that felt as if it had never been full. Now it is full-blown pain, and that is something with which you are familiar. You crawl across the bed and grasp the dangling limb.

* * *

Alice shrieks in horror as the cold hand closes on her exposed ankle just above her shoe. It is slick with blood, so she kicks free with a shudder and tries to wriggle out of the window frame. The hand grabs again, and this time the hold is like a band of iron. Then the face of her husband swims into view. She squirms in horror and screams.

His mouth closes over her calf, but she kicks her foot in his grasp, and he is left with just a taste of her slacks for his effort. He sits up and grabs at her hand, which she uses to bash away at him. She strikes his head and arm, but the blows do nothing to stop him. He leans over to take a chunk of her neck. She pulls away but catches a hint of the reek that comes from his bloody mouth; it's like old rotten meat.

She falls out of the window and hits the ground with a thump. The breath is driven from her body. Her hand is outstretched to break the fall, but it just skids across the bark that covers the ground, picking up several splinters. Her elbow hits next, and it's a real ringer. The pain takes half a second to reach her brain, but when it does, she gasps and cries out.

She landed badly, the breath knocked from her body. She rolls over and looks at the window, and sure enough, there is her devoted husband Ken looking to follow his love out of the window. He is clamoring onto the windowsill with little grace, more like a sack of potatoes trying to exit the tiny space.

She rolls over onto all fours and comes up slowly, panting, gasping for breath.

"Ken! You need to stop this!" she yells, but he ignores her and slides out of the window to the space she occupied not half a minute ago. "Dammit, Ken! Leave me alone!"

She turns and runs up the driveway to the car, past her beautiful rose garden, past what is left of the old tire swing, chopped to pieces by Anthony when he was in a 'destructive' phase. She reaches the car and hears Ken closing in from behind. She reaches for her purse and—OH FUCK!—her keys are on the kitchen floor, in the house.

They may as well be a mile away. She turns around just as Ken barrels into her.

* * *

So close, you almost had a mouthful. You can almost taste the meat, the fresh blood. It's going to be a feast unlike anything you have had. The pain in your gut has become unbearable, and all you can think about is filling it. But the cold meat inside the house doesn't do the trick; you want the live thing.

You've managed to get outside after your prey, but now it is running away. You walk as fast as you can, but something is off, and you realize it is the arm with the backward hand. It doesn't swing right, so you drag it close to your chest and set out at a half-run, with one foot dragging a little bit.

The meat reaches the big metal shape but stops and stares at her side for a moment. You pick that moment to collide with her at full speed.

* * *

Caught, and on her side. She claws at the arm across her body, scratches Ken's face, which is right in front of hers. Then her hand shies away as he tries to bite her questing digits. She gets her hand under his chin. It is covered in cold, sticky blood. The ragged hole where his throat had been squishes under her palm; she wants to wipe her hand on her shirt in revulsion. He bites at her, pulling his head back, trying to shake her hand loose. She fights him off, holding his neck as tight as she can. She squeezes and squeezes to cut off his air supply, but he doesn't seem to care. He is cold, so cold in her hands, and there is no pulse of life.

She manages to roll onto her back and push him to the side, but he is back on her in a flash. Then his mouth is close to hers, and that cloying stench hits her in the face. She gags as a piece of flesh falls from his mouth and lands in one eye.

"NO!" she screams and withers beneath him like an animal caught in a trap. He gets his hand around his body and presses it down on her mouth. It's the broken one, so it grinds, bone against bone. The sound is too much, the smell is too much, and the fight has been too much. Horror tugs at her, and she knows she is going to die. She is about to be eaten by her husband.

She barely holds him off as he gets his mouth on her shoulder. The fabric of her jacket prevents his bite from going deep, but he nuzzles at the fabric like a rabid dog seeking warm, salty flesh. Soon he will bite into her neck, and they will be the ragged-neck twins, joined in matrimony with holes in their breathing apparatus.

Movement behind him. The sun is shut out for a moment before a large black shape smashes into Ken's head. He rears up, eyes crossing for a moment as if in confusion, then the shape plows into his head once more, with authority, and Ken drops like a felled duck onto her torso.

She slithers out from under him as quickly as she can, her body shaking as adrenaline rushes though her system. There seems to be blood everywhere. She automatically checks on Ken, worried that the blow killed him, then she thinks on this and bursts out in hysterical laughter.

There is a guy standing over Ken's body holding a skateboard. Alice recognizes the shape from earlier, the person who flew in front of her car, and doesn't that seem like a lifetime ago? Only that wasn't a guy.

"You okay?" the girl asks. She is young, maybe sixteen, with a row of metal studs dancing up each ear. Black eyeliner paints her eyes like a raccoon, giving her a frightful look, but at this moment Alice thinks she could adopt the child. Her clothes are ragged, but fashionable, like she paid extra for the holes. Jeans in tatters, a black t-shirt with a picture of a skull on it.

"Oh poor Ken, I don't know what's wrong with him!"

"He's got the thing, the disease or whatever."

"There is no such thing; it's all lies—the leak, the gas. Maybe he just ate some bad chicken." And even as she says the words, she knows how ridiculous they sound. How hollow they ring, how shock and dismay are fighting to control her mind.

"We should go; I don't think I can finish him off." The girl holds her skateboard close. "I just have to go check on my mom; she was acting weird this morning, like she wasn't herself."

"Is it the same …" Alice can't finish the sentence.

The girl drops the board on its wheels and puts one foot on it.

"Good luck."

"Wait, just wait a minute." Alice can't leave this defenseless girl alone on the street. And as if to punctuate this thought, a loud scream echoes through the neighborhood. A scream of terror much like Alice's shrieks not so very long ago.

"Just let me get my keys, and you can ride with me." She takes one shaking step toward the front of the house. "They're on the floor. I know where, give me just a minute."

Her arm throbs where Ken tried to bite her. The thick fabric of her shirt prevented his teeth from puncturing her skin, but it still hurts like hell.

"Did he bite you?" The girl backs away.

"He tried, but I don't think it broke the skin. What's wrong?" Alice meets the girl's eyes. They are filled with terror.

"I think that's how it spreads, the thing. I think if one of them bites you, then you die and come back as one of them." The girl trembles, her hands clutched to her chest. She glances behind herself as if she is ready to bolt.

"Don't be silly, there is no such thing. See, I'm fine," Alice pulls up her shirtsleeve. There is a ring of bite marks, but it's just a red-rimmed series of bruises that aren't even bleeding. "Now just wait here, and I'll grab the keys. We can go see your mom first if you want, to make sure she is okay." Alice is babbling, thinking at twice her normal speed, her words barely matching her thoughts. If she keeps vomiting words, maybe she won't have to think about Ken on the ground.

Ken moans, and one hand moves beneath him. It is the broken one, now protruding at an angle from beneath his body. Alice doesn't understand how he can be functional; the arm must hurt like hell.

"Okay, I just want to get out of here," the girl says in a small voice. Alice wants to take the girl and hug her.

She runs to the front door on leaden limbs, hands shaking as they close around the frame, and launches herself into the familiar house. The hallway shows signs of the battle. There are drops of blood in a steady pattern on the carpet, on the wall. How will they ever get it clean? She will have to come back later with a bucket of cold water and try to get the blood off the walls.

She runs to the kitchen and stops to snatch up the contents of her purse. She stuffs them into her bag and then her eyes light upon the shape of her son lying on the dining room floor, and a cry of agony goes out. She crawls up the stairs and stares into the empty eyes, gray lined and filled with blood. They don't look anything like the boy she raised, the trusting eyes he had as a youth. The mock-serious stare he could give her when she told a bad joke.

Gone, all gone. The house they built will be empty, Ken and her son dead. She was fooling herself about coming back to clean up; she never wants to set foot in this house of horror again. She stares at the still form and notices the gun on the floor. It looks as if Ken used it to end their son's life, but how could he do it? How? It's murder! Oh God, they are both dead!

She grabs the automatic and studies the cold steel, the dull barrel, and the black frame that seems built for someone with much larger hands. She drags herself to the bottom stair and looks at the gaping hole as if she has found salvation. She studies the chunk of metal that is the hammer, how it is cocked and ready to fire. Then she points the gun at her forehead, finger resting on trigger and contemplates oblivion.

KATE

"What's in the bag, Bob?"

"Lil' friend of mine I like to call 'Peace.' 'Cause when people see it, they want to be left in peace."

He unzips the bag and takes out a giant revolver. The barrel is nearly eight inches long and shines like fire in the light of her old lamps. It's getting dark out, but she doesn't want to turn on the bright overhead lights just yet; she is enjoying Bob's company and the intimate ambiance of her otherwise dull living room. He hefts the thing, sights down the barrel at the picture of a drunken clown on her wall. It is truly the most hideous thing she has ever owned, and yet she refuses to get rid of it.

"Shit, that thing is huge."

"This is a .357 magnum, and it will blow your head clean off … almost as well as the .44 that Dirty Harry carries," he says, trying to emphasize his words with squinted eyes and a raspy voice.

"Bob, if you seriously need to take a crap, go to your apartment." She laughs at his face. It looks like he is dealing with a case of constipation.

"Clint Eastwood playing a cop who shoots first and asks questions later."

"Oh. Yeah! No, not familiar."

"I'll bring a video over sometime."

"I hope it isn't one of your client's videos." She smiles and it feels good. Maybe it's just the wine. Like usual when Bob is around her, she feels warm but confused. She would like to open up to him more, but she is also terrified at the thought. She can never let him know what lies buried within; she can never let him into her space.

"A Clint Eastwood video, silly. I kinda like you, so why would I subject you to one of those videos?" He opens his eyes wide and rolls the word 'those' with a full dose of sarcasm attached.

"And in your, um, professional opinion, what would be a good video to show me?" She echoes his sarcasm.

"Oh, you know, something with horses and people dressed up in furry costumes who like to meet in parks and fuck like giant bunnies." He starts laughing, and for some reason the sound is infectious, so she joins in.

"Second time you've brought up furries, you sick fuck. I think you're the one with the weird fetish." She holds her stomach and tries not to spill the wine because she is laughing so hard.

The beer first, now the wine—it is all going to her head. She collapses back into the couch, trying not to spill the glass. Wine splashes out anyway and rolls down her robe, which is apparently spillproof. Well, it will just have to wait for a washing, because there is no way she is running around in her t-shirt again. Weird fetishes aside, she doesn't want to deal with the looks.

"Okay, so the gun, what's the deal?"

"Nothing, I just like to have one around. I grew up around them. Dad and Granddad always had guns around. It's a surprise me and my brothers didn't blow our heads off. Grandpa even had an old World War II Luger he kept in a drawer."

"Isn't that something you hawk up?"

"Hah, no, it's an old-style automatic that the Nazis carried. Supposedly he got it off a dead German when he was a paratrooper. He jumped into Italy a couple of times."

"You don't have to explain to me. I'm not some liberal crackpot who thinks guns are a threat. Hell, if you want to have a rocket launcher, more power to you, just don't use the goddamn thing on me."

"Gee, a voice of reason. Have you thought about running for office?"

"Nah, I'm too gay for that."

"Hey, gay is in."

"Really? Do you have a man in your life, then?" Her eyebrows arch up in sarcasm.

"I don't even have a woman in my life. I have bad luck with girls. They tend to wake up one morning and realize I am a thirty-two-year-old slacker who collects money from old men for porn companies."

"Hey, it's a job."

"Yeah, that's true." He hands her the gun, and she takes it with no hesitation. In fact, she takes the big heavy silver thing and holds it in one hand like she has handled one a number of times. She points it around the room, aiming it at the few paintings on the wall of her sparse apartment.

"It's beautiful," she breathes as she holds it by the grip, her other hand on the silver barrel. She studies the side, pushes on the little button to release the chamber. It is empty, the six holes staring back at her like hungry little mouths.

"Smith and Wesson make that particular model. I've only fired it a few times up at the range in Montlake Terrace. It yanks up like a bitch when it fires, but the big heavy barrel keeps it down better than a shorter barrel. At least, that's what I think based on my twelfth-grade understanding of physics."

"I can see how it would help," she says as she caresses the barrel like a lover. She spins the chamber and then slaps it shut and whips the gun up to aim at the wall. "Bang," she whispers. She imagines she is aiming at one of the disgusting sweaty men she meets.

"Anyway, with all the craziness going on, I thought I would show you the gun and—if you didn't freak out—show you how to load and handle it."

"Ah gee, Bob, if I wasn't hot for chicks, I would consider that downright romantic. 'Hey babe, wanna play with my big pistol?'" she intones in a deep voice that is nothing like his.

He chuckles and takes the gun back. He pulls out a box of shells, folds back the paper lid and slides the box out. It is obviously heavy with its load of long shells. He takes one out and hands it to her.

"These have a lot of stopping power. They are just the standard load, and to tell you the truth, I don't know the first thing about bullets. I just asked for the right ones for this piece, and that's what they gave me. I have fired off at least a hundred of these things, and they will supposedly stop a man at fifty paces. Not only stop him, but turn his guts wrong side out."

"Gross." She studies the bullet. It is nearly as long as her pinky finger. Except it isn't gross; she wants to see what it would look like.

"In case you ever have to use it, and I hope you don't, just load it, close the barrel, shoot. You can pull the trigger to fire it, but it's a bitch to squeeze, so cock it first if you are in trouble."

"Do you really think this is necessary?"

"I don't know, kitty cat, I just think it is better to be safe than sorry. So there ya go. You can now kill a bad guy six times if you have to."

"Don't call me kitty cat."

"Sorry, kitty cat."

She sighs and fights the urge to grin. Fights the urge to smack him one. Fights the urge to sit in his lap.

She hands the bullet back, and he slides it back into the box. Then he puts the gun and the bullets into the gun bag and zips it up.

"If it comes to having to fight, I think I'll just stick with my swords."

"Swords? I know you are into martial arts, but I didn't know you were a ninja."

"That's me, Kate the ninja." Then she pops up and goes into her room. She opens the sliding mirrored door of the closet and extracts a bundle that is wrapped in a colorful oriental print. It is blue with white circles and women dressed in kimonos on it. She returns to her chair a bit dizzy from the wine and beer, but she wants to show Bob that she has a big cock too.

She unwraps the cloth and lays the swords on her lap. Her robe has fallen open, but she doesn't care because the sheaths are cool on her bare leg. She picks up the smaller one and pulls it out slowly so he can see the light reflect off the folded metal. While some swords are for show, perhaps to be placed on a mantle or a table, this one is not. This is a real weapon created by a swordsmith she found online. While hers will never be mistaken for genuine master swords, they are nearly as sharp and just as deadly. The edge has a wicked gleam that ripples like water.

"This is my wakizashi, and it is used in conjunction with this sword, my katana." She indicates the longer scabbard on her lap. They both have simple pommels done up in black cloth. The string is wrapped over and over to form a strong grip. Even drenched in blood, the grip will prove firm and secure.

"Nice. Did you pick those up at the Asian store downtown?" The inane question doesn't anger her. He just has no idea what they mean to her—and they mean a lot. She has studied the art of kenjutsu for quite a few years. It and her other martial arts have become her center, her religion. Without them, she would be lost. The other would take over, and Kate would cease to exist.

"No, I ordered them from a swordsmith online. It took six months, and I had to put a thousand dollars down just to get the order started. They are quite real, and I know how to use them."

"No shit?"

"No shit. I have been training with the things for years. I also take an Indonesian martial art based on penjkat silat, so I can pretty much kick your ass in multiple languages."

He stares at her for a few seconds in shock, then a full smile cracks his lips, and he laughs out loud. "My but you are full of surprises. Sort of at odds with your other interest," he says, looking at a welt on her leg.

"That's me, nothing but surprises. And yeah, I have no misconceptions about the irony. I guess you could say I am conflicted."

He continues to grin at her like she is bat-shit insane. Then an image flashes into her mind of her coming up on the balls of her feet, whipping the longer blade out of its scabbard and slashing it across his throat. She would draw and slice in one smooth motion, something she has done a million times in iaido class.

She slams the sword back into its sheath and then wraps the weapons before he can ask any more questions. She sets them in the corner of the apartment as far away from where they are sitting as possible while still keeping them in the same room.

She returns to the couch, but Bob must have seen something pass through her eyes. He stands up and stretches while trying to look nonchalant.

"Well, I should get going."

"Okay," she replies lamely, wishing the words she has been thinking for the last minute would bubble past her lips and she would say them. The words that she can't trust, yet wants to ask anyway. Please stay, Bob. Then they will go to her bedroom and he will make gentle love to her, something a man has not done in many years. He will fill the voids in her, the one that aches between her legs and the one that resides in her soul that is broken, unable to be mended.

"Night, Bob." She walks him out, and when he opens the door, he turns to say goodnight, and she meets him with a soft kiss on the cheek. She has to stand on her tiptoes to place one right against his scratchy half-beard. The image of him crouching in front of her earlier goes through her mind, how she wanted to part her legs and pull his face between them. Then the image is her slashing his throat, and she is indeed ready for him to go.

"Thanks, kitty cat."

"Don't call me that."

"Sure, kitty cat," he says, just like always. "Any trouble, any at all, and you come get me. I mean, not that you need help." He smiles at her. "On second thought, if there is trouble, I'll come get you." He turns toward his door, and she closes hers gently.

She shoots the bolt and then stares at the wood door for a full minute. Protect her! She is more than capable of taking care of herself.

She is strong, fast, a natural fighter who has honed her craft over many years of sweat and pain.

Kate picks up her swords and slips them from their sheaths one at a time. She polishes the steel of the wakizashi and tests the blade against the fine down of her arm. It leaves a bare spot. Then she takes out the longer katana and repeats the process. When she is satisfied, she kneels and spends twenty minutes practicing an iaido move that has her drawing the sword in reaction to a surprise attack from behind. She turns in one swift motion, sword drawn, rotates around without slicing her leg off, defends, comes back to her original position and then sheathes the sword, all in a blur.

She centers herself and does it again, then again until she is one with the movement, with her sword. There is great and terrible beauty in the form. She doesn't break a sweat, and after a while, her body loosens up, so she rises and goes to bed.

INTERLUDE: JEFF

"Is that a sick clown, Mommy?" young Jeff Hallack asks.

Christine glances up at the guy with the painted face and grimaces. He coughs and leans against a wall as if drunk. He presses his hands to the side of his head and rubs them as if the pressure will make whatever is hurting him abate.

The sun is drooping in the sky, and she should really think about getting her son home. He will be cranky if they stay up too late, and tomorrow is his day with Dad.

"Yes, dear heart, that clown might have the flu," she replies and takes Jeff's hand in hers.

The Seattle Center is crowded, even for a Tuesday. Frank, her latest in a long line of boyfriends, will be at work for a few more hours. She wanted to take Jeff to the science center so he could play with the exhibit on electricity. He once saw a man with his hair standing on end and thought it was funny. But they spent so much time on the rides that she won't have time. Not on this visit. Maybe they can come back next month when it is a little bit cooler.

The clown coughs again and reaches down to scratch his leg. He pulls up the bloomed-out pant leg and runs a hand over an angry-looking bite mark. Strange thing to see on someone, Christine thinks. The mark is also round as if given by a person. It has been there for a few days, though. Christine is a nurse, and she has seen much worse in the ER. In fact, she has seen worse bites inflicted by lovers during foreplay.

She doesn't like clowns, but she feels obligated to check on the man in patchwork clothes. He looks weary, even with all the makeup; his body language speaks of pain. He coughs again into his hand and looks at her as she approaches.

Jeff smiles and waves at the clown. He has never seen a live one before, and as with most new things, he is ready for the experience.

Unlike his father, he excels at being outgoing, even at nine—so outgoing that Christine keeps a tight grip on him at all times. Occasionally he likes to wander off and talk to new and interesting people.

"Are you okay?" she asks the clown, who wears the requisite white face paint, black eyes and a bright red smile. He holds a long stream of green faux-dreads and cradles them in his arms like a wounded animal.

"I think so. Damn kid was acting weird, and he bit me," he mumbles in a smoker's voice that is deep and raspy. He coughs again, and she can hear the deep rumble of phlegm stuck in his throat and lungs. He wipes at his mouth, and his hand comes away red. It is not just the lipstick; there is blood there as well, underneath the bright crimson of makeup gone wrong.

"You don't sound too good. Maybe you should lie down somewhere," she says, and she automatically wants to check his forehead to see if he is hot. She knows he is a performer for the center and probably clean. They probably make that part of their employment contract. She shies away from physical contact. No sense in risking getting herself or Jeff sick if he has some sort of virus.

"Good idea," he says and sinks to a sitting position. He rubs at the bite mark again, and she sees it is livid, punctured through the skin in a couple of places. These are gray-lined and angry, and she thinks of cancer for some reason, even though skin cancer is usually just spots that are off-color and asymmetrical. At least that's how the easy-to-recognize stuff starts.

A family wanders by, an older couple with two teenagers in tow. The girls wear dark lipstick and don't smile. One walks with her arms crossed under her budding breasts and looks straight ahead, since no one can understand the misery she must be feeling at … well, at being a teenager. Christine remembers this stage well—minus the black lipstick.

The family shifts out of the way as if the clown is contagious, and Christine can't really blame them. He does look very sick, and as he slides down, he sort of slumps and then falls over.

"Cold," he might have said, but it is so quiet she might have mistaken the words. How could anyone be cold in this damn muggy heat?

She drops to her knees and feels his neck, then his chest, and both tell her he is not breathing.

"Oh fuck!" Jeff repeats the words after her without hesitation.

She doesn't have time to spare him a glance. She grabs her purse and empties it on the ground. Dragging her pocketbook from the mess of lipstick containers, gum, baby wipes, her iPod, a mass of coins from the games, and a pile of tickets, she tears it open and takes out the privacy guard she keeps there.

She rips open the package and drapes it over his mouth. Then she starts pressing on his chest just as she has been trained to do. Thirty times, counting out loud. Jeff stands at her side and watches. He leans close and touches the clown's face.

"SOMEONE CALL 911!" she yells to the spectators that gather around. The teenage girl with black lipstick who just passed stops and stares back at the dying man. She stands in place, looking around as if unsure what to do. Others pass and stare, but Christine appears to have things under control, and hey, it's a nice evening, so why get involved?

She reaches thirty and then leans over and takes a breath. Not her favorite thing here, folks, move along and watch the freak show down the road. Then the briefest of hesitations before she plants her lip over the guard and gives him two quick but strong breaths.

She pulls up but not before she catches the stench from his mouth, something she has smelled before, illness, stomach acid and underlying it all–death. She has seen bodies brought in that defy description when it comes to being mangled. She has seen the dead in all their various guises, and she knows that she is seeing it here.

"One, two, three ..." she counts out anyway and then is in for another kiss against those cold, dead, plastic-covered lips. She gags this time and almost throws up, but it must be working, because he moves.

She repeats the count to thirty, and his arm twitches. Then the hand rolls over onto the ground, his palm rubbing at the hard surface. She drops her head to his chest, but there is no sound. She jerks up quickly as if stung. That's not possible unless it is just postmortem spasm. Then the hand moves again, but this time it is not a spasm. It is a full movement that pulls his hand closer to his body.

She listens to his chest, and there is a loud whump as his heart fires up, but then it is silent again.

"What the ...?"

She sits back and starts pumping his chest, but she loses count after three, because the man is staring at her with blood-filled eyes. It's like the pupils have been swallowed by red. They don't blink, but his head moves. That's when she starts screaming.

Her screams don't finish until he has taken Jeff by the hand and torn out his stomach with his nails and mouth. The only reason she stops screaming is because she faints dead away.

MIKE

"You are an idiot. You know that, right?" her voice murmurs from the pillow where her head is turned toward mine. She lies on her stomach so that the sheet rides low on her hips. I lean over and kiss her right between her shoulder blades, then kiss down to the small of her back.

"Am I?"

"We could have done this a long time ago."

"I think it was worth the wait."

"Me too."

We are silent for a while. I run my hand over her back where I just trailed my lips. I'm lying on my side, perched up on one elbow. She is slim, in terrific shape, and I am all too aware that I have become lazy over the last year and that there is a layer of extra weight I need to drop. She didn't seem to care earlier when she took off my clothes in a rush, a breathless rush that had us in a tangle of limbs while we sorted out my pants.

"I need to work out," I think out loud, looking down.

"Yeah, you do. You can start now," and her arms are once again around my body. I pull her to me, on top so that her breasts are crushed against my chest, and she discovers that I won't need much help getting ready for her as she slides her legs down to straddle my chest.

* * *

Later we raid her fridge. She has a bucket of cold chicken and some potato salad. I expected her to stock nothing but health food, so this is quite a surprise. "Weekend food," she informs me. I'm dressed in a pair of boxers, and she has on a t-shirt that is dangerously short. I can't take my eyes off her as she moves around the kitchen. I feel free to stare at last; I have denied myself for too long.

Stomachs full, we hit the wine again and get a little tipsy as the evening fades. It's only nine, and I try not to think of Rita. We are on her couch, me sitting up, her lying against the other side so her legs trail over my lap. I have my hands on her calves and feet, and she teases my crotch with an ankle.

"How long have you looked at me that way, Mike?"

"Like this?" I ask and scrunch up my lips like a fish and cross my eyes.

She falls back laughing and jabs her foot into my side.

"You know what I mean."

"I do, but I just figured I was too old for you."

"I'm thirty-one, Mike. How old are you, thirty-seven? I think you're still young enough to train."

"It's not the years. It's the wear and tear."

"I like you just the way you are, wear and tear and all. I've always liked you. You made me laugh my first day at work when you asked if my purse was made of genuine giraffe."

"I never got an answer, either," I state in mock seriousness.

We trade banter for a few more minutes, then she sits up and puts her hand behind my neck and pulls me down for a kiss. I breath her in, taste her, revel in her, and I am the happiest I have been in years.

GRINDER

The show is going well so far. About fifty fans stand around for the first band, a local group called simply Ballard. They play a brutal sludge metal that has the singer-keyboardist jumping into the crowd when they don't yell loud enough, of which Grinder approves. The smell of pot drifts across the stage.

The next band has double the fans, some of them cheering at the top of their lungs. Anti-Pope-Reviver has a hot female bass player who likes to wear tiny miniskirts on stage. In the light of day, she isn't nearly as attractive. Face a bit long with a high forehead. Pale skin from being on a bus all day and stage all night. She is slim and trim, and Grinder is pretty sure she is a total cokehead.

Grinder doesn't do drugs, not anymore. The music is too important to him. Sure, he takes a hit of weed from time to time, but that doesn't count. If it is natural, from the earth, what harm is it? Hell, half the country smokes it. He does like to drink, though, and he loves to start when the second act is winding down.

He has the bottle of Wild Turkey in hand that he stole from Wil earlier. He sips it while he warms up his vocal cords; this amounts to a lot of humming and then some ungodly howls. One of the roadies has already fetched a pint of ice-cold chocolate milk and dumped a few shots of Baileys in it. What would the fans think if they knew he got his evil growls not from the devil but from chocolate milk, which thickens the mucus in his throat?

The liquor burns a nice line of fire into his belly just as Anti-Pope-Reviver is finishing up. They play the last few beats, and then there is the promise of "See you again soon!" for which the now-full venue cheers.

Half the kids out there are either drunk or wired up on the drug of their choice—most likely both. Some of the girls do ecstasy at the show and get all touchy feely. Grinder will be looking for these after their hour-and-a-half set.

The roadies for the other band are tearing the place apart as fast as they can, since there is only a twenty-five minute window before Corpse for a Day takes the stage. The guys move into the main room with instruments in hand. Eric wheedles on his guitar, Sid plucks at the thick strings of his blood-dripping bass. The thing looks like it could have been carried by a Viking, and Grinder has always thought it was just as cool as fuck.

Allen strums his guitar lovingly, fingers dancing up the frets, then whipping down again. The guitar is shaped like an ax, and it goes well with Sid's. When they headbang together, it is a wicked sight.

They pass the remains of the whiskey around, all except Eric, who doesn't drink anymore. He was a heavy alcoholic but avoids the stuff now like it's acid. The rest of the band has heard the stories, how he was a mean drunk and started shit with fans every night. Not good PR, man.

The club manager pokes his head into the room. "Five minutes, guys."

Grinder answers with the devil horn salute, index and pinky finger raised high.

The band doesn't say a prayer, they don't have a pre-show ritual, they just wait for the signal and then march to the stage. There is some posturing, hair being loosened or tossed back as if they are already on stage. They walk with big, purposeful strides as if they own the place. There is an attitude to being in a band like this, an attitude of unbridled intimidation.

The little hallway reeks of cigarettes and beer. From one corner comes the stench of old piss, and instead of shying away or looking grossed out, Grinder snorts in a familiar way that says, "This is my house now."

The stage is tiny, a postage stamp, and through the little curtain that separates the left and right sides, they can see the crowd is a seething mass. There may be only six hundred out there, but they are fucking loud. The ground shakes in anticipation, and Grinder almost gets wood. This is why I do it for, for the love. Then the music starts. It sounds grandiose, like a sweeping chorus from a Lord of the Rings movie.

The lights start to flash, a strobe that turns the howling mob into demons. The front row is pressed up against the stage so they can barely move. Sweaty faces and upraised fists are the order of the night. When the lights go down, there is a massive wave as the latecomers jockey for position against those who have stood their ground all night while pressed against the stage. It's not just men, either. Girls in leather and stilettos fight for the front with as much passion.

BOOM! The first volley as the music crescendos and the stage flashes brightly from behind. Wil slithers between a stack of amps and creeps up on his drum kit. When the next splash hits, he is already on his throne.

BOOM!! And the lights flash again. This time Wil raises both hands in the devil horn salute. Then the stage goes dark and they step onto it. Grinder struts to the microphone as the music builds. He doesn't look at the crowd, who are going nuts; he just offers his fist.

The last BOOM shakes the building and the music stops, the lights go out, and all they can hear is six hundred people screaming at the top of their lungs. Screaming for them, and Grinder wonders how in the world Sid can even think about giving this up. He glances Sid's way, but his head is down, long curly black hair obscuring his face and upper body.

The lights go up, and the band launches into their favorite opener, a staccato-paced piece called The Sleeper Awakens.

If Grinder were in the back, he knows exactly what he would see. Four heads bobbing up and down to the music as they bang the shit out of the venue. Then the first line comes up, Grinder gathers phlegm, pulls the microphone to his mouth in a tight fist and lets loose his growling vocals.

It's going to be a great night.

* * *

Chuck is a gorilla of a man. He stands outside of El Cid with his hands crossed over his massive chest while the third shitty band of the night batters the brains out of the kids inside. It's dark thanks to a series of streetlights that failed months ago and have never been fixed. There is the rush of cars along Eastgate Avenue on their way to I-5, but fewer than usual, owing, perhaps, to the shit going on up on Queen Anne.

A tour bus is parked outside behind a camper on the back of a big Ford F-350. The bus is old, seen better days. It must house the main band, a gift from their record label. Here ya go, boys, enjoy riding in style in this twenty-year-old bus that probably used to ferry old people to Vegas once upon a time.

The camper is just plain pathetic. Who would want to live that kind of life? Not Chuck Malanski, that's for goddamn sure.

He has been doing this job for a long time, and he has seen a lot of shit. He wears his old black t-shirt every night with something approaching pride. It has a single word on the front and the same word on the back:

SECURITY.

This magic word allows Chuck to get away with all kinds of things. He gets to pull people out of the mosh pit by their hair. He gets to sucker punch drunken ones who don't listen when he yells that they need to move the fuck out of his way. He can start fights, he can stop them. He is big enough that no matter how fucked-up the little metal heads are, they usually don't mess with him. He is all too familiar with their type—all the attitude and ego. It's all for show, and when he confronts them, they always back down with a whispered, "Wish that mother fucker would have touched me" as he struts away.

He hates the music at the place, although he would never say that to his employer's face. Truth be told, he is a good guy when he is away from this sinful cesspool. He enjoys church on occasion and would consider himself a God-fearing man. He lives his life by his own code, one that allows him to do bad things to people he considers beneath him, people like those at the concert tonight.

When he goes to work, he is a different man. He sees himself as some sort of avenging angel, the kind that uses his fists for words and his size 14 metal-tipped boots when he has to. Tonight is no different. It's another band of losers playing for a full house of equally brain dead losers.

He watches the back entrance to make sure none of the little shitheads tries to sneak out for a toke. He likes the way the music washes over him from inside. It is muffled and mindless with a beat he can still feel in his chest.

A couple of girls walk by in miniskirts, black tank tops barely holding in their boobs. Both sport six-inch heels. They look like whores, but he watches them just the same. Nice ass on the blonde— too bad she is probably a skanky bitch who is trying to get backstage so she can blow one of the band members.

A man wanders into the alley and slips on a pile of refuse. Oh great, another drunk. The guy staggers and then walks into a wall. He stands there, face to the red brick surface, and doesn't move for a minute. He is stocky, built like a linebacker except he can't be taller than five foot six. He wears a pair of blue coveralls that look like a painting uniform. There is a patch on the front, but Chuck can't read it in the poor lighting. The man turns his head ever so slowly, eyes passing the beefy security guard, sweeping past him and then staring at the moon as if he were a werewolf about to howl.

Chuck doesn't offer a smile or even acknowledge the guy, who is clearly drunk. As if to confirm this, the guy lets out a moan and then staggers toward him. Chuck leaves his arms crossed, because no one is stupid enough to mess with him. He may give him a dirty look or try to bum a smoke, but Chuck is confident he will get a load of his size and move the fuck on.

"You okay, buddy?" he asks as the asshole wanders toward him. Now that he is closer, Chuck thinks the man doesn't look so hot. In fact, he looks like hell with blood-red eyes sunken into their sockets. His face is ashen, devoid of emotion. Is that blood on his shirt? Chuck likes to kick ass and not take names, but he hates to get blood on himself. Please be spilled tomato juice.

"Just calm down, buddy. We are full up in there, all right?" he says in the tone they taught before he washed out of the Seattle police academy for lying on his job application. It was just a big misunderstanding—him and that kid. If she had just kept her mouth shut … but she had to tell her dad. It's not like they even did anything. He only put his hand between her legs because she said it was cool.

The drunk moves quickly, and Chuck steps back into a fighting stance. He draws back to throw a punch, but the guy now has his mouth wide open, and it is a bloody grin of horror.

He howls just before he leaps in the air, but Chuck throws his arm forward and catches the guy full in the face with one giant fist. Cartilage snaps, bones shift, and the guy should be down for the count. He drops like a lead weight and doesn't move. Chuck didn't mean to hit him that hard. In fact, he threw the fist up as protection more than anything else. But the guy was moving so fast the momentum turned into pain and, it seems, broken bones.

Oh shit, how hard did I hit him?

He wanders over and nudges the body. No response.

"You okay, buddy? Didn't mean to hit you so hard," he lies in case the guy is still conscious.

He drops to one knee on the side of the road and checks the guy's chest. Holy crap, no heartbeat. He puts his hand near the drunk's nose to test for breath, because that's what they do on TV. As soon as his hand is near, the guy opens his blood-filled eyes and darts his face off the ground. Pulped nose notwithstanding—and not bleeding—he snaps like a viper and takes off the last finger of Chuck's large hand. It just pops off in the guy's mouth, and as the pain starts to register, as the revulsion starts to sink in, the drunk moves forward. Hand whips up and wraps around one of Chuck's massive biceps; mouth darts up and nips off the tip of the big security guard's nose.

There is chewing, there is screaming, but the thing doesn't let go. It tightens its grip and pulls closer as Chuck tries to stand. He comes to his feet, and the thing bites him in the neck, severing his vocal cords and sending his blood flowing down his black SECURITY shirt. At first he is shocked that a short guy attacked him at all, and then his mind turns to the blood rushing across his chest. Not someone else's blood, but his own. His mind tries to cope with the shock, with the pain. He thrashes, but the thing latches on and won't let go. It bites into him over and over, and his world is nothing but blinding agony.

Then he dies, and he doesn't think of anything at all.

LESTER

Lester staggers out of the house, breathless, exhausted, and pissed. He storms across the yard, into the gate and promptly trips over one of his bags of pilfered goodies.

"Mother fucker!" he screams and stands up and kicks the bag. This results in him stubbing his toe against a very hard tin can. He wants to pound on something, but he goes silent as moans from the front of the house scare his breath away. He gasps and freezes. What did he just do? All that creeping about only to lose it for a minute. Stupid!

He grabs the bag and grimaces at the way it crinkles. He shuts the gate quietly but for the little snick as the latch catches and locks. He storms to the back of the house on light feet, teeth clenched so hard they grind together. He almost bowls over Angela in the process. She backs into the doorway, wide eyes fixed on him. Lester studies her for a moment, her hair hanging in her face because she hasn't been able to wash it since yesterday morning. Her face is lined with tiny wrinkles, particularly around the eyes and lips; she looks at least ten years older. Her eyes are sunken in; red blood vessels make them look like they are glowing. What the fuck are we doing here? They need to get out of Dodge, because there ain't no sheriff coming to rescue them anytime soon.

Even for her tired look, he can't get mad at her. She is so good to him and fucks like a little monkey on speed. She is the best time of his life, a life he has pretty much wasted in the pursuit of the next scam, moneymaker, or drug deal. But being locked up in the little house is going to get real fucking old real fucking quick.

"Sorry, babe," he mumbles and limps into the house. She stands aside as he walks past.

"What happened? I heard gunshots!"

"I found our neighbors."

"Oh God, are they all right?"

"Well, John had half his brains lying on the floor but was still moving. I had to beat the shit out of Jan; she attacked me."

"Jan?"

"The wife. Jane?"

"Her name is Justine."

"Oh. Well, I had to beat Justine to death with a DVD rack. She came on too strong." He tries to grin but instead starts laughing big hysterical guffaws that come fast and breathy. Tears blur his vision, and he isn't sure if they are from the stress of the last half hour or the ridiculous way he had to massacre his neighbors.

Angela puts her hand on his back and rubs it. He doesn't stop laughing, and pretty soon she is giggling along with him.

"It's not funny!" He tries to sound serious as tears of relief stream down his face.

"I know." She laughs with him.

★ ★ ★

"Start, bitch!" Lester grumbles again as he yanks the cord on the generator. This time he must have gotten it primed right, because it roars to life. They placed it upstairs in the empty bedroom near an open window, exhaust pointed out. He already ran a couple of extension cords downstairs. Once satisfied with the fuel level, he shuts the door with the cord running under it and stuffs a folded towel into the space. There is no way he is going to run that thing outside with the back door open.

"We got juice!" he calls out.

"Can we heat some water?" she calls back hopefully.

"I don't think so, maybe a little at a time."

He dragged the smaller TV downstairs earlier and put it on the shelf where the big flat screen sits. The bigger TV looked like a shadow of the smaller one. Then he hooked up the cable box and fed everything into a power strip. Now it looks like a weird squid left in the center of the room. The connection is rigged to the generator through a long extension cord that snakes across the floor and up the stairs. He pushes the switch on the strip, and the little amber light comes on. He wonders how much electricity that thing can put out, so he switches on the TV first, then the cable box. They have juice!

Both come to life, and the room is filled with artificial light for the first time in days. One of the local channels comes on, but it is just a channel identification sign. The next channel is running a sitcom he has seen a few times. He watches it for a minute, trying to appreciate the humor the way he does when he is high, but it just isn't that funny now.

"Oh wow, things must not be that bad if they are showing this crap."

"Huh?"

"Well if the shit really has hit the fan out there, then we would see nothing but coverage of it on every channel. I mean, maybe it's just us and there's help on the way."

Angela is quiet as she looks at him. Her face is painted a hopeful shade in the shallow light of the TV. He wishes he could be more reassuring. He picks up his pipe, wincing at his various bumps, bruises, and scrapes. He is going to be one sore puppy in the morning. He changes the channel again but runs up against another channel identification placard. The next two channels are just colored bars. When he finally reaches CNN, the screen switches over to a live studio where a smiling blonde is talking about the latest celebrity gossip.

The local news channel is next, and—bingo!—here is what he has been waiting for.

The newscaster looks concerned. His eyebrows are pulled together, but before Lester can listen in, the screen flips to a live outdoor camera. They are at the bottom of Queen Anne Hill, where the police have set up a series of roadblocks. Farther up the road, people drift down the hill on foot, bags and boxes in hand. A few of them ride bikes, and one is on an electric scooter.

"As you can see, the authorities are still blocking access to the Queen Anne neighborhood while the leak is taken care of. Residents are being asked to leave in as orderly a fashion as possible and to take only what they can carry. This is day two of Crisis on the Hill."

The newscaster goes on to explain that the leak has caused people to become sick, disoriented. If approached, please be cautious. If attacked, try to be as humane as possible by locking them inside or securing them to something.

Lester smiles around a puff of smoke. The acrid odor burning down his throat makes him want to choke and cough. At least it isn't that bad out there. He is sure the government will be able to take care of them in no time.

Then he thinks of the bodies in front of the house. Oh shit, did they say to treat those fuckers humanely? Hide the bodies, his mind whispers, just stash them when the street is clear. They'll never know where the shots came from with all the chaos. His mind sinks into a haze of marijuana that allows him to escape from reality for a while. Yeah, man, soon as the government gets here.

ALICE AND KEN

The gun warms in her grip; she has been sitting for several minutes, thinking. Her life is gone, her husband, her son; her house will never be the same. She stares down the barrel and thinks about the end.

Just a squeeze and it will all be over. What will it feel like when the bullet enters her forehead? Will she feel it exit? Will there be pain or just a blast of nothingness? Will she hear the boom as the gun fires? She has fired this pistol before, and she remembers how loud it is, not like the shows on TV where they fire guns in closed rooms and can talk afterwards.

What about the girl? Will she be okay? She seems to be doing a hell of a lot better than me. She sighs as she thinks about abandoning the child. She lowers the gun, grabs her keys off the floor and makes for the door. She comes around the corner of the room and nearly crashes into her rescuer. She runs down the hall full tilt, and they both scare each other into little screams. Alice stares at her and then almost chuckles at the frightened expression on the girl's face. It is probably a replica of the one on hers.

"Where were you? He was moving, and I don't think I can hit him again."

"I'm sorry. I had to get something."

"Can we go now? I need to check on my mom," she says in a small voice.

"Is she like my husband?" Alice stares into the girl's raccoon eyes, realizing that they are a pool of emerald green, red rimmed and filled with tears.

"Yeah. But I have to do something."

"Why don't we check with the police and see if they can help us out first?"

The girl follows her like a lost puppy as she storms out the door. Alice comes around the corner, and the little silver car is sitting just as she left it. The street is quiet, the sudden silence shocking set against the chaos of the last few minutes. A crow caws in the distance, then another answers. For some reason, this sends a shiver down her spine.

"Where is he?" the girl asks under her breath.

Alice spins around in a full circle and realizes that her dear husband is nowhere to be seen. They run to the side of the car while images from bad horror movies of people unable to get their keys into locks hit her. But the door reacts to the electronic key she carries, so when she puts her hand on the door, it immediately opens.

The girl waits at the side of the car, turning her head back and forth in a frantic scanning motion.

"It's open. The doors are automatic …" Her voice turns into a scream as Ken rises from behind the compact.

His head is off kilter, just to the side. A portion of his skull sticks out; his hair is matted with blood and dirt, and for a mad second, she wishes he would take a shower so he can go to his grave looking clean. The girl dances away from the car as Ken closes in on her. Alice doesn't really think, she just opens the door and slides inside, then triggers the automatic lock.

She stares at the shambling thing that was her husband as he bears down on the girl. The teen picks up her skateboard and swings it in a menacing manner. It thumps against Ken's dangling hand. It does the job of pushing him off balance. He almost falls but turns back around faster than Alice has seen him move before. His mouth opens, as does the girl's, but the car drowns out any sound.

Alice hits the button on the dash, and the car starts, but she freezes in horror, unable to move as she sits in the safe confines of the car.

"Run, I'll pick you up!" Alice yells.

The girl looks at Alice as she scrambles backwards, but she cannot make out Alice's words. Alice pumps the gas and spins the wheel to the left. A moment of clarity pops into her brain in which she imagines herself running Ken over and saving the girl. Oh God, Ken, how did it come to this? She slams her hand on the dash. It sends a jolt of agony up her arm from the bite mark. The car jerks forward as the shock drives her foot into the accelerator.

Ken shoots his head to the right at the sudden sound, and the girl takes the opportunity to run. Only she doesn't make the first step, as her foot comes down on a large rock, which sends her sprawling. Her skateboard slides away, and her hands splay out in the gravel.

* * *

Your heart thunders in your chest just once, then after an eternity, the great organ shudders to life and thumps again. It comes in intermittent beats, but each one is a blast of life. There is no pain, barely any thought—you are driven by pure instinct. Your prey has been difficult, but you don't care. There is damage, but you work around it.

You hovered near the ground patiently, something telling you that they would return, and return they did. Talking, jabbering, noises that don't make sense. The smaller one is on the same side from which you emerge, and all you can think about is her warm blood oozing down your throat, the feel of flesh between your teeth. The gnashing and tearing. Something to fill the tremendous hollow that has become your world. The emptiness beats at you like a furnace that radiates from your center and makes you want to scream in frustration.

You are on your feet, unsteady but moving. She is just there, her flesh warm and glowing. One foot in front of another, you move as fast as they will allow. She glances into your eyes, and hers go suddenly large. She stifles a scream and backs up. She swings her weapon at you, but misses. A loud noise, a distraction, you turn your head toward it, and she uses the moment to turn and run. Only her run turns into a fall as she goes down.

Triumph! You nearly howl with need as she goes flat. You are on her in an instant, hands digging into her body, mouth seeking her flesh. She tries to swing her elbow back, but you ignore the pitiful blow and take in a mouthful of hair. Then your lips close on the meat that has been taunting you forever, and you tear into it with genuine relish.

* * *

Alice howls as she comes out of the car. She has the gun in a shaky hand and raises it mechanically. "KEN, NO!" she screams and moves around the car door. Ken wraps around the girl like some hulking wraith gone mad. He moans as he chews. The girl struggles. She tries to scream, but all Alice hears is hoarse cries. Ken digs his face into her neck and worries at the skin like a beast. He pulls back, and there is a horrible ripping sound.

Alice staggers forward, aims the gun at her husband and doesn't pull the trigger. Tears flow from her eyes as she struggles to hold the pistol straight. Her vision goes blurry, but she can't pull trigger. What if she hits the girl? Don't be silly, she says to herself. The girl is done for. The realization that she has failed to protect the young woman rocks her back. She failed the girl with no name. She realizes it with a sudden staggering breath—she never got the girl's name.

She aims the gun as best she can through her tear-stained vision and pulls the trigger. Nothing happens except Ken tearing another piece of meat out of the girl's shoulder. She remembers the firing range and grabs the slide on top. She yanks it down so hard her hand slips off and scrapes along the rear sight. Then she aims again and, with a roar, it speaks. The shot clips Ken's ear, then ricochets off a rock. The sound is loud. Her husband howls in frustration as his head pitches forward from the blow.

He recovers and raises his head again, so Alice takes aim. The next shot throws her arms up into the air. She has the sights lined up, but fearing the recoil, she glances away just as she fires. The bullet punches into Ken's shoulder and smacks him down once again. The girl screams as loud as she can and manages to push Ken off. Her shirt hangs in shredded, bloody red ribbons, and then Alice realizes that it's her skin that is dangling in strips.

She gathers the girl up, one shoulder under her good arm, and presses them both to their feet. She hurries the girl as fast as she can to the side of the car. She pops the door open and helps her into the seat. The girl moans and presses her hand to her wound, but blood continues to leak in a steady stream. Splashes of it hit the car seat and door, but Alice doesn't give a rat's ass about the car anymore. All she wants to do is get the girl to a doctor so she can have her wounds tended.

Ken rises to his knees. Alice deposits the pistol in her jacket pocket, takes a couple of running steps and plants the flat of her sneaker in Ken's back. "Asshole!" she yells and kicks him again just for good measure.

She rushes to her side of the car and jumps in the driver's seat. The new car smell has been replaced by the reek of blood and dread. It's palpable and hangs in the tiny space like a curtain. Alice drops the car into drive and puts the pedal all the way to the floor. The car responds by kicking in the gas engine. Gravel flies as she rips toward the street. She glances in the rear view mirror in time to see pieces of rock pelting her husband. He is on his feet once again, his mouth wide open in fury.

God, what in the hell just happened? Alice pounds on the dash. She wants to scream at the top of her lungs. Everything has been turned upside down; her life is gone, and she has no time for grief. She pushes the urge to scream aside with a will and instead pats the girl's knee. She is all that matters now. She will become the center of Alice's world. She never should have let the girl out of her sight; she should have had the gun drawn and ready for Ken's attack. She should have seen it! Alice slams on the brakes and stops a few blocks from her house. She turns to her side and looks at the ashen face of the girl.

"I'm so sorry. I should have protected you better."

"Nothing you could have done," the girl cries, her voice weak and tiny.

"I'm taking you straight to a hospital. They will take care of you."

Alice whips the towel off her own wound and turns it over to the clean side. She ties it over the girl's ragged wound. The girl tries to turn her head and makes it halfway around. Alice wipes away the girl's tears and then tries to move her so she can cradle her in her lap.

"I need my mom," the girl gasps. Alice feels blood, warm and thick as it soaks into her pants.

"Can you hang in there for a little bit?"

"Yeah."

They sit like this for minutes while the blood continues to run out of the wound. Alice weeps over the girl. She hugs her close as the girl goes from sobbing in weak shakes to quivering all over. It feels like she has a terrible fever. It gets so bad, just a few minutes later, that Alice wonders if she is an epileptic. Then the girl's body clenches tight, a brief respite before she starts shaking again.

"I forgot to get your name," Alice says in a whisper as tears pour down her cheek.

There is no answer.

* * *

The parking lot at Queary Park has one other car in it. A beat-up Chevy Astro that has seen better days. It is red but looks like someone tried to spray paint half of it black. No one has walked through the park, although she did see someone poking around in the bushes at the edge of the tree line to the west.

Alice sits in her car and looks at the shrubbery near the parking lot, the leaves swaying in the mild breeze. It's late, night will be here soon, but she is too scared to leave the neighborhood. Since she pulled up here and put the girl on the picnic table, she has heard screams, cries for help, and more than a few gunshots. But the noises have been in the distance. Far away from her and her fragile state of mind. She still has the gun in one hand, and she has stared at the barrel more than a few times.

She pulls into the park just as the sun is setting. There is no one to shut the gate, so she picks up the girl from the side of the car and carries her to the closest table. The girl shakes the entire time as if cold, and Alice wants to drop her right then and there. It can't be true, what they are saying, what the girl said about being bitten, it can't be! At the same time, she has to make sure. She has to know!

Dark now, night has arrived, and the girl is sitting up on the table. Her legs shifted first, then her hands, then her arms. Alice turns on her headlights and then her high beams. The girl's eyes are blood red. She opens her mouth, and a horrible cry pours past her lips.

A tear slides down Alice's cheeks as she puts the car in reverse and backs out of the park.

GRINDER

They are halfway through their set, and the place is insane. The floor is moving with the music, heads are thrashing up and down; a respectable mosh pit has opened up where body after body throws itself into the fray. People collide, fly away and are back in a few seconds. When they finish a song, Grinder jumps on one of his PA amps at the front of the stage and stands like a god before his flock.

"Come on, you mother fuckers! I can't fucking hear you!" And "Do you want some more? 'Cause I want to see some pain!" And "Don't make me come down there and show you pussies how it's done." And he will do just that if he has to. He will stage dive right off this rinky-dink rise and land in a mass of people.

They eat it up, and he eats up the attention. Each song is short, but each is a brutal assault on the senses. The tension, the rhythm, the pace never lets up. They just finished their ninth song of the night, but Grinder loves the crowd, so he decides to do something special.

"Let's go waaaay back and play some shit from the EP!"

This isn't on the set list, but he glances at Sid, who has a goofy grin on his face like this is what they were made for. He steps up to the mike and bellows, "Fuck yeah!" Grinder looks at the person with whom he grew up and wishes things could be different, wishes they could bridge the distance that has grown between them. That look on Sid's face, the glee as they are about to crank through one of the first songs they ever wrote together. This is the way Grinder will always remember him.

The band knows all the songs. They have practiced them countless times, but this one is old and rarely added to the set list. Still, the band members look at each other, and Pounder beats out a double bass line to get the place rallied up.

"This is fucking BLOOD BATH!" and the opening chords erupt like a bat out of hell, crushing the audience like a fresh assault.

There is a commotion in the back as Grinder steps up on his mic stand and starts grunting the lyrics. One of the security guards wades into the crowd from the back, and he flails around as if in pain. Then the strobe flashes as the chorus kicks in, and it looks like he is attacking people. Another figure crashes into the back of the crowd. The kids adjust, sucking the combatants into their fold.

More thrashing, and the guard is down and being pounded to the ground by a rush of fans. Other guards wade into the crowd, pushing and shoving as they try to reach their comrade. Sid looks at the crowd, then at Grinder. Grinder looks back at him, then gives him the horns. Fuck yeah, man, rock and roll.

The big man is up, but he attacks one of the other security guards, a much smaller man with the same black shirt on. Did he just bite him? No fucking way did that just happen! No way. The venue is dark; he probably just imagined it.

The crowd seems to be losing steam as the fighting goes on. Now there is another person down, and is that blood? The band slows and stops playing; soon only the drummer is pounding on his kit until he realizes everyone else has stopped. There is a scream from the back row, then more pushing.

"I'm about to come down there and sort that shit out!" he yells into the microphone. His voice bounces around the venue without the instruments to back him up, and close to six hundred heads are looking at him, but he doesn't feel like a rock star anymore. He feels like a normal guy in front of a bunch of strangers.

A scream from the back of the room saves him from embarrassment. A fresh fight breaks out as the big bruiser who started the shit in the first place comes to his feet and shrugs off two sweat-covered guys in black Corpse for a Day shirts. He is covered in blood, so much that Grinder wants to know how he is still standing. The lights are coming up, and it is apparent that the song they just performed is over. In fact, the whole set is done. Maybe it is a joke, some kind of prank the audience decided to throw. If that is the case, Grinder IS going to start kicking some ass.

A second security guard, the skinny one, is on his feet as well, and he starts attacking the kids around him. Meanwhile, the giant guy has a girl in both hands. She looks young, nineteen at the most. She is tiny and grabs for a boy in black next to her. But the security guard doesn't seem to care as he tears her away and then picks her up, both hands gripping her upper arms, and brings her to his mouth. She fights him, hitting his face and chest to no effect. The brute pulls her close and bites into her forehead.

"WHAT THE FUCK?" Grinder screams, but his mouth is far enough from the microphone that the sound isn't very loud over the din of the fans, whose screams have turned from cries of adulation for the band to shrieks of terror. The guard's hand slips off one shoulder to slide along her arm and then grasp her neck. She fights like crazy, arms thrashing, flailing against the big guy. The boyfriend punches him, pulling at his arm and hitting him in the neck, face and chest as hard as he can.

The guard shrugs off the blows, raises the girl higher and tears out her throat with his teeth. Then he starts eating her from the neck down, and the crowd goes insane. There is suddenly a mass of people trying to get out or at least away from the crazy guy who is ripping chunks out of a woman as if she were a prime rib. He chews and swallows, then, as if realizing what he is doing, drops her on the floor. Several others have risen and are now attacking the crowd. It's a free for all as fans and security guards alike go to town biting and chewing, all while bathed in blood. The stampede reaches the stage, and the band is forgotten as they are pushed out of the way.

Grinder remains rooted in place. He stares at the carnage, at the mayhem, at the blood and bile. He wants to turn away, but he can't; he can't pull his eyes off the horrible spectacle. A sweat-drenched man in full leathers bowls past him as he tries to find the backstage area. The rest of the band joins the exodus, hauling ass for anywhere but here. Eric may have a felony on his record, so he doesn't want to talk to the cops. The others are clean and clearly not living up to their full potential if the fans can be chased off this quickly. Maybe they need to add some shock to their shows—but in a more controlled way.

"What the fuck are you doing, man?" Sid steps in front of him, breaking his view of the carnage.

"Dude, what I just saw, I don't know how to describe it."

"I know, man; we need to get the hell out of here. Yeah it's fucking horrible, but we need to haul ass."

"No, Sid, this is beautiful. This is what we have been searching for. If we can capture half the horror, the passion of what we just saw, in a record, just fucking think about what we could accomplish," Grinder yells over the din of the screams.

"Grind- ... Duane, Duane! Look at me! You're in shock!"

Another scream as a concertgoer falls. Then, to his disbelief, the girl he saw get partially eaten comes to her feet and makes straight for the stage. There is a hole in the crowd now, as though they have opened up just for her. She is howling, but there is barely a voice, only a wheeze as she makes her way toward them through an ocean of bodies that are trying to clear out of the place.

Sid still has his back to the spectacle as others rise off the ground. The place now has a new smell over the old taint of piss, booze, and stale cigarette smoke. It has a fresh odor to add to its past, the smell of death.

The girl takes the stage by slowly crawling onto it. Grinder watches in fascination as she comes to her feet behind Sid. All he has to do is say something, pull him out of the way, push him aside, grab him and tug him to the backstage area. But he doesn't. He watches in complete rapt and morbid fascination as the girl grabs Sid around the neck, jumps onto his back and sinks her mouth into his sweaty hair. She pulls hard with her arms, and Sid's face becomes a mask of terror, then one of pain as she rips off his ear.

She pulls back, and he spins out of control, unsure what to do. He reaches for her, but she darts in and takes another chunk. He backpedals, eyes pleading with Grinder until he crashes into the drum kit. Then she is on top of him, and her mouth tears at his neck. Why the neck? Grinder wants to yell at her. You're no fucking vampire.

"Sorry, Sid my man, my brother. I'm going to miss you. Don't attack me when you come back, buddy, okay? I need to get a new album written, and you are going to be the star." On some level, Grinder realizes how crazy he sounds. He knows that if he ever breathes a word of this to anyone, they will lock his ass up for a good long time in a place where they give you lots of medication and ask you about your feelings.

Sid thrashes around, trying to grab his neck as blood spurts out like an overblown horror movie effect, and the sight finally snaps Grinder out of his reverie. Grinder steps up and kicks the girl in the head as hard as he can. Her head snaps back as his giant boot connects, but he doesn't strike in rage, not in anger. He doesn't blame her; he just wants to get away and not end up like old Sid. The kick is a beauty that makes the girl's head pop to the side and then snap. She falls over in a heap on top of Sid.

Grinder looks at his friend one more time. Sid stares at him, clutching his neck as blood runs out in gouts. He presses his other hand there, but the stuff doesn't stop pouring out. Grinder doesn't touch him. He steps around the blood slowly, carefully, and then walks calmly to the back of the stage.

One glance back tells him that the place is in complete chaos. There are bodies everywhere and people on top of others feeding as if they are in some bad zombie flick, but Grinder couldn't care less. He has seen the face of death, and he is ready to move on to the next phase of his life.

* * *

The backstage area is a mess. People have run over everything, tracking blood and viscera with them. There are screams from the main area, but Grinder walks with the confidence of a man in charge of his destiny. A man who has a newfound respect for life, or the dead. Yeah, that's it. He now sees the beauty that is inherent in death, and he is pleased.

Eric is grabbing gear, tucking things under one arm. He has a bottle of Jack in his other hand. He chugs back a huge double shot worth of fire and then grimaces as he appears to be holding down the contents of his stomach.

"Jesus fuck, what the hell is going on out there?"

"No Jesus in the house. That is pure evil out there. They got Sid. He's gone."

Eric drops everything under his arm but holds onto the bottle. He stares at Grinder as if slapped.

"There was nothing I could do, truly."

"Oh jeez, man. Fuck, that's crazy. Are you sure?"

"Oh yeah, I'm sure. This chick jumped on him and tore out his throat, and then she chewed a half dozen times and swallowed."

"You saw it? Why didn't you help?"

"I did help. I killed the girl, planted my boot in the corner of her head. She went down like a sack of potatoes."

"No way, man, no way. It's just the shock talking. Let's get back to the tour bus and get the fuck out of here, man. I don't want no shit with the cops, you know? Just watch, Sid will turn up in a minute and we can leave."

Eric tosses back another shot of Jack and runs down the hallway. Grinder follows at a sedate pace. What's the hurry? He has become some sort of evil angel, and he will soon bring the word of the dead to the faithful.

* * *

Out in the night, people are still streaming out of the club. Several stragglers across the street wander slowly as if confused. Grinder knows all too well what that look means. They have already turned; hell, the whole city is bound to go before the night is over.

He gets to the tour bus and pounds on it. Three fans wearing expensive hockey shirts with the band's name emblazoned on them stream past Grinder as if they don't see him. Each has blood on him, and they all look terrified as they run past the lead singer of their favorite band.

"HEY!" Grinder calls out.

They stop and stare at him for a second before recognition dawns. They approach slowly as if he is one of the creatures. He smiles a wicked grin full of evil intent and beckons to them. Before any of them can speak, he drops the grin, gives his best badass metal face and grunts, "We are the chosen. Take back the night. Go forth and kill, my children. Kill the infected." And with that, he turns and pounds on the tour bus door.

The driver recognizes him and opens the door. Marcos doesn't speak; he just reaches for the lever that closes the door to the bus, but before he can shoot it closed, he yells out, "Come on, Sid, we are getting the fuck out of town."

"No, Marcos, WAIT!" But it is too late. Sid staggers onto the bus. Grinder backs up the aisle, suddenly unsure. Maybe Sid wasn't as dead as he thought. He is, however, covered in blood; his hair is matted and stringy with gore. Sid's eyes are bright red, the pupils nearly obscured by the blood.

Eric hops up from the little chair at the two-seat table where he has been hitting the bottle of Jack. He looks like he wants to hug Sid, even offers him the bottle like he is a returning hero.

"Oh Sid, man, I heard you were dead." Grinder tries to yell a warning. His eyes are wide, his mouth open in a great big O.

Sid moves fast. He grabs the proffered arm and instead of taking the bottle, he bites into Eric's forearm and tears off a hunk of meat. Eric screams in shock and drops the booze. It clatters to the metal floor and rolls over and over, spilling alcohol. Sid latches onto Eric, and they fall together in a tangle. Sid's head dives in and takes a chunk of Eric's cheek with his next bite.

This is not fucking good. He can't be trapped here with these things. He needs to get off the bus so he can spread the word to the faithful, not to mention the fact that he has no desire to die just now. Eric withers beneath the assault, and instead of standing aside, Grinder steps up and starts pounding on Sid's back. He grabs the man's long hair and tries to drag him off poor Eric. But Sid has a death grip and is eating the drummer alive.

Eric howls in pain as blood spurts in every direction. Sid is drenched in the stuff, and it starts to sicken Grinder, so he lets go and rubs his hand on his pants. Then he looks down to see the red smeared on his clothes, and he wants to scream.

Wil and Marcos have joined Grinder, but they stand behind him in the tiny space, unsure what to do. The bus driver jumps up suddenly and hauls Sid off by his legs. Eric thrashes on the floor, hands against his neck as he tries to contain enough blood to stay alive. The effort seems futile. Blood pours from his body at a terrible rate, and Grinder doesn't think he can last much longer.

Sid turns over and comes to his feet. Grinder sees the move, and it isn't like before, when he was moving as slowly as a drunk. He comes up fast and latches onto the bus driver, chomping at his shoulder through the driver's thick shirt. The driver goes crazy, punching and kicking Sid, but to no avail. Sid's grip is unshakeable as he tears through the fabric and rends the man's skin.

The small aisle is completely blocked; there is no way to get past the two. Wil steps right over Eric, who is staring at nothing as the blood flow slows. His legs kick as the bus driver and Sid dance around in their deadly struggle.

"What the fuck is wrong with Sid, man?" Wil screams as he tries to pry Sid off the bus driver. Sid's teeth hold fast.

"It's all wrong, man. They're already dead. It's all wrong," Grinder mumbles as he witnesses the carnage. His gaze is fixed on Eric, who is no longer moving except for his eyes, which are blinking very very slowly.

Grinder backs up past Allen, brushes against the sides of the little sleeping areas and then reaches the back of the bus. He stares in horror, in wonder, in dread as Eric dies. There is a last gasp, a bubble of bloody air that escapes his torn throat before his death throes arrive. This is a scene to which Grinder is growing accustomed, a scene he is falling out of love with—quickly.

Eric dies, and they all know it because his bladder lets go, releasing the unmistakable smell of urine. Then a worse sound as Eric shits himself.

Allen is down on his knees beside Eric when he dies. He looks up at Grinder, then at Sid and the bus driver who are thrashing it out. The smell of blood is palpable, overwhelming, it mixes with the horror in a way that sends poor Allen over the edge. He turns his head, and vomit erupts in a geyser across the table and chair legs. Grinder is all the way at the back of the bus now, and scared to death. He knows what is about to happen and is powerless to stop it. He can see the scene like a clairvoyant; he can see Eric's eyes snapping open as the newly dead man reaches up to attack and eat Allen. When the driver is down, it will just be him and his dead bandmates.

As if reading his thoughts, Eric does open his eyes, and a half-scream roars from his mouth in a breathy gasp echoed by a wheeze as air escapes the giant hole in his neck. Then he snaps up and latches onto Wil's neck and holds on like a dog with a large rope toy. His head whips back and forth and comes away with a mouthful of flesh.

Blood rushes down to spray Eric's face, and Grinder decides he has had it with this hellish scene. He jumps up onto his bunk, grabs his iPod and his worn notebook with all the unfinished lyrics he has been working on. His leather jacket is next as he whips it onto the floor. The men on the bus are alternating moan and scream, and it is truly something out of a nightmare.

Sid must be done with the bus driver, because he drops him and stares at Eric, who has his hands wrapped around Wil in a death grip. Wil howls as Eric feeds on his face. He snaps at an eye, gets hold of an eyelid and rips it off. Wil kicks and punches, but he is obviously running out of steam as the blows fall weaker and weaker.

The driver is trying to drag himself out of a puddle of blood, shit and vomit. The smell is unbearable. Grinder has an exceptionally strong stomach, but he wants to empty it. He wants to turn his head and give the bus a farewell by projectile vomiting all over it.

Sid turns his blood-filled eyes on him, and Grinder is done with this scene.

He jumps up on Wil's bunk, which is at the very back of the bus. He lands on the bed, then hunches his body forward and rests his foot on the back window. There is a safety release, but he remembers the bus driver telling them that it wouldn't work and they would have to use one of the pop-out windows at the front of the bus if they got into trouble.

He rears back his leg and kicks the window as hard as he can. Safety glass explodes outward. He looks back, and Sid is closing the distance. He slides out of the hole and drops the notebook and jacket on the ground. He jams his iPod in his pocket along with his high-end headphones and prepares to join the night.

Blood is caked in Sid's hair, smeared all over his face, congealing in his eye sockets. Red froth and drool dribble out of his mouth, and there is a piece of skin stuck to the side of his lips. Whose is that? Is that part of Eric or the bus driver? Eric is on his feet, and he has nothing but malice in his empty red eyes, which are set on Grinder.

He takes a quick peek out the window, but there are no others on this side of the bus. He slips his feet out first, then his legs follow. Sid staggers down the walkway with murder in his eyes. At least that's what it looks like with the amount of gore on his face. Grinder, who loves horror and torture-porn flicks, is convinced he has never witnessed a scene more graphic or disturbing in his life. He slides out just as Sid closes the distance. Eric is right behind him, and Grinder wishes he had a camera to capture this Kodak moment.

"Adios, mother fuckers!" He gives them the finger before he drops to the ground. It is a short drop, just a few feet, and he pulls it off with aplomb and grace. Behind him, Sid pops his head out the window and groans like a fat man passing gas. Grinder turns around as he slips his leather jacket on and offers his middle finger once more before pounding into the night.

PART TWO
DAY 1

MIKE

Night and I can't sleep.

She lies next to me in a heap of sheets, the blankets having been pushed to the end of the bed during our lovemaking. I turn on my side and open my eyes to find Erin's face inches from my own. She sleeps much more quietly than Rita ever did, and I curse myself for comparing the two. I don't jump into bed with women unless I am in a serious relationship. My mind latches onto that thought. A serious relationship. Am I ready for that?

Rita was another person, another life ago. I should have done it a while back, but I do it now: like letting someone adrift in the sea, I set her free in my mind and wonder what my future might hold with Erin.

The condominium is cool. Her air conditioning unit hums along in the bedroom window. First on, then off, the sound seems to kick in every time I drift off. The city is devoid of the crickets and frogs I usually hear at home, and I find the silence a bit unsettling. Light from the streetlamps paint the condo a hazy shade of dusk and yellow. It only adds to the feeling of gloom. But I lean over and stare at Erin, and I forget all about that.

I could get up and see if she has blinds behind the curtains so I can cut out the light, but I don't want to wake her.

Erin's bedroom, much like her living room, is sparse. A single dresser with a rectangular mirror mounted in oak hangs over it. Minimal artwork, a nighttime shot of New York that stretches nearly three feet across one wall. The other has some abstract piece with swirling shapes competing for room on a white background.

She doesn't snore but sleeps with a contentment I wish I felt. Don't get me wrong, I am very happy with our lovemaking. In fact, the word ecstatic comes to mind. I worry about other things. Rita. I wonder if it will affect our relationship back at work. If I survive the weekend, that is—she seems intent on draining me dry. I sit up and look at the clock on her side of the bed, and the digital display informs me in big amber numbers that it is just after midnight.

There is a scream from outside, but this is the big city and I'm sure it's just kids leaving a bar or playing around. Erin rolls over and tugs a blanket up. I stare at her face in the pale light and watch her sleep. A lock of hair falls across her eyebrows, and I use a gentle touch to move it out of the way.

I give up on sleep after another twenty minutes, slip out of the bed and find my boxers. Moving quietly across the wood floor, I go to the living room. My laptop is in my bag, so I take it out and fire it up. It has a built-in wireless broadband card, which I use to get on the web. I make myself at home on her lazy boy, or what passes for one. It has a soft cloth cover in blue that is much more comfortable than any chair I have ever owned. The laptop finishes loading, and I start the wireless service. After about twenty seconds, it shows a connection failed error.

I hit connect again, but I get the same result. She has a computer, but it is a Mac and I am Apple-dumb. I know how to load an iPod, but my knowledge ends there. I close the laptop and set it aside.

Night and I am wide awake.

I should be exhausted after the things we did, but instead I feel wired. I wish Erin would wake up so we can talk, but I will let her sleep. I peruse her bookshelf, which turns up a pretty wide assortment. There are books by Stephen King, Crichton and some large cookbooks. She has a couple of 'chick lit' books, something by the author of Sex and the City, or so the cover proclaims. There is even a lone Harry Potter book. I wonder how Andy would have liked those, if he would have grown up to wish he were a boy wizard.

I pull out a book on depression and palm through it. It seems to be commonsense advice, but it makes me wonder why I have never dealt with my own. They gave me drugs after the accident, Zoloft and then something to help me sleep at night called Klonopin. They were fine for a week or two, but I found myself transformed into a drugged-out zombie while Rita refused to take anything except Wild Turkey. Then it was scotch, and then she finally settled on vodka as her food of choice.

"See anything interesting?"

I nearly jump out of my skin. I am in the act of putting the book back like a child caught with my hand in the cookie jar. My face flushes red, and I turn to face her with the book clutched at my side.

She has slipped into a skimpy black nightie that clings to her in the pale light. It plunges deeply around her breasts and barely reaches her thighs. There is lace everywhere, and the night does interesting things to her shape, making her ethereal, unreal. I put the book down and go to her.

"You scared the crap out of me. I didn't mean to snoop, just couldn't sleep."

"I thought as much. It's always tough to sleep in a new bed, or someone else's. Not that we got much sleep earlier." She stretches her arms above her head, which makes the hem of the nightie ride up her hips. I wrap my arms around her waist; she comes up to about my nose, so I lean in and kiss her very deeply. We stand in the room for a while, reacquainting our lips with each other's, and I feel a stirring below.

"Let's go back to bed. I know how to help wear you out." She grins with devilish intent. She breaks free and does a little pirouette for me, then she pads down the hall on bare feet. She slips the black film of the nightgown over her head in a languid manner that has my complete and utter attention. Her legs are fine, long and lean, and I can't take my eyes off her.

* * *

A gunshot makes me sit up in bed. I come up from a deep but dreamless sleep, eyes wide open. Erin sits up as well, and we stare at each other like strangers. There is no sluggishness in my mind this time; I know exactly where I am.

She clutches at me, so I pull her close.

"Was that a gun?"

"Yep. Does that happen often?"

"No. I've never heard one, at least one that close." She nestles her head on my shoulder and pushes her forehead against my neck. "It sounded like it was right outside."

The air conditioner picks that moment to kick in, and the room is suddenly filled with its low hum. Then another shot makes me flinch, and I am out of bed in a flash. I move to the window, heart pounding in my throat, and I'm ready to dive to the floor if I have to. Sliding the curtains aside, I struggle to see something below.

The night hangs over the hill with the barest hint of light from the sliver of a moon. From this side of the building, there is a clear view of Puget Sound. A ferry is on the water, speeding away from the city, and a cargo ship sits silhouetted against the backdrop of the island across the way. I try to see over the side of the building to the street, but what little I can make out is clear of people. Another pair of shots, these close together, and one is a loud boom that sounds like a shotgun.

I stand at the window for another minute, but there isn't anything I can do. If people are sorting their feelings out with bullets, I don't need to get involved. I go back to the other side of the bed, the side on which I am not used to sleeping, and slip beneath the covers. Erin drapes her warm body over mine so that one leg arches over my waist and her arm rests on my chest. I slip an arm under her neck, and she slides her head next to mine.

I am wide awake again. I glance at the clock, and it is close to 3:00 a.m. As she pointed out, it is very hard to sleep in another bed, but I can't think of a single place I would rather be right now. We chat quietly about nothing, just lovers enjoying each other's company. She tells me that she has yoga in the morning but she may skip it, I tell her I need to go home and feed my cat, Buster, and make sure he didn't eat the bird. I invite her to go with me, and she agrees with a long yawn that reminds me I should be sleepy. With her nuzzled against me, the last thing I want to do is escape into slumber. I want to feel her next to me and savor every moment.

She will have to drive, but she says it is okay. I tell her that if I am going to stay in the city for the rest of the weekend, I should bring my car in as well. I don't come out and ask her if I should stay, but she asks me to immediately, then I offer my larger house for us, and she is silent for a moment.

"Maybe not right away," she says with a slight hesitation, and I can imagine why. The house was mine and Rita's and Andy's, and while I am the only inhabitant now, there are pictures of us in every room. It would probably be uncomfortable.

With Erin's scent filling my nose and the thought of being with her all weekend fueling my tired thoughts, I drift off a half hour later, all too aware that my arm is going to be very sore in the morning and yet unwilling to remove it from underneath her neck. As I drift off, I am pretty sure I hug her to me one more time.

* * *

Mornings are a bitch for me. I hate the gummy glue in my eyes, the cotton balls in my mouth, the grogginess as I want nothing more than to sink back into sleep. The lag as I stare at the clock and wonder how many times I can hit snooze. I hate that I am so alone that I am glad to see my cat, which is ornery enough to take a dump by my shoes if things aren't going his way. Glad that he decides to make a bed in mine most nights so that when I wake up he can grace me with a look from his luminous eyes.

This morning starts in a similar way. I wake to sunlight, which is annoying. I press my head into the pillow, but I know it is still bright out there. The smell is different, not my familiar washing liquid or softener or the stupid little sheet I sometimes put in the dryer.

Then I realize the smell of coffee is permeating the room. It is odd, because I never figured out how to set the timer on my fancy coffee maker that does all that stuff for me. Only to lose the setting the next time there is a power outage.

There is something else different this morning, and that would be morning wood. When is the last time that happened? I roll over and stare at Erin's curtains. They are cracked open just enough to let in the morning but not enough to blind me.

I can smell her everywhere. A clean scent of soap and shampoo with hints of vanilla. I don't remember her ever going crazy with the perfume or fancy hand cream. She has a very smooth complexion, and come to think of it, she rarely piles on the makeup—or she is an expert at subtlety.

I think of last night, how she got on top of me and leaned over so her breasts were in perfect view. I sat up a bit so I could nibble at them, and then she rolled her head back and rode me with my hands circling her slim waist.

This isn't helping the current state of affairs in my boxers, so I roll out of bed and find the bathroom. Splashing some water on my face and hair helps. Then I look in the mirror at the one-day growth of beard. The gray that nestles there is a full decade early. The wiry light brown hair that almost crinkles as I push it forward. My eyes are wide awake for a change; one thing with which I was blessed was good vision, so there are no daily rituals with contacts or keeping glasses clean as Leonard is apt to avoid. Once I am somewhat presentable, I find my shirt and slip it on. It smells like yesterday, and I wish I had a change of clothes.

I walk into the living room and find my way to the kitchen. Erin is dressed in a flowery robe that hangs around the seat of the chair. She faces away from me, and she has one lovely leg bent at the knee, foot perched on the chair in front of her. She reads what looks like a newspaper, probably the Seattle Times.

She turns as I enter the room. Her hair hangs around her face, looking like she just came from a salon. She is fresh faced, and her eyes sparkle. She is, without a doubt, the most beautiful thing I have ever seen.

She smiles, and I have to pause, dizzy because I am confused by what I feel for her, by how deeply I feel for her. I have denied myself so long that it is a bit overwhelming.

"Are you okay?"

"Yeah. Waking up in a strange place and all ..."

"Is my condo really strange? I mean I don't have any shrunken heads on the wall, no Voodoo dolls. My vampire outfit is at the cleaners, and the time machine left without me."

She is always such a smartass. I lean over and kiss her on the lips without preamble. Her eyes go wide, and she kisses me back.

"Thanks for the update on weird; I guess I'm behind the times."

"I should say so," she smirks. "I have been dropping hints for months. I considered dropping a large weight on your head but thought better of it, you know, in case there was anything up there."

"Erm."

"You aren't a morning person, but I can work with that. Grab a cup of coffee."

"That sounds fantastic. I need about a gallon this morning."

"That tired, eh? I guess I did try to wear you out."

"You did a wonderful job. I'll be sure and return the favor today." I grin at her.

I flip through three cupboards before I locate the coffee cups. My mood is already great, but the coffee makes it even better.

LESTER

Daylight has been pouring through the blinds for at least an hour. Lester rolls over a few times. He tugs the covers over his face, then tries to use a pillow to block the cursed rays out. He sits up after another half hour of tossing and turning. Angela is asleep on her stomach. There is only a thin sheet covering her naked body. He follows the line of her ass up to her back. His head pounds, and he has a smoky taste in his mouth, which is as dry as a sponge left in the sun for a couple of days. The only thing he wants is about a gallon of ice-cold water.

He hauls himself out of bed and walks naked to the bathroom. He fills and drains a tall glass with lukewarm water a few times, belches, scratches his balls and considers going back to bed.

There is a tiny window over the toilet, and as he relieves himself— a long steady stream of piss that echoes around the quiet room—he glances at the road. He expects to see a few of the deaders walking around, but there is no one in sight. Thank God that's over! There is a loud sound off to the east like a car crash. He tries to peer around the corner of the window, but he can't see anything. Oh well, it's not his problem. He flushes, leaves the lid open and looks in the mirror over the sink. Dark circles line his red eyes, not red like those fuckers outside, but the red of the recently exhausted, previously stoned, and very much hung over.

The bed is warm and inviting when he returns to it, and he even snuggles over to Angela. She murmurs to herself, turns on her side and starts snoring softly again. He slips his arm around her slim waist and pulls up close to spoon. Within minutes, he is fast asleep.

* * *

"Babe, we need some hot water!" Angela calls from the bathroom.

165

The water was running, but it was a low-pressure stream that barely rinsed the soap off his body. The water felt like ice needles when he stepped in, and it was probably the fastest shower of his life. As he stood shivering in the warming house, he couldn't help but laugh at Angela's squeal when she stepped in. He watched her move under the water for a couple of minutes as he dried himself. Her nipples stiffened under the cold, and goose bumps stood up all over her body.

He goes back to the bedroom, half hard and slips into a clean pair of sweats he finds on a shelf in the walk-in closet. They are up top, half hidden behind a couple of old pillows, which have a slight musky smell. He finds a shirt that isn't too ratty, a long-sleeved thing that he leaves open in front. They have a plan today to soak a pile of clothes in the tub, wash them in the shower and then hang them up to dry all over the house. As it warms today, they should dry. They aren't in a hurry, after all; there is plenty of food for a few more days.

Dressed, he heads back to the bathroom for another peek.

"Hot water would be such a luxury," she says with chattering teeth.

"Want me to warm you up?" he puts one hand in the shower and runs it over her wet back and ass.

"No I don't want you to warm me up! I'm fucking freezing in here, and all you are doing is thinking with your cock!"

"I was just playing around, babe. You know, trying to keep it light."

"You wanna keep it light? Keep it light by getting us out of here, Les. I'm sick of being cooped up, and you said yourself it wasn't that bad out there. So let's get the fuck out there!" she pleads, pointing in the general direction of Seattle, voice going high in a way that he finds unpleasant.

"Why are you mad at me? I been doing my best, babe. I went to the house and got all that shit for us. Christ!"

"I don't want to be stuck here anymore, that's all. I appreciate it, babe, but I want to get out. Let's go see some smiling people for a change. We haven't even left the house in a couple of days."

"Do you really think it's such a good idea to go out there? Those fucking things are everywhere. We are so much safer here." He wants to lose his cool and yell at her, but what good would that do? He'd gag her, but she would probably tell him she isn't into any weird shit and storm out of the room.

"How do you know? How do you know they're everywhere? Maybe they're just in this area or in our neighborhood. Maybe no one knows and we need to get word out. Remember what the news said? They are normal people that are disoriented. We're supposed to be nice to them."

"Now you just sound fucking stupid. If you saw that bitch attack me last night, trying to bite me ... I'm not kidding you; she attacked me like I was a steak dinner on a deserted island. It's bullshit. Whatever the news guys are telling us is a lie."

"Don't you call me stupid, asshole." She frowns as she steps out of the icy water. Hints of conditioner run down her face, over skin blue from the cold and lips pale as milk, which cover chattering teeth. She stomps her foot, shaking suds all over the floor. Normally he can't take his eyes off her naked body, but right now he wants to push her down and scream at her. Stupid bitch, like he got them into this.

"Tell you what, babe. You go ahead and go out there and spread the word that we're trapped here. Meanwhile I'll be downstairs trying to get the goddamn TV working so I can find out something, okay!?" He yells the last word and turns to leave. A single sob stops him in his tracks. He turns around, and she is wiping tears from her eyes. He should say he is sorry, but he doesn't.

* * *

Les fires up the generator and follows the cable out of the bedroom, down the stairs, checking each connection as he goes. He hits the power strip when he is in the big living room, and the TV comes to life. He flips around, but there is little in the way of news. Some channel has reruns of an old primetime drama about doctors. This makes great background noise as he opens a can of corned beef hash.

Their four-star meal this morning will also include mandarin oranges and some fried potatoes. Last night they put the little propane stove near the fireplace and tested it. He can't remember if this is one of the devices that can cause carbon monoxide poisoning, so he plays it safe by maneuvering the thing right under the fireplace vent.

He goes through a bag of spuds and finds a couple that are just on the verge of going soft. They have little roots growing out of them, but they are easily snapped off. He peels them into a plastic bag. That will make another sack for the guest bedroom upstairs later. They get a dash of salt and some pepper, and then he tosses them into a shallow layer of oil that shimmers in the morning light. The smell makes his stomach rumble. As they get close to being done, he dumps the can of corned beef hash in and starts salivating like a St. Bernard.

Angela makes it downstairs. She's dressed in jeans and a tight t-shirt with the word 'Paramore' on it. It was her band of the week a year ago. Her hair hangs in her face, blond and frizzy. Probably needs a hair dryer to fix, not that he cares. She looks fresh from the shower, if a bit like a lost waif.

She stands at the bottom of the steps for a minute and closes her eyes. She inhales and smiles a shy smile as if she has a secret. Then her face goes flat and she walks toward him. Wondering if he is due another argument that will snap his considerable patience, he prepares for the worst.

"That smells amazing," she says and stops to stare up at him. Without heels, she stands a full five foot two, not that he is a giant by any stretch. Just seven inches on her, which is considerably less when she wears high heels.

"Thanks."

"Look, I ..." they both start and then chuckle, and for a minute Lester feels like he is on some sitcom where everything is scripted and they follow roles. The words were there, somewhat rehearsed. He was going to apologize, but instead he waits for her to do it first.

She sighs and sits down on the couch. He dishes up a plate of food and hands it to her. She eats and stares at the TV, which is now broadcasting nothing but snow.

"Where's the news and stuff?"

"Don't know. They said there was a problem, and it just went dead a few minutes ago. I'm sure it will be back s-" he is interrupted by a loud rattling near the front of the house.

"What the hell?" He goes to the front door and pulls aside the curtain covering the little window.

"Oh fuck! Fuck! Fuck!"

He turns and runs across the room to find his AR-15, which is against the wall, near the kitchen. He snaps it up and grabs an extra magazine while he is at it.

"Get every bullet you can find and pile them up on the table," he commands as he runs back to the door.

"What's wrong, babe?"

"Get every gun, every bullet you see. Just fucking do it!" he yells.

"God, Lester, what is wrong with you today?" But she stands and picks up the Glock and a box of shells that are on the coffee table. She brings them over to Lester, who has the magazine from the automatic. His hand shakes so badly he can barely get the damn gun loaded. He snaps bullets in as fast as he can, but some fall and clatter to the wood floor. She sets the gun down and studies him for a second.

"What is it, babe?"

"Get the other guns!" he screams in her face.

"Oh my God, you have really lost it today!" She storms to the door and pulls the curtain aside. She stares outside and then looks at him in disbelief. The blood drains from her face. "We are so fucked, Les." She heads upstairs. He hopes she is going to get more ammo, not to get high.

* * *

Lester is ready for war. He has the AR-15 loaded and an extra magazine in his back pocket. The Glock is in the band of his pants, and it tugs them down, but he couldn't give a fuck less. There are boxes upended everywhere with shells sorted. He has the old shotgun he bought at Walmart a year ago ready and near the front door. He gives Angela a quick rundown of how to cock the thing, eject the shells and reload it. The shotgun will be a last-ditch weapon just in case the deaders make it as far as the house.

"Why, Angela? Why are they here now?" he asks for the third or fourth time.

"Maybe they're starving and they know we have food."

"That is the stupidest fucking answer ... wait a minute. Holy shit, you are a genius."

"What?"

"It's the noise, the generator, it sounds like a goddamn chainsaw, and they are attracted to the noise! Go kill it. There's a switch on the side; hit it until the thing cuts off. Go!"

"I'm going, Lester. Jesus." She stomps off.

He steps to the door and puts his hand on the doorknob. He takes a deep breath. He just needs to get a quick count, see how badly they are outnumbered. He turns the knob and steps out onto the porch with the gunstock pressed to his shoulder.

There must be a hundred of the fucking things. They are a moaning mass that presses against the chain link fence, arms out as if they can reach the house from there. They range in size from short and female to large and fugly. He thinks he may recognize one or two of them from the neighborhood. Maybe he has seen them at the market or when he stopped for gas.

A scream from the other end of the street, and a woman in a floral print sundress runs in his direction. She whips her head back at a pair of deaders that are hot on her heels. She recoils when she sees the mass in front of his house and makes the mistake of trying to run the other way. She slams to a stop, dodges one way and is picked off by the other deader. She goes down howling, her screams echoing up and down the street.

"Oh God no!" he says and raises the rifle to his shoulder, but there is no shot. They tear into her, and her screams attract others. Some leave his fence and join the mass on the ground. Before a half-minute is over, the woman stops screaming and the street is quiet again but for the sound of tearing cloth—or it might be skin.

"You mother fuckers," Lester mutters, hands shaking in rage. Not going out like that. Not going out like that.

One of the women in front has her shirt ripped off so her tits sway freely as she is pressed by the mass from behind. She may have been attractive at one time, but now her body is drenched in blood, and there is a dry mess down her stomach that may be puke. Hell, for all he knows, it is brain matter. Her hair is black on one side and hangs to her shoulders. There is nothing on the other side except bare skull where her scalp has been torn off.

There is a pair of Asian men who have identical bite marks on their necks, but they are as far from twins as they can be. One is tall and has reddish hair and a chunk of his neck missing. The other is short, older, serious-looking and missing a chunk from the other side of his neck. They stand together and howl at Lester. It's like a sea of deaders that stretches away from the house and across the street ... and more arrive by the minute.

He presses the gun to his shoulder, tight, aims and—BAM—the shirtless woman goes down. Her body flops over backwards from the impact, then lands in the mass of deaders.

BAM and one of the Asian twins falls. That shot was a beauty, took the guy's brainpan and shoved it out the back of his fucking head. BAM, the stock hammers into his shoulder and another one drops.

"Get your ass out here and drop some deaders!" he yells.

A shot in the distance tells him someone else is having the same kind of trouble. Maybe it is the Guard dudes on the way. At this point, he would welcome them with open arms. Hell, he won't even get mad if they want to stare at Angela's rack while she serves them lemonade. He giggles maniacally at that image and then fires again.

Angela whirls through the door with the 9 mm in hand, aimed just like he taught her, arms out straight, elbow slightly bent. She takes up a wide stance and stares down the barrel, but she doesn't fire.

BAM. A balding black guy loses the top of his head and flops into the heap. The others ignore his body and clamor to their feet. The stock hammers into his shoulder over and over as he drops one after another until all thirty rounds have either found marks or flown off into the distance. He pops another magazine in and then goes automatic by pulling the gun forward with his left hand, gunstock barely resting against his shoulder so he can 'bump fire' the weapon. Most of a magazine disappears in the wave of deaders as the gun bounces off his chest. His finger over the trigger means that with each recoil it fires again, and again.

"Shoot 'em, Angel!" he pleads.

"I can't shoot people, I can't!" she cries.

"They aren't people, Angela, they're deaders. DEADERS! If they reach us, we are fucking dead." But that's not the only reason. He thinks of the woman he saw torn to shreds, and he is pissed.

"Oh no. I can't!" she cries.

BAM, he drops a skinny guy who claws free of the mass. He is covered in fresh blood, and most of his chin is already gone. Strips of flesh hang as the bone works up and down. BAM, the gun rocks him back again, and he has lost count of the shots. How many does he have left?

"Do it! I need to reload soon!"

He looks out the corner of his eye, and she still has the gun leveled. She takes a breath, sights, and then the gun bucks in her hand so hard that she nearly drops it. The pistol flies up, but she recovers and lowers it. A woman with a missing arm drops to the ground, shot through the neck. It is a beauty; the bullet enters through a tiny hole and then exits with part of her spinal cord to pelt the deader behind her. She aims at that one and blows his face open.

"Oh my God, oh my God, oh my fucking God," she cries as she fires.

Lester smiles and wishes he could take a minute to reassure her, but there are more pressing matters at hand, like a shitload of deaders.

He fires again, and the shot slides along the face of a woman with red, frizzy hair and takes off part of her ear. She howls and staggers forward, flops over the fence, and just like that the tiny barrier that has protected them collapses in the middle. Several of the deaders pressing against the fence fall forward and land in his yard in a great rippling wave as the chain link tinkles together. It was just a matter of time, gonna have to shoot them all now. He sights the center of her head and squeezes, but the impact for which he is prepared doesn't happen, as the hammer clicks on empty.

He reaches up and, with hand shaking, tries to hit the release. His finger fumbles over the latch, and it doesn't come loose. The woman has a hard-on for him as she staggers forward.

Timothy W. Long

Fifteen feet.

He hits the damn release again, and the magazine hits the porch.

Ten feet.

He grabs the metal magazine. Fumbles it in his hand and nearly drops it. He dumps a box of bullets on the small tabletop. Beer bottles from the day before fall on the deck and roll around like loose bowling pins. He grabs a handful of the shells and starts ramming them in as fast as he can.

"Lil' help here, babe!"

Five feet.

The girl gets closer. One slow step at a time. She might move faster, but she is dragging her left leg, leaving a streak of blood with each step. Her eyes aren't white; they have been consumed by that bloody pupil that looks like a crimson marble, which he is getting sick and tired of seeing. He gets half a dozen shells in, and it will have to do for now, because Angie is in her own world.

"BABE!"

He flips the magazine over.

Two feet.

He rams it home with trembling hands. Angie squeals, turns and blows the top of the deader's head off.

"Sorry."

"Jesus, that was a great shot." He smiles at her and fires the six rounds as fast as he can. Then he has a few seconds to do a full reload.

She clicks on empty, so he rams the full magazine home and steps forward, resting his waist against the wood fence that encompasses the space. She sits back in the chair in which she lay tanning yesterday and reloads the pistol. Her hands shake, and she drops as many shells as she puts in, but she gets the job done. Lester watches from the corner of his eye and grins when she gets the gun loaded.

There is a crash from the back of the house that scares the crap out of him. Lester wants to run around the side of the house and see what the hell is going on. Probably nothing, probably just a dog wandering around. Yeah, that's it, a dog. A big-ass dog whose only purpose in life is to scare the shit out of Lester. This is worse than a movie, worse than anything he has ever seen before. He fires again, and one of the deaders drops in his tracks. There are so many, though, and they are coming over the bend in the fence.

Another wanders into the yard and then another. This one looks like your garden-variety stay-at-home mom minus the kids and soccer-mom-approved minivan. He shoots three times, and three answering holes stitch up her chest until one takes out her throat and she flops down, hands at her side.

He adjusts his aim and fires at a big guy who is missing part of his head. How the hell do they survive damage like that? Then there are five in the yard, then seven. Angie fires as fast as she can draw a bead on each one. Lester, being only halfway decent at math, runs the numbers in his head and realizes that they can't fire fast enough to stay ahead of the deaders. Nope, not unless someone shows up with a big Gatling gun or maybe a flamethrower. On the next episode of cooking with the drug dealer, we have a fantastic recipe for Deader Flambé.

"In the house, babe. We can't stop them here."

She is in the seat again, leaning forward as she reloads, trying to focus on the magazine and not the yard. She looks up and yells when she sees the deaders swarming. She stands up, knocking over the box of shells and nearly losing the gun as well. Lester takes it from her shaking hand and puts the magazine in his pocket. He grabs as many of the bullets as he can and drops them in the box. He opens the door and ushers her inside.

As he turns to dash inside, the rest of the fence gives and the entire world pours into his yard. The first one reaches the stairs, and instead of giving them the finger, he opens up in bump fire mode again and takes chunks out of the first row. It's like someone started a chainsaw. Bodies twist and flop under the impact, and for a half-second he thinks of Tony Montoya at the end of Scarface. That's right, bitches, my little friend has some advice … fucking die! Some drop, but most reel back, recover and keep on coming.

Then he is through the door, and he slams it shut. He rams the deadbolt home and leans against the door, panting.

Now what the fuck are they going to do?

KATE

Fever-dream, pain and salvation. The men she has lured to hotel rooms wander into her mind, one after another. They weep and plead for another chance just before she cuts off their cocks. They beg her for mercy just before she forces their own members into their screaming mouths. Then they rise up with blood dribbling from the centers of their waists. Gaping holes that yearn to be filled by the handle of her flogger.

They fall to the ground and worship her, and then they try to eat her.

She wakes with a scream. At least she thinks it's a scream. Maybe it is one of the victims in her head, perhaps the guy from last night—Walter. What will his wife think when he doesn't return? What will she say when the police deliver the news that he was found dead in a hotel room? Will she scream or cry, deny it, say it isn't possible? Will she weep instead and close the door quietly in their faces, then smile, knowing that her vile husband and his obsession with hurting women is over?

Maybe she knows about him; maybe he hides videos on the computer that she knows how to find. Maybe she has seen the emails and stories from girls he met on Craigslist. On the singles sites. Maybe she chooses to ignore them in the interest of keeping peace in the house, of not asking too many questions, perhaps of being afraid of the answers.

Maybe she has a large insurance settlement on her precious Walter and now she is a rich woman. Maybe he is just dead and the wife was a lie. She will never know.

She will never care.

* * *

First things first: coffee, coffee and more coffee. She slams the first cup after splashing it over a handful of ice, then sips the second as she cooks a pair of white bread slices to a dry crisp in her toaster. When they are done, she will slather them in butter and let the bread sit and soak up the greasy mass. She likes to lay out a big pile of raspberry jam and scoop it up with the soggy bread. Later she will make grilled cheese toast and dip it in tomato soup and try not to think about the color of blood.

Once the toast is ready, she will eat the edges first, the crispiest sides, then she will eat the centers, licking melted butter off her fingers as it dribbles down. Third cup poured, she flips through the Seattle Metro and reads the eclectic mix of stories. Then she pops on the TV and turns to the news channels. They are running stories that look just like the crap they ran yesterday. A shooting in Tacoma. Well, what day doesn't have that? She flips over to a local news station that is playing a mix of local and world news, entertainment, gardening, sports, and even a section on high school athletics. Right now there is a live broadcast featuring a military man behind a desk with a concerned look on his face.

The video quality is poor, as if they are using some old equipment to broadcast or the signal is degraded. The sound comes through, though, and that is all she cares about.

She sits her bruised backside and legs down on the ancient couch and kicks her feet up as she adjusts the volume.

"… and if you have containers, please fill them with water and set them in a cold, dark place for now. If you have stores of food, particularly canned goods, save those for last, eat what you have in your refrigerator first, move on to the freezer, then the canned items if you have to. My people will be around today checking up on the elderly, and delivering food and water to shelters. Remember, folks, if you see a man in military uniform and he calls out to you, please take a moment to identify yourself by stating your name, and you will be free to go. This way we can quickly identify those who are sick and get them the medical attention they need."

What the hell is this? Are they going to start asking for papers with German accents next?

The Asian reporter stares at him in rapt attention, but when the focus shifts to her, she goes into what Kate likes to think of as robot mode, reading the screen back with a plastic face.

"Going back to our top news story, a sickness has struck some of the citizens of Seattle. It appears to have originated in the Queen Anne district, where a gas leak started several days ago. Although city employees are working around the clock, they have been unable to stop the leak. Those sickened appear disoriented and may become violent. The authorities are asking that you treat them humanely. Those who are ill appear to be in distress. We are asking the people of the city to stay put for now. When everything is under control again, we will bring you more information."

Kate flies out of her chair as the story repeats. She turns on her aging computer and waits for the Windows XP screen to appear. After what seems like forever, she enters her password and opens a web browser. The little icon in the top right corner spins, and the status bar at the bottom shows one green bar. After a few seconds, she gets the infuriating 'This page cannot be displayed' message.

She goes to CNN, MSNBC, and BBC, then tries to open Google and Yahoo, but none of them loads. She checks her router, but she barely understands the thing. She followed a simple guide to set it up, and when everything worked, she left it alone and didn't bother to go back and read the manuals. There seemed to be no point, since support was just a phone call away.

The TV stays on in the background, but they just repeat the story over and over again.

She knows enough to reset the computer's router and reboot everything. They always say to leave stuff off for thirty seconds, but no power is no power in her book, so she boots everything after barely a second and gets the same result.

She throws on her robe, belts it in the front, walks across the hall and bangs on Bob's door. There is silence for a good minute before the eyehole goes dark. Then the door pops open, and there he is in the same robe as last night, hair disheveled and beard scruffier than ever.

"Nice shoes," he smirks at her feet. They are encased in her favorite oversized Sylvester the cat slippers. They are huge, black and have big ears poking out the top. She got them as a gag gift from an old friend and just never got around to giving them up. They are warm and comfortable and make her feel young. She would have killed for a pair of these in her youth—well, maybe 'killed' is the wrong word, since she didn't come into that particular interest until a few years later.

"Yes they are. If you have Tweety ones, I'll chase you around."

"Hmm, let me check." He chuckles. "Anyway." He smiles. "Net down?"

She nods.

"Yep, me too. Wanna come in?"

"What the hell is going on out there, Bob? You're a smart guy; you always have things figured out. So what are they talking about on the news?"

"The mysterious illness, you mean? No idea. I mean, they aren't saying much. Well, they are saying a lot, but it's a lot about nothing."

"Huh?"

"Okay, look at it this way. They are going on about what to do, how to get by, what to store. They warn about what to look for, avoid the violent ones. It goes on for a long time, but they aren't talking about what caused it. Well, they say a gas leak, but who the hell goes insane from smelling gas? Even the major radio stations are running national news and making mention of what's happening here, but there's an emphasis on staying put, riding it out. For Christ's sake, it's Saturday. Half the city should be heading out for the day, but do you hear cars on the road?"

"I haven't been out yet." She spreads her arms wide as if he hasn't noticed she is still in her fucking bathrobe and ridiculous slippers.

"Okay, how many airplanes have you heard fly overhead in the last fifteen or twenty minutes?"

"None, but I usually don't hear ... " and then she realizes how quiet it has been. "Wait, I heard some traffic choppers earlier."

"Those were military: black helicopters with weapons mounted on the bottom. There is some serious shit going down."

"Do you have one of those radios, the meat one ... erm, HAM?"

"A HAM radio? You must think I am really fucking pathetic." He grins.

"Cell phone!" She snaps her fingers. She will call the bookstore and see if they're open today.

"Doesn't work. I tried mine already, and all I get is a fast busy signal, like the last time we had an earthquake and the lines were overwhelmed."

"That's strange."

"You think so, Captain Obvious? We have cell towers on just about every building. You couldn't get away from a cell phone if you tried. I would be willing to bet that other providers are having the same problem. I have Verizon, how about you?"

"AT and T of course—iPhone." She smiles.

"So try it."

Kate heads back to her apartment and retrieves her cell phone from her purse. She autodials the shop, but it just rings. Then she tries her favorite pizza joint and gets a fast busy. She doesn't have a land line anymore, so she tries one more number.

"You have reached 911 emergency. Please stay on the line and someone will be with you shortly. We apologize for the inconvenience."

After a minute of the message repeating itself and Bob's eyes staring into hers, the line goes dead. She shrugs. "I guess 911 is too busy to take calls right now."

Screaming outside preempts whatever she was going to say next. Bob moves through his apartment to the sliding glass door on his patio. She is hot on his heels. Kate has been in his apartment before, but she still feels like an intruder. He has decent furnishings. His couch is newer and pale brown leather. A matching lazy boy chair seems to be the centerpiece. It sits five or six feet from a big flat panel television mounted on the wall. There are a bunch of wires all over the place, because he may have every gaming console known to man.

He also has a good-sized computer desk covered with discs and parts. There are several cases on the floor, and some of them are open, revealing hard drives and fans of all shapes, sizes and colors.

He slides the drapes open, and they both crowd around the door. On the street below, a girl backs away from a pair of men who are … Is that blood on their shirts?

The girl turns to run, but one of the men pounces, moving fast as a cat. He grabs her by the hair, and they both tumble to the ground. Bob rips the door open and is on the deck in a heartbeat.

"Hey asshole, what the fuck?" he yells, and there is some east coast attitude in the voice. Kate has never asked him where he is from, but she is betting on New York now.

The guy stares up at him, and the other one actually hisses in their direction. Kate thinks about the gun he showed her the night before, but a feeling of helplessness washes over her, as she has never used one before. Now if she were on the street with her swords, it would be a different story.

"Identify yourself!" a voice shouts, and two soldiers dressed in green fatigues round the corner with guns drawn. One fires into the air, probably a warning shot, but the second guy just tries to stare them down. The first attacker has collapsed on the woman, who is not small; she rolls over and tries to fend him off. Being that she outweighs him by about fifty pounds, it seems likely she will succeed.

The man tries to bite her, but she presses her forearm against his throat.

"Help!" she screams as the guy continues snapping at her. He is in a frenzy like a dog. The other guy moves in and reaches down to grasp her foot. He drags her off the first man and then across the ground with her kicking the entire time. He is a slight kid, maybe sixteen years old, and Kate wonders how he can be so strong.

"Hey asshole, let her go!" Bob calls out again, but he obviously feels like she does. Helpless. He turns to look Kate in the eye, and she sees pain there, as though he were the one being assaulted. Must be nice to have feelings. A heart.

"I said, identify yourself!" One of the soldiers calls again, and when they don't answer, he tightens his grip on the gun and a single shot echoes across the neighborhood. The attacker on top of the woman rears up from the shot. His head whips back, then he falls to the side.

The first one leaps to his feet but is brought down by two shots, one from each gun. The two soldiers glance at each other, then one of them, visibly shaken, talks into a small device in the collar of his shirt. Voices, tiny and tinny, drift upward. The other man moves in on the woman, with his gun still pointed at her.

"Are you hurt, ma'am? Did one of them bite you?" His voice is small from where they stand, but Kate can tell it has a waver in it as if he is trembling.

The woman groans and rolls over and tries to get up on all fours. Her hands seem unsure, and Kate is positive it's just the adrenaline running through her body. The woman sobs and tries to stand, but the soldier closes in on her and points the gun at her face.

"Are you bit, ma'am? Did one of those things bite you?" She looks up at the gun and shies away, but she can't seem to find her voice. The other soldier continues talking into his little radio as if oblivious to the spectacle before him.

"She's in shock," Kate says but only loud enough for Bob to hear. She wants to jump off the little balcony, drop the fifteen feet to the ground and smack the shit out of the black guy who is pointing his gun at the lady.

"Ma'am, I am not going to ask you again: Are you bit? HAVE YOU BEEN BITTEN?"

She comes to her feet, and Kate can tell she is struggling. There is blood on her, but judging by the amount, it probably isn't hers. She tries to speak, tries to form words, but nothing comes out, and she just stammers for a second.

The soldier backs away from her, one slow backward step after another until he stands by his partner. They confer for a moment, and the woman, with shaking hand, lifts her pant leg to show the bloody bite mark. It's livid, and there is a small stream of blood flowing down.

Kate is only twenty feet away from the poor woman and feels shocked at the spectacle. The first soldier looks up in a panic and points up the street. They talk back and forth quietly in a heated argument that doesn't last long. The soldier with the radio looks at the woman, who now acts odd. Foam comes to her mouth, and she shakes in place. She drops to one knee as if in sudden pain, and her whole body trembles. She coughs loudly before a stream of blood spews from her mouth. It's red and ropy like it is thick with mucus. Strands of it hang down her chin and coat her shirt.

The soldier slams his gun against his shoulder, aims and shoots her in the head. She is whipped around by the force of the shot, her body flopping back at an impossible angle, knees flat on the ground. Her sightless eyes fix on Kate as her head falls back with a crack that seems as loud as the gunshot.

Kate backs up in horror and struggles not to scream. She wants to grab Bob's gun and shoot both of these assholes in the head. How would you like that, mother fuckers? She has seen death before, has caused it herself, but she was not prepared for the cold-blooded murder she just witnessed.

"Folks, get everyone out of your building and get away from here. They're coming!" he yells at them as if unaware that he just shot an innocent lady in the head.

"You shot her, man. You just killed some innocent woman. What the fuck gives you the right ..."

"You don't know what is going on out here, man, so just shut the fuck up. I did her a favor, 'cause now she can't turn into one of those things," the soldier yells back at Bob. "Just listen, grab what you can carry, warn everyone you can and get out of that building. This place is going to be overrun in a few minutes! This ain't no joke! If you want to live, you need to grab your girl and haul ass anywhere but here!"

An Army Humvee screeches around the corner followed by a second one. A truck also arrives, one of the big ones with a canvas top. It slams to a halt, and men and women pour out of the back. They are young, all of them and they look scared, but they seem to have the drill down as they stand in a line at attention. Meanwhile a couple of them haul a big gun out of the back and start setting it up. Another truck arrives, and men jump out and start dragging big sandbags into the street.

Kate turns to Bob, and he says the words she is mouthing, their voices parroting each other.

"What the fuck is going on?"

MIKE

The morning wears on and we manage to make it into the shower, together, which means it takes about three times as long as it should. Then we retire to her room to finish what we started under the pulsing blast of steamy water. Later as we lie close, comfortable, together, we talk about all manner of things while I trail my fingers over her warm flesh. We doze for a bit, and then she suggests that we head to my house.

We have been completely preoccupied with each other, unaware of what is going on out in the world. I get up from the bed naked as the day I was born and look outside to see if the weather has changed. This is Seattle, after all—if you don't like the weather, wait five minutes.

I expect to see cars on the street, and if I lean far enough out, I can probably make out Denny, which is a major road stretching between the waterfront, Seattle Center and I-5. What I don't expect to see are a couple of green trucks pulling onto the main street. Men in uniform get out, and I think of the other trucks I saw yesterday, on their way to destinations unknown. Now they are here and very real. I have to wonder what they are up to. It's creepy, seeing the damn things two days in a row. There is something going on, something huge.

I can feel Erin's eyes on me. I turn, and she smiles at me. A genuine smile that makes me feel a sudden overwhelming rush of affection. I walk to the bed, lean over and kiss her. I stare into her eyes for a moment, content and yet lost at the same time.

"I'm sorry it took me so long."

"It's okay, Mike. Next time I'll just hit you over the head with a club and drag you back to my lair."

"I think you did that last night." I laugh.

After a moment, she gets out of bed and dresses in jeans and a light-blue polo that looks amazing against her dark skin. I watch her slide into her clothes from the other side of the room. She stares at my state of undress and smirks; one eyebrow arches up. I go to her and hug her for no reason other than that I can. We kiss for a moment, and then she advises me that I can't stay naked all day.

We chat for a moment about how we will spend our time after we swing by my house. We come to the conclusion that we should take a scenic drive, maybe to Mt. Rainier. We can pick up goodies for a picnic on the way. Our plans settled, she goes to the bathroom to get ready, and I am left to my own devices. I can't wait to get out of the city. We seem to be making the assumption that whatever brought the soldiers to this part of the city won't keep us here.

When I am dressed and seated on her couch, I switch on the television and try to find the news. The local channels are showing sports and infomercials, but a red banner runs across the bottom of the screen. It keeps repeating something about a sickness. People are hurt, confused, and they might be dangerous. Dangerous? I hunt through my pants pockets, which are in a heap on the floor, until I find my phone. The little text message icon is lit and, sure enough, Leonard has sent several. I back up to the first one of the day. It came in around 7:00 a.m.

Mike, it's real, the virus. They have been covering it up, shutting things down … Cell phones are flaky, so I'm sending messages from mine just in case it works. They have nicknamed them deaders, and they have already taken over a couple of neighborhoods. The virus attacks the nervous system, shuts down the brain. Makes them appear dead. The people slip into a state that is like death, then they reanimate.

I nearly drop the phone at the message. Things like this happen in books and movies, not in real life. He is just setting up a joke. The next message is even more disturbing.

They are shutting down communication in the city so word doesn't get out, but you can bet your ass it won't last long. The virus, they are calling it Registrop, spreads through saliva. A bite from one of the victims takes about thirty seconds to do complete and irreparable damage. It is mutating. It seems to get stronger with each generation of infection.

The last message is from an hour ago.

Get out of the city. Go home, find a place to hide. If one of them attacks you, kill it. The Army guys are doing that now. They are shooting anyone who appears to be infected. They are stronger than us, faster. They want our blood. I know it sounds absurd—just get out, Mike.

Erin is still in the bathroom fixing her hair. The hair dryer clicks on and off, then there is the clink of things being placed on the sink, and she is actually humming. I want to go in there and pretend like nothing is wrong. I want to hold her and protect her. It can't be real, can't be. I read the messages over and over. It is not like Leonard to make jokes like this. But how can he think I will take it seriously?

I poke my head in the door to see what she is up to. She has a toothbrush hanging out of her mouth and is putting earrings in her lobes. They are short silver loops. She spits and shows me her pearly whites like a child.

"Okay, I know Leonard can be a little crazy at times, but this one takes the cake." I show her the message. She reads it and then reads it again.

"He must be joking."

So I show her the next message. She reads it and hands it back, no longer smiling. Gunfire from outside the building interrupts us, and we both jump. These aren't the distant shots we heard last night. These are much closer and much louder. More shots, and I rush to the bedroom to get a glimpse of the street, but I can't see over the side of the building. Besides, the shots sounded like they came from the other side.

"Let's just go to your house," she suggests, and I don't care anymore if Leonard is serious. I just want to get out of the city, go home, and watch the news. Surely the trouble hasn't reached as far as Auburn. It looks like we will have to postpone our picnic.

"Is your car close?"

"Yeah. There is a garage in this building. We can be out of here in a couple of minutes."

She squats and takes a small red plastic bag out of the cabinet under the sink and then starts sweeping items in. Hairbrush, wet toothbrush, toothpaste and a bottle of pills. She grabs a lipstick. I decide I have seen enough, so I go to her room to find my shoes and socks.

We meet in the hall, and she dashes past me to load another bag with clothes. I down my coffee, which has grown cold. A glance at the clock tells me it is nearly eleven.

She locks her condo, and we make for the elevator. It zips us to the parking garage, and there is her little red Honda Civic. I take her bags and put them in the trunk, then we pile into the car and she squeals out of the place and toward the garage exit.

She zips up the little driveway that rises to meet the street and almost runs into a man who wanders by as if in a daze. He doesn't bother to look at us.

She slams on her brakes, and we are both thrown forward. The guy doesn't even acknowledge us or the shriek of the tires. He walks into the street, on which cars are stretched in every direction. They are all at a standstill with more piling up behind them by the second. Horns honk, and people get out of their automobiles to stand around looking toward I-5. Others get on hoods and try to make out what the holdup might be.

Erin pulls up the little rise, but we aren't going anywhere. I pop out of the car, and it is easy to see why everyone is stopped. The camouflaged trucks I was worried about are more troublesome than I thought. They block the road, men piling out of them in an orderly fashion.

"What the hell is this?" Erin mutters.

"The gas leak maybe?" I know how dumb the words sound, but I refuse to believe what Leonard sent me earlier. I roll the window down and yell at one of the men in green who is going car to car, telling people something, pointing down toward the waterfront.

"What's going on?"

"You should get out of here, sir. This place is about to become a battlefield. The deaders have overrun Seattle Center. They're headed this way."

"Deaders?" I shrug my shoulders. Isn't that what Leonard called them?

"The ones with the virus. Just get out and head for the waterfront with all the others. More National Guards are on the way, so you should be safe." He doesn't sound very convincing.

When I look back, he is gone and more men pile out of the military vehicles. They look motivated. Some appear concerned, but they also seem confident as they pour into the city street with large guns in hand.

Has the city gone completely mad?

LESTER

Angela is sitting on the couch crying when Lester runs into the living room. He spares her a glance and then dashes to the back of the house. The generator is dead thanks to her pulling the plug. This leaves the TV cold and black. He runs to the sliding glass door and watches as hands feel along the top of the fence. The thin slats of wood that have fallen into disrepair are all that separates his house from the green belt. Where did they come from? The fingers move, shift, slide along the top, and it freaks Lester right the fuck out. He shivers violently.

"Ange, we're going to have to move upstairs. Grab everything you can and haul ass, babe. Get the guns and anything that looks like a weapon."

He runs to the kitchen and starts throwing as much food as he can into a box. The back fence groans and rattles, but it doesn't give. The front of the house is not as silent, because the rabid people are banging at the front door and pounding on the steps as more of them move onto the porch. He hauls the box into the living room and catches Angela lighting a joint.

"What the fuck?"

"If I'm going to die, Les, I'm going to die stoned and drunk." She tosses the handgun and a magazine into the box, then marches into the kitchen and comes back with a half-full bottle of Scotch. Lester doesn't comment, because after they get upstairs he may just join her, figuring it will be better to die drunk off his ass. He almost goes back for more booze, but the banging from the door scares the shit out of him. He gathers up the machine gun and heads for his secret stash.

There is a painting in the hallway of a pair of herons on a blue seascape. He yanks the frame up and then to the side to shake it off the four nails that hold it on the wall. It's a stretch as he reaches into a hole he cut there. He hooks his elbow and leans in until he feels the strap, then he pulls out a zippered black bag.

Reaching back into the hole, he comes out with a small .38 hammerless pistol. It is compact enough that he can stash it in his front pants pocket. It's a last-resort weapon, but right now he doesn't want to think about what he will do with it if he has to.

Angie puffs the joint while she continues to load stuff into a box. They grab bags and cardboard boxes they have both been filling and haul them upstairs. Louder and more desperate banging causes him to stumble and nearly fling the contents of one of the boxes all over the floor. A window shatters. Lester stops, one foot poised, and stares toward the front of the house. Deaders moan and wail. It sounds eerie, like a hard wind whistling through a cracked door. Lester watches the stairs, waiting for them to flood inside.

"Holy shit, Ange, I know how we can stop them!"

He grabs her hand, drags her into their bedroom and starts hauling drawers out of the oak armoire and tossing them on the floor. Then he runs into the kitchen, retrieves two towels and spreads them on the hardwood floor beside the heavy piece of furniture. He tilts it so all of his porn videos slide out of the double doors on top. Joining these is a pile of prescription drugs and a couple of sex toys Angela had brought over.

"What are you doing?"

"Help me drag this to the stairs!"

He pushes while she pulls, and they slide it on the towels. Lester hopes they will lessen the friction. One end has a decorative lip, and it drags across the floor, leaving a noisy furrow. When they reach the door, Lester quickly changes places with her and tilts the armoire over so it lies on its side. The thing is as heavy as an obese woman on a waterbed, and he ends up dropping the end. The sound reverberates across the house.

Downstairs, another window breaks.

He is in a panic, and when Angela doesn't move fast enough to help, he lashes out at her. "On the other end! Jesus fucking Christ!"

"Don't yell at me. I don't know how to move this big-ass thing!"

He sighs in frustration and sits with his back against the heavy wooden box, then pushes against the floor with his feet. The cabinet budges and then slides as he puts his back into it.

Angie stands back with her hands on her hips and watches. She finally gets the idea and drops down next to him. She digs her feet into the floor, but they slide as she pushes. It's better than nothing, though. It budges, and they are able to maneuver it out into the hallway. They push the old thing until it is out of the room, and then they both take hold and stand it up with a lot of groaning, which—ironically—sounds like the moans coming from downstairs.

"Fuck, that thing is heavy. We just need to slide it to the stairs."

"I think it's too big, babe." Angie observes, her eyes dropping a little.

"I hope so," he replies, shoving it closer to the stairwell. When it is lined up, he presses the top until it tilts and falls forward. It slams against the wall with a crash, takes a chunk out of the whitewall, and promptly becomes lodged in the stairwell as it slides to a halt at the bottom of the stairs.

"More shit, we gotta jam more shit in the stairs so they can't get up here," he gasps and runs back to the bedroom. The two nightstands join the first obstacle, then the bed frame with its bookshelf that is used to hold a stereo and CDs. Then everything in the guest bedroom joins the pile. An extra dresser he never found a use for. A mattress is jammed into the space above the furniture, and they back it all up with boxes of crap that he was planning to toss someday. Glad I put that shit off. A weight bench that has never seen use and even the standing ski machine Angie brought from her old apartment.

Soon a mountain of stuff blocks the stairs. There is no way those brain dead things are ever going to get up there. Of course, it also means there is no way he and Angela are getting out. They sit at the top of the stairs and study the pile they have created. Lester wipes at a river of sweat that is dripping down his forehead and wishes he had a line of coke right about now, just to stay sharp. He stares at the blocked passageway and starts laughing. After a couple of seconds, Angie joins him. Nervous energy leaks out of him like air from a balloon as he considers the giant mess they have made.

"Now how the hell are we getting out of here?" Angie turns to him. Her eyes are heavy and bloodshot. It's not just the pot. She is tired, just like him, and the problem is that he has no idea what to do next.

"I can't stay here with those things around," he replies. "I say we shoot our way out."

"Babe, there are too many of them. I mean, there are seriously like a hundred of those angry people out there. Ain't no way we can get them all. What we need is a really big car like John's. If we had that, we could ram our way out. We could head to town, find some cops—find some of the Army guys that are supposed to be in the city. Anything but hang around here."

She is making a lot of sense, and he knows it. John's overpriced luxury car probably weighs a ton or three.

The door finally gives below, and the deaders stumble into the house. His house. Bastards.

"John's SUV is still in his garage. I don't know how we can get to it, though."

"Jump the roof," she says.

"Too far. Probably a fifteen-foot jump."

"I can do it," she says.

"No, babe, you can't jump that far. No one can."

"Hmmm."

"Seriously. Imagine jumping to the end of the hallway from here, look how far that is."

He points to the wall at the other end of the hall where a painting of a spooky old woman hangs. She is dressed in the kind of stuff they wore a hundred years ago, severe black lace up to her neck. Her face doesn't have even a glimmer of a smile. Lester doesn't know who she is, but he liked the way the frame looked, so he left it, gave the place a dark feel as if the old lady were some kind of ghost. Now he couldn't care less about ever seeing anything scary for as long as he lives.

"Okay, I see your point."

The deaders mill around below, walking into stuff, knocking things over. There is a crash from outside as the wooden fence gives. They both jump up and run to the guest bedroom, which looks over the other side of the house, and sure enough at least fifteen of the people are making their slow way toward the house.

"We better think of something fast."

They are making a lot of noise below, and it is really pissing Lester off. He wants to take his gun, clear a space and start dropping the fuckers as they wander by. He has the nasty little surprise in his black bag as well. A little something that would take out a chunk of them for the small price of the destruction of part of the house. Well it's not like the house is even mine.

Stupid generator. Hauled the thing over here and all we got out of that deal was the attention of every deader nearby. Should have stayed put, waited it out, hunkered down and stuck with the weed and alcohol. Hell, we have a closet full of stuff we can drink.

The fence below is pretty close to the overhang of the roof on the other side of the house. He is pretty sure that if he hangs off the edge, he will be able to put his feet on the top of it, then drop down to John's yard, enter the house, avoid looking at the corpse of his former MILF neighbor, run to the garage and jump in the SUV.

Fuck! The whole idea is filled with fail because there are so many things that can go wrong. He doesn't have any cool James Bond toys.

He can't shoot a wire across the roof and have it stick to something, then slide across the gap.

"Come to the window with me and watch what I'm doing."

"Okay." She follows, eyeing the stairwell as they pass. Every step brings a creak in the wood no matter how softly they walk, and she has a look on her face that says she is sure the things below are about to break out the deader chainsaws and go to town on the barricade.

He slides the window open in the guest bedroom and then works the screen up and down until it comes loose. He starts to pull it in, but the thing slips, falls outside and slides down the roof, rattling as it goes like a string of firecrackers. He grimaces and holds his breath, but the screen just stops at the gutter and stays there.

He swings out of the window and carefully walks along the old tile. It is gritty for the most part, but there are signs of wear, which make it slippery under his Nikes. He stares down and avoids the spots as much as he can until he is near the edge. He looks over, and there is the top of the fence, but he sees the problem right away. He will only have one shot at this. One chance to drop over the edge, swing his body away from the house and somehow make contact with the top of the fence. Lester is all too fucking aware that he is anything but an acrobat. In fact, he is one of the most uncoordinated people in the world.

Angie, on the other hand, was a dancer at one time and is quite light on her toes. He motions for her to join him, so she slithers out the window and just as carefully as he did a moment ago, creeps outside, following in his footsteps.

She isn't wearing shoes and seems to have a better grip than he does. She joins him, and he leans over and whispers in her ear what he has in mind. She looks at him, shock painting her face before she looks down at the drop, at the fence and then at the roof.

"Okay, let's do it," she says with conviction. Lester wishes he felt as confident.

MIKE

There is nowhere to take her car. The streets are at an absolute standstill, and the National Guards are directing the cars that have been sitting to get out of the way, up onto sidewalks if they have to. More military trucks are trying to maneuver through the alley that has been cut in the stream of automobiles. People stand around talking, joking, pointing at the men in green. A helicopter thumps in the distance, and we raise our heads, hands in a salute to cut out the sun as we watch the copter rattle across the sky. It weaves into view like a black wasp, pods bristling with weapons. Another arrives behind it, and it is an older one, the kind you'd see in an old Vietnam movie.

This is surreal, and the only thing I can think of to compare it to is the WTO riots ten years ago when the streets were turned into a battle zone. Only then it was an army of police against an army of civilians, and the civilians didn't come out so well. I can't believe that these guys are telling me that virus-infected crazy people are on the way and they are the only thing that can stop them. Call me a bleeding heart liberal, but you just don't use machine guns to stop sick people.

I notice that most people have cell phones and are holding them up as they capture the scene on video. Some of the guards ask those near them to stop. Some comply, but others—most likely thinking that this is America and they can do whatever they want to—continue to film.

One overzealous Guardsman decides he is in the right, so he snatches a phone with a look that promises violence. He throws it on the ground to the indignant cries of the owner—a man in shorts and a tank top with a Seattle Mariners hat turned around backwards. The guy grabs the Guard on the shoulder, and the Guard responds by reaching up and by some twist of the wrist pulling the guy's hand off him and then forcing him nearly to the ground with as much ease as if he were flicking a fly off his clothing.

Some stop filming but others, farther away, turn their cameras on the drama.

A pair of men comes into view, and they look very sick. One of them is dressed in shorts and a pair of flip-flops. His shirt is filthy, torn and disheveled. The tails flutter around him in the gentle breeze, and he glances about as if confused, then he walks into the back of a car, recoils, goes around it and continues advancing on us at a sedate pace.

The other man is much taller and dressed like someone who works at a ticket booth or concession stand. He is young and would have more of a gangly gait if he weren't leering at everyone he passed. A group of Asian tourists are walking at a fast clip when one of them stops and points. Tiny phones snap pictures as the skinny kid takes notice of them.

One of the men steps out of the group and says something I can't hear. By way of answer, the sick guy strikes him across the face and then falls on him like a vulture descending from the sky.

I can't see what happens to the kid after that as the others surround them. There is screaming as the group tries to pull the guy off their companion. This is all starting to remind me of the video we watched yesterday of the attack and the crowd's response. One of the men reels back from the group with a long gash across his face.

They are a good fifty feet away, and I take a step forward as if my feet have a mind of their own, then Erin is there to grab my hand and pull me back. I look at her face, which is a picture of misery as she watches the men and women fight.

A couple of guards peel away from their group and approach with rifles pointed down. They are large black machine guns—I'm guessing M-16s. One of the tourists lets out a real scream and falls away with blood pumping out of a stump of his arm. The rest of the limb is in the hands of an attacker, who is chewing on it, his face contorted with insanity. He snarls and moans as he eats. There are maybe fifteen or twenty spectators on the road, staring and pointing. Then one of them screams, and suddenly there is a stampede as the onlookers realize what they are seeing.

This isn't a staged performance! This is real.

The kid jumps off his victim, flies back as if kicked and lands on his back with a thud but continues to clutch the length of arm, blood trailing from it to splatter his shirt, his face, and the road. That kick was hard enough to break bones, and the man behind the boot is an enormous black soldier.

To my surprise, the kid leaps off the ground from a crouch and is on the other Guard in a half-heartbeat. The guy thrashes back, falls under the attack, and then his hands pummel the crazed man.

"It's one of them!" the soldier screams, and all guns are suddenly pointed at them both.

"No," I mutter to myself over and over. This can't be happening.

"No," Erin echoes my thoughts in a loud, high gasp of shock.

"NO!" screams the guy who is being attacked.

The Guard lashes out his foot in a front kick that connects with the kid's head, flinging him to the ground. He aims his machine gun, and it spits three or four times. The attacker is driven into the concrete, then snaps up as each bullet punches into his head. Then he is still, and so is every onlooker.

A fresh scream sets off a slow exodus as the pedestrians watching the scene start backing away. I'm rooted in place, horrified and angry. The Guard who was attacked staggers to his feet. He holds his neck, hands pressed to the side where a geyser of blood squirts from a ragged tear. The Guard who just executed the attacker looks over his shoulder as if for guidance, face a mask of horror. I want to hate this man, this killer, with every fiber of my being, but the agonized look draws me up short.

He turns back to his companion, who has dropped to his knees, one hand on the ground, the other held out before him as if begging for a coin from a passerby. The black Guard shakes his head back and forth, over and over, then raises his gun and shoots the guy in the back of the head. He falls forward and is still.

The attacker's companion has been making a beeline for the Army guys, one hand at his side, the other clutched and crooked, his hand a claw. He has a look of dread on his face, and then I see his eyes, which are blood red. Not bloodshot—they are completely red without even a hint of white.

That's when two of the National Guard draw aim and blow the man's head off his shoulders.

Then the stampede starts.

First a couple of bystanders turn and walk away swiftly. One man has two little ones in tow. He grabs one and presses the young boy's head to his thigh as he draws away from the crowd with a brisk stride. A threesome of black-clad teens stare in disbelief. One has her black-lined lips open in an O while her friends drag her away even as she stares back over her shoulder.

Erin tugs at me until I turn to look at her. "We need to stay a little bit longer," I tell her. "The paper … We are small, but this story is huge and I don't see any news cameras here. Where the hell is the media?" I have to raise my voice for the last as the helicopter with the machine guns hanging out the side closes in on us again. The whump whump whump is so intense at this range that I can feel the ground pulsing under the gust from the blades. The wind picks up dust and detritus and flings it in every direction. I have to squint and cover my eyes with one hand so I'm not blinded by an abandoned beer can or empty Big Gulp cup.

A few of the National Guardsmen break away from the rest and approach the tourist group. The tourists move together, but they are in shambles. One holds his hand to his head to stop a flow of blood. He looks confused and falls to his knees as if dizzy.

One of the girls wears a short, bright yellow skirt. She has lost a pump, so she half-walks, half-stumbles toward a tall Guard, who motions for her to stand back.

Then she moves so fast that it seems like a blur as her legs flash, yellow buzzes across the pavement and she slams into the guard like a Mack truck. If she weighs ninety-eight pounds, I'd be surprised, yet she takes him off his feet with the skill of a linebacker. The impact should have thrown her, but she holds onto his head in a death grip. She moves like a banshee. I have never seen anything like it. She is crazy, arms flailing as she tears into his face with her fingers. She punctures his eyes, then squashes one in her hand as she digs it out and tries to eat it.

The guy thrashes beneath her, punches, drives his knee into her, and each blow is like hitting a tiny brick wall for all the good it does. She ignores his struggles, leans in and rips part of his face off with her teeth. With his cheek a ruin, one eye blinded, one gone altogether, the man howls like the damned. His pain is cut short, however, when gunfire ripples out from the soldiers. Suddenly it is a bloodbath as the people in the small group are all gunned down. Horror grips me as Erin's hand tightens on mine so hard that it hurts. I can't even look at her. I want to shield her from what we are seeing, but I can't even hide my own eyes.

People turn and run away from the shots. They crowd Denny Avenue by the hundreds, all running together in an all-out panic. In hot pursuit are more of the things.

I've seen more than enough. I tug Erin, and we run north along the street until we reach another roadblock, this one much more orderly. A man in uniform with a big bullhorn calls out orders to the approaching people, telling them that if they are okay they should raise their hands or find some way to show that they are not infected. Some peel off from the crowd and run in different directions. Some run past the line. People bob and weave around us as if we are on a tiny island. Then I raise my hands above my head and run forward. Erin does the same, and we make it past the line.

A gun opens up, and one of the infected—at least I hope she is—falls backward, feet swept out from under her as a shot takes off most of her head. I am horrified when I realize it is a young girl, probably no more than thirteen. There is mass panic as more shots erupt along the line. A Humvee pushes its way over sidewalks, between cars and people.

"We should go back to my condo!" Erin yells in my ear. I grasp her hand in mine, turn and nod.

"We never should have left. I'm sorry, Erin."

"Don't be. There's no way we could have seen this coming. We should get back and see what the media is saying now that this is out in the open," she yells as we jog away from the nightmare. I wonder if we can somehow cut back across an alley and angle back to her place. More guns open up, and it is very confusing for a few minutes as blood sprays from bodies, people dive for cover, families huddle and hold each other. The Humvee, which is less than thirty feet from me, opens fire, and I feel like I am inside a dryer as the sounds rattle and ricochet around my head. My ears start ringing at once. I slap my hands over them, but it barely helps.

There are more of the things everywhere, an army of people who are easy to pick out, as they move more slowly and most have blood on their clothing, hair, and faces. It's like they are drunk or drugged. They stumble, stagger, some fall and move on all fours. A few crawl with legs stretched behind them like a parade of the damned chasing a slow-moving river of refugees.

One takes the initiative and moves, fast. He is an old man with a gray ball cap on his head. Even at a distance I can see the age spots on his craggy face. He looks like he should be in a wheelchair, but he moves like a field runner.

He overtakes a woman with brown hair so long that it sweeps the line of her waist. She wears a Beatles shirt that says All you need is love. The man pounces—that is the only way to describe it. One second he is loping along; the next he is airborne and then on her back. She crashes to the ground, arms outstretched to stop her fall. She cries out in pain as they slam to the ground and roll across the unforgiving asphalt.

Then the man attacks her, hands striking. Tearing. Her hair comes out in bloody clumps that he tosses aside. He tears at her clothes until the white skin of her back is exposed, bra pulled up and away as she flails in torment. She screams for help, and someone tries to pull the crazy old man off of her. Her savior is a fit-looking guy around my age. He looks behind himself just long enough to see the swarm of infected bearing down on him, and his screams join hers.

I'm shaking so badly that I want to throw up. I am beyond furious. I have rarely wanted to hurt another person, but right now if I had one of the soldier's machine guns and knew how to use it, I would open up on the attackers.

The refugees are closing in. They are at twenty feet, and some are running. The National Guard has set up a roadblock with the wooden slats that warn of danger, but they will be precious little defense against the oncoming horde.

Some Guards raise guns; others stand on top of cars and aim at the … at the monsters. There is no other way to describe them. They aren't people to me anymore, not after what I have seen.

I feel real dread, a deep terror when I realize that the first innocents attacked are coming to their feet with the same blood-red eyes, the same hollow look and the same hunger for flesh. An Asian girl snatches a child from a running woman and bites into its back. The little girl, who can't be more than four, howls as she is torn apart. Part of the attacker's intestines are hanging out of her stomach, and blood sprays back and forth with the sway of her guts as she moves.

It is too much, and instead of thinking about how much it turns my stomach, I lean over, hands on my knees, and throw up.

KATE

Blood stains the street around the two corpses. The two men who gunned them down shoulder their weapons and move back to their line. The younger one glances back, and Kate is pretty sure she can see fear and regret in his eyes. He meets her gaze and looks away quickly.

"I can't believe what I just saw. I need to get down there and put some of this shit on video and get it on the web. People need to see what's happening here." Bob stares at the bodies.

"No kidding."

"I'm going to get dressed and head out there."

"Me too. Meet me in the hallway in a couple of minutes." She is freaked out by what she just saw, not the shooting or the blood, but the way they executed the pair. She is all too familiar with death, but that was just wrong. Or was it? What if the stuff about a virus isn't bullshit? What if they really need to put down the infected, the deaders? What if they all need to be shot like rabid dogs? the other whispers.

She is back in her apartment in a flash. She dresses quickly: panties and loose jeans that won't rub on her sore backside too much. She slips into a tan bra and a white tank top. She slides on a jean jacket even though it is warm. She dumps her purse on the bed and drags a larger beige bag out of the closet. It is covered in Sub Pop stickers with obscure band names. She dumps out the crap in it. Old clothes, some makeup—colors she hasn't worn in a year (mostly black and bright reds from her semi-goth days), since back when she couldn't decide who she wanted to be. Back before she became Kate the Killer.

She stuffs in a change of underwear, an extra bra; she grabs a t-shirt and a thicker shirt just in case. Another pair of jeans that she finds in a heap on the floor, not exactly clean, but she will deal with that later.

She takes money from a hiding spot under her nightstand. She has to turn the thing over and peel the tape off an envelope that is folded over several times. It contains her life savings. She has always suspected that she would one day end up under investigation for her nocturnal activities, and this is her escape plan, pitiful though it is.

There are ten crisp hundred-dollar bills and ten twenties. More and it would be too much to hide, less and she wouldn't make it a week. She divides the money into several piles and hastily stuffs it into her jeans pockets.

She puts the bag over her shoulder, grabs a one-liter bottle of water from her fridge and stuffs it in the bag, jamming it down among the clothing. She thinks of Bob and grabs one for him as well—no telling how long they will be gone.

Her swords go under one arm. Wrapped in cloth, they look long and bulky, but she isn't going out there without them. She skids into the hallway, almost running into Bob, who is stuffing the big pistol in the back of his pants. He tugs his Hawaiian-print t-shirt out and lets it fall free to hide the butt of the pistol.

"Should have bought a holster for this thing, it's heavy as a bowling ball," he mutters.

She tosses him the water, and he hands her a couple of protein bars. They are only neighbors, but she is impressed with the teamwork. He smiles at her, and suddenly the distance between them seems smaller.

Gunshots call out below—hot, fast and furious. There are screams, but it sounds like they come from inside. Doors slam, and the other tenants start shuffling around so loudly that the old building seems to be alive. More gunfire and a long, loud scream that sounds like something from a horror movie. Someone else shouts out on the street, and Kate doesn't need any more encouragement. A doorway opens at the end of the hallway, and a man and woman of Hispanic descent emerge. The man carries a young child; the woman holds a plastic grocery bag that swings around her body ponderously as she whips the door shut. She locks it, then heads for the exit, a stream of Spanish going back and forth as if they are in a heated argument.

There is pounding on the floors above as people flee. More gunshots echo, and Kate doesn't wait around any longer. Stuffing the bars in her bag, she whips it over her shoulder and takes the bundle of swords in her right. Bob shoulders his bag, which looks light as well, and then they are pounding down the hallway. They take the stairs two at a time as the other residents start to stream down them. Bob is right on her heels, and the flood of residents is just as hot on his.

"It's too early for this bullshit," a guy calls from above, but no one laughs. Nervous energy seems to ripple thought the tenants. It's palpable, and she can almost taste it.

They fly down the last set of stairs, into the dilapidated lobby, which almost turned her off the place the first time she set foot in it. The walls are brown, old, peeling, but the super had promised he would redo it when summer was over. Of course, he has been promising this since Kate moved in. She doesn't really care; it's easy enough to ignore the decor, which is decidedly seventies.

Past the mailboxes, and she has an urge to check hers.

Bob grabs her arm and steers her out the front door. Her first impulse is to knock his hand away, because she is a fiercely independent woman and doesn't need a man's help. Only his hand is firm, warm, and it brushes her breast as he guides her down the short set of stairs. She tries not to show it, that she is excited by the danger, that she likes how his hand feels on her and would like to explore the feeling more. That might not go well for Bob, so she pushes the feelings aside.

He lets go, and she almost pouts, but another Army truck comes tear-assing up the street. Men pour out before it even comes to a complete stop, men in green fatigues armed with large guns and grim faces. She follows as if she belongs with them, long strides in her sneakers, no clacking of high heels today. She rounds the corner and thinks that she has suddenly left the main street and entered Hell.

There are dozens of them walking with hands at their sides, vacant eyes that even from a distance show bright red. Most are drenched in blood—red and angry, some dried to a rust patina as if it has been there for a while. They are all shapes and sizes and in various states of dress and undress. There is a well-built man who looks like he is from Jamaica. His dreads hang down his back and one side of his head. He wears just a t-shirt with an old picture of an El Camino on it. His dick dangles free, but it is shriveled and drawn up just like his balls. Her eyes are pulled there automatically, because she has been taught from the time she was a child that it is a naughty area. Now she is just sorry she looked.

An older man with a bullhorn cranks up the volume and shouts at the approaching people, who are still a good twenty or thirty feet away. "Identify yourselves or we will open fire. If you understand us, then raise your hands over your head and drop to the ground. Lie flat, and when we clear the area, we will come for you."

He repeats a variation of the same address once more, but the people keep coming. Some signal is passed, something Kate doesn't see or hear. Guns start firing along the line the men have set up. Most lie prone on the ground, but a few are on one foot with a knee on the asphalt.

Shells eject and hit the ground, a tinkle that is barely audible over the sound of the gunshots. The blasts assault her ears, and she tries to cover them with her hands, but her eyes don't flinch away.

People jerk and fall as bullets slam into their bodies.

A large man dressed like a cowboy takes a shot in the leg just above his knee. Then one hammers into his side. He spins to the left from the impact, but recovers and keeps moving. Another shot hits him in the center of the chest. This stops him. He is pushed back, but his only reaction is to stare down at the sudden bullet hole. He stands in the mass of bodies as if listening to something, then a blast of automatic fire rips across one shoulder, almost separating his head at his neck as it zips past.

The guy goes down at last, and when he hits the ground, his head nearly shears off from the impact. She should look away; that's what normal people do. She is aware that Bob has been standing next to her, that he cried out as some of the folks on the street were struck, screamed when some of them fell. She risks a glance at his face, and it is ashen, as pale as the walkers that just fell under withering gunfire.

She knows what she is doing. She is aware that it is not at all in her character, and yet her hand finds itself reaching across the vast gap that separates them and taking his hand in hers. It is no longer warm. It has gone cold as if his blood is frozen. He turns to her and squeezes her hand tight. His eyes are two great pools of sorrow. Who knew that Bob the collector had a heart, or a soul?

One of the shooters turns to them. He looks young, barely out of high school. His voice wavers and his hands shake visibly. "You should get out of here. There'll be more of them soon, and if they get behind our lines, we can't protect you ... or ourselves." The last is muttered as he turns around to pick off another one but not before she gets a good look into his eyes, which bear wounds, things he is not proud of. There is sorrow there; it calls to her for help, but she has no idea how to answer.

She doesn't remember what sorrow feels like.

"You just shot them. American citizens. You shot them like they were animals." Bob moves close so he can scream in the guy's face. His hands are up in front of him, and Kate wonders if he is about to attack the soldier.

The guy stands unmoving under Bob's tirade. His face is blank, and when Bob stops shouting, he doesn't yell back. Instead he wipes his mouth with a trembling hand and looks Bob in the eye. He even offers an olive branch in the form of a hand placed on Bob's shoulder.

"I know what we did, and it will haunt me for the rest of my life. I'll tell you the truth, man, because they can't keep this shit secret much longer. Those things are dead. It's like someone killed them and then they reanimated or some shit."

"That's impossible. What kind of sick fuck comes up with a story like that?" Bob steps back, knocking the soldier's hand off his shoulder.

"Did you see those things?" the guy pleads. "You can shoot them fifty times and they don't go down. Try it. Take that gun out of your pants and shoot one in the chest. He'll smile an evil fucking grin and then try to take a bite out of you."

Bob turns away and throws his hand in the air.

"More on the way, sir!"

"Go hot, go hot!" he shouts, then picks up the bullhorn again and starts yelling his previous orders. "Show your hands in the air or run IN another direction!"

More of them shamble into view, and Kate understands that the guy isn't crazy. They are monsters, nightmares of walking flesh. A woman has her arm blown off, but she keeps walking. It's insanity! Gunfire pops along the line, and the things drop like rag dolls, then more come until they fill the street. There must be a hundred, two hundred!

"Left flank!" one of the soldiers screams, and all heads pivot in that direction. As sure as shit stinks, there are twenty or thirty of the things, and they are much closer.

Kate will say one thing for the military guys: they have their shit together. Five of them detach from the main group and move to form a new firing squad. Then the guns sound again and Kate is deafened.

Bob rages against the injustice, pounding his fist against his leg in frustration and begging the men and women to stop firing, but they can't hear him over the gunfire … or maybe they choose not to. She tugs at his hand, drawing him after her. He follows dumbly, and once they come around the corner of the building, he seems to recover, to snap back to himself. Bob is trying to be a man about the situation. He wants to be the alpha dog of their duo, but he has no idea that he's dealing with a strong alpha cat with a few deadly secrets.

"I'm sorry, it's just such bullshit!" he says furiously.

She extracts her iPhone from a pocket, turns on the video camera and hands it to him. "There you go, Mr. Cameraman, document away." Maybe giving him something to do will focus his anger. He snatches the phone from her hand and rounds the corner again. He holds the camera up at the firing squad, then pans it over the bodies on the ground and over the approaching people as they fall in bloody heaps.

"See what they are doing in Seattle? This is real, people, this is real shit happening right now, and we are powerless to stop it. Our government wants you to think they are saving us, but what they're really doing is slaughtering innocent people. Why aren't they gathering them up and putting them in trucks or something? Huh? Why aren't they …" and he sputters out as several of the walkers manage to elude the storm of bullets and close on the line of fire.

A deader howls and jumps on top of a soldier who is shooting to the left of the main line. The soldier collapses beneath the bloodstained man, a guy in a bathrobe who is spitting blood. His eyes are livid, filled with rage. Blood-red rage. He snaps his head down and bites into the soldier's arm, then rips his mouth upward in a furious pull that manages to break through the heavy fabric and find skin.

The soldier goes crazy! Dropping his machine gun, he fights to stand but ends up flipping the thing off his back. It clutches his arm as if holding on for dear life and takes another bite. The soldier screams as cloth and flesh are torn; both hang in strips below his elbow, and his green sleeve turns crimson.

The soldier kicks the attacker in the chest with one heavy boot. Then he takes a large step forward and kicks the guy's head like it is a soccer ball. The blow should put a normal man down, but the guy hardly misses a beat. He leaps to his feet and snaps at the soldier again. This time the man in green is better prepared. He throws one hand in a big hooking punch that pops the attacker's head around. Then he kicks him in the chest again, this time with more force. It knocks the deader back a few feet.

The soldier's ruined arm hangs useless at his side, so he reaches across with his left hand and removes his gun from his holster. The others still fire, but some have stopped at the spectacle in front of them. One turns and fires a quick shot at the walker, hitting him high in the shoulder. Then he turns and trains the gun on the approaching horde again.

The distraction is enough. The soldier aims his gun, cocks it carefully with his damaged hand, and then shoots him in the head. The biter falls, and the soldier steps forward and shoots him a few more times, which finally does the trick. The deader's head turns into spaghetti as blood and gray matter splatter in every direction.

The soldier stares at the mess and looks like he wants to puke. Then he studies his arm like he is looking at a science experiment.

Behind him, the deaders advance at a steady rate, and it doesn't seem like the soldiers will be able to keep up. Some eye the rear, probably trying to find a suitable place to which to retreat.

The injured guy stares at his arm for a few more seconds, then jerks as if hit by lightning. "Oh fuck, they got Ramirez!" one of the young female warriors shouts over the gunshots.

Ramirez pulls the gun up and tries to put it under his chin, but he is shaking and can't seem to lift it. He looks at his companions in dread, horror etched all over his face. Then he looks up at the sun, almost smiling, rips a pin out of one of the grenades at his waist and falls on top of it.

Kate is standing ten feet away when the explosion rips through the air.

LESTER

They have lain in bed for a few hours in silence, studying the ceiling as the temperature rises. Unlike yesterday, there is no desire to have sex. They stare and consider, and Lester takes the time to go over the plan in his head again and again, but what he is really waiting for is the alcohol to leave her body and for her to come down from her high.

"More water, babe?" he asks, holding the bottle out. He wishes it were ice cold and sweating in the heat like he is, but they have to settle for room temperature.

"No, I'm good. I want to take my purse with me. That thing was a lot of trouble to get."

"The Coach thing from Marlene?"

"Yep."

"Sure, okay. We can put stuff in it. When you're on the other side, I will toss the bag to you. Just drop it, grab the rope and pull it tight so I can slide down. You may have to wrap it around your arms and then sit down, pull it away from the fence and brace your feet against it." He sits up and demonstrates what he means.

"I got it, babe." She smiles, but he wonders if, inside, she is ready for this.

"Hey, don't worry, I got your back. I'll be standing above you with guns blazing. None of those fucking things will get near you."

"Les, I know we haven't been together long, and I know I can be a bitch, but do you love me?"

The question is just about the last thing he expected to hear from her. They have fun together. Sure, she has a knockout body and is willing to do just about anything he asks. She isn't a prude even though it took him a couple of weeks of persistence to get her panties off. In the end, it was worth it. After that first night, they were as busy as horny hamsters on X.

The first night, he peeled off her clothes like he was unwrapping a Christmas present. He couldn't take his eyes off her, and because she was so fucking hot, he barely lasted an embarrassing thirty seconds. Afterwards he slipped a Viagra down his throat and dry swallowed it. He spent fifteen minutes with his head between her legs in an attempt to show her he wasn't complete shit in bed. After that, he was ready to go, several times. If she was impressed, she didn't say so, but after that night, she sort of set up home base and stayed with him. That was compliment enough.

She did a little coke with him but stuck mainly to pot and booze when they partied, which was just about every day. He always let her have access to his stash, and she never took advantage of it. She had a job in town, but it was assisting a paralegal and it didn't pay well, nor did she do it full time. Still, it was money in her pocket, and whatever else she needed, he was happy to provide.

They may die today when they attempt their escape, and if that's going to happen, well, he wants to go out in style. He sees himself taking a dozen of them with him as they tear him apart. Sure, there will be pain, but if it comes to that, he will cap his girl and then himself. So where's the harm?

"Yeah, babe, of course I love you."

She beams a big smile at him, rolls over and climbs on his lap.

"Too bad we can't squeeze one in."

"Sweetie, I'm too fucking freaked out by those things downstairs to even get it up right now."

She looks down at his body and draws little circles on his chest, which is mostly bare of hair, going a bit to flab and pale as milk.

"I bet I could change your mind if I put my mind, or should I say my mouth, to it."

Lester grins, but instead of thinking with his dick, for once in his life he does something smart and slips his hands around her slim waist and eases her off. She lies next to him and kisses him on the cheek.

Lester stretches and grabs the knotted sheets they have bound together and wraps them up like a big weird rope. He also has the rope he found in John's house, but it doesn't seem thick enough for her to hold onto while he shimmies down it.

"I'm gonna get set up. Come out in a few minutes and we'll put this crazy plan in action."

"Okay," she says as she sits up.

He hauls the bag and rope to the window. Then he takes the sheets out the window and into the blazing sun. The bodies in the front yard and street number at least fifteen, and when he steps out and the deaders see him, they go a little bit crazy, moaning and reaching for him even though they are at least a dozen feet away. He could sit up here and drill the things all day if he wanted to. If he had enough ammo, he could clean the entire street. That might not be enough, though, unless this crazy disease is only affecting this part of Seattle. Lester has doubts about that. He has been hearing distant gunshots for most of the day.

A small circular air vent sits on the house near the top of the roof. He secures the rope to it and then rigs up a sling so he can thread the sheets into it and cinch the nylon stuff tight. He makes knot after knot in the rope until he is certain it will take a crack team of Eagle Scouts to undo the mess. He tugs on the rope and sheets as hard as he can, over and over, just to make certain.

Angela joins him on the roof a minute later and walks to the edge. She will have to be near one of the shortest parts, and if the deaders have half a brain among them, they will probably be able to reach up and pull her down when she drops over the edge. In fact, to those things, she will probably look like a juicy worm dangling from a hook.

"Damn, babe, you are pretty fucking brave to do this."

"I don't feel brave. I feel like crapping my pants."

"That makes two of us."

They smile and laugh at the little joke as Lester hauls the rest of the gear onto the roof.

* * *

The noonday sun has given way to a couple of clouds, so it's not such an oven, but the humidity is high, which makes them almost as miserable. From here, Lester has a perfect view down Cole Avenue, but it is empty of people and there hasn't been an Army truck in a day. He wipes sweat off his brow, then wipes his hand on his pants. From this side, he can see a section of downtown Seattle, but his view is partially blocked by trees. A few helicopters hover around the city. That can't be good news.

He leans over the other side of the fence and shouts, "Over here, asshole, come one, come all! Step right up, ladies and gentlemen, and see the great Lester and Angela disappearing trick. Come on. OVER HERE!"

The deaders look around for the voice and follow in his general direction. He takes the Glock from the waistband of his pants and aims at one. He has a clear shot of the top of the bald guy's head, can't miss. Instead he drills the guy in the shoulder so he is able to get up once the bullet's impact knocks him on his ass.

"Over here!" he yells again and shoots another one for good measure. Too bad he doesn't have any firecrackers. That would get them good and riled up. Some of the deaders are coming to investigate the noise as he hoped they would.

"Ready, babe?"

"Yep!"

He dashes across the roof, feet more sure of the gritty surface. He sits down next to Angela and leans over the edge of the roof. There are no deaders there now.

"Okay, babe, it's all you."

"Great."

She slides her legs over the edge of the roof, and Lester holds on to her arm. She has the rope wrapped around one wrist just in case, but he worries that it will snap if she slips. He helps her shimmy her hips over the edge so just her upper body is on the roof. She slides down a little more and then glances down with giant eyes, but there are still no deaders.

She drops a little farther, arms holding on to Lester and the rope. She is trembling, or maybe it is him. He can't stand to lose her like this if she slips. His words earlier, that he loved her—maybe he meant them. He has never loved anyone before, but he is pretty fucking sure it isn't rocket science. You have feelings for someone, they either go away or stay, and his are right where they started a few months ago. Can he imagine his life without her? Sure, but he doesn't want to, and maybe that is the whole idea.

She dangles free, and her hands slip down to grasp the edge of the roof where the tiles meet the edge of the fence. He has to lean all the way forward but has a bright idea.

"Hold on, babe. Let me get in a better position. Hold on to the rope like your life depends on it."

"My life does fucking depend on it!" she shoots back as she grasps the rope to her chest, one forearm bent to hold her on the rooftop. Lester drops to his front, chest flat and stretches out his legs, then spreads them so he has more surface area. His body weight is focused on his left foot, but he uses it like a rudder to steady his body. He can't see over the roof, however, so he sidles forward.

He grabs her arms as she swings free, focuses on her face to show her everything is okay. Lester has good peripheral vision. He can see a pretty wide area around the side of his head, but he doesn't panic when he gets in position. He doesn't glance over in dread. He focuses on her face as if she is the only thing in the world, as if he can't see the pair of deaders that have taken interest in her.

"Just slide down a bit. I got you, babe."

"Okay." And her straining arms slip down. He holds her tighter than he probably needs to. He can still see the shapes moving toward her from the corner of his eye, but he resists the urge to scream at her to hurry the fuck up!

"Okay, now just reach out with your leg, a little farther, the top of the fence is ... just ... right—THERE! Good job, babe!"

She dangles at the end of his reach, one leg on the fence, one leg swinging free. She kicks the other leg back, catches her foot hard and then slips off the fence. Lester is pulled toward the edge of the roof as she swings, her momentum carrying her toward the house. Her foot slams into it with a vicious bang.

"Ow! Shit!" she yells.

She scrambles around and gets her foot on the fence again, and Lester risks a look down. The pair of deaders are staring up at her, but they don't reach for her. Thank God those things are stupid. Then one of them stretches a hand upward but fails to brush her foot.

She swings the other foot over, and this time she ends up with both feet on the top of the fence. Now Lester sees one crack in the plan. When he lets go, she will have to fall either forward or backwards over the fence. Right now she is stretched tight, but bent over slightly at the waist. Just as he realizes the predicament, she looks down and lets out a scream.

"Oh shit! Pull me back up!"

"Angela, we may not have another shot. I'm going to push you, and I want you to try and roll backwards and fall off the fence. I know you can do it, babe, just be brave!"

"You be fucking brave! Pull me up!"

Lester ignores her plea.

"Please, just try it, baby. Please! I love you!"

"I don't care! Pull me back up!"

"Babe, just do it! We may not have another chance. Please!"

She starts to say something else, to argue, but she risks another look at the deader that is reaching toward her and seems to make up her mind. The man only has one arm, and he is having a terrible time using it. He reaches up but can't seem to find her leg.

"Goddammit!" she screams. "Push me!" and Lester does. He shoves as hard as he can from his precarious position, which doesn't leave a lot of wiggle room. No chance for a do-over. If this doesn't work, she is going to die. He looks down, and another of the things has joined the party, so three of them are in on the plan.

Angie seems to have enough momentum. There is a split second where it seems she is about to fall, but she sticks her butt back and leans away from his push. Gravity does the rest of the work as she tumbles back off the fence and out of view. There is a loud cry of pain and what he hopes isn't the sound of bones snapping. He can't see her and has a terrible feeling of panic.

"Ouch!" she calls back just as he comes to his feet and is trying to look over the edge of the fence.

"You okay, babe?"

"I am not fucking okay. My ass is going to be bruised for a week!" He breathes a sigh of relief and gathers up the rope and cloth. He tosses them over the edge and is greeted by another loud "Oww!"

"A little warning!"

"Sorry, these things are making me nervous. But you did it! I am so proud of you, babe, you saved our asses."

"At the expense of my own," she says, but she still sounds upset.

The rope and cloth go taut. He can tell right away that there is a problem. The sheets that seemed so long when they were knotting them together aren't quite long enough. He will have to trust the rope.

"Pull that rope tight, babe!"

"Hold your goddamn horses."

He tries to be patient, but he wants to get to her as soon as possible. She has no weapon, no way to defend herself if he doesn't make it over the fence. He wishes there were more time so he could have her run onto the neighbor's roof and then tie the rope to something over there. Then he could 'Indiana' it across the gap. Just call me Dr. Jones.

Speaking of drugs, he should have gotten more of his stash, something to bargain with. Maybe he can come back later and retrieve some of it. Come back with a fucking army and take back the neighborhood. Not that he knows many people here. He doesn't really have friends, just acquaintances who stick around his house for a few minutes to be polite when they pick up an eighth of weed or a dozen hits of ecstasy. In fact, with the exception of Ronnie, who is dead in his front yard, he can't think of many 'friends' who would go out of their way to offer him water if he were parched and dying in the desert.

The rope goes taut, and he realizes what a stupid idea this was. How the hell is he going to shinny down that line, reach the top of the fence, and then get down without falling on Angela? If he lands on her, she may just take the keys and leave his sorry ass behind. Angela's stock has seriously increased over the last day. Not only is it the best sex ever, not only is she beautiful, she puts up with his shit and she is a zombie slayer extraordinaire. He ought to marry her.

"You ready for me?"

"Yes, just hurry up so we can get out of here, babe. I want to get on the road and back to the real world."

Lester wonders if civilization will still be there when they arrive. Is this really a good idea? Maybe they should lock themselves up in John's house, nail everything shut and then sit it out. He knows the house has food and running water, and they must have some booze stashed somewhere.

"Wait, I almost forgot the goods."

"Send them down."

He has a sudden but brilliant idea.

"Babe, do you see a water pipe on the side of the house over there? It should be near a meter of some sort," he guesses since there is one like that at his house.

"Yeah, it's behind me."

"Will the rope reach it?"

The rope is nearly torn out of his hand as she grabs it and pulls. He rubs his palms against his pant legs.

"Yep."

"Tie that sucker tight, babe. I'm going to slide down, and you can help me if I get stuck."

The rope jitters around in his hand, and he takes a look at his audience. The deaders have been gathering below. There are now six or seven and more on the way. He looks away, then reconsiders and gives them the finger.

Lester pulls out his .38, points it at each one, and mimes pulling the trigger while he waits. When he has killed the fifth one with a fake shot, complete with 'bang' noise, she gives the all clear. Lester uses some hangers to jury-rig the bags so that he can slide them down the rope.

First goes some of their food. Then goes his black bag and Angela's new Coach purse. Next up is some of the ammo, then another bag with more ammo and his handgun. He keeps the little .38 in his pocket just in case.

The AR-15 and shotgun are last, but Angela stands under the fence and catches the guns with both hands and lowers them to the ground. Then everything is over, and he is ready to make the leap.

He runs to the other end of the fence and calls to the deaders again. "Hey you dead freaks, come to papa!" Then he hoots and hollers, jumps up and down, and generally makes an ass of himself. They wander over, some with split mouths, grinning like clowns at a circus. Some of them moan, but most just mill around as if confused. They don't seem to get really excited unless they are on a level playing field with their prey.

He dashes to the other side, but a couple of them are still hanging around. He draws his .38 and puts bullets in both their brains. The gun may be small caliber, but it does the job nicely, and they both flop to the ground like rag dolls tossed aside.

He grabs the rope, leans over and drops so he is hanging over the yard. He now knows how terrified Angela was a minute ago. His balls have shrunken into his stomach. He loops his foot up and over the rope and slides down it inch by inch. None of the deaders is around, but they may see him any second.

His feet touch the top of the fence, and he is home free.

Then there is a snap and the rope comes loose, shaking him so violently that he nearly lets go. He yelps but recovers quickly and puts one foot back on the fence while he ponders what to do next. He is dangling a mere seven or eight feet off the ground, but on the wrong side of the fence. He has no leverage, no way to stand up straight, so he slides farther down until his legs are on top of the fence. He gets an idea. He will lower himself until he is sitting on the fence and then drop to the other side.

Another pop and the rope loosens even more. He dangles free again but recovers just as before. "What is that?" he hisses.

"It's the pipe," she whispers back. "It's coming loose from the wall. It's breaking … And it's not a water pipe, babe."

It's not a … then the smell hits him. Gas. Fuck! Gas, brilliant! How many shots will it take to cause that shit to explode?

He starts jumping so he can get on top of the fence. His legs are pressed over the edge, and he has to slide down to get his thighs on top of them. The bouncing has produced a lot of noise, and the deaders are moving in on him.

One of them, a guy who must be close to six foot six reaches for him and gets ahold of his shirt. Lester makes a squeaking noise that is half scream half girlish yelp. He pulls away and takes one hand off the rope so he can slap the deader's hand aside. Angela must realize the danger he is in, because she grabs his leg and pulls. Her hands on his ankle and calf scare him so badly that he jumps and nearly kicks her in the head.

The deader grabs him around the waist and pulls. Lester is half dragged off the rope. One hand still hangs on, wrapped around it in a death grip.

He reaches across his body with his left hand and pulls the .38 out of his pocket. The deader gives him a fierce tug; he tries to hold on but is ripped off the rope.

His legs slide along the fence, and there is a blinding flash of agony in the left one, just above his ankle. He hits the ground hard, and the breath is punched out of his body. He manages to get his head up just before impact, but he still feels it in his neck. The deader loses his grip when Lester falls. He looks around for his prey, then his gaze is inexorably drawn to his victim. The thing's mouth drops open, and Lester sees a portal to Hell in that maw.

The deader drops on top of him like a giant tuna, cold, dead, reeking of shit he doesn't even want to try to identify. The guy goes for the throat, but Lester shoots his hand up and holds him off, gripping the deader's neck, which is cold and slimy. It is covered with old blood and possibly drool. The smell of death hisses out of the bastard's mouth right into Lester's face, making him want to puke his goddamn guts out.

Angela is screaming on the other side of the fence, and he knows he needs to get the fuck up and save her if another deader has managed to get to that side of the fence. His peripheral vision picks up movement to his right. The army of deaders he attracted to the other side of the house must have gotten wind of him. If he doesn't get the fuck up, he is going to be one sorry drug dealer. He wedges a knee up between him and the deader and manages to roll the big guy to the left.

Hand free, he fumbles the gun, nearly drops it. He recovers it in his right, pulls it up and without even a half-second to aim, puts the gun in the general direction of the deader's head and pulls the trigger. The little hammerless revolver isn't the most powerful thing in the world. It doesn't pack a wallop like the Glock, but it does an admirable job of blowing a hole through the deader's head.

"That's right, you fuck!" Lester growls as he rolls to his feet. The big man drops face first to the ground, and Lester gets a look at the thing's brain, since pieces of it hang out of the hole. They are gray with bright red flecks running through them. It looks like a ropy mass, nothing like he would expect.

"Les! Are you okay? Les? Please answer me. Oh God, PLEASE be okay!" Angela pleads from the other side. Then the gate rattles as if she is trying to come for him. The doorway is a mere three feet away.

"Just a second, babe." He tries to yell, but he barely has breath, and his voice sounds raspy in his throat.

"LESTER! Are you all right? Was that you?"

Another deader is almost on him before Lester realizes it. His body aches as though he were being pummeled by fists from three different directions, and for all his heroics, he has just about had it.

He sucks in big breaths. Big ragged, gasping breathes. His stomach hurts like he just tried to run a mile, and he is stupid-tired. He can't seem to pull enough air into his lungs, and stars dance in front of his eyes. He wonders if he was seriously hurt during the fall. He turns halfheartedly as another thing moves on him, this time a kid with black hair wrapped around his head like a tornado of hair gel hit him. He is dressed in black from head to toe, and both of his arms are covered in bite marks as if he had enough of the horror and just offered himself to the deaders.

Lester staggers toward him, and he feels a sense of irony at the thought that if anyone were to pass by, they might mistake him for one of them. They would see his weary form shambling like the mindless things and probably try to blow his brains out.

Weariness drags at Les as he takes the two or three steps that will bring him to the gate. The deader in black seems intent on making sure that doesn't happen. Lester walks right up to him with his gun in one outstretched hand. He slips on a rock that throws him off balance, and the twisted ankle sends a fresh bolt of pain up his leg. Because he no longer gives a fuck, Les points the gun at the kid and shoots him in the throat. "Fuck you, emo-boy!" he rasps as the kid drops to his knees, then falls forward in a pool of blood.

Angela finally gets the gate open and peers out with giant eyes as if she expects one to jump on her the second she cracks the door. Les rips the gate open and staggers onto John's lawn. He slams the door shut, but the latch doesn't catch, and the door bounces back, striking him across the flat of his back. Fresh pain joins the host of injuries all over his body. He doesn't even bother to curse. He just stares straight ahead with teeth clenched so hard he is sure they will crack.

During the mayhem of the last minute, a group of the things has gathered at his back, and now they push through the pitiful wooden structure and onto John's lawn.

Les grabs Angela, and feeling like he is coming off a three-day drunk/high, legs heavy as lead, chest full of water, he steers her toward the back of the house. He looks back and sees at least five of them following close behind. He draws a bead on the last one and pulls the trigger, but the little five-shooter has seen its day, so Les throws it at the deader, striking the thing in the head. He may as well have thrown a sponge for all the good it does.

They reach the door, which is cracked open just a hair, and they tumble inside. The door moves fast and bounces off of the jamb. Les spins around and slams it shut, but he does it too hard and the door bounces back. At least the damn thing doesn't break.

He tries again, this time smashing a deader's fingers as she tries to slip a hand inside. The woman is of middle years and has a wig hanging half off her completely bald head. She has a ton of makeup on and is as skinny as a rail, and the word cancer springs to mind. At least she isn't feeling any pain; the bitch is dead as can be.

Fingers drop to the carpet, but he is beyond the point of horror. He just looks at them in a numb fugue. He slams the door again and this time shoots the lock home. The deaders press up against the glass door and cry out for them. Angela does the only thing she can and closes the blinds on the creatures. She spins the little rod so the slats close lengthwise and they are no longer in view.

Les grabs her in a fierce embrace, pulls her tight and feels like weeping. But he isn't a girl; he is the man in this relationship. He is one in-control motherfucker as far as he is going to let on. Inside, he feels like he is on the verge of falling apart.

"You got deader shit on me," Angie says. She stares down at her shirt, which now has red stains on it. Les thinks that is the funniest damn thing he has ever heard in his life. Deader shit. Those things aren't even alive, how can they take a dump? But what else do you call the goop those goddamn things wallow in?

Laughter bubbles out of his lips even as his chest burns from the fall. He tries to catch his breath, but the laughter interrupts, and soon he is gasping between fits. Snot bubbles out of his nose with a pop, and this just makes it worse. Tears stream down his cheeks.

Angela doesn't seem to understand why he is laughing, but it infects her, and soon she joins him with a tentative giggle that turns into full laughter complete with at least one snort. They hold each other for a minute until he can sit down in John's big lazy boy. He looks around and there is Jane/Justine lying flat on the ground just as he left her.

"Honey, I'm home," he says to her vacant eyes, and that is the second-funniest thing either of them has ever heard.

The deaders pound on the door as if they are the big bad wolf about to blow the place down. For the moment, Les ignores them as he and Angela enjoy a laugh at the morbid spectacle they have become.

Once Les is back in control of himself, he steps over the body of Jane/Justine and moves into the dark kitchen. He finds a roll of paper towels and wipes the tears and snot off his face.

"That scared the shit out of me, Les. I thought you were dead when you fell."

"I feel dead now. Every inch of my body hurts."

"As soon as we get somewhere safe, I will go over your body and check every square inch," she swears. "I never want to go through that again. Sitting on the other side wondering if you were being eaten by those things, I didn't know what I was going to do. I can't shoot worth a damn and, well, I don't even know how to load the guns that well. I am one useless bitch."

"Oh, stop. I'm fine, and I like you just the way you are. Besides, you aren't a bitch. You are my girl, and nothing—I mean nothing—is going to come between us. If I have to torch the whole goddamn neighborhood to save you, then that's what I'll fucking do," he says with sincerity.

"Well holy shit, Les. That is the sweetest thing you have ever said to me," she says with conviction, and then they burst into laughter once again.

He goes to her and kisses her, but she pulls away and crinkles her nose.

"You smell terrible. Let's get out of here. Let's find a hotel with warm water so we can soak in a tub for a few hours."

The pounding on the back window dies down for a moment. Les figures it's because they can't see anything in the house anymore. He feels warmth on his left back pant leg and looks down and twists his leg to see a bloodstain. Pain rips through his leg, and he staggers. He yanks the pant leg up, suddenly terrified that he was bitten, only to find that—to his relief—there is a piece of wood sticking out. It's not a large piece, just a chunk of the fence from when he was hanging over it.

He sighs in relief. Had it been a bite, he isn't sure how he would have offed himself, since the guns are outside and there is no way he is about to go retrieve them. They would have had to improvise, find another way. He'd have had to hope Angela had the guts to put him out of his misery. Probably with a knife, and man oh fucking man would that suck.

"I don't suppose you got any of our stuff from the side of the house."

She shrugs and looks down, but he can't blame her. There was no time to get anything after he fell off the fence. No guns, no ammo, now what do they do? He had assumed they would get to the house and be safe for at least a few minutes, have time to plan out this escape. He thought they would have time to go over the house in more detail and take their time locating the keys for the big Escalade in the garage.

Keys, shit.

"We gotta find their keys. You start with her stuff and I'll go upstairs."

"What makes you think they're up there?"

"Because that's where John is." He heads for the second floor before she can ask any more questions.

KATE

The sound of the grenade exploding is so overwhelming it jars her, shakes her body. The ground moves beneath her, and she feels like the earth is about to rush up and smack her in the face. She feels flushed and removed from the scene, as if it isn't real. She is in a dream again, like the ones that take over when she has a man in a hotel room and the other Kate comes a-calling.

"That took some balls," she mutters, her voice muffled in her own ears.

Bob is backing away from what looks like a hundred of the things. They fall to a swarm of gunfire all around the uniformed National Guardsmen. One of the trucks backs down the street, and a Hummer takes its place with a rumble. The smell of diesel rattles out like a smoke stack. The gun turret on top swivels around as a man pops out of the hatch and then opens up with the giant gun. It makes a chugga chugga noise followed by the sound of shells rattling on the top of the Humvee.

Gunpowder, acrid and hot, assaults her nasal passageways. She staggers back, moving away from the people who are going crazy around her.

The gunner stops after a half-minute, and she follows his line of sight in horror. Bob is running toward her with fear etched on his face. The walkers have reached the line of fire, and the soldiers are abandoning their post, backing away while firing indiscriminately. Bodies jerk, shuffle, stutter and fall. There are screams, but not from the dying. They are from the civilians whom the things pursue.

She scoots back as if keeping her front to them will protect her. What can she do except run? If those things reach her, she will be done for. She will be dead, and that is not acceptable. Not remotely acceptable.

The soldiers fall back, and one of them turns and runs. The man next to him follows with his eyes, fires a few more rounds, and then runs as well. Kate watches them and wants to join the retreat, but she can't seem to look away from the carnage, from the bodies of those who fell in the path of the army of the dead. Some rise up and join them, others run ahead, and some are clearly worn out, because they are sucked into the mob. They stumble over corpses, over soldiers who are trying to back up, over parts of Ramirez where he lies on blackened asphalt.

Several of the things grow bold, faster, and more energetic as the men turn from their firing positions and run. One of the soldiers barrels past her in a flat-out sprint, gun held to his chest as if it were a newborn. She keeps backing up, eyes on the creatures that have broken through the line. One of them pounces on a soldier, then another one leaps and is on top of a woman who manages to draw her pistol and empty it into the man's body. She panics, and as bullets punch through the deader's body, it manages to tear into her face. She howls in pain and horror.

The Hummer opens up on the lot, smashing them to the ground, then the gunner pounds on top of the vehicle and shouts, "go go GO!" The big car shifts into gear with a grunt as if in pain and then roars backwards. The gunner has his eyes fixed on the men he killed, and Kate is pretty sure she sees tears in them.

The walking things are now running things, and they are screaming for blood, a faceless hideous mass of people who seem to be rushing to a street event. Only the event has turned into something out of a horror movie.

It's chaos all around, and Kate is terrified. She breathes deeply, and her hands tremble as she tightens her grip on her bundle. Bob comes into view, grabs her arm and starts pulling her away from the spectacle. She follows but is unable to run. There is something she should be doing, some task she needs to complete, but she can't wrap her mind around it. It's the blood, the screams. It's the pain. It's the suffering, the anger, the pure mindless terror, and she knows why she is hesitating. She knows why she needs to stay.

She knows she has work to do.

She drops the bundled cloth from her swords and takes one in each hand. She has no way to store the sheaths, so she slips the swords out and drops the wooden holders on the cloth, then tucks them up against a corner of a curb.

The swords gleam like liquid in the sunlight. They are beautiful and they are terrible. They are razor sharp, and if she isn't careful, she could take one of her appendages right off.

"Keep them off me." A pair of women who were falling back take an interest in her weapons and stop to see what she will do. They stare at her as if she has gone fucking crazy. Kate stares back at them, hard. Each meets her eyes, and they must see something there, because they both nod lightly.

Kate spins and strides toward the few remaining stragglers, who seem determined to make a last stand while their comrades escape. She slips between a pair of men who are walking backwards while they fire, rifles sweeping from left to right as they pick targets. They are shouting back and forth, working as a team. "Wait, you can't go that way!" one yells over the din of gunshots.

She ignores the men and hopes one doesn't shoot her in the back by accident.

The first one rises up before her, and she slashes the sword up in a perfect stroke that opens the man from groin to ribcage. The shorter sword dives in and severs the vertebrae in his neck by way of his throat. It's a beautiful blow that she continues through, pulling the short sword to the side as she passes.

"Holy shit!" the other man yells as deader guts spill onto the ground.

Then a woman is almost on her, and she steps back a half-pace and whips the katana around in an arc that takes the questing arm off at the wrist. The shorter sword sings again, moving like lightning to sever the woman's neck.

The body drops at her feet, but she is already past. A gunshot echoes, and a man charging from the right drops. Although Kate saw the charge in her peripheral vision, she is all too aware that she would have had trouble turning fast enough to do damage before he was on her. She silently wishes a prayer upon whoever shot him.

She is a dervish, moving into the crowd like a tornado. The katana is a trailing whisk of fire that rips into deaders, leaving her cruel mark on all she touches. The wakizashi trails it, and if one of the old masters of the kenjutsu school could see her now, he would surely nod in approval, or so she assures herself. She fights in the old style, something developed over six hundred years ago called nitōichi, or two swords as one.

"Move back!" she yells as she closes in on the remaining few. They stare at the woman covered in blood who is wielding two swords, and she is sure she hears one of them mutter, "Fucking hell."

Kate charges the mass of people with a roar that would make her sensei proud. She dashes one way, jitters to the other and takes one down with a spinning blow to the neck. Kenjutsu taught her how to fight face to face with precise movement. Silat taught her how to get behind an opponent and screw up his day.

She lops off an arm, and then one's leg at the knee. The man falls but seems immune to pain. Kate has to back up from a pair that has taken a liking to her, then she moves to the left, fast, slippery as a snake, and punches the razor-sharp long blade into his shoulder before the other snaps out and slashes him across the throat. Her aim becomes more precise, because she has found out the hard way that they don't go down fast if you just wound. Every stroke has to be a killing one.

This suits her just fine.

She is one with the weapons, and she is one with death as she delivers killing strokes in force. The next opponent is much larger, but this doesn't deter her. She shifts right, then her foot shoots out and she snap kicks him in the knee. Though she is already moving, she knows the precise time at which the blow will land and goes from a relaxed state in her hips to spinning full power. The torque carries her around, and every muscle in her body tenses with sudden rigidity. A loud "Saiii" floods past her lips. The force is concussive and snaps the bone like a twig. She moves past him, mere inches from his body, then half moon steps to the left so she can yank the katana across his back and sever his spinal cord.

He goes down without a peep.

Bloodlust, dread, cold precision, and horror. All of these feelings course through her body and are one and the same. Goose pimples flush her body at the excitement. She can do what she loves in a way she has never before been able. She can kill with impunity, with a will. She smiles and slashes another to the ground from right to left. A blow that nearly cuts the creature in half, the thing that is just a girl. A young one at that, maybe sixteen if a day, but she has been howling for blood. Mouth open, nearly panting, enraged. And when the girl falls, Kate looks down at the body and wants to feel shame, but the feeling doesn't arrive. Then she looks up through a haze of red that is the blood pounding in her body, the adrenaline pumping though her veins, and there are more of the fucking monsters coming.

One of the soldiers had been dragged back into a mess of them, and now he comes to his feet like Lazarus him-fucking-self. Kate decides this is enough to freak her out as the guy turns, eyes blood-red, skin the color of putrid gray left to rot. He opens his mouth, and an inhuman howl erupts.

"Clarke's a deader, kill him!" one of the soldiers behind her shouts, but she is probably in his line of fire.

The guy is huge and comes at her with considerable speed, and yet he is unsteady on his feet. She waits for him, almost patiently, as he gets one foot in front of the other. He staggers and almost goes down but manages to recover like a drunk suddenly asked to take a sobriety test.

She steps forward, left foot in front of right, slightly spread, a close fighting stance. The swords' points hang toward the ground, and she feels like a samurai on the field of battle. But she isn't fighting guys dressed in armor of bamboo and wood. She is fighting the dead.

She smiles.

Then he arrives like a charging bull, and she raises the swords, pivots her body to present her left side and, as he moves in, sweeps her leg in a crescent that creates an obstacle that will use his own momentum against him. As he falls, she is already moving, katana rising high then slashing down to catch him across the neck. He goes down without his hands in front to stop the fall and ends up skidding across the black road on his face. Good thing he's dead. Fucker just lost his good looks. She takes two strides and buries the sword in his head.

Work to do, blood to spill, death to cause, she thinks, but as she shakes crimson drops off her main sword and whips the wakizashi through the air one more time to shake it clean, she realizes the people running at her are glancing back, scared. They are the living, and they are being pursued.

She falls back as one of her guardians steps up with her machine gun, slams a magazine home with the palm of her hand, slides back a little bar on the back, pulls it tight to her shoulder, and drops two of the deaders in rapid succession.

"I need to get me one of those," she mutters, but the other, a statuesque woman with gentle lines on her face, shoots her a look. She has auburn hair that slips free of her helmet and falls around her ears. The hair is slightly curly, and there is a moment when Kate wonders what her own mother looked like before she ran away from her husband, the asshole who abused Kate into her teen years.

"Can't have her, she's mine." And the other girl shoots her a look, a secret smile that Kate just gets a hint of.

"I mean the gun," she pants.

"I know, I'm just teasing." And the three of them turn to study the pile of bodies they have created.

The rest of the men and women in uniform have gotten things under control, and a large black helicopter arrives with a great whump whump of blades striking at the air to keep it aloft. It hovers over the chunk of road at building level with soldiers hanging out the side. One swivels a large machine gun and paints the scene with it, but he doesn't fire, as he sees that the running folks aren't deaders.

Another one points up the road, and the chopper lifts into the air and moves up Denny Way to investigate. He will be over Seattle Center soon, and Kate realizes with horror that the people moving in on her location were probably at the Center enjoying the sun, the rides, the food, and each other's company. Then some of those things got in there and ruined everyone's day.

She staggers away from the scene, weariness suddenly dragging at her body. She is in good shape, but the surge of adrenaline leaves her shaky and cold. She snatches up her sheaths and does her best to clean the swords of blood and gore.

Bob wanders over with gun in hand, and it is obvious he helped out. She tries to smile at him, but he just stares at her in horror. Then she leans over, plants her hands on her knees and vomits everything out of her stomach.

Bob looks away but rubs her back.

Standing up, she wipes the back of her hand across her mouth. Without warning, she leans over and throws up again. Big gasping breaths rattle into her chest as she tries to breathe through the burning puke.

"You okay?" she asks when she recovers.

"Yeah, I did that over there. Not very manly ..." He tries to keep it light, but his eyes are cold and haunted. His hands shook as he touched her a moment ago, and they shake still. In fact, his whole body is quivering as if in pain, but she can't do anything for him now. The pretense that they will ever be more than friends is gone forever, cleared away on the edge of her twin blades.

"I don't understand what you did out there, how you walked into that mess, that hell, and hacked people down. I had the honor of standing back and picking them off with my pistol," and he shows her the gun. His hand shakes so badly he can barely hold it up.

"But you got up close and personal. I don't know how you did that. It was so brave and so stupid at the same time."

"I know," she sighs and looks at the bodies, at the blood, the parts. People are streaming past now. Some run, others walk with kids in hand or at their sides. Women hold babies to their chests, strollers forgotten.

A man runs past, bloody from a head wound, but his eyes are bright and alive.

The soldiers try to keep track of who is whom, try to catch a glimpse of everyone's face as they stream past like a river of flesh. The older guy with the bullhorn is calling out his litany from before. "Raise your hands, show us you aren't one of them," but he can't keep up with the influx of people.

"What are you, Kate? I thought I knew you, as a friend, and I won't lie to you, because I don't give a damn anymore. I wanted us to be more than friends. I wanted to tell you so many times, but I was scared and I know you don't like men."

She tries not to laugh out loud at the last, because she certainly does not like men.

"Bob, look at me. I can't ever be what you want. I'm the person you just saw." She pauses to collect herself. She glances at the ground and then back into his eyes. "I'm the one who is a monster, not those poor people out there who are infected."

He continues to study her and then nods once as if he has convinced himself of something. He wanders over and helps up a woman who has stumbled to the ground. A man walks toward him as if in a daze, and then a fresh ocean of people streams into the road.

Drivers have given up any pretense of getting through the mess, and many have abandoned their cars in the middle of the four-lane road. Most cast their eyes away from the bloody bodies, the puncture wounds, the separated body parts, the heads that look like dropped melons. Some hold their children close and try to shelter them from the sights and from the pain. There are still shamblers on the loose, and some of the men pick up weapons and go to work.

There are screams in the distance from the direction of the Seattle Center, then more from the center of town. It seems Seattle is under siege, and Kate doesn't know what that means for her. She sets her eyes on the sun that rises over the Puget Sound and walks toward the water that stretches into the distance. She has no particular intention in mind except to lay eyes upon the sea. Her two friends strip off their camouflage shirts to reveal thick, white, sweat-stained t-shirts beneath, and under the baleful gaze of some of their colleagues, they follow her.

MIKE

Erin grabs my arm and starts pulling. I don't need much more encouragement, but it comes anyway, in the form of gunshots. The men and women who were sent out to protect the population instead begin slaughtering them.

The deaders drop like flies under withering gunfire, but like all gunfire, it is impersonal, and the moment the trigger is depressed and the gun bucks, there is nothing they can do to alter the course of the small hunk of lead. Some innocents wander into the line of fire or are mistaken for deaders. Some fall to the ground when the shooting starts, and others run in every direction like a flight of frightened crows.

Bullets punch into flesh, tear at muscle and appendages. I want to scream at the men to be careful, to watch what they are aiming at, and to look out for children even though some of those are attacking.

The deaders reach the front line just as more vehicles arrive, smashing through stopped cars and trucks, careening off taxis and buses. One is a Humvee with a machine gun mounted on top. As soon as it stops, there is a great pounding that shakes the ground as it fires into the crowd. I look away as the big gun rips off chunks of people, leaving bloody holes behind. I don't know how many are hurt or dead. Many lie in heaps, some crawl toward loved ones, and some pull cloth over gaping wounds, screaming in pain and horror.

The men on the front line take the assault by shooting point blank at the attackers. Some strike out with knives and the butts of their guns when they have to. One of the men goes down with two deaders on him, and I am nearly tugged all the way around the corner when I see her wade into the fight and save him.

She is slight but moves with confidence as she unwraps a pair of swords. She swings them around her body in a pattern that does not look too complicated, yet she does it with so much grace that it is beautiful to behold.

"Mike, we need to go!" Erin tugs at me so hard that I nearly stumble over a curb. I can't take my eyes off the female warrior. She is as beautiful as the blades she wields.

The first deader is on her, and she swings the longer sword around so fast that it is a blur. The guy falls away with his neck half off his shoulders. There is an enormous spurt of blood that sprays the concrete around them, but she seems to be able to predict the path and step out of the way.

She moves forward to swing at a larger man and slashes twice, once with each sword. She glides around him, and I see her true face for the first time. She has delicate features, a small head with a little button of a nose perched below vaguely Asian eyes that arch naturally. Her eyes seem lit from deep within. Her lips are parted, and I think she is smiling.

"MIKE!" Erin breaks my reverie.

We stumble away from the madness and head down Broad Street for a block as others run or walk before us. There are people poking their heads out of businesses and restaurants as the gunshots become louder and closer together. There is screaming behind us, something with which I have become far too familiar in the last few minutes.

Erin starts to run away from her condo, and I stop her by pulling her into an alcove in front of a store that has chairs and office equipment in it. She looks at me, eyes scrunched up.

"Where are we going?"

"That way." She points down Fourth Avenue at the departing backs of folks on the run. "We can't go to my place. It will be overrun in a matter of minutes. I say we head for the center of town and hope there is a better law enforcement presence. I can't believe what we just saw. That was insanity, Mike. How could they shoot those people down in cold blood?"

We start walking again. This time I don't protest. I go along because I can't think of a better thing to do. I realize that my mind is not working at one hundred percent; I think I may be in shock.

My mind continues to play tricks with me as I see the bodies fall, the guns firing into the crowd, inhale the smell of spent rounds, hear the sound of shells striking the ground—tinkling in numbers I don't want to think about. Then I lean over and puke again. Erin pats my back, and I appreciate it even though I don't want her to see me as weak. I stand up and wipe my mouth with my shirtsleeve and immediately wish I hadn't done it, since my change of clothes is miles away.

I walk beside her again and catch a glimpse of her from the corner of my eyes. She is crying quietly. Tears run down both cheeks, and when she sees me looking, she wipes them away with stabbing motions as if to clear the things she has seen.

"I can't handle it, all those people. All those poor people crying out for help, and what kind of a goddamn virus makes people act like that? It's like they are on PCP or something. They actually wanted to eat each other!"

"Don't forget that the virus seems to be spread with a bite. Did you see how fast those Asian tourists fell and then got back up and started attacking others?"

"No, I was too busy watching a class of kids—couldn't be more than ten or eleven, trying to stay together as a group but getting peeled off one at a time as they yelled for help. And the only help were those assholes with guns shooting anything that moved."

I can understand how upset she is, but I know the National Guard was doing their best under terrible circumstance. As I think of the people falling, we step up our pace, and soon we are a few more blocks into Seattle. I can see the line of proud skyscrapers rising like gods into the sky.

There are clusters of people all around us. Some are on the other side of the street, and some move down side streets. Not that we have any destination in mind, but I can't help but wonder where everyone else is going. One of the Guardsmen mentioned the waterfront, but I don't want to be blocked in on one side. Then I remember the ferries, and suddenly that sounds like the best place for us.

"I know what we should do! Let's get to the ferries, and we can be on Vashon or Bainbridge in an hour." I have only been to Vashon Island once, and it was a long time ago. Still, either destination will be a dream compared to here.

"You're a genius!" she exclaims and plants a kiss on my cheek instead of my lips. I'm sure she is thinking of the fact that I threw up just a few minutes ago. Still, I will settle for it. Hell, yesterday I would have fainted dead away if I thought Erin would be kissing me anywhere.

"I have my moments."

I spot a Chase bank and take Erin's hand in mine. I pull her with me to the cash machine on the side and dig out my card. I punch in my pin, and it gets rejected. Then I realize I am shaking so hard I mistyped the code. So I try again and it goes through. I quickly take out my daily limit of three hundred dollars.

Erin has the same idea and extracts a load of cash. I don't pay attention to how much, nor do I glance at her balance. We have been together for one day, and I'm sure the last thing she wants is me creeping around her finances. We walk away from the bank quickly and down a street that was built on a hill. We end up almost running by the time we get to the bottom, from fear or adrenaline, probably both.

We make haste for the waterfront, but there are screams behind us. The thing is spreading, and I hope it doesn't overtake us.

Two blocks later, we are running along Alaska Way past the piers. The smell of the sea clears my head, makes me feel like I am back in Seattle, no longer in a nightmare. There are boats on the water, but most of them have come to a halt. People are specks in the distance, but they are following events with binoculars. What must they be thinking? Can they make out any of the carnage we just witnessed?

We move briskly. I know from last night that she is in great shape. I have also seen her eat a ton of junk food at work. She loves to eat at Taco Time on a regular basis, and sometimes I have seen her wolfing down a Big Mac. How she does it is beyond me. Sure she has mentioned yoga, but my guess is that she runs or does calisthenics at a gym.

By comparison, I am in okay shape. I do work out but not as much as I should. Still, I eat well and manage to stay off the junk food. My waistline is a bit larger than it should be. I keep up with her even though I'm a little bit winded, so we make good time passing Ivar's Seafood and the great big pedestrian bridge that crosses over Alaska Way so people can get to Pike Place market.

The other people on the sidewalks have expectant faces. They glance around as guns fire in the distance and helicopters fly overhead. As if to punctuate the fact that something weird is happening, a gray Navy cruiser moves along the coast as if hunting prey. Men stand on deck holding large binoculars as they stare at different points around the city.

We approach the pier for the ferry and take the stairs to the Vashon side, mainly because it is the closest one. We enter, and there is already a line. We aren't the only ones thinking about getting away from the city in this manner.

"Made it." Erin's voice is distant, distracted. She keeps looking behind her as if she expects one of those things to enter at any time.

"I bet they have it under control up there," I say and almost believe it.

"You think so?"

"Sure, they probably brought in more men, trucks, guns," and as soon as I utter the last word, I am sorry for it. "I mean they have to contain the thing somehow, whatever it is."

"What is it, Mike? What causes people to go rabid and bite each other like that? It's like one of those movies about walking dead things."

She is standing close to me and speaking in a low volume as if the rest of the people here aren't aware of what is going on. We are all crowded into a large waiting room, and I spot a soda machine across at the back. Suddenly I am parched, and all I can think about is something ice cold.

"It was insane. And why don't they feel pain? It's like they're immune to it. Some of them were missing body parts, but they kept coming in the face of all those guns. I saw one of them dragging crushed legs behind him. And what about that crazy girl with the sword? I hope I never run into her in a dark alley."

I pause as I try to think of something to say, but all that comes out is, "She was amazing."

Erin stares at me for a minute as if I am insane. She doesn't speak, so I ask her if she wants something to drink.

"God, an ice-cold Coke would be great."

"Diet?"

"One day, Mike, and you already think I need diet soda."

"I didn't mean ... oh, very funny. Unleaded it is." I'm glad to see she is keeping her sense of humor with me after all the horror we have witnessed today. I hope I am able to do the same. I am learning that Erin has depths I would never have imagined.

"Good. And none of that sugar-free crap. I need my fix."

"Liquid sugar coming right up." This draws a grin. I feel much better with our banter restored. Say one thing for Erin and me, we are always willing to tease each other for a cheap laugh. Our sense of humor is remarkably similar.

I smile and peck her on the cheek then go to fetch my love a drink.

LESTER

The house isn't half as creepy in the light of day. Sunshine streams in through curtained windows. Most of the draperies were closed, but Les went around and tugged them back. Last night was terrifying, and he still feels a sense of fear as he ascends the stairs, but he has scoped out the entire house, so there is no reason to screw around looking for stuff. He knows exactly what he needs.

He goes straight to the room with John's body, tears open the door and is immediately assaulted by the smell of all the potpourri lying in piles around his corpse. Chunks of wood, flowers, buds of plants and even some seashells make up a wide variety of colors—red, blue, fuchsia, pink. If it's a girl color, it is on the floor.

The flowery crap barely stifles the stench of John's dead and rotting body. There has to be something about the virus that adds to the foulness. He can't imagine that anyone smells this bad after being dead for just one night.

He drops to his knees and pats down John's jeans with his fingertips as if afraid he will get burned. John is staring straight at the ceiling with one eye; the other is missing (having been replaced with a bulging bullet hole), and the socket is puckered and bloodless, as if cauterized.

He pokes around while staring at a brown spot on the ceiling. After a second, he realizes it is probably dried blood. The closet is a horror, but worst of all, John's pockets are empty.

He stands up and closes John's tomb.

He makes a cursory search of the bedrooms, opening anything that is closed—drawers, jewelry boxes, closets. He runs back downstairs, where Angela is in the process of turning the house upside down. There is a loud bang at the sliding glass door, but they both try to ignore it.

"Nothing?" he asks.

"Not a damn thing. Well, I found a flashlight in one of the bottom drawers," she shows him with a beam of white light. How do they have so many of these things and he doesn't even have one?

"Cool, may come in handy. Did you find her purse?"

"I didn't see it anywhere."

"Ah hell, the keys have to be here somewhere."

He scans the wall for any of those fancy key hook things that the affluent think to buy. Not Les, though; he prefers to hunt for his keys on a daily basis. He goes through the drawers in the kitchen and finally looks for any bowls in the hallway. He pats down Jane/Justine's body and is horrified when his hands wander across her chest and he thinks about feeling her up. Deader tits, nothing like live ones. He starts laughing at his own joke, which earns a strange look from Angela as she turns over the cushions on the couch. Each times she tugs one out, it sounds like a loud fart as the leather slides together.

He risks a peek though the sliding glass door, and now there are a lot of them. They mill about, but the two that chased them inside are still walking into the door over and over. One meets Lester's eyes with his blood-red ones, and his mouth opens in a big, bloody O that makes Lester shudder. He gives the deader the finger and slides the curtains shut again. The other one sees the movement and starts banging his head against the glass in frustration. He howls, and others join him, pounding on the door.

"We gotta go, babe. Those goddamn things are going to get inside."

He has another brilliant idea, but he is afraid she will freak out when she hears it. He dashes to the front of the house and looks outside. There are a few in the street, but they are milling around in the opposite direction of the house. If he can run fast enough, he may be able to get around the side of the house, grab some of their gear and make it back.

Before Angela can freak out, he puts his insane plan in action. First he checks the locks to make sure he won't get stuck outside, because that would be a real shame. She would probably leave him out there for being a dumbass. He opens the door as quietly as possible, checks either side of the house, lets out a long, heavy sigh, wishing he had a double shot of tequila for courage, and then bolts for it.

He runs like his ass is on fire. Around the house, slamming his shoulder into the corner as he does. Pain nearly blinds him, and he almost crashes over a water hose coiled on the ground. Vaults over that, comes down hard, flat-footed, and then he has the prize. The gun and bags are lying in a heap. He grabs the black bag and the purse and slips the AR-15 over his shoulder. He snatches up the first box he sees, not even sure if it has ammo in it, and knows his time is up because one of the deaders has taken notice of him. He would love to bring the gun up and shoot a couple in the head. He is pretty sure that would be monumentally stupid, considering the fact that gas is pouring out of the busted pipe in a steady leak that sounds like a tea kettle. He heard once that they added stuff to the gas to make it smell. That way if there is a leak, it will be easy to detect. So the entire area reeks like a pack of dogs stopped by and took a massive shit in the yard. He thinks that maybe he should be holding his breath.

Too late for that now. He runs back around the side of the house with the box clanging, almost falling over the same hose. He clears it and comes down on his other foot, which sends agony coursing up his leg thanks to the giant splinter. Brilliant, Les, think you could take the thing out before the next time you try to be a hero? Every step is agony as the wood bites deeper and deeper.

He rounds the house full tilt and runs past the garage again, but he has caught the attention of the other deaders on the street. One of them howls, which sounds to Lester like it is calling for his blood. They swarm into the yard a couple of layers thick. A ragged band of refugees dressed in the remains of clothes not torn off by the deaders that tried to make meals of them. Fucking heat or not, if I get out of here, I'm dressing in thick leather. See them bite through that shit. He jumps the two steps of the porch. Screams when he lands on his bad foot, again, and almost drops the box he is carrying. Manages to hang on, barely, because he crashes into the door with it. His hand slips on the doorknob as he tries to turn it, slides off because it is wet with sweat. He tries it again, with a grip this time, and opens the door just as one of the deaders reaches the first step. He slams the door in the thing's face. A horrid face that is covered in fresh blood, thicker than the gore on the fucker that chased them out of the back yard.

Angela comes into the hallway and stares at him as if he is insane. She looks like she wants to throw something at him, and he can't really blame her. What he just did was stupid; if he had been captured, they both would have been done for.

He pants, the last of his energy used up. He leans over, hands on knees, and takes shallow breaths. They wheeze in and out of his lungs, causing a crushing pain in his chest.

"Oh God, Les, what the hell did you just do? What the fuck did you do?"

"We needed some stuff, babe, a gun at least."

"But you didn't say anything. You just ran off. I thought you were leaving me." And she bursts into tears.

"I wouldn't do that. Jesus, Angela, what kind of an asshole do you think I am?"

"Just don't do anything like that again! Promise me!"

"Fine. I promise I will warn you next time I'm about to run off and do something that fucking stupid." His voice drips sarcasm. She stands with her arms crossed under her breasts as tears run down her cheek. He takes the step that separates them and folds her in a firm embrace. He holds her tightly as she shakes against him. She pounds on his back once with her fist, but he doesn't feel it, since the piece of wood buried in his leg is a constant drone of pain. He breaks away and promises her once more that he won't leave her like that again. She seems mollified and even kisses him on the cheek.

He drops to his knees and unzips his black bag. It's small, about the size of a lady's handbag, and much like that object, contains goodies, things without which he won't leave home now that the world has gone to hell. While he is down there, he yanks his pant leg up and studies the piece of wood stuck there.

"FUCKING CHRIST!" he screams as he tears it out. Blood dribbles out of the wound, and he would really like to get a bandage on it. Putting the pain aside is hard when his entire body is one big mass of hurt.

He pulls out a small box of .38 shells and tosses them aside. Lot of good that will do with the gun outside. He takes out a smaller box of Glock shells and tosses them as well. There is a half-ounce of pot, a small baggie of coke, some X, a few hits of meth—not that he does meth, it's for that 'just in case' scenario. Just in case he needs to stay up all night cleaning shit. Just in case he needs to trade it for something more important … like lobotomy tools, because he would have to be fucking nuts to get hooked on that crap.

The real prize is a genuine Army-issue fragmentation grenade. The latter came from a deal with some soldiers from Fort Lewis. At first they had tried to trade him some night vision goggles, but he was worried they would be too traceable if he ever tried to unload them. A grenade, though, who has one of those? So every once in a while, he hauled the thing out when his buddies came over, and they would toss it back and forth to freak out Angela.

He puts everything back in the bag and straps it over his shoulder, then checks the load on the AR-15. There are about fifteen bullets, and if it comes down to shooting their way out, they are fucked. Of course, they have been fucked since the bastards got into the house.

"Keys. We need those damn keys." As if to punctuate his statement, the deaders start banging on the sliding glass door again. "Maybe they're on the garage wall."

He stands, grabs Angela by the hand and pulls her along to the garage door. He has the rifle in his other hand and is ready to draw it if one of them so much as looks at him wrong.

Les takes a deep breath and pulls the garage door open, fully expecting the space beyond to be full of mindless things howling for his blood. Weariness drags at his arms as he yanks the gun up to his shoulder and takes aim into the darkness. He clicks the flashlight on with his other hand, holding the gun awkwardly, and pans them around. In the back of his mind, he is pretty fucking sure no deaders snuck over here in the middle of the night. Not even the cat is in here anymore.

There are shapes in the dim light, but none of them moves. Faint rays stream in from the edges of the twin metal garage doors, drifting lines of yellow that penetrate the darkness. It is still murky, but at least he can see better in the daytime.

Boxes are stacked up on one side just opposite the expensive SUV. The rest of the space appears remarkably clean except for the mess he made the night before while going though the shelves. Sorry John, pardon the mess. I'll clean it up once I come back with a shovel to bury your ass.

As if reading his thoughts, the deaders manage to figure out how flimsy their defense is. The glass door shatters, and two of them fall into the room. The same pair that chased them into the house from the back yard come scrambling to their feet. He rushes into the garage with Angela hot on his heels. No time to get a shot off now. Besides, Angela would be in the line of fire.

The two get to the garage door just as it is about to slam shut. Lester is first. He takes the steps like a pro, but Angela doesn't expect to have to run down a pair of stairs and stumbles. One of the things is on her tail and fares no better.

The creature reaches for her as she stumbles into Les, but she reaches the bottom of the little landing without breaking her ankle. Lester nearly goes down in a heap as she collides with him, but he manages to stay upright with her pressed against his body.

They stumble forward into the back of the car, and his face smacks into the back window hard enough for him to see stars. His front teeth slash into his upper lip, tearing the flesh and drawing blood. He gets out one "fuck" as blood floods his mouth. He staggers around the side of the car and heads for the door. He grabs the handle and is surprised when something in this whole fucked-up day goes right and it opens.

"IN, ANGIE, GET IN!" he screams, hoping she is heading for the other side.

He slams his door shut and sinks into the plush interior. He leans over and looks at every button on the door to find the one that will unlock the car in case the driver's-side door is the only one left open. What am I doing? he wonders and leans across the console to open the door for her instead of trying to find a button.

She makes it to the door. Her hand reaches in and touches the seat. Wan light from the sides of the garage door hits her beautiful face, which is painted in terror, eyes wide with fear and utter revulsion. Her mouth opens in horror as one of them grabs her hair and drags her down. She screams, and Les tries to maneuver the big gun in the small space. "You fucking monster, I'm going to kill all of you!" he screams in rage as Angela howls in pain. He can barely see the other two shapes bobbing around in the dark. He knows it is too late and there is nothing he can do for her. He slams the door shut and pounds the steering wheel in frustration. He hits buttons on his side until he hears the doors lock, and then he screams as loud as he can until there is no breath left in his body. Then he drags in another breath and does it again.

MIKE

The line has not moved one foot while I was gone. I have two Cokes and a couple of bottles of water in hand. Erin takes one of the sodas and drains half of it in one lusty gurgle that impresses me. I manage a quarter of mine before she toasts me with the tip of her plastic bottle.

We have been inside for at least fifteen minutes, and we haven't heard anything from the overhead speakers. No one has come out to assure us that everything will be okay. People mill around nervously, and there is chatter, but it is hushed. Others keep to themselves, glance at their cell phones, check laptops or just watch the calm water on which the ferry rests. To avoid the long line at the unmanned counter, I purchase our tickets at an automated machine.

A woman has been standing near us for the last few minutes, ever since she wandered in, looking dejected. She has a cardigan draped over the top of her dress, and I'm pretty sure I can see spots of dried blood behind it.

She glances at me, then looks away quickly but not before her eyes settle on one of the bottles of water I am hoarding. I look away, but then I remember some of the horror I have witnessed today. I wonder if she has lost someone or if she got away from one of the things. I turn to her and hold out a bottle.

"I ... thank you," she says, and I think she is about to break into tears. She is older than I, a bit overweight and what I would think of as frumpy. But her smile is genuine, and it makes me smile in return.

"Did you have an encounter with one of them?" I ask in a tentative voice. I don't want to push her away, but if I am going to report on this entire story, I need to talk to people.

"Yes." She pauses to take a sip of the water. When the first drink rolls down her throat, she looks into the bottle and gives a little sigh, tilts it back and nearly drains it. "I haven't had anything to eat or drink since this morning. I just forgot about that stuff."

I wait because she deserves it. I don't want to intrude on her life, and yet I want to hear her story. A terrible thing has happened to her; I can tell by the fear and despair in her eyes. She is distant, in shock. I wish I could help, but the best thing I can do, I think, is to just wait.

"My name is Alice. Alice Paulson." She speaks in a small, quiet voice. She has her glasses shoved right up against her eyes, and it gives her something of a piggish look, but I imagine she was very attractive in her youth. "I came home from the ... from the grocery store, and I was bringing in bags. He was lying in a heap on the floor next to our son ... and I couldn't believe he was home for a change."

She takes a breath, then exhales slowly. "There was a gun on the floor, next to Ken and I saw that ... that he was dead. He had a big hole in his ..." She pauses for a moment and presses her hand to her nose to stop a sob.

Erin looks up at me, but I gesture with one hand in a downward motion that I hope means let's give her a minute.

"Ken wasn't himself. He attacked me, and I ran into the bedroom. I slammed the door in his face, but he bashed it down. He came at me, but I was climbing out the back window so I could run to my car." She looks up at me after a pause and then goes on.

"His throat was a mess. I mean, it was torn and chewed on. He was covered in blood, and I don't know how he could walk, how he could even move. I got away from his attack, but barely. He was so strong ... like he was on drugs or something."

I nod at the familiarity of her story after witnessing the same phenomenon not half an hour ago.

"Then I ran to the car. It was parked on the street. But he was right there. He knocked me down and tried to attack me again. He tried to ... He tried to eat me."

Erin holds my hand to her side again, pressing her breast against my upper arm.

"I got away when one of the neighbors hit him in the head with a skateboard. She was just a teenager, and I used to see her on the thing all the time. She cut me off a few times, and I would get mad, but now I wish I could talk to her just one more time and tell her how brave she was."

She sobs to herself for a few seconds, and Erin reaches over and rubs her shoulder and upper arm.

"I got away and ran to the house. We found my keys ..." the story is a little disjointed, but I don't say anything. "... and went back outside, but he wasn't there. I got in the car, and as the girl tried to get in, Ken attacked her again, and bit her. Killed her."

"I'm so sorry for your loss." They are the only words I can think of.

"I didn't get her name. I have no idea who she was, but she died. I just wandered after that. I drove to town and thought it would be calming to see the water. Then I thought it would be nice to get on a ferry and just, you know, go." She looks down, and I feel uncomfortable.

"When this is all over, I bet you will be able to go back and find out what the girl's name is. I bet she has some identification on her. We can track down her family, and we can tell them how brave she was."

"No point. I think she is one of them now."

A small crowd has gathered around us, and some of them start telling stories as well—stories of loss, pain, sorrow. I listen as Erin slips her hand around my waist. After a while, Alice wanders away and sits by herself. When her eyes find mine again, she tilts the water bottle at me, and I smile.

★ ★ ★

Another fifteen minutes pass, and no workers show up. I check the schedule for the sixth or seventh time. The ferry should be departing in a few minutes, but they still aren't even boarding. Others stand around and, like me, look impatient. There is a scream from outside, and some go to look. Down below the terminal, cars sit in straight lines waiting to board.

Some National Guardsmen pull up in a Humvee. They jump out and start talking to drivers in the parking lot, motioning for them leave. The problem is that the lot is not designed for that. Cars can't just turn around and leave.

A man covered in blood runs into the terminal. There are gunshots below, and people duck, drop behind cars, look around in fear. A couple of deaders have moved into the parking lot, but the Guards draw firearms and make short work of them. Score one for the good guys. Or are we? The deaders don't know any better. They are just being treated like cattle. Then more deaders arrive and gunshots call out. Another man and his female companion run into the terminal, and they are breathless.

"What the fuck!" the guy yells. The woman looks around at all the expectant faces. There are at least thirty of us here, and not one of us is moving. The man walks up to the closed ticket window and bangs on it as hard as he can, but there is no answer.

"Where is everyone? Those things are out there. We need to get on the ferry and get out of town goddamn pronto."

I couldn't agree more.

"We don't know." Alice sits up and offers her wavering voice. "We are all waiting."

"Well those things ain't waiting." And he leaves in a huff. There is a scream as he slams the door open and one of the deaders lurches toward him.

The man backs up in a panic, hands in front of his face, palms out in surrender.

The deader doesn't look interested in surrender. His bloody mouth drools glistening crimson saliva. He moves with quick steps and makes a grab for the loudmouth, who steps aside and plants one big fist in the deader's face. There is a pop, and momentum from the swing translates to force that throws the man to the floor. I hear a crack and wonder if it was the attacker's jawbone.

The man steps forward and kicks the deader in the head as hard as he can, a great big reared-back kick that connects like he is aiming right at a goalie. The deader flies back and lies in a heap for a moment, and the man backs up. The deader struggles to his feet. The woman who came in with the fighter makes a panicked move through the door, but she re-emerges with a gray-skinned man pushing her. He has one hand wrapped around her throat, and he is grabbing at her chest. He pulls down, tearing off her top and the pink bra beneath, leaving her exposed. I think to look away, because that is what polite men do, but I can't. I don't care about her losing her top; it is the attacker that interests me.

One of the men waiting in line advances on the deader, and I am right behind. I wish I had some sort of weapon. Looking around, I see something I may be able to use. My new companion pulls the guy off by his hair and throws him to the floor. I scoop up one of the supports for the rope that defines the line, a heavy silver pole with a weighted base. I unsnap the hook as I swing it up so that the thick yellow dividing rope falls to the ground in a pile.

I hate what I am about to do. The deader is trying to get to his feet, and as I start the overhead swing, I see that he is an older man in shorts and an AC/DC t-shirt that has seen better days. He is probably a father. Maybe he has a daughter or two. Perhaps he is a good man who goes to church and would never hurt a fly. Is it his fault that he has been changed by this cursed virus? I swing for all I am worth anyway, and the heavy end of the pole makes contact with a sickening crunch.

When I hit the guy, his head dents inward. He stops moving and just falls forward as if the strings that controlled his puppet body have been severed. I want to throw up again. The sound was terrible—like a hammer hitting a melon.

"Nice swing, buddy." The man I helped holds out his hand. It is rough and strong when I shake it. "Name's Trevor." He is taller than I am and wears a cowboy hat, cowboy boots, jeans and a Lone Star State t-shirt. His porn-star mustache covers most of his upper and lower lips.

"Mike."

"I drive a truck, see, had a big ol' delivery for Vashon. Beer. They love their beer over there. Anyway, I was going to take the ferry, but I been waiting here a long time, and I don't think that damn thing is going to sail. I say we get people out of here before one of those things gets in and we can't stop it."

"We should wait here." A woman with a large black hat that droops over her head speaks up. She is clad in a black dress that covers her from neck to ankle. It is slit up both sides so her white legs flash free. She must be warm in that thing in the July heat.

"You can wait for one a' the things. I'm gonna take my chances finding a place I can hole up in with some guns. Right, Mikey?"

"He's right." Erin joins me. "We have nowhere to go from here except to the sea. We should find a hiding place until this is cleared up or the CDC or whoever can get in here and start administering vaccines."

A pair of men dressed in camouflage gear stumbles in the door. One of them, the larger of the two, is supporting a soldier who is bleeding from his arm. His other arm, the one that appears uninjured, is draped over the big man's shoulder for support. They both collapse and set their machine guns on the ground. I go to their side, but I'm not sure what to do. Erin joins me, and we both crouch next to them.

"Do you need a bandage?" I ask and notice that I am not sickened by the blood like I was earlier today.

"I got it," the guy says. He is a black man younger than I am. I put his age around twenty-six, if that. He takes a white-wrapped package from a pouch on his belt and rips it open with his teeth. He helps the other guy peel off his shirt, and that's when I realize it's not a man but an older woman. Her jacket top is covered in blood down the injured side, and I can see the puncture wound in her bared arm, right below a big tattoo of Olive Oyl, the girl from Popeye.

I back up in a flash, thinking she may have been bitten.

"I'm fine. I think a bullet nicked me," she groans as he lifts her t-shirt sleeve and applies the bandage. It has an adhesive back that covers a large area. He presses it hard and puts her hand on top of it while she makes a face at the pain.

Another guy crashes through the terminal door, and it is clear he isn't one of us. He snarls like an animal as he sees all the people lined up like cattle for the slaughter. The soldier grabs his machine gun and does something to the side, maybe hits a safety. Erin drags the woman back from the door as the other soldier opens fire.

In the terminal, the sound is nothing like it was outside. In here, the shots echo around the room in sharp booming retorts that make my ears ring. The deader scoots back, a little crab walk on his butt, and then comes to his feet in a rush. The first couple of shots were in haste and they struck the man in the chest. Somehow the thing stays on his feet, so the man aims and drills one right through the skull.

The deader's head snaps back from the impact, and then he is down. The last bullet had punched through the entryway, shattering the glass, and we can see people rushing to the entrance.

"Grab the gun!" the guy yells at me. I lean over and pick it up, but I don't know how to fire it. A howl echoes across the room as two more come in. The soldier backs up, firing, so I raise the gun to my chest and try to figure out how the damn thing works. There is a slide on the back that I assume chambers a round. Then I look near the trigger and find the safety, so I pop it in the opposite direction. I raise the gun to my shoulder, shrug it tight and pull the trigger when the deader comes into view. I expect the recoil to smash into my shoulder, and I probably squint my eyes at the last second. I am not prepared, however, for the sound that greets my ears.

Click.

Oh shit!

LESTER

Lester sits in the dark car. It is closed up and as hot as an oven. He stares at the passenger-side mirror where he last saw Angela, but he can make out nothing but indistinct shapes in the dark.

Lester can't seem to make the dots match up in his head. When he started the day, he had no idea he would be fighting for his life. He had no idea he would lose Angela to those fucking things, and he certainly had no idea he would be contemplating suicide. It's like he drew the lines, but somewhere along the way he missed a few numbers.

They didn't really have a chance anyway. He had no keys, no destination in mind, just the assumption that if they managed to get out of the horror they were in, they would reach some wondrous place of safety and freedom.

Now everything is lost. He is stuck in the car, in the dark, and if he steps out in the garage, he is dead. So he will do the one thing he can.

Les maneuvers the rifle onto the floor and sets the stock against the floorboard. He leans forward and slides his hand down the stock until he finds the trigger guard. He checks the safety and then leans forward so he can put his mouth over the gun barrel.

Movement to the left draws his gaze to the window, where one of the deaders stands, mouth gaping open, bloody drool dripping from his teeth as he claws at the window. Lester gives him the finger and turns away.

Just a quick squeeze and it will all be over, one less meal for the deaders. He won't end up a mindless shambling thing. Not Les, he plans to go out in style with his brains painting the ceiling of a fifty-thousand-dollar car. He looks in the mirror on the passenger side again, looking for some sign of his girl. Is she now making her return to life? If she is, there isn't much he can do about it.

He shifts his foot back so he can lean into the barrel and make sure the bullet goes straight through his head. He would hate to fire the gun and have a bullet go astray. Hate to have to lie in shock as he bleeds out in a slow painful death.

As his foot moves back, it hits a lump on the floor that clinks a familiar song. Lester knocks the gun aside, reaches down between his legs, feels around the carpeted floor that doesn't seem to hold a speck of dirt, and closes on a ring of keys. He places the gun on the floor, tilted up so it leans against the seat.

He lifts the keys to his face as if he has discovered the holy fucking Grail itself. His hand trembles, setting the keys jangling. He feels each one until he finds an oversized key that he tries to slip into the ignition.

It doesn't go in, so he tries another key. After that doesn't work either, he reaches up and feels around until he finds the overhead light. It clicks on, flooding the car with bright white light that forces him to close his eyes. Of course an expensive car like this has a floodlight in it.

Shapes move around the SUV but are just as hard to make out in the wake of the interior light as they were in the dark. They bang their heads on the car, one so hard that it trails a line of blood down the window on his side. Lester locates the key with the Cadillac symbol on it and slides it home. He turns it so hard he worries it might break off. His hands shake with a combination of exhaustion, anger, loss, and misery.

The SUV roars to life. He revs the engine a couple of times just for the reassuring sound. He fumbles with controls until he finds the right one, and the garage is flooded with bright lights. One of the deaders is standing in front of the car, and another staggers just to the left.

Well, only one way out of here. He aims for the deader with the center of the hood and punches the gas pedal to the floor. The big V8 roars and tires spin as he drives straight into the deader, smashing him into the metal garage door. Then he is through with a rending crash. He spins the wheel to the left and hits the brakes as he comes out of the garage and drives over the door, which flops ahead of the car. Let's see what this bitch can do!

The Escalade bucks as it keeps pushing the big metal door ahead like a giant bulldozer, so he slams on the brakes, but the garage door's forward momentum continues after the car stops, smashing into the deader and several others that are feasting on various body parts. The smell of burning rubber permeates the car. He drives into yet another deader, ramming the thing before he can hit the brakes. The balding guy was chewing on an arm, blood staining his hands, shirt and chin when Lester rode him down.

He screeches to a halt again and looks back for Angela, hoping against all hope that she was not bitten but instead escaped and hid in a corner or behind a box. His fears are quickly confirmed, however, when she stumbles into the light, her shirt ripped open to reveal one of the perfect breasts on which he'd sucked happily just yesterday. The other one is torn and hanging by threads of skin. Her face is a nightmare of damage. Bite marks and open wounds leak fluid down her chin, and one of her hands is completely missing.

Les can pull his gun and put her down from where he sits, but it would be dangerous to lower the window, aim and fire. There is a chance he will miss and have the window open for too long, giving the other deaders a freebie to make mincemeat of him.

He has a better idea. He unzips the black bag around his shoulder and extracts the fragmentation grenade. It's green with the pin set in the angled arming device. He remembers the guy who traded it for some weed telling him how to arm it. Pull the pin and hold down the latch, because there is only a four- or five-second delay before it goes.

He does so now, then hits the button for the automatic window so it slides down, mechanical motor a steady whine. He holds his left arm out, releases the lever and is greeted with a click from deep in the heavy shell.

Then the smell hits him.

"Oh fuck!" He slings the grenade into the garage and is already hitting the pedal. The car lurches forward, shimmies a little—probably damage from driving over the garage door—then seems to straighten, and he is off like a shot.

The smell!

He forgot about the pipe they knocked loose earlier, the one that fed gas into the house. He zips up the street past at least a dozen deaders who stare after him as if they are about to wave goodbye. He is almost fifty yards away when the already bright daylight sky turns brilliant orange. The sound washes over the car and is gone. He stops and turns to look at the orange ball of fire roaring into the sky. Then he puts the house behind him and sets his destination for downtown, because Lester is going to find a bar and get good and fucked up.

MIKE

The soldier drops a deader with a shot from less than ten feet away while I fumble around with the gun like an idiot. Erin has retreated behind a set of chairs with the injured girl. The woman has a pistol in hand, but it's her left and it looks very unsteady, like the gun is hard to handle. She aims it at the door nonetheless while Erin crouches next to her.

"Like this!" the soldier yells then mimes pulling back a mechanism on the back of the barrel. I notice that his nametag says Nelson in white letters that are covered in blood.

I pull, but it won't slide back. I notice a small button on the slide, so I push it in and the thing finally pulls back. "Thanks. I have never fired one before."

"No shit, Sherlock. Just pull it real tight against your shoulder, tuck your arm hard like you are hugging that bitch with the crook in your arm—like it's your girl." He demonstrates with his arm out, then at his side. "When you get one in your sights, squeeze the trigger with a light stroke. You don't want to hold it down. Don't waste ammo if you don't have to."

"Okay. How is it out there?"

"Fucked. The virus is spreading like wildfire. We were supposed to contain it, but we lost the city in the first five minutes. The things are too fast, and the virus is mutating. It seems to get stronger with each generation, which means those fucking things are stronger than the ones we fought half an hour ago."

"Is there a plan?"

"Yeah, fight until they take you down, then off yourself. That's what I'm gonna do."

He moves to the door on light feet and peers out the shattered window. A fresh pair of deaders gets wind of him, so he falls back firing. There are more behind those, and I know we will lose the terminal if we don't stop them.

I raise the gun like he showed me and peer down the barrel. How hard can this be? Just like a video game, right? Line up the back sight with the front and squeeze. One of the things is in view, and it is a young kid no more than eleven or twelve. His mouth is covered in blood, and he snarls. I shift my aim to another deader, a man who could very well be his father. His blood-red eyes meet mine, and I fire the gun. It punches into my arm and makes me stagger back. The guy is still coming; the bullet might have struck his shoulder.

"HEAD!" Nelson screams, so I raise the barrel and fire again. Bingo, a hole appears in one eye, and he flops to the ground. I just shot a man. I can't believe it. I just aimed down the barrel of a gun and shot him like he was a dog. I don't have time for shock right now, so I push aside the feelings. I will deal with them later, something I am very good at.

Nelson takes out a woman with a cast on one leg, then shifts his aim and blows the kid's head off. Another one stumbles in, and I drop him with a mere three shots. If I can figure out how to aim, I might be dangerous in a day or two.

Nelson looks outside and runs back. "Listen up, everyone. They're all over the place, but a couple of Humvees just arrived, so we are moving the fuck out of here. If you have weapons of any kind, get them out. If not … fucking improvise. Above all, do NOT let one of those things bite you. If you do, I will drop you myself." He stares from face to face, and some of them nod, others look away.

I'm impressed with how quickly he takes charge. The sliding glass door pops open again, and more of the things arrive. We fire at them, dropping bodies as they enter. I don't know how many shots I take, how many times I kill. Each one makes me feel sick.

"Get everyone out of here, down the side," Nelson roars, shooting his hand toward the Bremerton side where the deck leads to stairs to the street. The forty or so people are already in a panic, and now they move like the place is on fire. They push and jostle but somehow avoid a stampede.

More of the things are coming in, probably drawn by the screams and gunfire. They howl like banshees, and some of them actually lope like weird werewolves without the fur. I get better at killing them, but before I know it, the gun clicks dry.

Nelson pops one between the eyes, a kid with a baseball cap on backwards. Then he runs to me and hands me his gun; we swap quickly. "Keep 'em busy, man!" he yells while he hits a release on the bottom and changes magazines. I provide backup for him, and before I know it, he switches guns with me again.

"We need to get the fuck out, man; we don't have the firepower to stop them here forever. Start falling back with the others."

Erin is helping the injured National Guard to one of the side doors, and as I move in that direction, a warm blast of summer air hits me hard.

The room we are in is quite large and could hold three or four hundred people, but it has become a claustrophobic nightmare as the bodies pile up at the main entrance. The normally salty air is livid with the reek of fired gunpowder, blood and human waste.

Nelson backs up a few steps and pops two more as they come in, then he hits the release and the magazine clatters to the ground. He reaches for his belt, but it looks like he is out. He turns the gun around and uses the barrel like the neck of a bat, swinging the stock into the face of one of the deaders, smashing it to the ground with a sound I don't want to even think about.

He draws his pistol and shoots it in the head. The doors are wide open, and the deaders rush in. He shoots the first few, and when his partner sees he is in trouble, she rips loose from Erin and moves with purpose to his side. She reloads on the run and starts firing, then the two of them are side by side and the swarm is on them.

The woman who staggers through the door is enormous; she must weigh close to three hundred pounds. Part of her face is missing, leaving a horror of bone and muscle that leers like a cadaver used by medical students. She barrels into Nelson and knocks over his partner in the process. I shoot at her but only manage to catch her cheek.

Nelson screams louder than the pack and falls back, rolling out of the way. They are on his partner, however, and he looks like he is going to dive in and haul her out, but a single gunshot comes from the mass of bodies, and then her legs are no longer kicking.

He rolls to his feet and backs up to join us. I am at the door with Erin pulling me, trying to get me outside. I jerk my hand out of hers and raise the gun. I take steady aim and shoot two of the deaders, including the big woman, in the head. I'm pissed, and the sacrifice of the female Guard weighs heavy on my mind. Nelson stalks toward me, picking up his empty machine gun in the process. He doesn't speak, but when our eyes meet, I see approval there.

We are all out on the deck when I decide to do something stupid. I run back inside the lobby. It is filling with deaders very quickly. I grab a gold pole and rush back outside. The nearest one was four or five feet away, but I don't think I have ever been so scared in my entire life.

My scrotum is shriveled up under my gut, and I'm shaking like a leaf when I jam the thing against the door in the hope that it will hold them back for a few seconds.

The parking lot is surprisingly calm as we descend the stairs. Nelson slaps me on the back once, then peels off and joins his comrades. The National Guard guys are pushing back a group of civilians who try to jump on the ferry. A guy with a bullhorn is ordering calm, but no one is interested in that. Three or four of them leave the ferry and jump onto the dock with guns at the ready. More pile out of trucks and make a beeline for the deaders across the way.

A group of deaders prowl the street under the viaduct. They seem to be going car to car as if hunting like a pack. A siren goes off at that moment—a loud shrill that reminds me of the old air raid sirens you hear in videos about World War II. It howls, and every deader in view stops to stare into the sky as if searching for the source.

"Please proceed to the football stadium. You will be safe. Please proceed to Qwest Field football stadium. You will be protected. You will be safe." Then the thing repeats. The sound echoes across the waterfront and rolls over the city.

"At least we're close," Erin says as we jog across the parking lot through which a stream of people walk and run. Many have cell phones pressed to their ears, but there is no talking. Some stare at their screens, but they are probably having the same problem as earlier. No signal. Could it be that the military has cut it? Or maybe the government decided to …

"Oh my God!" I actually stop and grab Erin by the arms. She looks at me as if I have lost my mind, and I wish that were the worst of my problems. "They are cutting off the city!"

She looks at the Guards standing by the ferry entrance, and as if on cue, the massive boat slips free of its mooring and putters away on the calm surface of the Puget Sound. There is no fanfare, no howling whistle, just a calm departure under ideal sailing conditions with the exception of one problem: there are no passengers.

We dash down the sidewalk with other runners, all of whom seem unaffected by the virus. The deaders are still across the street, a street filled with cars that can't go anywhere. Some of the guards take up positions on top of the stalled automobiles and open fire. The infected ones drop, but there are many more to replace them.

Some of the deaders have figured out that people are hiding in these cars. They roll up windows as the things pass, and some even start their engines, probably to run the air conditioner. Then one of the things leans over and peers into a car, a little blue compact with shiny rims.

The deader bangs his head against the window a few times, and the couple in the car recoil in horror as the blood-drenched man leers at them. It strikes a few more times, and the window shatters. The girl in the car jumps out of her side but is swarmed by a waiting horde. The one that broke the window leans in and pulls the struggling man out by his hair and one shoulder. He thrashes in his grip and punches at the deader with little effect.

One of the monsters, a woman missing her hair and part of an arm, grabs a screaming infant from the back and hauls it out, then tears at the soft belly like an animal with a fresh kill. I can't help myself; I break off from the crowd with my gun held high and walk into the middle of the street. The rifle comes up just as I have learned in the past fifteen minutes. I aim carefully and stroke the trigger.

The woman falls when one side of her head disappears in a spray of blood. Then I aim at the one who is tearing at the driver and shoot him through the throat. A spray of blood erupts from his back like a consumptive's cough.

I drop the last one and turn the gun on the man and woman who were attacked. My arms shake and then my body reacts violently, and I nearly fall over. With an effort, I stagger forward and put my hand on a car hood to steady myself. The shakes are setting in badly. One of the National Guard approaches me, a slim man with a shaved head. He puts his hand on my shoulder. I turn to face him, and he gives me a dour look.

"That was a brave thing you did, man. Fucking brave."

I don't feel brave. In fact, I feel small and used up. The day has been a nightmare, with the exception of the time I spent with Erin, and isn't it ironic that just yesterday I had the best day of my life? Erin has been a dream today. From the shower, the night of lovemaking, to seeing her in the kitchen moving around with a soft smile on her face, unaware that I was watching her.

"I just did what I had to," I tell the guy.

"Sometimes that's the only thing you can do." I think I understand what the brotherhood of battle does to warriors, because I suddenly feel very grateful for his reassurances. "Here, man, take what you need," and he drops a belt at my feet.

It is like his, loaded with magazines and a handgun.

"Don't you need this?"

"That was Stewart's, but his black ass is dead. I know that because I shot him myself after one of those things bit him. Just take it, man.

It's weighing me down, and I need to keep my arms free." We walk at a brisk pace to the sidewalk as we talk. Erin is at my side again. She turns to stare into my eyes, but I don't want to think about anything right now, so I don't bother looking for anger or pity.

I buckle the belt on, and it fits better than I expected. I have to loosen the buckle an inch or two, but it is snug on my waist. I check the pouches and magazines; there is a handgun that I hand to Erin. She takes it without a word, pops the magazine like she knows what she is doing, and then slams it back home. She pulls the slide back a bit and peers into the chamber. Satisfied, she carries it at her side.

"Shit is getting crazy, man. They're everywhere. Most of my guys are gone, dead. We fought them off as long as we could, but there are too many of them and more by the minute. Get to the football field and you should be safe. They are going to ship people out from there as soon as things are sorted out."

"How did this happen?" I ask. I'm exasperated with how calmly he is informing me that the city is losing its battle with the monsters.

"I don't know. All I can say is we've been running all over the damn place trying to contain it. We had some neighborhood in Queen Anne locked up for two days before the things got out."

Of course, the ridiculous gas leak they talked about on the news. But how did it start there? I will ask questions until I get what I am looking for, and then Erin and I will write the story of the decade told from the viewpoint of the survivors on the street.

Assuming we survive, of course.

Screams erupt behind us. The things have broken out of the terminal, and there are more running down Alaska Way. A lot more. In fact, I can't count how many. My new friend waves and runs off to join his companions. Gunfire starts up again, and this time there are many rifles firing.

We run straight up Yestler Avenue. There are none ahead of us, but they may be coming up one of the side streets soon.

We make it to Occidental, then First Avenue before going north. In the distance, Mount Rainier shows clear as a picture against a deep blue sky. The roof of the football stadium is dead ahead.

There are crowds of people walking, running, on scooters, and even a pair on Segways. Behind me, there is a yowl that sends chills down my spine. I glance back, and there they are. It's like a sea with hundreds of them in pursuit. Someone catches my eye, a familiar figure with two blades in hand. She is being followed by one of the female National Guardsmen we saw earlier. Hot on her heels are at least a dozen of the things, and they are howling for blood.

"We have to help her!" I yell at Erin, and before she can answer, I run to a red BMW stuck in the middle of the street. I slam my upper legs against the car, raise the gun and begin firing at the deaders pursing her. One or two drop in a heap. I miss one by a lot, as I jostle the shot at the last minute, but the bullet smacks into a thigh and the thing goes down as well.

The girl looks behind her and puts on a burst of speed straight toward us. Erin raises the handgun and fires. I watch this from the corner of my eye, and it is a beautiful sight. She aims, fires and shifts. Then aims and fires again. So smooth and so calm. When I first held the machine gun, I wanted to lean over and throw up.

Then the girl is there, and she shoots us a look of gratitude. She is covered in blood like she just showered in the stuff, and for a split second I wonder if she is one of them. But her moves are far too coordinated. She moves like nothing I have seen before, fluid and deadly.

There are far too many people ahead. We will never make it before we hit the back of the mob, and then we will be picked off. As if thinking the same thing, the deaders advance in numbers so great that they fill the avenue.

"Let's go up a few streets and cut over," the girl yells.

We nod and join her, and she is suddenly our leader. I follow gladly, since I am not cut out for that the way Nelson had been. We run up Yestler, and the street ahead is clear. Then we hit Second, Third and cut toward the football stadium, which is now just to the northeast. The girl with the rifle slows first. She looks behind, but there are none in the immediate vicinity. She leans over and puts her hands on her knees, drawing in deep breaths.

"I'm Kate," the girl with the swords says. She is much younger than I thought earlier. I do introductions. The other woman doesn't say anything, and I don't ask. Her eyes look more haunted than those of the woman in the ferry terminal, Alice. I wonder if she lost someone or if she is just sick of the killing.

"So Mike, you are pretty handy with that machine gun … wouldn't know it from looking at you." Kate grins. She wipes blood off her face and smears it on her jeans as if it were just water.

"I'm a fast learner, sort of on-the-job training. Normally I'm a writer."

She nods, and we start walking again. Three helicopters zip by us, and for the first time, I see that one of them is a news chopper. I wondered how long they would be able to keep this a secret.

"It was a real bad idea to take the whole fucking city off line," the woman says and hefts her machine gun up and onto her shoulder.

"They were trying to isolate the city, weren't they? That occurred to me when the ferry set sail and there were no passengers," I say.

"That was the plan. Fucking stupid one if you ask me. Said they didn't want a panic, they thought they could contain it, but we all knew that was bullshit," the woman in green fatigues offers.

We continue walking, trying to catch our breaths. There are none of them behind us, and I welcome the respite. I could go the rest of my life without seeing another deader and be as happy as a clam.

We are very close to Qwest Field; I can make out the river of people streaming into it. Here and there, cars race along sidewalks, jitter into streets that aren't blocked too badly and swerve around people when they can. I can't wait until Erin and I are safe inside so I can tell her how much she means to me, even though our feelings have only been out for a day.

"Must have been hard to cut everything off and not raise a panic," Kate says.

"Not from what I heard. I heard that homeland pulled the plug just like pulling a telephone cable out of the wall."

"They can't do that ... There are rules," Erin says with indignation.

"Fuck rules, this is the end of the world. If one of those things gets outside the city and spreads the virus, how are they going to contain it? And what do you think the odds are of them getting all of the dead fucks? Not a chance, man." The soldier spits on the side of the road.

"It can't be that bad." There is disbelief in my voice, but I think about what she said and wonder, just wonder how fast it would spread. I have seen one bite take someone and change him or her in a matter of minutes. She's right; if it gets out, we are all screwed.

"Here they come!" a kid with long blond hair and a black t-shirt yells as he careens down the street. He grips a tire iron in one hand, and there are spots of blood all over his pants.

"Where ..." I start to wonder out loud, and then I see them running down Main. There must be hundreds, and they are all moaning for blood.

"Oh holy fuck!" the woman whose name I still don't know screams.

Some Guardsmen come around the corner on their way from Fourth Avenue and set up a line of fire. They open up, and the staccato sound is loud. A Humvee pushes into the street, and the big machine gun on top starts rattling like a chainsaw.

We don't wait around. We are close to the stadium. A few blocks and we will be safe. Then more of the things arrive on Fourth Avenue, and we start to run toward the water again.

* * *

Pioneer Square is just ahead, and it is relatively clear of people. The 'park' has a notorious history of brawls and feuds spilling onto the street from one of the countless bars that surround it. There is also beauty here, with its Victorian Romanesque architecture, art galleries and tourist attractions like the Seattle Underground.

Some cars have had to pull over in the spaces close to the firemen statues. We are running catty corner to the roads in an attempt to cut our route short when a pair of deaders appears. I stop, raise my gun and shoot one. With the next shot, my hammer clicks on empty, and I have to drop back to figure out how the release works.

I'm glad I watched the other soldiers change magazines earlier, because it probably saves my life. I drop the magazine, fumble around in my ammo belt and find one the same size. It goes in with a satisfying click, and I am ready to be a warrior again. I take aim and drop the first one at eight feet. Then I shift my aim and miss the second one. He is almost to me when I put a bullet in his forehead and he slams to the ground at my feet.

Behind us, the deaders close in. The guy with long hair comes across a body curled up around the statues. The dead man is missing the top of his head. There is a gun barrel on his shoulder, and the means of his demise becomes apparent. Undaunted, the longhaired guy picks it up and tests the weight in both hands. He fiddles with it until he can point it at the approaching deaders. Then he raises the big gun to his shoulder and fires.

"Fuck yeah!" he exclaims as recoil smashes the gun into his shoulder and the deader falls away with a hole the size of a small saucer in his chest. He jacks a pump under the barrel and fires again.

Kate goes into ninja mode, sweeping the sword around her in a deadly arc. She moves one way, and the sword always seems to be in a different place from her momentum. She weaves among them with grace, dances around them, leaving nothing but body parts behind. I wonder if the things feel pain. She takes an arm off near the shoulder, and the kid doesn't seem to react. He just watches it drop, then renews his attack. She is already behind him, and her smaller sword finds the back of his head. She is silent except for an exhale that sounds like the word 'sigh' spoken out loud. He is also silent as he falls backwards, red eyes already glazed and staring at the sky.

The deaders grab for her hands, reach for her clothes, but they are more apt to lose an appendage than to get a piece of her. She falls back to us, and we fire into the disorganized mess of people.

There is blood everywhere, and the stench of the things is unbearable. It's like we stumbled into a fish market devoid of cooling. We are slowly pushed back toward the statue. We surround it even as the deaders surround us. The young guy drops down and paws through the dead man's clothes before coming up with a handful of shells. "Fucking party time," he exclaims and loads the gun.

"Had one of these in a video game once, but this is so much better." Then he raises the barrel and starts shooting again, great booming blasts that tear into the mob. The wind ripples over us, and it carries the smell of death. How comforting, I think, knowing we will likely join them soon. I wonder if it will hurt when I change.

Erin is at my side and going through the belt pockets before she finds what she needs. She leans close to my ear as she slams one of the magazines into the handgun and brushes her mouth across my ear, sending chills up and down my spine despite the danger we are facing. Then her voice is a whisper as it penetrates my mind, the words she offers simple and somehow surreal.

"I love you."

I look at her and mouth the same as the kid fires again, the blast wiping out my words. She has tears in her eyes as she looks past me at the wave of deaders.

Behind us are more of the things, an ocean that stretches as far as I can see. They are dragging individuals out of crowds and devouring them alive. Screams echo across the square, and I wonder how mine will sound when it joins them. I'm furious that I won't be able to protect Erin, much less myself. I feel helpless, and I want to scream at the injustice.

Kate is pressed back by the mob. She turns and swipes her short sword across one guy's neck. He is dressed in a black leather jacket with no sleeves. Then she drives the longer sword into someone's chest and kicks him back.

"Wish I had a couple of fucking frags right about now," the National Guard woman screams, and then one catches her by the arm and pulls her into the press of deaders. Her screams aren't cries of pain, but rather a constant stream of swear words as she fights tooth and nail. There are tearing noises and she falls silent.

"What now?" Erin howls. I don't have an answer. I fire as fast as I can at as many as I can, but their numbers don't end. This is truly our last stand. After all we have seen today, to die like this so close to our goal seems like such a waste.

Erin puts her arm around my waist as I fire the last shot and prepare for the end. I bash one of the deaders in the face and am given a shower of cold blood for my effort. He is a tall man in his fifties with teeth spread too far apart. I knock a bunch of them out, and his nose squishes under the gun. Then he is falling away only to be replaced by a woman who howls as she reaches for Erin.

A horn sounds as a giant SUV comes barreling down Main Street. It slides onto a sidewalk, smashing into a couple of deaders that stand in its path. Then, like a four-ton angel, the car crashes into the group surrounding us and knocks them down like bowling pins. The SUV is black and beat to hell. The driver stares around like he is lost. He takes in his surroundings, and I can tell he is about to drive off again. He looks at Erin and the girl with the sword and seems to reach some sort of conclusion. The door locks sound, and he lowers the power window.

"Get the fuck in!"

The kid with long hair is the first one. He dives across the console, calling "fucking shotgun." Kate is next and jumps in with her swords crossed and at her lap. Erin is between me and the door, but she pushes me as if I were the obstacle. Rather than swap places with her and have both of us fall prey to the monsters, I jump in the car and haul her toward me. I toss the machine gun over my shoulder into the back of the big car.

Erin's hand is in mine, her foot on the runner. I slide over, pulling her as I move so she will be pressed close to me in the seat. I can feel the driver shifting into reverse. She glances behind as I draw her into the rear of the car. Our friend the female National Guard, whose name I never got, comes toward us, and Erin looks at her in shock. Then she motions with her hand and yells, "Come on!"

"No!" I yell, echoed by Kate.

Erin is snatched away by the woman. One second she is there, and then her big emerald eyes meet mine in horror and she is gone. She screams my name, but the car is already moving. I make a move to jump out of the car, to go after her, but Kate grabs my arm and slams me into the seat. The car whips around and plows over some of the deaders. The centrifugal force slams the door shut but not before one of them reaches inside. I grab the first thing I can, which is Kate's sword, and jam it into the mother fucker's face with all my strength. I howl in frustration and pain as I rip the sword free, then the door shuts and I sit with the bloodied blade in my lap.

Kate takes the sword back from me and pats my hand, but she doesn't say anything. The driver keeps looking in the rearview mirror, trying to catch my eye. He does once, and he nods at me.

"I know how you feel, brother."

How can the shaggy-haired guy who looks like he hasn't showered in a week know how I feel? I want to tell him to shut up, but inside I am grateful to him for saving us.

"The football field, man. That's where we're going. They said it is safe there," the long-haired guy says.

"That's what brought me here, dude. I ran into a Humvee by accident, and the driver said to hurry here, so I took every fucking back alley I knew," the driver says. "My name's Lester, by the way."

"I'm Grinder, or I was. My real name is Duane, but don't let that shit get out."

"Kate," Kate shoots back but doesn't say anything else.

"I'm Mike," I finish with little feeling.

"Mike, man, I feel your pain. My woman was ripped out of my arms, right out of them, not even an hour ago. Those fucking things. First thing I'm going to do when we get in there is find a gun and take the fight to them. I'm going to kill me an ocean of those monsters."

"Beautiful, man." Duane mutters.

He steers onto a sidewalk and runs over a couple of deaders. They smash off his giant grill and rebound into the street and walls. He seems to be aiming at some of them, which suits me just fine.

"Well we are a fine bunch," Kate says as we drive the two blocks to the stadium. There are people all over the street. He takes an alley, through which we barely fit. The big car scrapes a pair of dumpsters, then we are through and the fence is just ahead. There are National Guards everywhere, so it seems safe to get out.

We hit the ground, and I feel faint. I look toward Pioneer Square, where Erin died, and I wonder if she is one of them now. I feel a sense of loss, much like the day I lost Andy. I feel old, used up, broken. Kate swings around the side of the car and approaches me. She has her swords in hand, but her eyes betray nothing.

"Mike, I know it sucks, but we have work to do. We've all survived tragedy, but right now we need to get inside, regroup and then see what tomorrow brings. So are we all going to go in there together, or do we need to drag your ass in?"

Nothing comes to mind, no sharp riposte. I stare at Kate and her empty eyes, and I want to slap her. What does she know of pain and loss? What can she possibly know? But I surprise myself by stepping toward her and extending both my arms. She looks at them as if they are vipers and then into my eyes. After a moment's hesitation, she steps close and returns my embrace. I feel her crack, and one single sob escapes her body. Then she steps back, careful with the sharp blades in her hand. Her eyes are clear; no hint of emotion shows.

"What the fuck kind of name is Grinder?" Lester turns to the kid with long hair.

"It's my stage name. I'm the lead singer for Corpse for a Day."

"What an appropriate name," I mutter, and with my new companions, I follow the line leading into the stadium.

KATE

Kate stares at the man who dared to touch her as if she were some delicate flower. He is having a shitty day, but so are all of them. She has the urge to pull her short sword and drive it through his chest. She clenches her teeth and grinds them together. Rage builds up, and her hand trembles on the leather-wrapped pommel that is sticky with blood.

But is it Mike she wants to hurt? Or herself? What did she do back there? It was like she was another person for a few hours. It was like she was the other and herself at the same time. The other, who has never really explained herself to Kate. The thing that has grown and grown, the monster she ignores. She is pretty sure that a psychologist would love to lock her up and study her for a few years. Poke and prod and learn about her schizophrenia. Only it's not many personalities in one, it is just her—and the other, and she is all too aware of the other's existence.

She could turn away from that side of herself. She could change and become one person if she so desired. But she doesn't, and now she has a new lease on life. She can kill and kill and soak in a river of blood. She can takes lives, and no one will ever look at her twice.

Kate's old life is over. She will leave it behind just as she planned to leave it if she were ever in danger of being caught. She will become one with the other and learn a new life. And she will live for as long as she can.

Her new companions are nothing to her, a means to an end. A way to escape the horror so she can fight another day. As soon as she can, she will be on her own again.

She sees tears in Mike's eyes. She frowns at him and considers putting him out of his misery. Hell, she could put down all her fellow survivors. No one would know the difference. Just a quick slash and two stabs. They would all join the deaders in a matter of seconds, and she would be free to move on.

Kate releases the death grip on her sword and raises her hand to eye level. It shook a moment ago as rage flooded her. Now it is calm and steady, cool and controlled. Just like her. Just like the other.

EPILOGUE

Cold, and so are they.

Night fell like a curtain, and when the power finally came back on, there was an audible cheer from the stadium as if a game were in full swing.

The survivors huddled, talked, cried and expressed their anger at what had become of their city. Some crept out at night to rescue loved ones, some sat alone and stared into the fire barrels. Some plotted and planned their next move. The Army proper would arrive soon, and they would be in full riot mode, putting down anything that resembled an infected.

Kate, Grinder, Lester and Mike made an odd group. Gathered around a tiny fire, they talked late into the night. Food was fetched, drinks were filched, and at some point Lester, the shaggy-haired one, broke out a joint and all partook.

They spoke to each other in hushed tones while they waited for morning. When most were asleep or walking around glumly, a black guy whom Mike recognized came upon the group and sat down next to him. Mike greeted him as 'Nelson,' and the two shook hands like they were old pals.

Kate cleaned her swords while she talked about her friend Bob and her hope that he was okay. She spoke of the fight in front of her apartment, of the way she waded into battle without a hint of remorse. How she felt detached from the action as if she were watching it on a small screen.

Grinder talked about a concert, about stepping onto the stage and pounding through what he called a 'vicious set.' He went into detail about the attack on the fans, how they fought and died in the tiny hall. He should have been horrified, but when he spoke, it was in a tone that was almost reverent. Later he found paper and a pencil and started writing. When dawn rolled around, he was still scribbling notes with a goofy grin on his face.

Mike talked about his girlfriend the entire time he had the floor. He talked about how beautiful she had been, how he knew he loved her after only one day. Mike then spoke of his son Andy and how he missed him. How he needed to get out of the stadium and go find his ex-wife. He was sure that she was safe. The others listened but did not encourage him.

Nelson listened too, and before he turned to leave, he spoke to them in a hushed tone.

"I know you all have been through a lot. I know you think you have seen hell, but this is far from over, folks. There are a lot of people stuck out there, holed up in office buildings and apartments. Tomorrow the Army is going to start clearing the streets, and we can use help."

Kate looked up at him, and there was a gleam in her eyes that was unexpected, a look of eagerness. She seemed to be fighting a smile.

"I'm in."

Mike considered Nelson's words carefully. He had a half-plan in mind to go after Rita, to save at least one person in his life. He had failed Erin, and deep inside, he had always felt that he failed Andy. Now he had little to live for. Or maybe he needed something new on which to focus, because he was all too aware that he was capable of hating with as much passion as he loved.

Grinder didn't even think twice; he gave Nelson the devil horns and said, "Rock and fucking roll, man."

Lester sat quietly for a moment and then looked each of his new companions in the eyes. He knew that had he not come barreling into Pioneer Square earlier that day, they would all be dead. They stared back, and after a few seconds of silence, they looked away. They avoided trying to make him feel guilty, avoided trying to convince him that it was the right thing to do, but there was no need, because Lester was one pissed-off mother fucker. All he cared about was killing the things out there. Human or not, he wanted to roast the whole town.

"Get me a shitload of ammo for my gun and I'll help." Then he grinned the evilest grin he could manage just before he leaned over, hands on the barrel of his rifle and broke down in tears. "I'll kill every one of those fucking things, every one of them." His voice was barely audible.

Nelson, for his part, began to feel a bond with his new companions. There was a city to save and not enough people to save it. He knew that the local government had blown it when they tried to cut off the flow of information. Then the National Guards were called in, of which he was a part, but they were unable to cope with the threat. Now the federal government would have to come in and clean up the mess.

It was going to be a blood bath. They had to contain the virus here, in the city. It could not be allowed to escape. Nelson knew things that the others didn't. He knew where it started, how a doctor tried an experimental procedure on his wife and paid the ultimate price. He knew because he was called in with a group of others to help cordon off the place. But his men were unable to cope, and some were attacked, then they attacked others. And so it went.

His best friend died a horrible, screaming, mindless death. He had known the man for ten years; Nelson had been the best man at his wedding. He was there when the woman he married ran off with another woman. He was there when they took a little trip to Thailand to erase the memory.

He was the one who had to pull his .45 from his holster and shoot his best friend in the head, and whenever he closed his eyes, he saw his buddy howling for blood just before his brains were splattered all over the ground.

Broken, and so are they.

THE END

ABOUT THE AUTHOR

Timothy W. Long has been writing tales and stories since he could hold a crayon and has also read enough books to choke a landfill. He has a fascination with all things zombies, a predilection for weird literature, and a deep-seated need to jot words on paper and thrust them at people.

Tim is the author of the horror novel *Among the Living* and the forthcoming sequel *Among the Dead*. His other works include the deserted island 'zombedy', *The Zombie Wilson Diaries* and the apocalyptic novel *Beyond the Barriers*. He also co-wrote the post-apocalyptic novel *Wacktards of the Apocalypse* which was recently named the preferred version of the end of the world by a consortium of rapture survivors.

Tim can be found tooling around his website: TimothyWLong.com.

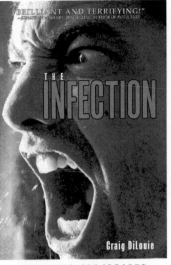

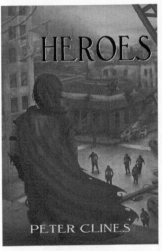

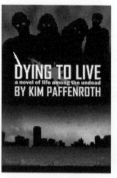

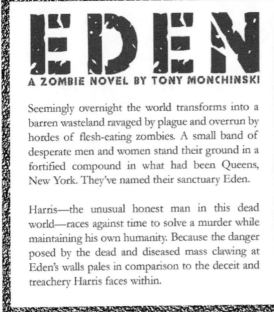

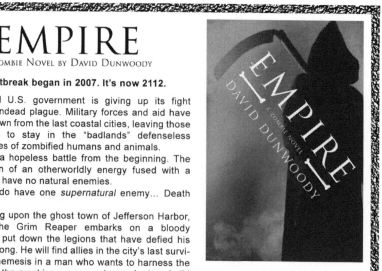
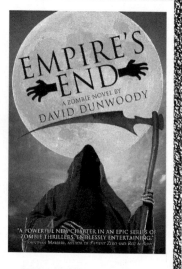

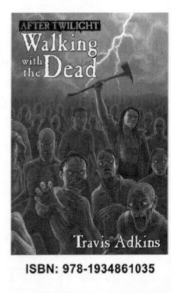

DEAD EARTH: THE GREEN DAWN

Something bad has happened in Nevada. Rumors fly about plagues and secret government experiments. In Serenity, New Mexico, Deputy Sheriff Jubal Slate has his hands full. It seems that half the town, including his mother and his boss, are sick from an unusual malady. Even more worrisome is the oddly-colored dawn sky. Soon, the townspeople start dying. And they won't dead.

MARK JUSTICE & DAVID T. WILBANKS

eBook Only

MARK JUSTICE AND DAVID T WILBANKS

DEAD EARTH: THE VENGEANCE ROAD

Invaders from another world have used demonic technology to raise an unholy conquering army of the living dead. These necros destroyed Jubal Slate's home and everyone he loved. Now the only thing left for Slate is payback. No matter how far he has to go or how many undead warriors he must slaughter, Slate and his motley band of followers will stop at nothing to end the reign of the aliens.

MARK JUSTICE & DAVID T. WILBANKS

ISBN: 978-1934861561

MARK JUSTICE AND DAVID T WILBANKS

MORE DETAILS, EXCERPTS, AND PURCHASE INFORMATION AT

www.permutedpress.com